Kiltman® 2

Maggie's Epiphany

Dear Reader,

I truly hope you enjoy
Kiltman's second
adventure.

Dermid Strain 1/1/23

Dermid Strain

ISBN: 9798579024008

PublishNation
www.publishnation.co.uk

Kiltman® 2 Maggie's Epiphany is dedicated to the amazingly special people who left us in 2020

Our gorgeous, kind, incredible sister, Margaret - the pain of loss will always be raw

Jack McVitie, a buddy, a leader, an inspiration in so many ways

Malcolm McConnachie, a beautiful mind, a gentle soul, a special friend

and to

Georgie, Max, Bruce, Anne, Angie and John

Let us make the most of our time together!

Mum, Margaret and George, watch over us all

Prologue

"Class! Class! Please can you all take your seats. We have a lot to get through today."

She scanned the room, row by row, counting the heads. The children were beginning to settle into their seats, gradually realising that no amount of screaming and shouting would stop Miss Kerr from starting the class.

29. There should have been 30.

She did not need to do a recount. She knew immediately who was missing.

"Where is she?" she announced to the room, pointing at the empty seat in the front row.

Nearly all the children turned their heads at the same time towards the window. Outside, a large scaffolding had been erected that morning to allow the roofers to fix the tiles and gutters, pounded daily by the incessant rain and wind blowing up the River Clyde.

Miss Kerr's hands moved to her mouth with a creeping sense of horror.

The seven-year-old was upside down, her legs wrapped around one of the metal bars, arms dangling downwards – as if pointing at the playground three floors below. Noticing Miss Kerr staring at her, she broke into a broad smile and waved energetically. The teacher's heart skipped a beat. She dared not speak lest she encourage a fatal slip.

The child threw herself into a half somersault to land gracefully on the wooden plank idly placed on the scaffold. She stopped to fix the pleats in her grey skirt, before ducking her head in through the open window. She climbed in nimbly, jumped down and was in her seat before Miss Kerr could remove her hands from her face.

"Young lady!" she croaked. "Why on earth did you climb out onto that scaffold and perform such a dangerous act?"

"Because I can, Miss," Maggie Wilson replied, innocently.

I

Six Months After Skink

December 21st

"Maggie, you're the coolest detective I know," Roddy said spraying half-eaten crumbs of baguette into his glass of sparkling water.

"Thanks, Roddy, that's a sweet compliment," Maggie replied. "But how many detectives do you actually know?"

"Eh, you're the only one." He reflected on her question before continuing. "But you would be the best no matter how many I knew." He looked over the brim of his glass at his father. Kenny winked in approval of a swift side-swerve he would have been proud of himself.

"Pass the butter, please, Roddy." Kenny nodded towards a pewter dish, classically over-engineered for butter-holding, but characteristic of the Ubiquitous Chip.

In his university days Kenny had enjoyed the banter and bonhomie of the eclectic bar upstairs. His trips to the bathroom would allow him a chance to observe the restaurant area, a luxury he could only have dreamt about. Now in his mid-thirties, he was happy to let the purse strings loose and settle into the peacefulness of the Chip's restaurant. Just off Byres Road in Glasgow's bustling West End, the lane outside offered the diners the lightest of clips and clops, people jostling along its cobbled stones. The noise was muffled just enough to add a subtle conviviality to the surroundings.

Sitting around a circular table towards the back of the dining area, Kenny, Maggie and Roddy were enjoying a special celebration. Kenny looked at Maggie. Her thick brown hair failing to stay scrunched up behind the back of her head, some rebellious curls drifting over her ears, others caressing her forehead as she spoke. Her deep brown welcoming eyes creased with mirth whenever Roddy spoke. Her mole and dimples, constant reminders of the first time Kenny had seen her beauty, now danced on her face with every word she uttered.

It was six months to the day since Cullen Skink had been arrested. He was behind bars in a special unit of Barlinnie prison, a few miles East of where they sat. They enjoyed a tranquil sense of safety knowing he was locked up and secluded from the outside world. A half year after this madman had been incarcerated, it seemed fitting for Kenny to treat Maggie to a celebratory dinner considering how much she had invested of herself in that investigation. She had faced death - and a fate worse than death - at the end of a nerve-shattering five days, taking them from Scotland to Rome then Estonia and back again. It had nearly broken her. Testament to her spirit and determination, she had recovered soon after Skink's arrest. She was in no doubt that Kenny and Roddy had played no small part in keeping her on track through those early weeks. She had grown to love this quirky father and son combination. And they had grown to love her.

Whenever they were in the vicinity of Byres Road, they would pause to remember her escape from the two thugs commissioned by Cullen Skink when she had been a young student. Long before Kiltman's arrival, Kenny's bravery and speed had saved her - and had cemented the foundation for a relationship that would take years before it began to blossom. The blessing they felt at their chance meeting that night outweighed the memory of the danger she had faced. It had taken her a long time to come back from the anguish left behind after the attack. In some ways she had never fully recovered, but over the last six months could feel herself repair and become stronger.

The Cullen Skink and Kiltman adventure had seemed surreal at the time. Now it just felt like a handful of days in someone else's life. She had moved on, and was enjoying the unknown of the future, rather than dreading it. When Kenny had suggested the Chip to celebrate how she had captured Skink, she had to remind him that Kiltman had done most of the work - she had helped where she could. As time passed, she admonished herself at times for feeling like a passenger in the chase to arrest their nemesis. She had been more of an assistant to Scotland's quirky superhero than a true detective inspector.

Kenny looked at Maggie, marvelling at how a dimple, a mole, a pair of brown eyes and a soft, full mouth could never become boring. He raised his glass. "To DI Wilson, the coolest detective the Morgans have ever met!"

He reached across and kissed her on the lips, while clinking his glass - brimming with Irn-Bru - against her champagne flute. Some of the amber, soft drink splashed into her Moet, but she did not care. She was genuinely happy and content, looking forward to a future as yet undefined or planned. Kenny and Roddy had become the cornerstone of her life, and she realised this afresh whenever they were together.

"Thanks, Kenny. And Roddy. I hope the Morgans always believe that!"

She smiled and sipped at her drink. She had not wanted to order alcohol, but Kenny had insisted, saying that she should not change her behaviour because he had to control his own. He enjoyed watching her become mellow and de-stress. He respected her self-control and discipline in having one, maximum two, drinks of an evening.

Three waiters arrived simultaneously, and ceremoniously began to lay large plates in front of them, each covered with a shiny metal dome. Roddy loved this part of the meal, his eyes widening in anticipation. He yearned for them to have mixed up the orders. That Maggie would get his fish fingers and chips, while he got her haggis and neeps. Although he would have quickly rearranged the plates if that had happened. He was proud to be Scottish, but haggis was a bridge too far for the sake of a joke. Her side-long, narrow-eyed look at Roddy, caught him by surprise.

A smile escaping the corners of her mouth, she whispered to him, "I'm not a detective for nothing, you know. If I get yours, I'm eating the chips. You can keep the fish fingers!"

Observing her, Kenny wondered how this evening was going to go. He had kept his Kiltman identity secret from her for six months, and it had been tearing him apart. He felt like he had been living a double life; not being truthful. Tonight, six months on from that fateful, longest day of the year when they had caught Skink, it now made sense to break the news. He was not sure how she would react, and this worried him. Would she focus more on the deception, or on the revelation? Over the half year, their relationship had grown faster than the days they had spent together – accelerating from friendship to love faster than either of them could have hoped.

The months had been relatively quiet from a Kiltman point of view. There had been occasions when he had to make an appearance, but they had been more ordinary in nature than crime-fighting. He had rescued lost hikers in the Highlands; and a Japanese mini-sub trapped in the depths of Loch Ness (the Drumnadrochit Loch Ness monster exhibition sitting high above its shores encouraged this type of madness through its many 'historic' photos of shades of grey, lumpy masses swimming in the loch); found a few missing pets; identified the structural faults in a newly-built block of flats in Dundee that prevented them collapsing after a couple of years. And so on. Humdrum and banal, yes, but after his Skink adventure he had been happy to enjoy some downtime. It did mean that Kiltman and Wilson had not interacted or even met one another over that time. She had been busy maintaining law and order on the streets of Scotland. He had decided that was okay. It should be Kenny that was building a real relationship with her. As opposed to Kiltman starting a weird superhero, Spidey-type awkwardness.

He was convinced he had made the right choice. These last six months had been the happiest of his life. She had seemed to blossom like a flower, letting Kenny and Roddy into her world in ways no-one before had been allowed. She rarely spoke of her younger years, but he sensed it had been rough. He did not need to use superpowers to read the pain in her childhood references. Her joy at seeing Roddy take pleasure from the simplest things was somehow allowing her to vicariously fill in the emotional blanks of her own upbringing.

The waiters paused for a moment before lifting the three metal domes. She and Roddy shouted, "Dennahh!" at the same time, to the bemusement of an elderly couple at the next table.

"Darn!" Roddy exclaimed, when he saw they had positioned the plates in the right order. She threw her head back and laughed, before reaching across to smack a wet kiss on Roddy's red cheek.

"Better luck next time, wee man," she teased.

"You two are unbelievable," Kenny interjected. "Every time we go for a posh meal, you get more fun out of the great plate reveal than the food itself. Sometimes I think we should just go to a magician and have a McDonalds on the way home."

7

"Great idea, Dad!" Roddy distractedly stuffed a large, gloriously oiled chip into his mouth. Kenny winked at Maggie just as she cocked a head knowingly towards him, quietly acknowledging the surprise arranged for Roddy's birthday in just under two months-time.

"Time to eat!" Kenny announced staring at his mince and potatoes, quietly reflecting on whether he may have too much on his plate.

The Great Reveal

The hum of the car's tyres on the damp tarmac of Great Western Road blended nicely with the Vaya Con Dios CD Kenny had inserted into the player. Gypsy jazz seemed appropriate for the mood he was in. He smiled at Maggie's slow foot-tapping. Initially she had not been Vaya's greatest fan, but over time she had grown to enjoy the jazzy beat. She had been willing to listen as long as he put up with her blend of 80's mish-mash when she was driving.

They had dropped Roddy off at Fiona's flat, only a five-minute walk from the Chip. He was in ebullient spirits as he bounded in through the doorway to hug his mother, before waving goodbye to them. Fiona had been her usual hospitable self, asking them in for a coffee, which they had to decline. Fiona and Maggie had hit it off from day one. Only the prior week, they had gone shopping for Roddy's Christmas presents, as if it were the most natural thing in the world, sharing dinner at the end of a day wandering up and down a busy Buchanan Street. Kenny was pleased not to have been invited. Shopping was not his thing. Although he was pleasantly surprised at how Fiona and Maggie had become such good friends. They both loved Roddy. They both loved/had loved Kenny.

Kenny had learned through Roddy's offhand comments that Fiona had someone *'special in her life'*. Roddy had heard the expression in a movie and could not wait to use it to describe his mother's new partner. His name was Angus, an islander from somewhere beyond Barra in the Outer Hebrides. Kenny's hackles had prickled for some reason he could not quite understand. Definitely not jealousy, he and Fiona were in a good place, conversing on a respectful level. It was more Roddy that Kenny worried about. Since becoming Kiltman, his protective instincts had gone into hyper-mode. Angus did not realise how high he would have to jump to meet the bar set for someone walking into Roddy's world. Kenny was giving him the benefit of the doubt, willing to wait and see. Fiona deserved a good man in her life just as much as Roddy needed to see his mother happy.

He was driving towards her flat in Townhead, a couple of minutes' walk from Strathclyde University, a quiet, sombre area of Glasgow in the evening, contrasting with the bustle of students during the day. He knew why Maggie stayed in this part of the city. It allowed the right amount of anonymity from the centre less than a mile away. It also provided easy access to the motorway allowing her to be at Pitt Street police station within a quarter of an hour. Physically she lived at a healthy distance from work, but metaphysically she felt just around the corner.

He was beginning to feel his palms moisten. The great reveal of the Chip plates was going to be nothing compared to what he was about to unleash on her. He had rehearsed the conversation multiple times. While he had learned his lines to perfection, the problem was that each comment depended on her responding in a certain way to the line before. He had tried his best to integrate her expected reactions into each of his sentences, in a mental YES/NO tree diagram. He knew the model was only as good as the degree of volatility his news would trigger.

He pulled up outside her flat in a convenient parking spot. As usual, he kept the engine running, until she said, "Well, Mr. Morgan, do you fancy a herbal?"

"Of course," he answered, smiling. No-one made chamomile tea like Maggie Wilson.

They walked into her second floor flat in good spirits. The evening had been fun, the conversation generally focused on Roddy. He had a new best friend at school and was tripping over his words to talk about how cool she was. Her name was Agnes, although she refused to answer to that. She preferred to be called Angie, seeing Agnes as old-fashioned. *Angie* came from her precocious, anachronistic love of 60's rock; and at the top of her list was The Rolling Stones. Yes, Kenny acknowledged, Angie was cool. Her father, Omar Lafit, a Middle Eastern immigrant, had come from the poorest of upbringings to become a Member of the Scottish Parliament for Glasgow East. He cut an impressive figure as he walked the streets of Glasgow. Tall, slim, handsome in a classical way, he carried an air of purpose in everything he said, quickly becoming a champion for Scottish independence. Kenny had seen him at parents' evenings and on TV in equal measure. A cool dad, with a cool child. Kenny liked to believe he and Roddy were moving into that category too.

"Here you go." She handed him a steaming mug, a teaspoon squashing the life out of a grey teabag. He only ever drank herbal tea when he was with Maggie. It always seemed to fit the mood, relaxed and subtly energising.

"So, Kenny, what's on your mind?"

She sat on the edge of the couch, half-turned towards him as she dunked her teabag methodically in her glass, gold-handled cup.

"What do you mean, Maggie?" he grimaced. This was not what he had expected, he was already losing advantage.

"I'm a detective. I know how to identify unnatural body language. How to interpret silences. What to consider unusual, versus normal. And tonight, my man, you've been acting in what we in the profession call 'a shady manner'. Come on, spill the beans, before I cuff you!"

She raised an eyebrow and winked at him. He usually liked being teased, but this was becoming uncomfortable.

"Yes, there is something I wanted to say."

He placed the cup on a yellow, clay saucer, a present Roddy had brought Maggie from a school trip to Oban.

"Well, go on then." A hint of discomfort began to tug at the side of her eyes.

"We've been together for six months, Maggie. And they've been amazing months. I've fallen head over heels in love with you. And you know that Roddy has too."

At this point he had expected she would be looking at him lovingly. Instead, he watched a shadow of anxiety drift across her face. And unusually, she was not speaking. She appeared to be in classic interview technique, waiting for the guilty party to 'fess up'.

"For me to continue to grow in love for you and for us to be all we can be together," he said, while thinking *crikey, this sounded so much better in front of the mirror*. "I want to… "

"Stop!" she raised both hands, palms facing him.

"What?" He had thought that he would at least be able to deliver the first line without interruption. "What's wrong?"

11

"I know what you're doing, but please don't say any more. I don't want you to spoil what has been a great night. And a great six months."

"No, Maggie, you don't understand. Let me explain."

"Kenny," she reached across and took his hand in hers. "I like you a lot. I really do. But we have to take this slowly. It's too soon to make big decisions. We have so much to consider."

It hit him like a mallet. While he had been planning the perfect conversation to reveal his Kiltman identity, it had never crossed his mind that there could be a misinterpretation of such colossal magnitude. He had touched the nerve she worked hard to protect, commitment.

He smiled, and squeezed her hand, realising what was happening.

"No, Maggie, let me…"

BZZZZZZZZ. BZZZZZZZZ.

Her phone, lying innocently on the coffee table, was vibrating with the unwanted interruption. The name displayed on the screen was Chief Constable Fraser.

"I have to take this, Kenny. Sorry."

She stood, quickly grabbing for the phone like a lifeline on a sinking ship. She flipped open the speaker cover.

"Hi Chief, Wilson here."

He watched her face contort with a combination of concern, anger, then dread. He did not need to ask what was being communicated, he could hear it already, by lifting his range a notch.

Cullen Skink had escaped.

Skink Unleashed

"Kenny, I'm sorry, but it's an emergency." Her face had drained to an egg-shell white pallor. He hoped the haggis was not going to revisit them.

"Are you okay, Maggie? What's wrong?" He feigned a quizzical look she would have seen through in a normal situation. This was not normal.

"Skink has escaped. I need to go to Barlinnie. A car is already outside waiting for me."

He stood and walked over to the lounge window. Lifting the side of the dark curtains, he peeked through the gap to see a police car, gleaming in the streetlights, parked behind his own. Its strobes were flashing, declaring a state of emergency no amount of spinning blue lights could overestimate.

"We'll need to pick this conversation up tomorrow. Is that okay?" She needed a hug badly. He wanted to reach out and hold her, give her some well-needed emotional strength. But he knew she would push back - she was focused on building her resilience not weakening it.

"Sure," he answered, half in response to her words, and half to himself recognising the enormity of this event. "Yes, of course, on you go. Let's talk tomorrow, if possible."

He leant across to kiss her on the lips. Her subtle head movement had him settling for a light peck on a pale cheek. She grabbed her bag and coat and ran to the door, calling over her shoulder, "Let yourself out, Kenny. Bye."

He waited a couple of minutes, continuing to twitch the curtain, until he saw her duck into the police car. It was already moving before she had closed the door. He grabbed his own coat and ran down two flights of stairs onto the damp, chilly street. Her car was turning the corner when he started the engine.

He drove a mile or so to Duke Street, one of those ancient Glasgow streets that everyone in the city has walked along at least once in their life. At over two centuries old, this traditional artery from Glasgow's East End to George Square in the city centre, is considered one of the UK's longest streets. If highways could tell stories, Duke would be top of the bestseller list.

He drove at slightly above the speed limit in the direction of Duke Street's destination, Parkhead Cross, a legendary area of Glasgow famous for its nearby football team, Celtic FC. Halfway along the route he turned left down a dark, secluded cul-de-sac and parked under an unlit streetlamp. He had removed the bulb a few months earlier, just as he had done with ten other streets dotted around Glasgow, creating dark corners carefully selected across the city for events such as these. He relied on the council not being in a hurry to replace the lamps; he was rarely disappointed.

He opened the car boot to be confronted with the parental residue common to fathers of twelve-year olds. Sweat tops, toys and footballs created layers of distraction before reaching a spare wheel buried deep in the pile of playtime flotsam. He wondered how messy his boot would be if he had not used the chaos to camouflage the wheel, guarding access to his Kiltman costume neatly stuffed underneath. Probably would not have been much tidier, he mused.

Within a minute, he was in full regalia, standing in the middle of Duke Street. He looked east and west for a taxi scouring the neighbourhood for a late-night reveller to round off the evening's takings. The quietness of the night seemed to bar anyone from wanting to disturb its peacefulness. Until he heard the crunch of gears and high-pitched whine of a vehicle heading towards him, fortunately in the same direction he was going. A green VW Beetle with flowers and 'Ban the Bomb' stickers dotted around roof and doors seemed completely out of place in early 2000s Glasgow. But then a grown man with a mask, cape and kilt was probably not too common either. He had considered upgrading his costume after the Skink affair but realised it fit his image just fine, no need to change. The blue and white of the saltire mask blended well with the St. Andrew's Cross, proud and bold on his cape as it fluttered freely in the wind. The bright green and deep black shade of the interwoven *K* and *M* on his chest fused nicely with the black and blue kilt, tempered with a hint of red. The sturdy kilt rested above hairy calves thickened with years of walking and running, and now with the unenviable job of supporting a bulk larger than he would like. He had squashed his socks down above his brown hiking boots allowing his legs to breathe unhindered, adding to the sense of freedom the kilt already provided. The sporran, his own design, made in the basement of Uisge Beatha, comprised a soft, strong leather pouch with three bouncy tassels. It was only penetrable by entering a code on a discrete panel on the back, protecting Hair o' the Dog from falling into the wrong hands.

He had already stepped out into the street, waving his arms as if directing a Boeing 747 along the tarmac into its departure gate. The car shuddered and jerked as the driver crunched the gears down before stopping at the side of the road alongside Kiltman. The passenger window struggled to wind down, barely reaching halfway before sticking. He could see the driver had leaned across to work the handle, straining to shift it another inch.

Kiltman leaned his nose in over the top of the glass and said, "Hello! Thanks for stopping. Can you please take me to Barlinnie prison?"

The driver, a blonde lass no older than twenty, was smiling so widely he wondered if she was practicing for a toothpaste commercial. Then he reminded himself that this is exactly what happens when you wear a kilt. People smile.

"Ja, of course! You are the famous Man of Kilts! Genau!" she responded. "I am Sandra, and I am from Germany." Of course, it suddenly all made sense. The smile, the car, the flower power motifs. "It is not normal for me to meet such a request, but I am happy to put you in prison if that is what you would want. Genau!"

At a different time, he would have found her perfectly punctuated, slightly off-point, English endearing. And would have asked what on earth 'Genau' meant, then would have told her that he found it appealing that someone who spoke fluent English still wanted to insert this German word every so often.

Instead he smiled back. "Well, let's not put me in prison. Just take me there, please. I know the way."

She opened the door for him from the inside, its creaky hinge reverberating around the tenement buildings surrounding Duke Street. He bent down into the car, finding himself flush against the dashboard. He searched around and eventually found a

15

handle to push the seat back and give him some welcome leg room. She barely noticed his front seat gymnastics, as she cranked the gears and sped through Glasgow's East End.

There seemed to be far too many irritatingly frequent traffic lights at red for a journey at that time of night. Sandra was happy to take his advice on not stopping and tentatively nudging through the junctions. He was less concerned about the length of the journey than the condition Sandra's gearbox would be in if she had continued to crunch it down and then back up again. Within fifteen minutes, they pulled up outside the prison gates just as her cassette stopped playing *99 Red Balloons*. He had not heard that song since it had dominated the charts twenty years earlier, yet inside a clunky VW Beetle, driven by Sandra, it provided the perfect accompaniment.

They had barely spoken a word to each other. She had been concentrating on not crashing the Beetle, while Kiltman had been considering the implications of Skink's escape. As she navigated to a stop, he reached down to his sporran and turned the dial to 1402. Extracting the flask, he lifted it to his lips, pushing the Celtic Cross to spring the catch over the mouthpiece. In his haste to extricate the container from its home, he did not notice the small buff envelope slip out of his sporran and drop onto the floor underneath his seat. He was rarely this ham-fisted - he would later put this clumsiness down to his being slightly out of practice of late, his mind racing with the events of the last couple of hours.

He put the flask to his mouth, where he had lifted his mask just enough to expose two parched lips. He quickly realised that Sandra had stopped the car and was gaping at him. He rarely performed his superpower libation top up in public, but he had no choice. It was safer to have a wee swiftie in Sandra's funky Beetle than outside the prison gates in full view of CCTV.

"Eh, sláinte!" he said before drinking a large helping of Hair o' the Dog. He closed his eyes and savoured the texture, aroma, and subtle charcoaling on his tongue. Each time he took a sip of his homebrew amber nectar, he thanked God for the random meteorite that had landed millions of years earlier in a stream feeding his homemade still.

"Ah, right! Off to work then. Vielen dank!" he announced, placing the flask gently back in his sporran.

Sandra continued to stare at him, barely comprehending what this kilted, masked man was now doing. If he had time, he would have counselled her on drinking in moderation, and certainly not when driving; and that in fact, his meteorically distilled whisky was actually non-alcoholic. But that would need to wait for another time.

He took her hand, squeezed it gently, and leapt from the car as nimbly as a well-rounded man can do while maintaining his kilt dignity, determined not to expose himself inappropriately to a poor foreign lass. He ran towards the prison entrance, looked back, and waved. Sandra was smiling again, raising two thumbs of support. He smiled when he focused on her license plate: FL4 W3R. Cute.

Sandra's innocence and good nature felt starkly at odds with the evil that Skink would happily unleash on innocents just like her.

Bar L of Laughs

Barlinnie, colloquially known as Bar L, had been Glasgow's main prison for over a century. From a distance, a long distance, it could be mistaken for a large, rural manse sitting above the houses of Riddrie, a close-knit community in north east Glasgow. A cluster of chimneys atop the building gave the impression of a homely environment, with everyone sitting around roasting chestnuts and marshmallows. Up close, Kiltman was in no doubt as to how far from a happy home this austere, commanding structure was. He smarted at the small windows built as an extravagance above sprawling brick walls, blocking access to the outside world.

He pressed the buzzer to the side of the entrance hearing the sharp, noisy whine disappear down through the prison's long corridors. He instinctively pushed against the gate as if he were entering someone's apartment block rather than a high security prison. After a few moments which he was sure involved a hidden surveillance camera examining this midnight visitor, the door sprung open. He walked through into a dark, lonely foyer to meet his welcoming committee - Governor John McCabe and two guards. Kiltman saw from their name tags that the taller of the two was called Officer Short and the smaller guard, Officer Lange. Considering the seriousness of the situation, he chose not to make jokes about the *lang* and short of things

"Evening, eh, sir!" Lange said. He was not the first to struggle with the nomenclature appropriate for a kilted superhero.

"That's alright, mate. No need for ceremony. Kiltman's fine." He prickled at how pompous he sounded.

"Hi, John!" He extended his hand to the Governor, who was holding a phone to his ear, barely registering the act. If he had not seen the stress on his face, and heard the fast thumping of his heart, Kiltman would have felt a tad aggrieved at the welcome. He knew John was normally polite and engaging, but he had just lost the nastiest and most twisted prisoner in Scotland. He had only come to the gate to make sure it was Kiltman, not some sort of hoax singing telegram. Annoyingly, a few of them had shown up around Glasgow after the Cullen Skink adventure. Some entrepreneurs cashing in on the superhero's newfound celebrity status. The only way to know they were not the real Kiltman was the fact they could actually sing.

"Okay, Kiltman, I'll leave you with these officers. They'll take you to Skink's cell. I'm trying to figure out if he is still here somewhere or has truly escaped."

McCabe walked off distractedly into the darkness, leaving him with the guards, who turned on their heel and proceeded to lead him down a nearby corridor.

Lange spoke over his shoulder. "It is not often we have the chance to meet a superhero in Barlinnie. It is quite the honour. While it is a shame that Skink's escape precipitated your visit."

Lange's accent, vernacular and pronunciation were not what Kiltman had expected. There was a strong element of a Glasgow accent, but the clarity of emphasis on each word reminded him of many of his friends growing up. The children of immigrant Irish parents seemed to have a softer Glasgow accent, mellowed by the sing-song nature of how their parents conversed at home. He wondered distractedly whether Lange had foreign parentage.

"Yes, Mr. Lange, I agree. Sometimes, we shouldn't need a reason to get together with friends," he answered, while not sure if Fraser, with his old school ways, would appreciate being considered a friend, rather than colleague.

Despite the situation he was looking forward to meeting the ex-Chief. While he had retired barely six months earlier after Skink had been imprisoned, it was not surprising the Chief was in the prison trying to piece together the clues. Over those five days in June, Fraser had lived and breathed every minute of the cat and mouse chase to snare Skink. If anyone had ever deserved retirement, it was him.

After what seemed an eternity of clanging doors and noisy marching through endless corridors, Kiltman found himself approaching the Special Unit. He had felt a strange vibe from the moment he had entered Bar L. He could not put his finger on it. It was not the sadness and despair of a thousand or so souls being locked up and separated from their families. At least, it was not only that. On walking through the gate, his sixth sense - evolving with every drop of Hair o' the Dog - had spiked. It was akin to an internal warning system that all was not what it seemed. Unfortunately, it was only a feeling with no connection to situation or circumstance: an alarm that was useful in indicating there was a danger, but not identifying what it was.

The Special Unit had been an area of Bar L created in the seventies, dedicated to the most violent of prisoners. An experiment to assess whether these individuals could be rehabilitated and reintegrated into society, it offered a range of support and therapy not afforded the rest of the prison population. Ironically, after 21 years when most people receive the key to the door, the Special Unit's key was thrown away and it was closed down. It was deemed to have served its purpose, encouraging long debates and mixed views as to how successful it had been.

Just shy of ten years later, it had been reopened to admit Cullen Skink. There was no discussion at the time as to rehabilitation, no such model would accommodate Skink's madness. When he was locked up, it was expected to be for life, no parole, or early release, contemplated. The simple truth was the Special Unit's location within Bar L allowed the Scottish Prison Service the best chance to isolate Skink and maintain the highest security available to keep such a maniacal villain under wraps. Until December 21st.

Kiltman walked into the small cell where Skink had lived the last six months, to find Chief Constable Fraser and DI Wilson sitting on the bed. They both stood when he entered. Fraser appeared younger than the last time he had met him at his retirement bash. He had put on weight, but in a good way, his face fuller and more relaxed. Kiltman was pleased to see he had trimmed his forestry eyebrows, which was something he had always wished he had the confidence to recommend. Fraser extended his hand.

"Good to see you, Kiltman. But how did you know? We've kept this watertight. At least we thought we had."

Kiltman shrugged, shaking Fraser's hand. He had not considered he would be cross-examined the minute he walked in and was not ready for this obvious question. Answering, *"well, I was having dinner with Wilson, when she thought I was going to marry her, and panicked, just before I tuned into her call with you*" was not going to work.

"Ah-hah, that would be telling, Chief. I have special powers, don't I? Nothing is beyond my senses." Before Fraser could react, he turned to Wilson, "Well hello, DI Wilson, nice to see you again. Despite the circumstances."

"Hello, Kiltman. You've been a stranger."

She was surprised that her voice displayed more than a hint of the hurt she had felt. They had become close on the Skink adventure; they both knew it. They had shared a kiss, for goodness sake. And then he had just disappeared, without a word of explanation. Okay, they had not dated as such, but they had spent practically every minute of five days together across four countries, saving each other's lives, and a country to boot. Surely that warranted at least one phone call. To conceal her growing awkwardness, she reached across and shook his hand.

"Good to see you," was all she could muster.

"Ahem!" an overly dramatic clearing of throat interrupted the bonhomie of an old friends' reunion. Leaning against the sink in the corner of the cell, the new Chief Constable, Gemmill, was pointing at Kiltman. "Who on earth told him? The last thing we need is a cartoon character showing up here attracting the media."

Gemmill stood to his full six-foot plus rugby stature, suddenly dominating the cramped cell. Twenty years younger than Fraser, Gemmill was handsome by any standards. His physical presence was complemented by a full head of thick, brown hair, a craggy chin and piercing blue eyes. He was the kind of guy most men would avoid standing beside in a singles pub.

He switched his gaze from Fraser to Wilson and back again, expecting one of them to own up to inviting Kiltman. The silence started to become unbearable and, Gemmill realised, unproductive. He drew a deep breath, shook his head, and pinched the top of his nose. Kiltman had never seen anyone so visibly resign themselves to a new turn of events.

"Right, you're here now, so we might as well use your knowledge and experience," Gemmill succeeded in grunting through gritted teeth.

Kiltman ignored the cartoon reference but locked it away in his memory for a future moment of revenge. Even superheroes have a modicum of childishness.

Kiltman cleared his throat then asked, "How could Scotland's most frightening criminal manage to escape from Scotland's most secure prison unit? And, in case anyone hadn't noticed, he did this, six months to the day after he was caught. Captured on the longest, escaping on the shortest. Exactly the kind of weird connection Skink loves."

All heads nodded - they had already noted that this was not a coincidence. Wilson was remembering a few hours earlier raising glasses with Kenny to toast the half year anniversary of his capture. She had not realised that a memory barely hours old could feel so painfully sharp.

"Okay, I'll take it from here," she said. "The guards had checked in on Skink at 10 this evening, on the hour as usual, and he was sitting on his bed reading. There had been nothing out of the ordinary in any of his routines. When they came back at 11, he was gone."

She paused briefly, aware of the parsimony of information she was sharing.

"That's as far as we've got. There was no indication that Skink was planning anything. In fact, he has apparently been the model prisoner." She splayed her arms wide nodding at the room. "There doesn't seem to be a single clue in here we can focus on."

"I see." Kiltman rubbed his latex chin. "No chisels or jagged saws? No birthday cakes with gaping holes in them? No acid residue around the door lock?"

"Look," Gemmill said. "You might think you're funny. But with every minute we're here listening to your havering, Skink is getting further away. If you're not going to be helpful, then get back on your high-horse and high-tail it out of here."

Kiltman decided not to question the high-horse and high-tail thingy.

"Sorry Chief, or should I say, *new* Chief. DI Wilson knows I try to ease the tension whenever I can. But don't let that fool you. I am completely incompetent whatever I do." He smiled, before remembering that Gemmill could not see his grin, then said, "Okay, let me focus, please."

Gemmill glared at Fraser and Wilson and raised his eyebrows, looking towards the ceiling. Kiltman walked over to the wall adjacent to the door. He removed his glove and pressed his hand against the bricks at the same level as the electronic lock located outside the cell. His fingers told him that the mechanism was high tech, code encrypted, designed so that it could only be opened by two separate control centres situated at different guardrooms in the prison. Both guards would be expected to engage on a verbal password routine before they triggered the lock electronically, and separately.

Kiltman briefly entertained the thought that the guards had colluded and opened the door for him. He shook his head and dispelled the thought, knowing that the trail would lead back to them before they could say 'game's a bogie'. He focused his attention on the brickwork and noticed on the edge of one of the bricks, snug against its corner, a hole no larger than a pinhead. He paused for a second to assess the process Skink must have followed to enact his escape, then stepped back.

"Okay, I've got it." He pointed at the hole. "There it is."

"What?" Gemmill said. "A brick? Yes, Einstein, we can see it's a brick!"

"Sorry," Kiltman answered. "Just there at its bottom right, that tiny hole."

Gemmill put on a pair of reading glasses. Wilson squinted. And Fraser did not even attempt to look at it.

"Em, I'll take your word for it, Kiltman," she said. "Assuming there is a hole, and I've no reason to doubt your hyper-vision, what does it mean?"

"Well, the hole allows access to the electronic mechanism which controls the lock." He turned to survey the room. "He would've needed a sophisticated piece of kit to insert into it and break the circuit. Once he had done that, he could reprogramme the lock to open the door from the inside."

He walked towards a cluster of cards, artfully arranged in a row along the one shelf Skink had been allowed in the room. Picking the first one up - a nondescript cover with no hint of Christmas spirit - he glanced at the writing:

I love you, Cullen, you are the future of Scotland.
Merry Christmas, their ass, I pray God it's their last!

William Wallace (the spirit of)

Placing it back on the shelf, he shook his head at an example of the following Skink's madness had inspired in a few delusionals dotted around Scotland. The next two cards displayed similar shows of undying affection. The last was one of the old-fashioned Virgin birth style, that appeared slightly thicker than it should have been. It was one of those musical cards, where you paid a couple of extra quid to annoy the recipient and their family. He prised it to its full 180-degree flatness and awaited some well-needed Christmas cheer. He was not disappointed. *Away in a Manger* rattled metallically around the cell. Turning the card upside down, he shook it gently, to see a small, flat squarish disc fall onto the shelf. The disc had a miniature dial and a neat little screen, with a thin but strong wire dangling beneath.

Kiltman turned to the others and pointed at the gadget. "There it is. Skink was dreaming of a *Flight Christmas*, and abracadabra, he is now on his way to eggnog and turkey."

"Seriously," Gemmill said. "Are you telling us, he was able to jimmy the lock with that little piece of plastic?"

"Afraid so," he answered, picking up the gadget and studying it carefully. "This little thing would have been nestled within the small sound box inside the card. If you look carefully at the wire, you might see it actually has a raised helical thread, just like a screw: allowing him to work it through the cement towards the lock mechanism. And most clever of all, there is a miniature camera at its tip allowing him perfect visibility of the task at hand."

He shook the card again. A yellow Post-it Note dropped from its inside onto the bed. Wilson picked it up in a gloved hand and read the hurried scrawl, "*I hope my escape allows you two crime-busters to get together again, Kiltman and Wilson. I left my ingenious technology for you to admire, purely out of arrogance and pride. I will be in touch! CS xx (one for each of you)*"

Governor McCabe entered the cell to a wall of stunned silence. He was pale and clearly off balance.

Fraser put his arm around his shoulders. "Take it easy, John. Keep your pecker up. What's the latest?"

"Fraser, with all due respect," interrupted Gemmill. "McCabe is feeling bad because he put naivety and nativity ahead of security."

Kiltman was beginning to realise that the new Chief was much less diplomatic and empathetic than Fraser. And he was not in the mood for taking prisoners, which felt like extreme irony, considering where they were gathered.

The Governor made a valiant effort at pulling himself together. "Bad news, I'm afraid. We've searched the prison from top to bottom, upended bunks and disturbed the entire prison population. He's gone. Disappeared. Not sure how he could have got from here to beyond the gate. But it has happened."

"Chief," Kiltman looked towards Fraser. "Skink would not have attempted to escape his cell unless he had a cast iron plan to get through the gate. We can spend time trying to figure out the how. But the reality is, it won't do us much good. We have to figure out where he is now."

"Eh, excuse me… Kiltman!" It was Gemmill. Kiltman had never heard his name pronounced with such derision. "I would appreciate if you would address me rather than the *former* Chief."

"Well, what I was going to say, Chief Constable Gemmill, sir," he enjoyed his own intonation, even with the voice changer in his mask. "There are two big issues here."

"Go on," said Gemmill.

"Cullen Skink has an accomplice on the outside. Until now, we thought he was on his own."

"Okay, I think we've got that," Gemmill answered. "And the second issue?"

Kiltman linked his arm with Wilson and turned to walk from the cell. He spoke over his shoulder as they left, "We have too many Chiefs and not enough Cullens."

The Kiss

"It's really good to see you again, DI Wilson," Kiltman mumbled through a mouthful of cheese 'n' onion crisps. He usually avoided crumbly, snack food when he was eating in costume, because of the time it took later to unpick the soggy crumbs from the inside of his mask. Unfortunately, the majority of East End pubs only offered crisps or nuts, all highly salted to keep the customer thirsty. "I've been meaning to contact you for a while now. How have you been?"

He was struggling to find the right words to manage the situation. He desperately wanted to reach out and hold her hand, give her a hug and say it would be alright; that they were a team and they would catch this mad escapee. He knew he could not reveal his identify at that moment - her reaction would be explosive on various levels. The last thing he wanted to do was to put her off tack when they were trying to build a picture of where Skink was hiding.

Sitting in O'Kanes pub in Parkhead after midnight, only a few miles from the Bar L, they were enjoying a rare lock in. Long before Kiltman, Kenny had known the pub from when he had rented a flat two floors above it, as a student in his first year at Glasgow University. He had chosen to live as far from the West End and his friends as would allow him to focus on his studies and minimise the accelerating number of reasons to party. On his second Saturday in the flat, he had decided to go to O'Kanes for a pint before going back upstairs to finish a particularly complicated essay on aromatic hydrocarbons. He was hoping for a modicum of tipsiness, just enough to inspire him to completion.

He remembered walking into the local, feeling pleased that his flat sat above a pub with *O'* in its name. He had an affinity for Irish bars having spent many long days in them with his uncles in Ireland when he was a child. Spying an empty stool, recently abandoned, judging by the empty glass and ashtray full of cigarette butts, he ordered a Guinness. Within minutes, he was enjoying the brown/black metamorphosis tantalizing his taste buds. Turning to an older gent on his right, he decided to strike up a conversation.

O'Kanes was half a mile from Parkhead stadium, home of Celtic football club, founded by an Irish Catholic Brother in the 19th century. Guinness, Irish pub and Celtic proximity prompted him to say, "So how do you fancy Celtic's chances this afternoon? They should pummel the Rangers based on recent form."

The older gent turned, barely hiding the menace embedded in his glare, and said, "Look, pal. I'm going to do you a favour. Listen. This is not a Celtic pub. In fact, it's very much a Rangers pub. Nobody in here wants Celtic to win today. And if they do, you better not be sitting on that seat if it happens. I suggest you finish your pint and skedaddle. Pronto, amigo!"

Now, nearly fifteen years later, and only the second time he had ever been in O'Kanes, he was settling into the late night, empty bar vibe. The silence of the pub and the normalcy it afforded, allowed him to maintain a distance from Wilson - and for them to approach their dilemma on a professional level.

Before he took himself off into the cellar to crate his empties, Tam, a long-haired, young, wide-eyed barman eager to please his late-night guests, had found a Van Morrison track to play in the background: *Brown Eyed Girl.* The perfect song for Wilson, Kiltman mused.

"Listen, Kiltman, I'm sure you've been busy. Just as I have." Her tone was more ardent than she had planned. "Life's been good the last six months. And to be honest, I had probably lulled myself into a false sense of security with regards to Skink. I feel like we have hit the ground with a crash tonight. So, if you don't mind, can we get on with figuring out our next steps. We can save the reminiscing for later."

"Sure," he said, more relieved than disappointed. "That works for me."

She took a deep, resolute breath.

"I want to know what you think. I've learned it works better that way. Rather than I tediously attempt to unearth a clue or perspective, when you are already ten steps ahead of me, waiting for me to catch up. We don't have time for game-playing."

If only you knew, he thought.

"Yes, of course." He paused and took a long draft of his Sugar Free Irn-Bru. He found it surprisingly tasty despite no sugar. "Okay, this is what I think. Skink has an ally; we know that now. I don't believe he, or she, was around six months ago. At least not as a potential accomplice. If Skink had been intent on burying himself in an underground bunker for years, then I am sure he had no ties with the outside world. Makes sense so far?"

She nodded. She had got that far herself; and did not need the reminder of the bunker and mind-altering equipment Skink had intended to use on her. She had worked hard to forget that year's longest day - over the last few hours it had come crashing back, rendering her more fragile than she appeared.

"Somehow," he continued, "in the last six months, he has been able to build a relationship with someone outside prison. This person is sufficiently clever to help create the gadget Skink used to escape his cell, and influential enough to get him through the gates. Agreed?"

She nodded again.

"That means," he said, "either there's some degree of inside help involved in connecting him with the outside world..."

"Or?" She raised her eyebrows, arms extended.

"Someone from the outside has had access to him on a relatively regular basis. In the morning we need to review all comings and goings in the Special Unit, particularly over the last few weeks."

"We don't need to wait until morning."

She leant down to pull a manilla folder from her bag. She opened it and placed an array of papers and photos in front of them. Kiltman nodded in recognition of her forward-thinking. He used his gloved fingers to spread the papers along the bar. The first photo showed Skink sitting across a table from a man in dark clothing. The man had placed his hand on Skink's cuffed hands, in a manner akin to what a parent would do... or a priest. The next three photos showed the visitor from the front, dressed in the clerical garb of a Roman Catholic clergyman. His face was always tilted slightly downwards providing a shadow dark enough to distort a clear picture. This was their man.

Alongside the photos there were copies of the access documents created when the guest entered Bar L. Each had been signed and attached to a photocopy of a passport, displaying the name, Father McQueen. Fr. McQueen had a thick, black beard, and a large pair of black 'national health' glasses. Kiltman was sure John McCabe would be looking at the same pictures, kicking himself at not seeing the disguise for what it was. Even more concerning, on a separate sheet of paper alongside a report on Skink's behaviour, the governor had made a comment: "Cullen Skink has been a model prisoner over the last few months. As a result, we are cautiously allowing him access to spiritual guidance. He has recently acknowledged his mistakes and is seeking divine forgiveness. Fr. McQueen has been an incredible rehabilitator, and ironically helped us remember the original objectives of the Special Unit. Skink has a long way to go, but these early signs of reconciliation are encouraging."

They eyed each other for a second longer than necessary.

"Well?" she said.

"If Father McQueen is a priest, then I am Pope John-Paul II reincarnated." He folded his arms in an effort to emphasize his point.

"Actually, JP II is still alive." She smiled. "But I get your meaning."

They spent the following half hour planning how to progress, recognising they had run out of road that night. They agreed to get together the next day and visit the prison to see what they could find on the fictional Fr. McQueen and his repentant prisoner.

Stepping off their barstools, Kiltman shouted, "Tam, we're done here. Thanks for the hospitality. Come and close the door after us, please."

Wilson dropped a twenty-pound note on the bar; and walked towards the exit.

"Thanks, DI Wilson," shouted Tam. "Come back anytime. You too, Kiltman." His broad smile showed that with one flick of her wrist Wilson had just left three months' worth of tips.

"So," she said, as they stood on a sprawling, empty Westmuir Street outside the pub. "Can I drop you somewhere?"

Memories of the year he had spent living and studying in Parkhead came flooding back. The rows of black cars outside the funeral undertakers next door to O'Kanes. And the all-night bakery across the road, an oasis of late-night sausage rolls and bridies. Those days seemed a long time ago when life, and death, had appeared much simpler.

"Actually, Wilson, I'll walk. I need to think some more and it's a nice evening."

His choice of O'Kanes had conveniently placed him less than a mile from where he had parked his car. She turned and stepped towards him, somehow placing herself closer than she had meant to. He noticed this and smiled, although she could not see his face. For Kenny, this closeness was normal. In fact, it was unusual for them not to be connected, either holding hands or arms wrapped around waists. If he had thought about it, he would have walked away. But Kenny got the better of Kiltman on this occasion. He could feel her warm breath seeping through his mask, and her eyes focused on him, as if egging him on. He lifted the bottom of his mask and leant across to kiss her on the cheek. Her head moved subtly, just as it had earlier that evening, but this time allowing him to kiss her on the lips. The moment lasted no longer than five seconds but was long enough to be meaningful. It was her who pulled away first, putting her hands to her head.

"Oh, God, look, I'm sorry. That wasn't supposed to happen."

"It's okay, Wilson," he appeased. "No need to apologise, it was lovely."

"That's the problem," she answered. "It was too lovely. This is not good."

"But… " he decided to spill the Kenny beans.

"No!" she answered. "I need to go." She touched him on the arm, with an air of finality. "Let's connect tomorrow and see where Fraser and Gemmill have got to in the Skink search."

"But, please, let me…"

"No!" She stepped back from him. "I need to go."

For the second time in a few hours, he was on the receiving end of a Wilson wobble.

She turned from him, hurriedly climbed into the car she had sequestered that evening, and within a minute she was driving towards Parkhead Cross, a spaghetti junction of juxtaposed streets - that characterised the confusion enveloping Kiltman.

Emotional Distancing

Kenny awoke early the following morning to the Proclaimers belting out *500 Miles*. Before he knew it, he was croakily singing along with his own version of the lyrics, *"I'm gonna be the man that wakes up on his own!"*

Uisge Beatha, his house named after the Gaelic for whisky, *water of life*, overlooked the spectacular Firth of Clyde, eight miles west of Glasgow. Its isolation on the Old Kilpatrick hills usually allowed him an uninterrupted sleep. That night, he only slept a few hours by the time he had picked up his car and driven home. His restless sleep had been full of dreams that drifted between his nemesis and Wilson - one a source of worry and angst, the other Skink. He reached across for the remote and clicked on the TV. After skirting the main channels, he saw that even now at 8 am, there were no published Code Green messages, Fraser's method of requesting Kiltman come to the station. It was becoming clear that Gemmill was a different animal. Where Fraser was happy to admit he was not the smartest person in the room and reached out for help, Gemmill was famous for his mulishness creating barriers to communication. If Kiltman was going to have an impact on this case, he would need to become more of a nuisance than normal. God help Gemmill, he thought.

Then there was Wilson. For them to work as a team, he would have to come clean and accept the consequences. She was feisty - he was in no doubt, that once he broke the news of who he really was, the odd kitchen utensil might end up heading in his direction. But there was no choice. His ham-fisted efforts the previous evening had proven that eloquence and timing were not his strong suit. He would have to use the direct approach. In hindsight, he realised this is what she would have expected, and wanted. As a detective, she spent her waking hours watching for gestures that spoke louder than words and listening for words not vocalized. How on earth had he thought he would beat her years of training and instinct? While his superpowers allowed him senses that could reach beyond any mechanical device known to man, they did not stretch to conflict resolution and tact. For those, Kenny was on his own.

His thoughts were interrupted by his phone buzzing, *Maggie Wilson* displayed on the screen. Picking it up, while swinging his legs over the edge of the bed, he took a deep breath. "Hi, Maggie. How are you?"

"Okay, Kenny. I'm already at the station. All hell's broken loose here. It was a late night going through the meagre morsels of evidence." Her voice sounded weary and fragile.

"Sorry to hear that. It really is scary that Skink has escaped. I can't imagine what's going on there in Pitt Street. Do you want to meet up at some point today? I know you're crazy busy, but I want to finish the conversation I clumsily started last night."

"Seriously, Kenny? Do you honestly think I can have that conversation in the middle of the current crisis?"

"But that's what I'm trying to say, Maggie." He took a deep breath. "What you thought I was going to say, was not…"

"Kenny, look. I have fallen for you. I really have. I adore Roddy and see you two as the most important people in my life." It was her turn to take a deep breath. "But overnight I did some thinking. I think it's better that we take some time away from each other. I need to work through a few things. Plus, the Skink escape is going to take up most of my waking hours."

"Maggie," he felt the hurt creep through in those two syllables. "I think I know what's going on with you, and I can help you work it out. It actually won't take long, I promise you."

"Seriously? What, you are a psychiatrist now? How on earth could you know what's '*going on with me*'?" She spoke the words mockingly, stressing the word *me*. "I wish I could say more, but whatever I say might come out the wrong way. I just need a break, Kenny. Please, don't push back. It just makes it worse. This is not about you. It's about me, and my issues. Don't you see?"

She stifled an intake of breath that was about to come out as a sob. Tears had been running down her cheeks long before she had picked up the phone to call him.

He waited to see if she had finished. He was becoming annoyed at the interruptions whenever he tried to get his message across. But another consideration was now gnawing at him, simple in principle, but crushing in impact. If Maggie Wilson was so fragile, how could he confidently expose his identity as Kiltman? He had unwavering trust in her, recognizing the high moral principles she lived her life by. Although he had to think about the Kiltman kiss some more. Could she really be considered as having cheated on him, with himself? He hardly even knew how to articulate the act, let alone understand it. But her fragility was a concern, and, other than Roddy, his Kiltman alter-ego was the most precious part of him. Once he had opened this box with someone, he could not get the lid back on.

He paused for a moment to collect himself and realised that the revelation would not be happening any time soon.

"Okay, Maggie. I don't want this to be about me. It wasn't supposed to be *about me*, but about us. I can wait. Take as long as you need to. Just remember, that every minute you are not in my and Roddy's lives, is a minute wasted. But if that minute can be considered an investment in our future, then I am willing to wait for the returns."

Why would he turn a lover's tiff into a financial analysis? Normally, she would have taken great pleasure in pulling him up on this. Things felt far from normal.

"Thanks, Kenny. I need to go now. Fraser is knocking at my door."

The gentle click of her phone nearly blew a hole in his ear drum. She was gone. If Laurel and Hardy had popped up in the bedroom, he thought, they would have nodded agreement at this being another fine mess for him to get himself into.

The doorbell rang, lighting up a display screen on his TV showing Fiona outside with Roddy and his friend, Angie. He jumped from the bed putting on a pair of running shorts and t-shirt as he ran downstairs.

He pulled open the door. "Hey, guys. Is everything ok?"

"Morning, Kenny," Fiona said as Roddy hugged his father's midriff. "Don't be alarmed. Everything is okay."

"Phew! I did get a bit of shock. Hi Angie. Great t-shirt." She was wearing a classic Stones shirt. "What's going on, guys?"

He opened the door for them to enter. Roddy and Angie made their way to the kitchen to help themselves to orange juice.

33

"I'm sorry. But I got a call overnight from Angus. He had been on lastminute.com late yesterday and managed to get us tickets for a day trip to London. Angie and Roddy had planned to work on their school project today, so I picked her up on the way. Today's the first day of their Christmas holidays, just shows you how keen they are. I hope you don't mind."

Angus, Kenny thought. Fiona had never mentioned his name before. It was only Roddy that referred to him.

"No problem," he said. "What's the big event in London?"

"Angus has always wanted to show me where he used to row when he was representing Oxford University. We're going to rent a boat and go down the Thames along the actual route of the Boat Race. You know how I've always loved rowing, and especially with today being such a beautiful day."

Oxford? Impressive, he thought, while silently chastising himself for not remembering Fiona loved rowing.

"Yes, rowing, your favourite sport." He nodded affirmatively. "That's fine. Just leave them here. I may have to pop out for a while, but I'll ask Shona from the village to look after them. She adores spending time with Roddy and his pals."

"Perfect!" Fiona turned to walk back to her car. "They are both so excited about their project, so they should be quiet. I'm away then to the airport." She spontaneously leaned in and kissed him on the cheek. "When I get back, I want to hear the latest about you and Maggie. She's a darling."

A blow to the groin could not have hurt more.

"Yeah, sure," he croaked. "Enjoy! And maybe soon I'll get to meet Angus."

She smiled and waved back. "Great, let's go out as a five-some next week."

Those blows kept on coming.

He heard Fiona's car quickly change gears as she exited his drive to head towards Glasgow airport on the south side of the river. Her shift from second to third reminded him he had to get out of neutral; and move his own gears. Skink was out there, somewhere, and would already be working on his next act of destruction. He would not be making allowances for broken-hearted superheroes' self-pity and wound licking.

Roddy and Angie

"Hi, guys, are you having fun?"

Kenny had just come off the phone with Shona, the babysitter of choice who lived half a mile away in the jauntily friendly village of Duntocher. She was already on her way to Uisge Beatha, ready to look after them for the rest of the day.

"Hi, Dad," Roddy answered, engrossed in a magazine entitled *Scotland's History.* "We're working on a school project, to be handed in after the Christmas break."

"Oh, really, what's it about?" Kenny studied an array of newspaper clippings, maps, and photographs, interspersed with sticks of glue, Sellotape, and scissors. They were scattered around the table in a pattern that clearly made sense to the two twelve-year olds.

"Mr. Morgan, we have been tasked to provide a history of Scotland, with a view to understanding what would need to be true to allow us to be independent again," Angie said proudly.

The apple does not fall too far from the tree, he thought. He could already see her following in her father's footsteps as a Member of the Scottish Parliament. Intelligent, articulate and engaging.

"That's a great idea for a project, Angie. And very relevant considering the discussion coming up next week in the United Nations." Kenny wanted to sound informed.

A UN meeting had been scheduled for December 31st, to discuss and vote on a resolution to adopt the parameters required for a country to self-determine its constitutional future. There were rumblings around the world of countries threatening revolution in a bid to break away from whatever superior power governed them. The UN had decided to begin a process that would allow a more transparent and logical self-determination program, within relevant constitutional regulations. At least to kickstart and open a dialogue, rather than have minority states feel they were stuck in a hole with no way out.

Scotland had been angling towards a play for independence for years, some would say centuries. And there were others: Catalonia and its Basques; Northern Italy's wealthy Lega Nord movement wanting to shake off the south; and Taiwan, which had been christened Republic of China to make sure it knew who was boss. Even Greenland wanted to break away from Denmark. How could anyone not want to be part of Denmark, Kenny mused? Whatever happened at the UN, it was going to be a rich discussion. It was also expected to be a fun event, scheduled for a late evening meeting, with a New Year's celebration at midnight. It was unusual for the UN to even attempt something like this. Apparently they were expecting the debate to become quite heated. By throwing a party, they wanted to raise the profile of countries working together and the importance of collaboration whatever the constitutional barriers separating them. A bold move, but one that the media had welcomed, even if it was just for the paparazzi to fill up their *Hello!* magazines with a swathe of merry politicians trying to look sober.

"Looks like you have everything you need," Kenny continued, pointing at the table. "No need for me to hang around and get in your way. Shona is going to be here in a few minutes. I need to pop out for a while."

"That's fine, Dad. Can we watch a movie later?" Roddy asked.

"Sure, pal. But no 15s. I don't like some of the superhero stuff in Blockbuster, it can be a bit too violent." He smarted at his irony tinged with more than a hint of hypocrisy.

"That's okay, Mr. Morgan. I prefer to watch documentaries," Angie said. "Don't worry, we'll find something we both like, 12 rating or under."

She turned to Roddy and they smiled at each other. Kenny sighed. It had started already.

The back doorbell rang, followed by Shona walking in through the kitchen as was her custom. A pleasant, lively lass just turned 21 the year before, she had been coming to the house to look after Roddy for the last few years, comfortable in the Uisge Beatha surroundings. She was wearing jogging trousers and a black t-shirt, ready to settle into a fun afternoon with her twelve-year old 'homies'. The only indication Shona was growing older was in the increasing number of tattoos joining up on her arms. He could see a new one '*love you Nan*' with pride of place on her forearm. He had humorously challenged Shona once about the increasing levels of body art. Her response of "*Mr. Morgan, I can't keep inside all the love I have for my family, it has to be on the outside too*" stopped him in his tracks. He knew he could not argue with her logic.

"Hi, everyone!" she called in her chirpy voice. "Who fancies baking a cake?"

Project Independence would have to wait, as Roddy and Angie ran towards her. She was already emptying cupboards and drawers tossing lots of baking instruments and containers onto the worktop. Kenny sighed, accepting that when he came home there would be a beautiful cake, or at least the remnants thereof, and a kitchen that resembled a mini-Armageddon.

He entered his garage and removed the cover from his motorbike. He had not taken it on the road in a while, but he did keep the engine tuned and ready to go, not knowing when an emergency would show up. He had christened his Suzuki 1100, MacWolf, and with a flick of a switch on the control panel he could change the standard banal number plate to KILTMAN, one of the little luxuries he allowed himself when he put on his costume.

He fired up the engine and shot out of the garage. Within fifteen minutes he was passing through Bearsden, an affluent suburb of Glasgow that enjoyed its own microcosm of accent and culture. He was enjoying the fresh winter's breeze wakening him up, helping him consider how he was going to blag his way into Pitt Street station, when his phone sounded.

Pushing a button on the panel, he activated the earpiece, to hear Tommy MacGregor's highland brogue, "You there, Kenny, hello?"

"Yes, I'm here Tommy. Long time, no hear."

"No, of course I'm not drinking a beer. It's nine o'clock in the morning," Tommy said.

"No, not beer. Long time, no hear!" Kenny shouted.

"Aye, it has been. You sound as though you're in some sort of tunnel."

"I'm on my bike, and it's a bit breezy. What's up, pal?"

"I just wanted to let you know that I got the lease on the pub on St. Vincent Street in Glasgow. 'Terviseks' is going international!"

Despite the wind, Kenny could hear the excitement in his voice. Tommy had recently come back to Scotland after several years in Estonia. He had been successful, opening a Scottish-themed pub in Tallinn, which hit the right note with the locals. Now he was opening an Estonian-themed pub in Glasgow. Both pubs would be called 'Terviseks', Estonian for cheers - a great way to start a conversation depending on how one pronounced the syllables, and with whom you were talking.

"Congratulations, Tommy. When's the opening?"

He was genuinely excited for his friend. He had worked hard to make something of his life, and this was the next positive step for him.

"Christmas Eve. I know it doesn't give us a lot of time to get the place ready. But we have already imported all the drinks. I don't want to miss December 24th because that's when Estonians celebrate Christmas. The theme will be '*two for the price of one*', since everyone will have another Christmas the next day." Tommy laughed at his own ingenuity. "Hopefully, you can make it. You'll get the chance to meet Marsha, and her brother, Digi."

Kenny knew that Tommy was besotted with Marsha. She was outstandingly beautiful. Tommy had shown him a photo taken with her when they were skiing in Otepää, a famous hill in Estonia reaching back to a settlement in the 6th century BC; now euphemistically known as the country's *winter capital*. She had made a point of introducing Tommy to parts of Estonia he had not seen before - it was clear she was wanting more than a short-term fling. No matter if she were Miss World, Kenny thought, she would need to be quite special if she was going to tame Tommy MacGregor.

"That would be good, pal, but something has come up. I will try. No promises. But I do quite fancy some of that black bread and seljanka soup you've been raving about."

"Okay, Kenny, I hope you can make it. I would love my best mate to be there, even if it's just for me to get a chance to treat you to a nice meal after all you've done for me over the years."

"Trust me. You've paid me above and beyond."

Kenny had a flashback to when Tommy had been instrumental in helping Kiltman capture Cullen Skink. It would not have happened were it not for Tommy's resourcefulness - and impressive ability to recover from a hangover. Kenny had decided not to disclose his Kiltman identity to his best friend. He trusted him with secrets just as much as Tommy trusted himself, which was barely at all.

They chatted some more, until Kenny found himself approaching another 'special' cul de sac in the vicinity of Pitt Street police station. Dialling off, he hoped he could be at the Terviseks opening, but realised there was a lot more chance of him being up to his eyes and ears in fish soup rather than seljanka. Skink would be aiming to make his mark soon after escaping. Being locked up for so long will have just fed his appetite for crazed schemes of destruction.

He parked the bike under a canopy at the end of the dead-end street, not far from Glasgow's bustling Charing Cross. He had created a fortified shed snug against an old warehouse once used for servicing trams. It was protected by a strong, canvas canopy, layered with iron mesh, sealed on all sides, and nailed into the tram tracks that disappeared under the wall. From the outside, it seemed innocuous and frail, but anyone nosy enough to try and enter would find it impregnable. When he approached the street, he had already checked to make sure there was no surveillance or prying eyes. He took off his mechanic's overalls and placed them in the panier, exposing his costume. Donning his mask and gloves, and activating his voice changer, he patted his sporran, checking Hair o' the Dog was still there. He opened it, removed the flask, and after a tasty slug, dropped it back in the pouch, closing the catch.

"Bring it on, Skink," he whispered to himself as he stepped out from under the canopy.

Pitt Street

"Oh, for goodness sake!" Gemmill said, putting his hands on his head, as Kiltman walked into the investigation room. Wilson and Fraser looked up from the photos they were studying of *Father* McQueen. Their visible relief more than matched Gemmill's rudeness.

"Hi everyone!" he announced cheerily. He decided that the best form of defence was attack. "I hadn't realised the name of the station had been changed."

"What are you on about?" Gemmill had a penchant for sounding grumpier with each syllable.

"When did it go from," he held it for a second, "Pitt Street to Pitbull Street?"

Kiltman heard the slight shuffle of feet as Gemmill twisted into position to lunge forward. Before he got the chance to move, Gemmill realised Kiltman had deftly put himself just far enough away to eliminate the Chief's reliance on surprise. He had the good sense not to throw the punch he had intended.

"Easy, easy, guys!" Fraser inserted his arms between the feuding parties. "Let's stay focused here. Nobody's slept much and our nerves are fraught. Let's take a chill pill."

Wilson glanced at Kiltman, controlling the grin threatening to upset Gemmill even more. *'Take a chill pill' - where did Fraser get that little gem?* crossed her and Kiltman's minds simultaneously.

"Look, Chief Constable Gemmill," Kiltman said, hands facing upwards. "I'm actually here for no other reason than to help you. If you find me obtrusive and not supportive, then by all means, tell me to go. But at least give me a chance to get involved. I know this guy, and he's warped and evil beyond belief."

He did not say that he had known Skink since they had studied together at Glasgow University. And that Skink was the only person who knew Kiltman's true identity. That was assuming he had not told anyone in the meantime.

"Okay," Gemmill's effort to compromise looked like he was bench-pressing 250 pounds. "Let's all work together then and see how we get on. But I'm warning you. If you turn this into a circus with your costume, gimmicks, and eccentricities, then you are off the case."

Eccentricities? Kiltman would park that alongside the cartoon character comments from yesterday.

"Sounds fair," he answered, nodding.

Wilson saw the moment to regain some momentum. "We've studied the photos of McQueen - and have reviewed the video footage from the various visits he made to Skink. Unfortunately, his beard and glasses covered enough of his face that we can't get a good idea of what he looked like. He never arrived by car, left no fingerprints on any of the documents he signed, and, other than the governor and the guards, met no other members of the prison service."

She paused and gazed at Kiltman then Gemmill, feeling a tad guilty she had turned her attention to Kiltman first, worrying that her boss would see this as a display of disrespect. Kiltman saw her unease and quickly threw in a verbal detour. "Thanks, Wilson, although the one thing you left out is the bit the guards will be kicking themselves about."

"And what would that be?" Gemmill asked.

"Well, I find it weird our prison guards didn't twig that Skink's accomplice had chosen as an alias the surname of the most famous escapee of all time."

"Eh, I don't think he signed himself in as Houdini, Kiltman." Fraser was perplexed at where this was going.

"No, not Houdini, Chief, I mean ex-Chief." He nodded towards Gemmill. "McQueen. Steve McQueen, The Great Escape. One of the best war movies of all time."

"Oh, for goodness' sake!" Gemmill moved his head to the side and looked at him with a puzzled frown. "Wilson, please go on."

"As for Skink's escape," she continued. Only Kiltman could see the slight twinkle in her eyes. She appreciated that he had thrown her a lifeline. "It's still a mystery. We have reviewed CCTV footage within a half mile radius of the prison and interviewed locals via door to door visits. We've come up with nothing."

Kiltman had expected this turn of events. When he had walked around the grounds immediately after the escape, he could smell Skink's scent all the way to the main gate. At that point the trail stopped, with the wind and rain diluting and destroying any hope of following the escapee's odour into the streets of Riddrie.

"Show me footage of the main gate," Kiltman requested.

She turned on the TV, did some rewinding and forwarding till she reached a frame that gave a clear shot of the front of the prison.

"Okay, now play the camera footage facing the gate from 10 pm onwards," he requested.

She found the spot and played the video. At 10.24, one of the guards left, huddled inside his great coat, and walked around the corner from the prison into the darkness.

"Who's that?" he asked.

"It's Officer Slevin, one of the guards, coming off duty," she answered. "We have checked and that was his knock-off time."

"Did he make it home?"

"Actually," she answered, "he lives alone. We called him this morning and we are awaiting a call back." As she said it, she felt a pang of concern at the pit of her stomach. She snatched her phone and pushed a couple of buttons. "Get someone round to Slevin's flat asap. Bang the door down if you have to."

"Wait a minute, are you saying you think he walked out the front door?" Gemmill asked. "Not quite broad daylight, but as good as?"

"Yes," Kiltman answered. "Check the prison again. You'll find Slevin somewhere inside. At best, unconscious. But I fear the worst."

Gemmill kicked the chair nearest to him, watching it smash off the wall. He was angry at how easily Skink had made his escape, but not nearly as incensed as he was at Kiltman realising it before him.

"We have to go back in there and ask the right questions as to how someone like Skink can just walk out the front door. Wilson, get your team up there right away. I need you focused on finding this weirdo."

Kiltman tapped his fingers, impatient to leave. "At this point, we're looking for a needle in a haystack. The good news, if there is any, is that his modus operandi is to send us little notes, with the worst form of poetry you can imagine. I would be surprised if one of them doesn't appear at some point today."

"How do you think he will get the note to us?" Fraser asked. "He has already scarpered."

"Unfortunately, I'm afraid the note will show up when we find Slevin."

Serenity in the Trossachs

"Welcome to your new abode, Mr. Skink," the man said. "Not quite as cramped as your recent digs, and certainly a better view."

He pulled back the curtain, to display a spectacularly vibrant hillside, heather and greenery fighting for space. Loch Achray, stretching underneath the hills, mirrored the beauty of the surrounding Trossachs, arguably one of the most scenic regions of Scotland. The small, snug cottage sat on the slopes of Ben A'an, overlooking the Trossachs Hotel, an extravagant manse of turrets, long windows, and imposing granite. At thirty miles distant, they were far enough away from Glasgow to remain incognito, and close enough to strike when needed.

"Yes, my friend," Skink acknowledged. "You have surpassed yourself." He raised his flute of champagne, pointing it towards his saviour. "To you and your ingenuity!"

The other raised his own glass and nodded his head. "Teamwork, intellect, imagination and sublime execution."

They both drank slowly and thoughtfully from their glasses, before he continued, "We are going to have fun on our upcoming adventure. Shall we chat?"

"Absolutely," Skink answered, placing his bubbly on the table. "That's why we're here, after all."

They turned to the wall facing the window. The maps, photos and chronological ordering of their plans were illuminated by the noon-day sun, bathing the room in a yellow light, contrasting with the darkness of the outcomes they had been designing. Above the display, spelled out in black felt tip pen, was written: *THE FRIEZE OF FEAR*.

"So here we are," Skink pointed at *December 22*. "The day I woke up a free man. And tomorrow, we strike here," he continued, flattening his thumb on the face of their victim as he posed for a photo in front of Edinburgh Castle. "I will take great pleasure in wiping that smile off his face. But there's one thing I have to do first."

"Oh!" His accomplice furrowed his brow. "What's left to do? We are ready. I have prepared all the arrangements: weapon, disguise, and logistics. Today should be a day of rest for us to prepare for the adventures beyond tomorrow."

"Ah, my friend, but I do have to check-in on the note I left for our Chief Constable and his helpers." He did not need to reference Kiltman and Wilson, this was understood.

"Really?" the other stepped back away from the frieze. "Why on earth would you leave a note for those imbeciles?"

"Because, my friend, that is how I do things. I like to play with my victims and taunt them. I like the mental acrobatics it creates, not to mention the sense of fun as they think they are close and then find they are still stuck in a vortex of confusion."

The other pressed his spindling fingers against the table, looking directly at Skink. "Your clues resulted in you being caught. Have you forgotten that small matter?"

There was no mistaking the flash of anger crossing Skink's features. It was barely there before it was gone. "There is nothing I dislike more than sarcasm, my friend. I should not need to defend myself. But, in the spirit of our cooperation and achievement of mutual goals, I shall take a moment to explain. When I was 'caught' as you say, I was minutes away from achieving my destiny. It was due to my underestimation of Kiltman's stubbornness combined with his enhanced sensory capabilities.

"If you had challenged me insofar as I had misjudged him, I would put my hands up and agree. He has a range of powers even he is struggling to comprehend. This time however, I have the measure of him, and will not make that mistake again."

Skink was thinking to himself that if Kiltman had not known him from their university days, he would not have made the link to the closed seminary in Langbank, and the location of his lair. But then Skink was not to have known that Kiltman was Kenny Morgan. Now he *owned* such a valuable piece of information, he was intent on using it at the right time. He had not shared this information with his accomplice: and did not intend to. This was his card to play, and his alone.

"Okay, tomorrow is your gig, Skink. I am your helper." He put his hands in the air with a sigh of acceptance. He pointed to the days beyond Christmas. "But when we move on to my agenda, I ask that you refrain from notes and clues."

Skink clasped his hands and bowed. "I would not expect it to be any other way. I'll be only too happy to help you in delivering and implementing your instruments of terror. After all, this is why you helped me to escape from that dump of a prison. You can rest assured I will honour my side of our Bar L bargain."

Skink smiled widely, displaying what remained of two rows of yellowy-black teeth, which would not have been out of place on an Egyptian mummy. And this was despite the free dental treatment he had been provided when he was 'in the can'. The dedication of the dentist had ensured he saved teeth that had barely survived years of neglect. In fact, he had made full use of the prison orthodontist in ways his accomplice would never know.

"I expect our hunters are only now finding the clue I left them," Skink sighed, and walked towards the fridge. "I will enjoy finishing the rest of this excellent champagne as I prepare for my trip."

The Clue

The buzz ricocheted through the silence that had descended on the investigation room. To a person, the four of them jumped. Wilson was the first to get to the phone.

"Yes?" She focused on the phone willing it to give her a steer on what to do next. "Where is he?" Her face drained. "Oh, that's terrible. We'll be there within half an hour. Don't touch a thing."

She put the receiver down gently, before looking at Gemmill this time. "Sir, they've found Slevin."

"Was he at home?" he asked, not sure what to expect.

"No," she shook her head. "He was still in the prison; he never left last night." The tremble in her voice belied their worst fears coming to life. "His body was found five minutes ago. He had been dumped in the freezer room in the basement below the kitchen."

"Right, you better get over there, Wilson." Gemmill could not stop a flicker of angst flashing across his features at the news. "And, eh, take your superhero pal with you. We'll need all the help we can get."

Kiltman was already walking out the door, as she gathered her notes and bag to follow him. She caught up with him at the elevator, just as he turned to wrap his arm around her shoulders.

"We'll get this maniac, Wilson," he said. "If God's my witness, we will catch him and make sure he never escapes again."

She felt strength in his half-hug. She needed it, on several levels. As they descended to ground floor and walked to the carpark, she was already rebuking herself for drifting towards self-pity.

"Right, let's go," she announced as they climbed into the car.

The engine had barely started when the sirens and strobes announced their departure. The flashes and noise probably saved them no more than ten minutes on the half hour journey; but those moments could prove precious when it came to whatever Skink had in store for them.

The next time they spoke was when they were standing alongside Slevin's body. Its frozen, crumpled dishevelment reflected how he had been thrown into the freezer room in a heap rather than laid out respectfully. No doubt, if Skink had more time, he would have created a clue in the shape of manipulated arms and legs. Instead he had gone for the unsubtle approach. A yellow Post-it Note - similar to the one that had dropped from the Christmas card - protruded from Slevin's left nostril. The edge of the paper was covered in a layer of white frost, sticking out of a nose bruised blue by the cold.

"Well, there's the clue. Zero out of ten for subtlety." Kiltman noticed that Wilson's expression was devoid of any emotion. He knew she practiced that look in front of the mirror to hide the sadness she felt inside in situations like this.

She took a pair of tweezers from her pocket and gently prised away the note, brittle with the iciness of the room, placing it in her free hand. The yellow against blue of her rubber glove seemed oddly elegant in the cold, soulless space. She stretched open the note, careful not to break it. As she spread the corners, she showed it to Kiltman, looking briefly at him to see how he was taking all of this. A waste of time, she realised, when a bland, blue, and white mask stared back at her, belying the fact his mind was racing. When was the next attack going to happen? Had they taken too long to find Slevin and were they now too late to intervene? All they had to do was decipher a clue that was literally unfolding in front of them. Wilson had used two pairs of tweezers to stretch the note and had placed some coins along its edges to keep it flat.

The words were miniscule in size to fit the confines of the Post-it Note, but there was no doubting the scrawl they had grown to loathe:

Dear Kiltman

I hope you've had a nice rest of late. You will need the reserves you've built up because your life is just about to get very busy. ☺

There lies a mystery in this town of victory
With a long street built by English,
at exclusion of Scottish ☹
Yet while Tom the Scot got so fraught

48

The time it cries is when the bullet flies
Your nemesis
Cullen Skink P   T   O

He watched her for a moment. "Does it make any sense to you?" He bent down to scrutinize each word.

She shook her head. "I've got no idea. I'll need to read it a few more times."

He had been wracking his brains to understand what *P   T   O* might mean. Until she nudged him to turn it over.

"Oh, yes," he answered, annoyed at himself for overthinking. Something he had been doing too much of recently.

Just one line awaited them.

PS. Don't waste time mourning Slevin. Every escapee needs someone on the inside.

She rubbed a hand under her chin.

"It's starting to make a bit more sense now. That's how he could get past security and out the front door."

"If this is how he treats his friends, Wilson," he spoke slowly, "I would rather not be his enemy." He meant to lift the atmosphere a notch, ease the tension.

She stared at him. "Kiltman, in case you hadn't realised. You are the enemy as far as he's concerned. He might talk to you in friendly words scrawled on bits of paper but be under no illusion what he would like to do with you." She halted for a second. "And me too, for that matter. But right now, we have other things to think about. Like towns of victory, long streets and a Scot named Tom."

She turned away from him, opened her phone, and pushed a speed dial. "Hello, McNeil?"

Sergeant McNeil, Wilson's second in command, was a policeman with a reputation for hard work and a no-nonsense approach. It was well-known that his IQ results were off the charts, and that he was a member of Mensa. Only his humility prevented him from boasting about it. Off-duty, he would let his hair down and join the bonhomie of his fellow officers in The Grove, his local pub in Finnieston. He was already en route to Slevin's home when she called.

"Yes, Ma'am. It's me." His deep baritone sounded refreshing at that moment.

"When you get to Slevin's place, bear in mind that it's part of the crime scene. Looks like he was an accomplice in helping Skink escape. Search for anything that might give an indication of where he's hiding out."

"Okay, Ma'am. Will do. Although based on his previous exploits, I doubt Skink will be there."

"Just be careful." She said closing the phone without her usual politeness.

Kiltman was working through each word of the clue, trying to find a hidden meaning, or some form of subtext to unravel the mystery, when he felt a tingling in his pocket. His phone was on vibrate. His Kenny phone - Kiltman did not carry a *superhero* version.

"Eh, excuse me, Wilson."

He walked towards the end of the room, far enough away to be out of earshot. Before he spoke, he glanced at the display, *Mum*. He flipped it open, ready to explain to his mother that he would call her back.

"Hi, Kenny?" a man's voice greeted him.

"Eh, yes," he answered. "Who's this? Where's my mother?" Panic rose in his chest as he realised that nothing was beyond Skink's resources and evilness.

"Kenny, it's George, your Mum's friend."

George had become a trusted companion for his mother over the last five years or so, building a strong friendship, more social than romantic as far as Kenny was aware. Although his mother would not have revealed to him if there was another level to their relationship. As far as Kenny could tell, George was an upright guy who helped his eighty year old mother find fun in ventures and trips she had given up on many years earlier, when his father had died in a horrific car accident. He had been five years old, left with only one memory of his dad, walking along the canal throwing bread out to the swans. When he remembered that walk, he actually saw it in black and white, somehow memorialising the event like an old photograph found in a drawer. More recently George had brought a spark to his mother's life. In turn, George would have benefitted from her yearning for fun; her incredibly tasty meat and three veg meals; not to mention her words of guidance which, like the food, you had to take whether you wanted to or not.

"Oh, hi, George," he found himself fighting a rising queasiness. "What's up?"

"It's your Mum, Kenny." He could feel George waiting, building up strength for the words he had been dreading to utter. "She's gone. I'm so sorry." George's voice cracked.

Kenny heard the muffled sobs between the words.

"George, what are you saying? I saw Mum at the weekend. We had tea in the garden. She was in great form. No, please check, please go back and look again, please make sure, please, please, please..."

"I'm so sorry, Kenny. So, so sorry. It seems she passed away peacefully in her sleep. I've just popped in to see her since I hadn't heard from her today."

George was no longer holding back his own tears. He had given up trying.

Kiltman's head was resting against the wall, his shoulders shaking, tears streaming down the inside of his mask.

"I'll be right over," he managed to say before he closed the phone.

"Kiltman," he heard from somewhere behind him, a remote voice invading his shock and rising grief. "I never knew you had a mobile phone." Her steps sounded loud crossing the room in his direction. As she approached he noticed her tone change from surprise to concern. "Are you okay?"

He sensed her hand reaching out to touch him. He could not cope with trying to explain. Even if he had wanted to, how could he unpick the layers of complexity intertwined with the shock of losing his mother and explaining to Wilson/Maggie. All he could do was lift a hand, flashing his palm towards her before turning and half-running, half-stumbling out of the room. He had to escape from the coldness of that space, the icy shards of grief wrapped tightly around his heart.

Rescued

It was shortly after noon when he burst out of the prison exit, into a bright, cold winter's day. He gulped the air greedily desperately trying to stem the flow of tears. The guards could hardly keep up with him when he ran along the corridors from the freezer room, rushing to get their keys out to open and close each of the doors and gates they had to pass en route to the exit. Later that day, they would share this story with their colleagues, surprised at how sensitive their local superhero had been to the sight of a dead body. In his game, they would muse, surely that was a run of the mill event.

He leant his back against the prison's exterior wall, and slipped down to crouch on his haunches, resting his head in his hands, crying uncontrollably. He had given up trying not to. It was beginning to feel good; the tears had a healing quality, tempering the sense of abandonment that had overwhelmed him in the call with George. Bizarrely, in the depths of his sadness, he realised he had not considered irrigating the inside of his mask for an eventuality such as this. He could feel himself falling into an abyss of grief, powerless to prevent himself drowning in the vacuum he felt around him.

Until he heard the clicking and shuffling of feet, and then the onslaught of high-pitched voices. He lifted his head to a surreal avalanche of cameras pointed in his direction, and most surprisingly of all, thirty Japanese tourists, animatedly talking, some shouting, "Kilt-ah-man! Kilt-ah-man!"

He clambered to his feet, bewildered by the group of foreigners completely out of place this close to the Bar L, in some sort of reverse kenopsia - large groups usually avoided gathering outside a prison.

At the front, a middle-aged man wearing a suit, shirt, and tie, approached him, bowed his head and said, "Hallo, Kilt-ah-man! The honour is ours for this great surprise to meet you."

Kiltman, growing more perplexed, was barely able to manage a nod, remembering how he had become front page news in

Japan when he had rescued the Japanese mini sub a few months earlier. Their search for the Loch Ness monster had been in vain, but they had come home with arguably a better, and more believable story, when saved by *Kilt-ah-man*, as he heard himself referred to in the news.

"Thanks," Kiltman mustered a half-hearted response, feeling the world closing in on him and his sadness.

"Today, we come to see Glasgow's famous prison," the man continued, oblivious to his hero's awkward posture. Kiltman was already beginning to sink to his knees again, succumbing to the weakness draining his legs of energy. "We love Victorian architecture, and Glasgow is one of best in your country. And Barlinnie uniquely so."

He rose from his bow, gawked at Kiltman, and continued to speak despite his hero's growing agitation. "And today, we meet you!"

The incessant noise of the cameras felt like they were piercing a hole in his ear drums. No matter how tightly he closed his hands over his ears, the cacophony of clicking continued with accelerating intensity.

The touch on his arm was gentle but firm pulling him up into his full height. He recognised the voice, although was surprised to hear it. "Man of Kilts, come with me! I help you escape!"

Sandra, his German lift to Bar L barely 12 hours earlier, was pulling him towards her green flowery Beetle on the other side of the road. The day was becoming too weird for words, he thought, resignedly accepting her prompting and direction. Within a minute, he was in the passenger seat with Sandra tearing along the side of the prison to escape the cameras and good-natured waves of the Japanese throng of happy Victorian architecture lovers.

He sat motionless, before turning to her, "Thank you, Sandra. But, eh, I didn't expect to see you, at least not so soon."

"Man of Kilts, genau! It is always my pleasure to meet you. You dropped this last night when you were in my car. I was coming back to hand it in to the prison for them to give to you, genau."

She handed him a buff envelope. He noted it was still sealed. Inside there were three tickets for the show he, Maggie and

Roddy had been planning to see at King's Theatre in Glasgow in January. Joseph and his Amazing Technicolour Dreamcoat, Roddy's favourite. He loved the Pharaoh Elvis scene and had been practicing it at home in anticipation of the show.

Fortunately, Sandra had not opened the envelope: otherwise she would have found Kenny's receipt, with name and address. He had stuffed it into his sporran when he had found it on the floor of his house a few days earlier, meaning to place it in a drawer. He was annoyed at himself - he could not afford for his clandestine personal life to be so easily disclosed.

"Oh, thanks, Sandra. I appreciate it," he managed to say.

"Are you okay?" she asked. He could hear the concern in her voice. She passed him a bottle of Highland Spring. "This might help."

He took it from her, lifted his mask and drank half the contents, enjoying the cold freshness. "Thanks. I needed that."

"Ah-hah!" Sandra smiled. "Maybe Man of Kilts cannot hold his drink!" She was remembering his hefty swallow of Hair o' the Dog. "Can I drop you at home? Where you can sleep it off."

"Eh, yes, maybe you're right," he answered.

He was beginning to feel himself recover slightly. He realised they were still driving around Riddrie's streets, while she waited for him to say where he wanted to go.

"Okay, Sandra," he coughed, and shook his head. "Can you take me towards the west of the city? I'll direct you."

She covered the handful of miles in record time to the cul de sac near Pitt Street, sensing the insistence in his voice. She was surprised that in spite of the urgency he waited with her for a few minutes in silence - until a couple of lads playing football had walked on towards the city centre. He thanked her for the lift and as he was about to exit the car, she reached across and gave him a strong hug, planting a kiss on his masked cheek. She felt his pain.

He clambered from the car and hurried along to the canopy to change into his overalls and uncover his Suzuki, which he considered a tad ironic considering his experience outside Bar L.

Sorry for his Loss

He manoeuvred the bike faster than usual heading west out of the city. He barely noticed that he had just passed Bouverie Street in Yoker where he had performed his first Kiltman rescue a few years earlier. Entering the town of Clydebank, on the outskirts of Glasgow, a couple of miles from Uisge Beatha, he felt its history envelope him. Clydebank was a world-renowned town famous for building some of the most iconic ships of the 20th century, including the Queen Mary and the Queen Elizabeth 2. Now he felt the pain of how quiet the town had become, the shipyards closed, its magnificent history written into the gritty tenements remaining from those legendary days. On his left as he approached the town centre, sitting above the river in splendid majesty, was the Titan, a huge crane surviving the dismantling savaged on the yards in the Thatcher years. It reminded all that Clydebank was the pride of the Clyde, and that the town had played a gloriously unique, and defining, role in Scotland's contribution to the war effort and industry.

The closer Kenny came to his mother's home, the more street corners and shops he passed with memories of moments spent with her over the years. He would enjoy her stopping to chat to neighbours and friends, always with respect and courtesy, sharing information and anecdotes to make their lives better from that conversation onwards. The tears were in freefall now, misting up the visor on his helmet. His mother had defined home and the town he grew up in. In her own way she had carried the scars of those depressed years when jobs were disappearing faster than the orders at the yards. She had remained strong throughout, just like the other mothers and fathers in the town, who did everything they could to help the next generations do better. To a person, they were titanic in how they defied gravity pulling them down, while helping their children up. He rubbed the inside of his helmet with his gloved hand, now better understanding what the Titan crane represented, testament to the people of this great town he was proud to come from.

He pulled up in front of his mother's semi-detached home, her pride and joy after over thirty years in bedsits, tenements, and maisonettes. Each of them became home very quickly with his mother adding her touch as soon as she had the keys to the door. But this semi-detached was the first time she had her own garden - the first time she could grow roses and sit in the sun outside her back door.

He felt the weight of grief in his legs, forcing himself to approach the house. George, standing at that door where his mother had welcomed and waved good-bye in equal measure, held out his hand.

"Kenny, I'm sorry for your troubles."

Age old words of commiseration that Kenny heard directed at him. He pulled George towards him and cried into his shoulder. Kenny felt his strong embrace ease some of the burden of anguish weighing on him so heavily. The hardest part was still to come.

"Is Mum upstairs?" he asked.

George nodded. "The doctor has just been and provided the death certificate."

Kenny studied George with an intensity born of fear. He did not want to ask the question, afraid of the answer. He could not get Cullen Skink and his malevolence out of his mind. He would not put anything past the levels of evil he aspired to. Please God, he thought, let my mother not be the price I pay for bringing Skink to justice.

"What did he say?" he asked.

"It was a heart attack, Kenny. In her sleep," George answered, his own tears streaming down his cheeks. "There was no sign she suffered; it looks like she passed peacefully."

He gave George another hug before entering the house to ascend the dreaded steps.

He walked into the bedroom, to see his mother, Molly Morgan, lying there with the covers neatly tucked in around her. She had been the unflappable rock who had helped him in so many ways. Her face had a hint of a smile, her features relaxed, her dimples and laugh lines testament to the joy she brought to others - how she relished the company of friends, family and strangers alike. He bent down to kiss her forehead, cold to the touch. The absence of any hint of warmth shocked him; there was nothing of her energy and love of life left. It had gone.

It was at that moment Kenny realised he would never again doubt there was a heaven. He had always been dubious and had kept the thought at a distance, since there was no existential proof that such a place existed. As a chemist, he had been blessed - some would say cursed - with the belief that all things had to have a physical basis. If it was not grounded in the chemical compounds we had documented and lived science by, then it could not exist. Now, looking at his mother's lifeless body, he knew he could doubt no longer. It was not possible for so much love, passion, joy, and kindness to disappear into nothingness. She was out there. She was just no longer with him.

He spent a few minutes trying to find the right words to tell his mother how much he loved her, but nothing came. The words sat too far back behind his sadness and confusion; nothing was working its way to his mouth. He knelt in silence at the side of her bed and rested his head on her bosom, like he had done so often before but barely remembered. He knew there was one thing left to do before he stood up and left. He closed his eyes, placed his hand on her chest and let his sense of touch take over, allowing himself to feel at one with his mother. It took a couple of minutes, until he sensed the exact spot where the artery had blocked and caused the heart to stop. He concentrated for a long minute, before exhaling a slow, deep breath. He was quite sure her death had been instantaneous. It had been a massive heart attack, with immediate consequences. His mother's huge, warm, giving heart had just stopped in an instant. The doctor had been correct.

He concentrated further, touching his hand gently to his mother's abdomen, waiting for a hint of a foreign substance in her body that could have triggered the arterial blockage. He felt a whisper of relief when nothing came back through his fingertips: he could not have handled the anger on top of the sorrow.

He kissed his mother once again and turned to leave the room. Before he left, he opened his mother's CD player, and found a Danny O'Donnell CD already inserted. Danny came from Donegal just like his mother. He knew all the songs his mother had grown up with. Only he sang them the way she felt they should be sung. Kenny moved the player to the song, *It Is No Secret*, and turned to leave, Danny's musical accompaniment filling the room. George was standing at the door waiting for him to have his moment.

"Kenny, the undertaker is coming later. If it's okay with you, I'll arrange the funeral. Your mother asked me to do this several years ago. She felt you would need the time to prepare."

"Yes, George, that would be good. I appreciate you doing that."

He felt a tinge of pain at his mother having this conversation with her friend, but not with him. But he also realised that he would need the time to grieve; and his mother, as usual, had got it right.

"The undertaker proposed the funeral to be on Boxing Day. Let me know if you want it changed. We'll post the notice in the Evening Times so that people can plan to attend." George waited a moment, before continuing. "You don't need to answer now but you may want to consider whether you deliver the eulogy yourself or leave it to the priest."

Eulogy? He had only found out less than two hours earlier that his mother was gone, and now he had to write a eulogy. He considered George with palpable incredulity, barely able to speak. "Look, Kenny, just think about it. It's a big ask, but it may help you."

"Help me?" He sounded more aggressive than he had meant to. "Help me? How on earth would it help me, to stand in front of all those people like a quivering wreck, bumbling my way through words I can't even imagine writing down, let alone speaking?"

He took a deep breath. "I'm sorry, George. I didn't mean to direct that at you. You are incredible. Mum loved you. And she would be so pleased to know you're taking care of the arrangements. She knows that... I mean, she knew that organising was not my strong point."

"That's okay, Kenny. If you need anything, let me know. I'm going over to New York for a couple of days after the funeral for the United Nations discussion on self-determination. It's a long story but I used to be in the diplomatic corps, and I've been helping draft some of the proposed resolutions. Anyway, until then I will be around. Call me, any time."

"Thanks. I need to go. If you want me to do anything, let me know." He turned to take one last look at his mother, before walking out of the room his bottom lip trembling, listening to Danny's gentle, soulful voice croon, the heartfelt lyrics following him down the hallway:

Footsteps walking with me,
Footsteps I cannot see.
But every move I make,
And every step I take.
I know they're there with me.

He walked out of the house into a world far emptier than it had been when he woke to Fiona ringing the bell only a few hours earlier. Then it struck him. He had to tell people. He had to tell Roddy his Gran was gone - she would no longer cradle him on her knee and soak his forehead in slobbery kisses; to tell Fiona that her mother-in-law/ex-mother-in-law, was no longer going to give unsubtle tips about the best way to make mince 'n' tatties. And Maggie. She had only started to get to know his mother but they had developed an immediate connection, both loving the Irish card game of 25's, and listening to Danny O'Donnell before bed-time - one of Maggie's dark secrets, which she had made him promise never to mention to anyone.

Kenny climbed back on his bike. He would be home in 15 minutes: and had to focus. Telling Roddy was going to be difficult. He knew whatever the words he chose to convey the message, he would never be able to explain the sense of vacuum he could already feel spreading out from him, enveloping his world.

He started to feel the urge to do something he had not done in years.

II

Off the Wagon

Glentocher 12

Kenny walked into Uisge Beatha around six o'clock in the evening. It had already been a long day. He knew it was not going to end soon. Shona, Roddy and Angie were gathered around a poster they had created timelining the key milestones in Scotland's history, stretching as far back as the Romans' failed conquest. The innocence of their smiles and light-hearted banter made him feel even more distant from reality. He was struggling to hold himself together.

He had called Angie's father just before he entered the house, to ask him to come and pick her up. He also mentioned that Roddy would need a friend after he broke the news his Gran had gone. Omar Lafit had sounded genuinely sad to hear this news. He had insisted he come right away to Uisge Beatha to take them both back to his place, assuming Roddy wanted to do that. Kenny needed some time to himself to regroup and collect his thoughts, without Roddy watching him grieve.

Omar would be there within the half hour.

"Hi, Dad," Roddy shouted and ran across to hug him. Kenny felt the love and loyalty seep into every bone and muscle in his body. He held onto Roddy longer than normal. His son looked up. "Dad, you've been crying. What's wrong?" Roddy's anxiety sat incongruously on his soft features.

"Shona," Kenny said, ruffling Roddy's hair. "I'll take it from here, thanks so much."

"I had a great time Mr. Morgan. I learned more from Roddy and Angie about Scotland's history than all my time at school."

She picked up her coat on the way out. He reached across and handed her a few notes. It was always an awkward moment for him, even though she had been looking after Roddy for years. Shona seemed completely unaware of his awkwardness, and melancholy, as she took it from him and left through the kitchen.

"Angie, your father will be here soon to pick you up. Can you start to pull your things together?" He was focused on taking one step at a time. "I just need a few minutes with Roddy, thanks."

Angie busied herself tidying the plethora of project accoutrements into her backpack, while Roddy held Kenny's hand as they walked through into the den. This small room was supposed to be Kenny's man-cave, but had become completely overrun with his son's comics, videos, and sci-fi instruments. Roddy had never lost his love of space, growing with every NASA rocket launch or meteorite shower presented in the science journal. Kenny directed Roddy to sit in the rocking chair Kenny sometimes used to while away time when listening to Phil Collins or Billy Joel ballads. The chair appeared unusually large compared to his son's fragile frame.

"Roddy, I have some news." He had decided not to insert the word 'sad'.

"Yes, Dad, please tell me. I'm getting worried." Roddy was squinting at his father, working hard not to let any emotions show. It seemed he was about to explode with the suppressed worry.

"I know, Son." He felt his throat constricting. "You know that Gran was always going to church, lighting candles and praying. One of the things she always prayed for was that when…"

Kenny's tears started to flow. Roddy did not interrupt. He just placed his hands under his father's eyes to collect the tears on his soft fingers.

"The thing she prayed for, other than you and me and your Mum, was that when God decided it was time for her to go to heaven, that it would be peaceful and painless."

"Yes, and she also asked me to pray for the same thing for me, Mummy and you." Roddy knew what was coming but waited for his father to say it.

"Well. Gran went to heaven last night. She is with God now. And she went so peacefully, just like she prayed for."

"Oh, Dad!" Roddy threw his hands around his father's neck. "I am so sorry, I am. But…"

He leant back to look at his son whose tears were unabashedly rolling down his cheeks. "Yes?"

"Gran also told me that when she went to heaven, she would be with us all the time rather than just when we saw her here on earth. She's with us now, and probably hugging us both at this very moment."

Roddy leant in and squeezed Kenny even harder. He never wanted to let his father go.

It was not long before the doorbell rang, interrupting their tears and hugs.

"Roddy, tonight your Mum will be coming back late from London. But Angie's father said you could have a sleepover at theirs. Would you like that?"

"But I'm worried about you." Roddy's concern rested in his moist eyes.

"No, don't worry, pal. I'll need to take some time to think about Gran and prepare for the funeral. It'll be on Boxing Day. But if you want to talk, then call me. I'll keep my phone switched on. And I'll call you tomorrow in the morning." He was surprised at how efficient he was sounding.

"Okay, Dad. Same for you! I'll keep my phone switched on too." Kenny and Fiona had conceded in giving him a mobile phone to help manage the two-house system.

Omar was standing at the door waiting for them when they walked back to the kitchen. Roddy grabbed his bag and gave his father another hug before going out to the car with Angie. He whispered to her as they opened the door. Kenny knew he was telling her about his Gran. His heart skipped a beat when she gave his son a crushing hug, nestling her head in his neck.

The tall, handsome man at the door spoke softly, "Kenny, I am so sorry."

Omar had come from the Middle East when he was younger as a single parent, Angie's mother not surviving to see her daughter grow up with poise and grace. He carried himself with an air of calm and thoughtfulness, inspiring trust, and an expectation of words of wisdom. His reputation as a powerful orator and bastion of fairness were considered his strongest qualities by the media. When he was speaking in public he could light up the room with his energy and impassioned views, displayed in his deep, soulful eyes. Kenny could feel himself enjoying the man's calmness and empathetic smile.

"If there's anything we can do, just let me know." He held Kenny's hand tightly. "Don't worry about Roddy, he'll be fine with us. Just do what you have to, to get the space you need."

He nodded his thanks; all his words had gone. He waved as Omar drove off down the drive, Roddy's innocent face in the back window, both hands waving. When they turned out of sight, he walked back into the house. He should have been hungry since he had not eaten since breakfast. His mother would have chastised him for this, he considered, with a shake of the head. He walked down the wooden stairs to the basement, smelling the welcoming aroma of Hair o' the Dog.

Opening a drawer underneath the boxes of glass bottles and tubes, kept as spares for the distillation process to produce his special whisky, he felt inside and found what he was looking for. A bottle of Glentocher 12-year old, three quarters full. He placed it on the table alongside a dimpled glass he had not used in years.

He had not decided yet if he would drink the whisky. It was a huge decision, and not one he would know how to reverse if he started. The last time he had consumed alcohol was the night before he rescued his favourite barmaid, Maureen, and her daughter, Sarah, from the raging fire consuming the first floor flat he had passed just an hour earlier. Alcohol had progressively taken over his life until that moment, fuelled by his employment in the world of whisky. He had lost sight of the things that truly mattered; and when the scales were finally lifted from his eyes, he had lost everything on that fateful day when he had lost his job, minutes after his wife and son had left him.

Paradoxically, the product that ruined his life saved him. Hair o' the Dog had unleashed in him the power to make a difference in the world. He had chosen to give back, to be the bigger person, help others live better lives while saving his own. Opening that bottle on the table would be the worst decision he had made in years, unwinding the positive journey he had been on and the new life he had built. He would not pretend to himself that '*just one wee dram would do no harm*'. He knew exactly how much damage would be unleashed the moment he let the genie out of the bottle.

He forced himself to break away from his flirtation with the whisky, as if being prised from the arms of a seductive siren. He pressed speed dial for Maggie's number. It rang a few times, before she answered abruptly, "Kenny, look please give me some time. You know I'm stuck in the middle of this Skink mess."

"But, Maggie, I need to…"

"I am in the middle of Barlinnie surrounded by police officers." She was still reeling from Kiltman walking out on her. "Give me a break, just for a day or so. Okay?"

He paused and sighed. "Yes, fine, bye. Take your break."

He pushed the stop button wearily, feeling isolated in his grief. He pushed the back of his head against the soft leather of the chair, trying to find strength for the next call.

Fiona was having dinner in an Indian restaurant in London, before taking the sleeper train back to Glasgow. He felt terrible at having to spoil her evening like this: he would have waited until the next day. If he could help her avoid a day of grief then he would have done so. However, Roddy would want a consoling call with his mother before bedtime. He would be feeling the loneliness of being away from home and the sadness of the realisation he would never see his Gran again. Kenny was proud of how stoical his wee boy had been earlier. But that stoicism would give way at some point to sorrow and floods of memories.

When he broke the news to Fiona, she did not even attempt to hold back her tears. Her expression of sorrow was genuine, she had adored his mother. Their relationship did not falter or waver after the divorce. They both knew that the marriage had dissolved long before the courts decided. Molly had been pleased to see them work hard to make sure Roddy was not punished for his father's mistakes. Before they hung up, she confirmed she would immediately call Roddy - and asked Kenny to look after himself. He knew what she meant by that.

As he moved to put down the phone, he noticed that there had been a missed call. It was from his mother's phone. He hit the message play button expecting to hear George's voice explaining the funeral details. He would rather not listen, but knew it was important now to focus on Boxing Day. How he was going to get through Christmas was beyond him.

He sat upright with a jolt when he heard the voice.

"Hello, sonny boy," his mother spoke falteringly in her Irish brogue, as strong as the day she had left Ireland sixty years earlier. She had hated talking to machines but had learned how to persevere, choosing to keep talking as if every call to an answering machine was a chance to practice. "Sorry to call you

65

so late but can you pop down tomorrow? There's something I want to talk to you about. Don't worry, no need to call back tonight. I'm off to bed. We can chat in the morning. Night, night, son. I love you."

The phone went dead.

He reviewed the message alert and realised she had called the prior evening at 10 pm, when he had been dropping Roddy at Fiona's. With everything that had happened since, he had not had a moment to check his messages. The sound of her voice brought a rush of tears to his eyes. They had barely dried since the last gush with Roddy. Whatever she had wanted to say to him, he would never know. It had gone with her to the grave, as she would have said, in her endearing Irish way of adding layers of drama to anything related to death. But what was it? Had she needed something? Had she felt the pangs of the heart attack threatening? If he had returned her call, would she be alive today?

That was it, he nodded to himself, as he twisted the cork from the bottle. There was only so much one man could take, he thought, as he poured a hefty dram down his throat not caring to savour or enjoy - only obliterate.

Pitt Street December 23rd

"What do you mean, he just ran away?" Gemmill asked.

He was not happy to be in the station at 6 am. And certainly not when he was compensating for a runaway superhero.

"That's what I said, sir. It was all a bit bizarre. I managed to get to the prison gate to see him disappear in a VW Beetle with a young girl." Wilson was still trying to make sense of Kiltman's disappearance. He had known the importance of working through the clue together, otherwise Skink had free reign to wreak terror. There was nothing more urgent. Yet, he had literally run away. In his absence, she had turned the clue upside down and inside out, repeating the words again and again, no further forward than when they had first found the note.

"Beetle! Young girl!" Gemmill shouted, barely hiding the gloat in his Glasgow glottal stop. "This is exactly what you get when you rely on a muppet to help with an investigation."

"Yes, that's correct, sir. I mean, the Beetle and girl. Not sure if I ascribe to the muppet comment though." This was her first hint of rebellion in Gemmill's presence. She continued quickly. "We tracked the girl down from her registration number. It was quite unique." She was never going to describe it in Gemmill's presence, red rags and bulls coming to mind.

"She's a German student who picked him up the night before when he waved her down on Duke Street. He had dropped something in her car. So, she came back to Bar L to give it to him. For some reason he left with her. Apparently, she took him to just around the corner from here, but he has not been seen since. She was very taken with him; and hinted that he had been acting kind of weird when she dropped him off."

"I'll say. Waving cars down on Duke Street? Running out of prisons?" Gemmill asked exasperatedly. "Is this guy for real? Let's forget him, we need to sort this clue out. Fast!" Gemmill leant over the Post-it Note and read the words aloud slowly:

"There lies a mystery in this town of victory
With a long street built by English,

at exclusion of Scottish
Yet while Tom the Scot got so fraught
The time it cries is when the bullet flies

"I've never heard so much drivel. Kiltman was right about one thing: this guy's no poet. He could be talking about anything."

Fraser had been quiet until that moment. "Downstairs, we have ten people working on this clue, and they're all stumped. It's typical Skink. A clue that he spends more time trying to get to rhyme than conveying a decent chance of solving it."

He slapped the table with his hand, feeling a familiar sense of déjà vu overwhelming him. Why on earth was he not on the banks of Loch Lomond with his fishing rod in hand, sipping from a flask of tea, listening to the Clancy Brothers? Skink had nearly broken him six months earlier when he was sailing towards retirement. Since then he had been lauded for his leadership in the face of escalating crime in the West of Scotland. A humble man to his core, he did not seek out praise and adulation, but he had to admit he had been enjoying it. If it had not been for Kiltman, the madman would have caused untold disaster. Fraser prayed that their superhero was okay and had not crumpled under the same stress Fraser was feeling for the second time in six months.

Wilson was walking back and forth in the room, dark shadows underneath her brown eyes. She did not need to look at the note, she had memorised it, having spent all night reading it out loud trying to find the slightest of hints as to where it might lead. She was also worried about Kiltman. The German girl had been right, his behaviour had been weird even for him. If only he had not been so secretive about the phone hidden in his sporran, she could call him to sort this mess out. Although she understood the secrecy. As soon as they had his number, they would be able to track him; it would not take long to unravel his identity. It all made sense but was just not helpful in the middle of a crisis.

BZZZZZZZZ. BZZZZZZZZ.

The sound of the phone startled them. Who was calling at 6 am?

Victory

He woke with a start, his right leg numb, his head screaming with pain. His first hangover in years, and it felt like it. He had been sitting in the chair all night. Rubbing his eyes with the palms of his hands, he encouraged his vision to start to focus. The first thing he saw was the bottle of whisky. The empty bottle.

He stood up gingerly and made his way to the bathroom, the pins and needles in his right leg helping in the wake-up process. He had hobbled a few steps when he placed his foot on an object in the middle of the floor. Normally he would have kicked it to the side, but his sleepy limb did not have the power to cope with unidentified fallen objects. The leg wobbled slightly before caving in underneath him, throwing his balance off. Fortunately, nobody was home to witness a clumsy half-somersault onto his back and his head slamming off the basement tiles.

"Owwwww!" he groaned.

The last thing his head needed was a pain on the outside as well as the inside. Lying on the cold floor, he looked back to see what the object was that had him taking a flyer. It was a running shoe - one of a pair he had bought a year earlier when he was determined to get back into an exercise routine. He felt the shame of realising it appeared as good as new.

Abruptly he jumped into an upright sitting position and grabbed the shoe. He lifted it to within inches of his face, studying the brand logo as if he had never seen it before. Nike. Why was this so important to him? Something was nudging its way from the back of his mind to the front, like a steam train with the brakes on. The harder he tried, the slower it seemed to come to him. Nike. Why was he suddenly fixated on that brand? New Balance and Adidas did not seem to do it for him. But Nike inspired him to have a hot flush. He was sweating, his hands damp as they turned the shoe over and over. Victory. Victory. Victory!

He recalled the first line of Skink's clue: *There lies a mystery in this town of victory*

Nike, the Ancient Greek word for victory. He remembered it from a pub quiz in Sweeneys years before. He had been the worse for wear throughout the night, sitting on his own at the corner of the bar, most probably mumbling to himself. One of the teams, short a player, had asked him to sit with them, hoping this genius chemist from Wallace Distillers would help the team win the £10 prize. They regretted their offer as soon as he sat down, spilling a pint of Guinness all over their answer sheet.

It was all coming back to him now. There was a second part to the question that night. Which European city had been called Victory?

A famous town. A coastal location. Somewhere exotic, but also accessible.

It rushed back to him with the force of a slap on the face.

Nice.

Nice, France, had originally been named Nikaia after the Greek Goddess of Victory. The Greeks had created a settlement there nearly four centuries before Christ appeared, one of their early forages along the unknown Mediterranean coastline. Over the years the hard consonants of Nikaia had evolved into the softer, more French version of Nice.

He climbed to his feet and turned on the TV, moving from channel to channel until he found the news on BBC. He only had to wait a few minutes before the newsfeed switched to a picture of a beautiful beach with a colourful, medieval old town in the background, its age contrasting with the more modern hotels and apartment blocks dotted along the seafront.

"Bonjour!" Grant MacTavish appeared on the screen.

Kenny nearly jumped from his chair at his ex-university chum's face taking over the majority of his wide screen TV. He had put on a bit of weight, cheeks more squidgy than a few months earlier. No doubt, dining out on the bonuses he would have earned in interviews and documentaries about Cullen Skink and his capture. Grant had become a self-christened expert on Skink, having had an uncanny knack of showing up during the chase when least expected. The fact he had known Donald MacKenzie at university, albeit from a distance, gave him a degree of credibility only Grant could milk as much as he had done. Other news channels and media had tapped into what they thought was a deep level of insight, when Kenny knew Grant told just enough truth to be plausible, happily embellishing the rest with his fertile imagination.

"What a gloriously beautiful day here in Nice, on the spectacular Côte d'Azur, the jewel of France's coastline. Our First Minister has picked the perfect morning to renew the Auld Alliance with Scotland's centuries-old ally. Several new trade deals are being signed this morning, recognising the solidarity and respect Nice and Edinburgh hold for each other. They have existed in parallel since they were twinned nearly 50 years ago, and now our leaders intend to take this partnership to a new level, working more closely together, both benefitting from the skills each country brings to the table.

"As I stand here on the Promenade des Anglais, I can see the town awaken with the knowledge that at the end of today, Nice and Edinburgh will be more Siamese than Dizygotic."

The camera panned over MacTavish's shoulder to the seafront, already busy with cyclists, joggers and rollerbladers, dodging the long row of palm trees offering a smattering of shade from the early morning sun.

MacTavish touched his earpiece, flinching at how loudly his producer had screamed at him to keep the jargon to himself. Kenny barely noticed this as he slapped his hand on his head, then yelped with the self-inflicted ache, remembering the second line of Skink's latest ditty. *With a long street built by English, at exclusion of Scottish.*

Promenade des Anglais. It was the longest street in Nice and ran all the way along the coastline connecting both ends of the city. It had been built by British expats in the early 19th century. The French had chosen to call it Promenade des Anglais rather than Promenade des Britanniques, which most likely made a few of the Scots at the time less than '*content*'. This omission may also have aggravated Skink, prompting him to use this as a way to remind everyone of how Scotland should be considered equal on the world stage.

Skink was going after the First Minister. The more Kenny thought about it, the more it made sense. It was exactly the international platform Skink thrived upon. As the interview with MacTavish closed, a breaking news report interrupted the start of the next programme to announce that Cullen Skink had escaped from Barlinnie prison. It provided a description: five foot six, completely bald, hooded brown eyes, with broken mahogany-yellow teeth. While useful for the media to distribute an alert and description, Kenny was quite sure he would have altered his looks quite dramatically already. Partially for anonymity, but mainly because he was no oil-painting.

Gemmill would have given it a lot of thought before disclosing that the menace had escaped. In all honesty, Kenny mused, he would have done exactly the same thing. Good to know he could agree with Gemmill on something. It would not stop the Scottish public from reacting badly to this news. They had barely recovered from his nuclear threat earlier that year and now he was at large again. There would be more than a busload of Japanese architect lovers outside Barlinnie prison in a few hours, reporters and public desperate to know how this could have happened.

He picked up his mobile phone, realising the battery had died over night. He plugged it in and waited a few minutes for enough power to call. He slipped on his Kiltman mask, activating the voice changer, triggered 'block caller ID', then dialled the number he had committed to memory six months earlier.

Half a Clue is Better Than No Clue

"Hello?" Wilson pushed the speaker button on the phone. "Who's this?"

"It's me. Kiltman," he said.

"Ah-hah! He's alive after all," Gemmill laughed without a hint of humour. "Decided to check-in on your part time job then?"

"Look, we don't have time for this," Kiltman continued, his head feeling like it was trapped in a vice. "I've figured out the first part of the clue, the first two lines. I know the location."

"Well," Wilson intervened, "don't keep us in suspense, Kiltman."

Her attempt to sound a tad light-hearted was missed by everyone including Kiltman.

"It's Nice, south of France," he continued. "The First Minister's there to reignite the twin city relationship between Nice and Edinburgh, with some minor trade deals being signed to memorialise the event."

"Ok, Kiltman," Fraser spoke up. He had been worried about his friend. It was not like him to go off radar. Even by Kiltman's standards, the exit at Barlinnie had been overly thespian. "Just help us catch up. Why Nice?"

"Hi, Chief," Kiltman responded. "Nice was originally called Nikaia, after the Ancient Greek Goddess of victory. There is a road running along the beach for the best part of five miles, called Promenade des Anglais. And our First Minister is there today."

Boom, boom, boom. He had made it sound so simple.

The Pitt Street investigation room fell silent. They had been spending their time primarily focused on locations where the Scots had been victorious in battle against England. The number of battles and victories had surprised them all, which they had discounted one by one, not finding a prominent event or reason for Skink to single one of them out for an attack. They had stopped to focus on what Kiltman had to say next. Nothing came. "And the rest?" Gemmill prompted.

"That's as far as I've got, folks. You need to notify the First Minister to cancel the meeting, or at a minimum to take it somewhere else."

His throat felt very dry.

"Seriously?" Gemmill again. "Even if your clue interpretation is correct, how on earth could Skink get from Bar L to Nice within 36 hours and have a ready-made plan to off the First Minister? This has all the hallmarks of creating maximum disruption in as short a time as possible, to put egg on our country's face, during an important international meeting."

Fraser stared hard at Gemmill. "Look, we have to at least notify the First Minister's office. They can then decide what they want to do. But you can't sit on this and see what might happen."

This was the first time he had confronted Gemmill. He had bitten his lip on several occasions out of respect for the new Chief, but the risks of calling this wrong were too high. What was the worst Gemmill could do? Fire an ex-employee?

"Well, *Chief*!" Gemmill's sarcasm was knitted into the solitary syllable. "Sounds as though we're building a consensus around our superhero's words of advice." He turned to Wilson. "Are you also a fan of Walt Disney productions here?" He pointed at the telephone.

She glared at him, quelling the anger rising in her chest. She knew Kiltman well enough to know he had a reason for running away. His instinct had made all the difference between them and Skink last summer. She trusted him implicitly.

"Sir, we have to let them know, with a strong recommendation to cancel."

Gemmill did not get to his position without some degree of common sense and compromise. "Okay, looks like we have consensus."

He stopped and rubbed his chin.

"Wilson, call the First Minister's office and explain our fears, and our recommendation. The First Minister is already there, he flew out yesterday. Get yourself on a plane right away and make your way to wherever he's at. Make sure you keep him wrapped in cotton wool until you get him back here."

They heard Kiltman exhale a sigh of relief over the speaker. He was the first to speak. "Okay, I'll get cracking on the rest of the clue. I'll let you know if I come up with anything."

"Kiltman?" She caught him before he hung up. "Do you fancy a trip to the south of France?" She tried to keep the angst in her voice to a minimum.

"Wilson, I look forward to you buying me a Niçoise salad on some other occasion. Not this time."

He was struggling to sit in an upright position, let alone chase down Skink. The thought of a three-hour flight made his head spin even more. He needed a mug of strong coffee and lots of water. His mother was in his thoughts every waking moment; he had to find a place where he could move forward. He was not even close to that spot.

"Ok," Gemmill intervened, rolling his eyes. "Let's leave date night for another place and time, shall we?"

Gemmill pushed the button to close the call. She felt Kiltman's absence immediately. She had handled many cases before he had come along, and she had been commended and promoted on the successes she had delivered. But with regards Skink - and no matter how odd Kiltman could be - she had come to rely on her kilted partner.

Maggie Wilson

Wilson shifted restlessly in the back seat of the police car, moving her position every few seconds. The call to the First Minister's office had not gone well. His team's focus had been on making sure the visit would not be disrupted. All efforts should be employed in that direction, rather than upsetting a meeting at the last minute that had been planned months in advance. There had been a hint of criticism in their tone. Yes, they confirmed, they would inform the First Minister of the warning and caution him on the risks to be considered. However, they made a point of emphasizing the low probability of an ex-convict less than two days on the run attempting to attack the trade deal signing in a town three hours flight away. But they appreciated her advice, nonetheless.

More than a little frustrated at their pedestrian reaction to her words of caution, she had reached out to the office of the Mayor of Nice, catching the benefit of the one-hour time difference before the flight was due to leave. The officer she spoke to had clearly just turned up in the Nice police station. She could tell he had not finished his first coffee or cigarette, or both. Between his broken English and her sparse memories of Longman's audio-visual French classes, she was pleased that he understood enough to put a few more officers on the event. There would now be an increased degree of surveillance, particularly on the promenade where the final stages of the meeting were to take place. He offered to send someone to the airport to pick her up when she arrived, which she accepted graciously.

She exited the car at Glasgow airport happy to enjoy the fresh westerly breeze buffeting her face, akin to an early morning massage. It was colder than she had expected. She had not dressed for the bracing wind billowing around the airport car park. Closing her eyes, she inhaled deeply working hard to calm her nerves, which had been on edge since Skink's escape. No, since before Skink's escape, she thought. Her sense of well-being and balance had tipped in the wrong direction when Kenny began his bumbled attempt to ask her to marry him. Or had he? She had been in so much of a hurry to close him down, she had not waited to hear what he had wanted to say. She still believed she had made the right call the following morning, to create some space between them. The kiss with Kiltman had been nice, she had to admit that. It was the treachery of those five seconds that had weighed on her every minute of the day since then. Kenny deserved much better. He lived a simple life, complication-free. It was not fair for her to bring confusion into his quiet world.

She walked briskly through to departures, noting that the airport was busy. In fact, it was much busier than usual, with travellers on their way to families and friends to celebrate the holidays. The innocence on their faces and carefree chitter-chatter seemed incongruous in the face of Skink being free. She had to remind herself that this was a good thing, no point in everyone feeling the anxiety turning her stomach inside out. Distractedly, she searched her carry-on bag for her passport. The airport police had her ticket; they had been alerted to the urgency of her trip. As she approached their office, she felt the phone vibrate inside her jacket pocket.

"Yes, Wilson here?" she answered just as she flipped open the mouthpiece, then saw it was Fiona's name on the display. "Hi, Fiona! Sorry, I'm at the airport, I didn't realise it was you."

"Maggie, can you talk?" Fiona's voice was brittle, barely louder than a whisper.

"Sure," Wilson felt the panic rise to her throat. "Is everything alright?"

"Have you heard?"

"No…" Wilson was now afraid.

"I've got some very sad news," Fiona was crying again. "It's Molly, Kenny's mother. She passed away; night before last." She stopped to take a breath. "Peacefully, in her sleep."

Wilson dropped onto one knee, cradling her forehead in her hand. "Oh, no! I'm so sorry. She was such a lovely lady, with so much sparkle and life about her."

"I know." Fiona paused for a moment. "Look, I've just picked up Roddy from his friend's house. I'm going to make him some breakfast. I wasn't sure if Kenny had let you know. But I'm worried about him. Especially now that I realise he didn't call you."

The weight of her words hung in the air. If Fiona had any emotional energy left, she would have prodded more deeply. But she was spent.

"Of course, Fiona. Don't worry. I'll call him. Take care."

They both closed the call at the same time. She felt the pain of remembering how she had hung up on Kenny the previous evening when he was most likely trying to break the news to her. How could she have been so self-absorbed to reject him in his hour of need? No matter what had been said between them over the last couple of days, she could not let him deal with this on his own. He adored his mother. She had seen them together on a few occasions: and admired their connection. They seemed to know each other better than any parent-child relationship she had seen before. Including her own. Particularly her own. Poor Kenny, she kept whispering to herself as she walked towards a corner of the airport far enough away from the check-in area to allow her some degree of quiet. On any other day, Wilson would have turned around, jumped in the car, and drove to see him.

She called. There was no answer. She did not leave a message, not prepared to commit to voicemail a babble of words she had not thought about. But she did on the second, third, fourth and fifth calls. By the fifth, she was already on the plane, being tapped on the shoulder by a heavily made-up air hostess, with an air of hostility that seemed at home on this particular airline. "Please, madam. I cannot tell you again. You must put the phone away; we are already taxiing to the runway."

She closed the phone down, just as the wheels left the tarmac. She peered out the window at the lush Old Kilpatrick hills where she could see the pinprick of Uisge Beatha sitting snugly under one of the mounds of rolling green meadows. How much pain and anguish dominated that tiny dot away in the distance? A black hole of sadness and loneliness, the sight of it caused her to put her hands to her face. Her crying prompted the elderly lady on her right to pass a frilly handkerchief, rubbing her arm at the same time. "Don't worry, hen. It's that time of year when we all feel a wee bit sad."

Wilson thanked her before muttering to herself, "Truer words…"

More Anaesthetic

Kenny tore the Kiltman mask off as soon as the call ended. For the first time, he had felt claustrophobic wearing it, the excesses of the night before constricting his veins, making his pulse feel like a hammer on his temple pounding against the inside of the mask. He could not stop feeling increasingly irritated at Gemmill. The Chief's approach to discussions was uniquely exasperating. In each conversation he seemed to start with the assumption that the person delivering the message had the least clue about what he or she was saying. He then made that person work hard to show why they might have a valid point, something worth communicating. Eventually, whenever he felt he had heard and seen enough to be convinced, he would grudgingly accept it and move on. Kiltman had never had to work so hard to communicate so little.

He had gone upstairs to the kitchen to feast on a cocktail of Roddy's Cheerios and Chocolate Stars, filling the gaping hole in his stomach, that had not seen sustenance since the previous morning. Three quarters of a bottle of malt could hardly be called nutrition. He recalled finishing the dregs in the bottle sometime after midnight, holding it upside down over his glass, trying not to waste a drop. If he had not been so tired, he would have gone back to the drawer and opened another. Fatigue had taken over and allowed him to avoid an even more excruciating headache.

Walking back down to the desolate sanctuary of the basement he could hear a number of high-pitched, staccato pings alerting him to a host of missed calls. He fell clumsily into the armchair he had tossed and turned in a few hours earlier, pushing the button on the phone to play the messages aloud:

"Hi, Kenny. I am so, so sorry to hear the news about your gorgeous Mum. I hope you're doing okay, at least as well as you can be. I feel so bad for not letting you tell me yesterday. Please call me back. I love you, sweetheart."

"Kenny, it's Maggie again. Please, call me back. I want to hear your voice and hear you're okay. Love you."

"Kenny darling, Please, call me. I'm about to leave on a flight and will have to turn my phone off. I'll explain later. I'm sending you lots of hugs and kisses."

The next one, he had to strain to pick out the words, Maggie's voice hushed and muted. *"Hi, Kenny. I need to close the phone down now. Love you. Will call again later."* A strange noise followed like a child trying to whistle for the first time. He realised she had tried to blow him a sloppy kiss while attempting to be incognito on the plane.

The male voice in the next message surprised him after her medley of voicemails.

"Hi, Kenny. Hope you haven't forgotten. Terviseks opens tomorrow night. Come round any time after 8 o'clock. I've got a table reserved for you, Maggie and a few other folks. Should be a laugh. Cheers." Tommy sounded in high spirits.

"Hi Kenny. We got back late last night so I didn't call. I hope you're okay today. We picked Roddy up from Angie's this morning. He's been worried about you. Me, too. If there's anything you need, let me know. We're all thinking about you and remembering your Mum. Such an amazing, lovely lady, like a second mother to..." Fiona's fragile, crackling voice drifted into the distance, followed by the message ending.

"Hi, Dad! I love you and have been praying all morning for Gran. Then I realised that I don't need to pray for her. Because she's a saint now. So, I'm praying to Gran that you'll not be too sad. I love you, Dad."

His tears had started again. He turned away from the phone after the last message, before pressing the feature to replay saved messages. His mother's lilting voice pierced the silence of the basement, *"Hello, sonny boy..."* He had forgotten her message had been saved.

He turned to the drawer, reaching down for a fresh dose of painkiller. He ripped off the lead covering and uncorked the bottle with the air of a condemned man lighting his last cigarette. He poured a dram into the sticky, crystal glass, studied it, then shook his head. He lifted the bottle to a steeper angle and added three more fingers of malt. It did not take long for him to work his way to the bottom of the glass. He then replayed his mother's message again, just as he poured another. And for the next two hours this duet of emotional destruction continued unabated, fuelling his memories and regrets. Drink, replay, drink, replay, drink, replay. Until the whisky was nearly finished. He studied the bottle, admiring the shade of green chosen to prevent sunlight from damaging the contents. He smiled a crooked grin at how green bottles were a waste of time in Scotland. They should have used clear glass and saved some money, keeping the more expensive green bottles for export to sunnier and warmer climes. He remembered the day they had launched this particular batch of Glentocher 12 during the Edinburgh festival. They had convinced the mayor of the city to allow the canon to be fired 12 times that day as part of the marketing launch. Their donation of five cases for a raffle to raise money for the city's worthwhile causes had clinched the deal.

The canon. The canon. The blast it made that day in Edinburgh kept repeating in his head. It was niggling him. In the same way the Nike running shoe would not leave him alone. Just kept reappearing in the recesses of his mind. Not wanting to be ignored, but then playing hard to get. Why was the canon suddenly so important?

Then his mind drifted back to his mother. In her later years, she had developed a travel bug, looking for any opportunity to visit far-flung places to see how the world really was rather than through a TV screen. She most probably had the desire to travel all her life, hence why she came to Scotland at an early age. Although that was probably more economic migration rather than vacation.

He remembered that she had gone to France a few years earlier with George, her travel partner of choice. He was quite sure George had kept a bag packed awaiting Molly's call. He always seemed to be available, even when she got last minute deals, which was more often than not. They had arranged a trip to visit Monaco - his mother had been a huge fan of Grace Kelly, not least because of her Irish roots, when she had been an actress in Hollywood in the fifties. She had wanted to see where Grace had lived when she married Prince Rainier in their fairy-tale wedding. It was late morning on the last day of their trip, when they were having a coffee in Nice, less than an hour from

Princess Grace's palace in Monte Carlo – she had decided to call Kenny.

Halfway through their conversation, there had been an almighty bang that made his mother jump with alarm. She hung up immediately, which made him panic, worrying there may have been some sort of attack - not a surprising assumption, he thought afterwards, considering the increasing levels of terror threats.

A few minutes later, his mother called him back to explain that there was nothing to worry about. He closed his eyes and remembered her words as if she were with him in the basement.

"Kenny, sure, you won't believe what that bang was all about. It happens every day at 12 o'clock on the dot, bang on the stroke of noon. Back in the 19th century there was a man who used to get so fed up that his wife was not back in time to make him lunch, he fired a canon from the castle at the top of the hill near here, to remind her to hurry up and get home. Now it's just a loud firework, but then it was a canon! Can you imagine? You wouldn't get away with that now, ha, ha! Good for her, keeping her man on his toes." She had giggled like a child. He had guessed she was enjoying a well-deserved Kir Royale with her coffee. "Anyway, the funny thing was that the man was supposed to be Scottish. George, George, eh, excuse me, Kenny. George, what was that fellow's name? Oh, yes, thanks, love. Kenny, you there, you there?"

When he had said, "Yes, Mum, keep going," he had been looking out the window towards the river sipping a coffee, vicariously enjoying her holiday.

"Well, got it here now, George wrote it down for me. Let me see… He sounds very posh; he had been knighted. Couldn't have been too many Scots knighted in those days. Sir Thomas Coventry-More, he was called. Sounds very hoity-toity! Anyway, thought I'd let you know in case you were worried about the bang you heard. Bye, son."

He rose from the chair faster than his body had anticipated. He sat down again, gulping deep breaths to halt the dizziness threatening to overcome him. He was recalling the last two lines of the clue:

Yet while Tom the Scot got so fraught

The time it cries is when the bullet flies

Whatever Skink was going to do was at noon, twelve o'clock exactly, according to Tom the Scot's reminder to have his lunch on the table. It had just gone eleven there, Wilson would be landing about now.

Kenny stretched his cheeks with pinched fingers to widen his mouth and avoid any hint of slurring in the call he was about to make.

He looked at himself in the mirror and spoke aloud in a croaky, tired voice, "*if you can keep your mind when all about you are losing theirs and blaming it on you, if you can trust yourself when all men doubt you*". He repeated this umpteen times until he felt he was achieving a semblance of clear diction.

Many years earlier when his English teacher had reinforced the importance of using Rudyard Kipling's poem *IF* as a means to improve elocution, he could not have realised just how appropriate the words would become for the distracted boy in the back row.

That boy, now a fragile man, picked up the phone.

Nice Time

Wilson had just cleared passport control and was hurrying towards the exit, where she hoped one of the local gendarmes was waiting to take her to the First Minister. She jostled through a sea of people on the other side of the mechanical doors, searching an array of scrawled nameplates for her driver. She wasted a few precious minutes in a futile hunt before giving up and hurrying outside to find a taxi. Leaning against the terminal wall, under a sign that read *Kiss and Fly*, a young, uniformed police officer was sucking hard on a Gitanes, enjoying that last hit before entering the building. Between his knees, she saw the letters *Wil* on a white board. She leant down and extricated it with a tug, to find the rest of her name there too.

"Ah," the gendarme said. "You are early! Bienvenue en France! My name is Pierre."

She wanted to explain that while most travellers experienced flights being late, it was not uncommon for them to arrive on time. And even, believe it or not, early. But she opted for, "Merci." And followed him to his car.

She settled into the backseat, momentarily distracted by the beauty of the drive from the airport towards the city centre. A panoply of towering palm trees and extravagantly painted buildings sat below the sprawling beauty of the riviera hills, wrapping their arms around a gloriously turquoise bay of calm waters dotted with fishing boats.

She was awakened from her Riviera appreciation by the vibrating buzz in her pocket. It was Kenny. Thank God, she said to herself, feeling her pulse quicken. She flipped open the phone.

"Hi Kenny." She knew she had to be strong for him fighting the tears welling up in her tired eyes.

"Oh, hi!" He slapped his forehead with the palm of his hand. His head was so befuddled from the whisky, he had neither turned on the block caller ID nor wore his mask with voice changer.

"Are you okay?" she asked. "I wish I was there with you. I am so sorry about your mother."

"Eh, thanks, Maggie." He hesitated for a moment. "I won't pretend, this isn't an easy time for me. It's breaking my heart." He did not have time for this conversation. "I know you're busy. I just wanted to say I got your messages. We can talk when you have time later. Okay, bye."

"Okay." She was surprised at how minimalist he had been in conversing. He must be so overcome, she thought, and with a heartfelt sigh, she whispered, "I love you."

"Yes, eh, ok," he replied. "I mean, yes, me too."

He closed the phone down before turning to put on his mask. That was a close thing; thank goodness she had spoken first. He had nearly started the call with '*Hello, Wilson*'. That would have sounded weird. He felt relieved he had done a good job in controlling his slurring.

She put the phone beside her on the seat. She needed both hands to apply tissues to her streaming eyes. Kenny had started drinking again. His deeper voice and noticeable slur were the classic hallmarks of a night on the tiles. He had sounded distracted and dazed, like he had gone three rounds with Mike Tyson.

The phone rang again, this time with No Caller ID flashing on the screen.

"Hello?" she announced.

"Wilson, it's me."

The sound of Kiltman's voice changer had a strangely distant, echoey sound over the phone. Despite his exaggerated self-belief that he had the ability to control his slurring, when he came off the prior call with her, Kenny had the good sense to put the phone on speaker at the other end of the basement, to allow a degree of distortion. She put the poor quality down to an international call over a mobile.

"Hi, Kiltman," she focused on pulling herself together. "Do you have something for me?"

"Yes, listen. Skink is going to make it happen at 12 noon. There's a controlled firework explosion every day in Nice at that time. It used to be a canon but it's now a firework. Anyway, the point is that the bullet will fly at that precise moment."

She peered at her watch. It was 11.20. She tapped Pierre on the shoulder. "Pierre, where are the First Minister and Mayor at the moment?"

"Madam, they are at the Promenade des Anglais, along from the Negresco hotel, posing for some photos."

"How long will it take to get there?"

"We will be there in 15 minutes," he answered.

"Make it 10! Come on, go!"

What Pierre lacked in picking passengers up in airports, he more than made up for in speeding through traffic. He nipped in-between the slowing lunch-time convoy of cars as if they were not there. On another day, she would have rolled the window down and savoured the passing palm trees and effervescent colours of the city.

"Kiltman, how do you know?"

He explained the clue - other than his mother's involvement - putting it down to another pub quiz coincidence. Wilson was probably developing a false impression of how difficult pub quizzes were these days.

She waited a moment. "I wish you were here."

"That's sweet, Wilson," he managed to say in a tone that belied his trauma. "Just put it on the postcard, please."

"Anything else I should know?" she asked, not understanding this weird guy who could happily disappear then pop up intermittently cracking bad jokes.

"No, I'm sorry. It's all down to you now, Wilson. Take care."

"Thanks a million," she said to the dull click of the line closing. He had preferred to push the stop button on the phone rather than his luck.

Line of Sight

He held his face up to the late morning sun piercing the narrow slit between his curtains. Even in December it was still warm enough to tinge cheeks that had not seen the sun in six months. One day he would come back to enjoy this beautiful city and picturesque coastline. He had never seen blues and yellows quite so dynamic and striking as they were in Nice. No wonder artists the world over made a point of checking into this haven of vibrant ecstasy at least once in their lifetime. He had not been blessed with the gift of drawing. His art was of a different nature, demonstrated in his application of skills to righting the wrongs of selfish, ignorant people who turned away from their responsibility to make the world a better place. A few well-planned events, and the right weaponry, meant he could play people like puppets. And take the odd trophy when he wanted to.

Today Scotland's aptly named *First* Minister would have the honour of being Skink's first target post-Bar L. He felt a tad guilty about what he was going to do. Not because he would extinguish the life of an innocent man, that was all in a day's work for Skink. No, it was more that this shooting was only a wake-up call. He had chosen this victim and event as a way of conveying the message that Cullen Skink was back in the game. He and his new accomplice had other, more damaging, acts on the horizon. The First Minister was merely the appetizer in a feast of mayhem.

The sleek rifle, fitted with a telescopic lens, sat inconspicuously under the blue towel, chosen to blend in with the curtains on either side of the window. It was already pointed at the podium awaiting its target to begin his speech, which would begin at the unusual time of 11.55. Knowing the First Minister, and how much of a hit he had for himself, he would be intending to use the noonday 'canon' bang as part of his message. Some drivel, no doubt, about the positive noise Nice and Edinburgh can make together. Blah! Blah! Whatever he was going to say, they would be his last words. Better for his legacy if he had something meaningful to communicate. Famous last words, and all that rubbish, Skink mused.

It was now 11.45. He stood up and twisted his upper body from left to right several times before cracking his knuckles and stretching his legs and arms. He was feeling fit. He had used his six months in prison to good effect, becoming healthier than he had been in years. His arm, broken by Kiltman when he had surprised him in the early hours of the longest day, had healed quickly, leaving a degree of callus protruding unnaturally on his forearm. Otherwise he felt perfect in every way, appreciating himself in the room's full-length mirror.

"Okay!" he said aloud to himself. "Time to tango."

On the fourth floor of the Negresco Hotel, he had a clear line of sight to the podium, a third of a mile along the resplendent promenade towards the town centre. He was far enough away, that when he fired the rifle, no-one would be looking for an assassin at that distance. Certainly not in the splendidly beautiful Negresco. At least, not initially. They would not even hear the sound of the bullet being released since it would coincide with the boom of Tom the Scot's legacy. He smiled at the irony of what was about to happen. Tom the Scot would camouflage the noise of the bullet that killed Scotland's First Minister on a promenade named after the English.

He had already checked out of the hotel that morning, with more than a hint of despondency. The reception had given him two hours grace before he had to vacate his room, which was more than enough time for him to pack up and make an orderly departure. The hotel was majestic in every way, neoclassical mingled with baroque. It defined the indulgence and opulence of the Côte d'Azur, somehow begging him to prolong his trip. Not this time, he murmured quietly to himself, as he settled down to cradle the rifle butt in his shoulder. He recalled the entrecôte from the previous evening, as fine a cut of sirloin as he had ever tasted. He had dropped a smidgeon of pepper sauce on his jacket sleeve, now just sitting under his chin where he held the rifle. He leant forward and extended his tongue to touch the stain, finding the slightest taste of fine cuisine to titillate his taste buds. He smiled, lowered his head, and squinted through the lens, adjusting it slightly to bring the First Minister into focus, centring the crosshairs on his victim's forehead. There he was bantering and blethering in the jovial manner people expected from Scots abroad. Blithely confident in his quick wit and dry sense of humour, he was always ready to have a poke at France and Scotland's mutual age-old enemy.

His mind drifted again, feeling a tad disappointed that Kiltman had neither showed up, nor convinced the French to cancel the event. Either his clue had been too obscure this time, or the superhero was out of practice. Probably a combination of both, he shrugged. Not to worry, Kiltman would get all the practice he needed in the coming days.

To his right, his phone alarm was set to 11.59 and 59 seconds. Tom the Scot's 'canon' reliably banged every day on exactly the stroke of 12. Other than on the odd April 1, when they would let it off an hour earlier. He had never quite understood why that appealed to the French sense of humour. At least today, that would not be an issue.

The First Minister ascended the steps, waving at a sprawling crowd, larger than one would have expected for an event of this relatively banal nature. There was no accounting for taste, Skink thought, as he glanced at his phone. 11.55.

Pebble Beach

Wilson threw the car door open and clambered onto the wide promenade sidewalk. Despite Pierre's good intentions and indisputable driving skills, the crowds and cars had become impregnable. All this for Scotland's First Minister, she thought. She had not expected such a large crowd. She understood that this was an important event for some members of the business community and for those politicians wanting to be seen to expand boundaries, but at the end of the day, it was hardly noteworthy enough to attract hundreds of people to the promenade two days before Christmas. Yet, it had done so, and had made her job much more difficult.

Stepping onto the perfectly paved pavement, she had no choice but to run the remaining half mile to the podium. After a few yards of bumping, ducking and diving, she gave up trying to navigate the traffic, human and vehicular, and jumped down onto the beach, feeling a sharp twinge of pain through the soles of her shoes. The 'pebble' beach had more large stones and small rocks than pebbles. This was not the time to chastise herself for not looking before leaping. She began to run and hobble in the direction of the stage, stumbling with practically every second stride. A quick glance at her watch raised her pain threshold to the 'deal with it later' level.

11.55.

She got to the beach just below the podium faster than she had expected, despite the rocks. Running up a set of iron steps, two gendarmes, one with arms folded, the other on his phone, blocked her access to the stage. Crikey, she thought, this was a problem. Neither a detailed explanation of how an assassin was about to shoot the First Minister, nor a Scottish police ID, would prove effective enough to convince them of her mission.

"Va vite! Va vite!" the gendarme with the phone shouted, making a space for her to run between them. He pointed at his phone for his colleague's benefit. "Pierre est ici. C'est bien." Thank God for Pierre, she thought. She saw the First Minister at a distance of no more than 30 yards, at the other end of a thronging swamp of humanity, walking up a set of stairs to the stage. She had no time to consider options. Sticking her elbows out, she rushed into the pack, reminding herself she was not there to make friends. She bumped into the first of many irate spectators, who had most probably stopped to see what all the fuss was about on this relaxed sunny day on the promenade. Only to be bundled to the side by a stampeding Scottish detective.

The First Minister was now in the centre of the podium without a lectern, looking out over the crowds, arms extended in an evangelistic, virtual hug. He entered into his speech with gusto, his oratory skill unquestionably one of his finer qualities.

"Yes, Edinburgh and Nice are joined as twins, and we have been in this close relationship for nearly half a century. While many cities see the twinning process as a formality, today our great cities, and countries, have taken it to another level."

He scanned to his right to his assistant, a handsome lady, with as stern a look as was appropriate when facing into a host of TV cameras. She nodded that he was on time for maximum impact.

"So," he raised his voice a notch, "let's all raise our hands and punch the sky. Because, mes amis, the sky is our limit!"

He threw both hands into the air above his head in the way a boxer would when the fight was called in his favour. It coincided perfectly with the legacy bang of Tom the Scot's 'canon'. As well as the painful wallop of 110 pounds of Scottish detective hitting his midriff. It was only Wilson who heard the whistle of the bullet as it missed her ear by an inch, just before it pierced the First Minister's flesh.

Nice Try

He walked out through the hotel doorway, turning left towards the town's bustling side streets, creating a healthy distance between himself and the promenade. People were still running as far from the shooting as their legs would take them, screams and shouts ricocheting off the town's walls. He smiled quietly to himself at how he could cause such pandemonium with one finger squeeze. An event like this really brought out the worst in people, he mused, watching them push each other out of the way in a hurry to escape.

He was working hard to control the simmering annoyance at how it had played out. He had done exactly as planned. The bullet had left the rifle just as the loud bang of the '*canon*' sounded across the sky. He had expected the First Minister to be thrown back against the Mayor, and to collapse into a lifeless heap. While he was not entirely sure, he thought he recognised the lady who had careered into his victim. DI Wilson. If it was her, then he could see the headlines the next day, *Flying Scotswoman saves First Minister*. Assuming she had done enough to protect him from his fate.

Skink strode purposefully towards the Rialto, the beguilingly shabby English cinema in Nice where many an expat whiled away a rainy afternoon, only a couple of minutes' walk behind the Negresco. He caught sight of himself in a shop window, pausing for a moment to appreciate his disguise. *Handsome* was not how he would describe himself, at least not in the classically good-looking sense of the word. But somehow, the brown wig, designer stubble and olive-green contact lenses made him worth a second look. He threw his head back and strutted in a gait John Travolta would have been proud of, before spotting his contact walking towards him.

Head down and moving at a brisk pace, the short, well-built man and Skink rubbed shoulders briefly before continuing on their separate ways. Enough contact for Skink to offload the rifle case. Just as they had done the day before when he had collected it. He had to admit, his new partner had thought of everything, in setting up this hit in Nice: the location, the disguise, the passport, the local support. When he arrived at the airport, he would make sure to buy a souvenir to thank him for his assistance. Skink sighed knowing his friend would not be happy: and expected a 'told you so' conversation. It was clear that they had solved his clue, he had to accept that fact. But Skink would remind him that even if the First Minister survived the assassination attempt, chaos and fear had been delivered in spades. He had witnessed it first-hand. The world would know that Skink was back.

What was more important, and truly niggling Skink, was why Wilson had intervened rather than Kiltman? Why was Scotland's superhero not swaggering around the promenade, taking credit for the intervention? Something was not right, and Skink was determined to get to the bottom of it once he was back on Scottish soil.

After a few more minutes of strutting and self-admiration, he noticed the temporary swell of worry begin to dissipate, fewer people spilling onto the side streets. In the distance he could hear sirens blaring, adding to the chaos that had descended on Nice. Not my problem, Skink smiled, walking towards a parked cab, its engine running. He opened the door with a confidence bordering on panache, before turning to wave at frightened faces peering out of windows from balconies and windows dotted along the street. Reluctantly he climbed into the back seat wishing he could have stayed to enjoy the panic and mayhem. As soon as he had clicked the seatbelt, the driver sped off at pace, only too happy to be going to the airport, away from all this madness.

His flight was scheduled to depart at 1.55, the time chosen to get him out of the city before the gendarmerie had the chance to begin a search, closing down airports and train stations. This also allowed him time to clear check-in and passport control at a leisurely pace before boarding.

Within half an hour of arriving at the airport, he found himself smiling appreciatively at how slick the experience was proving to be. He had cleared check in and passport control with an hour to spare before the flight left. He decided to wander through the duty-free shops dotted around the departure gates. He was quite disappointed at the lack of selection. Considering Nice airport was the last place visitors to the Côte d'Azur spent some time before going home, he had hoped to find a larger display of historical artefacts and meaningful mementoes. He was perturbed at how the shops were dominated by colourful towels and tablecloths. While he had only known his friend for half a year, he was quite sure kitchen trimmings would not be considered a thoughtful gift.

He had nearly given up when there it was.

The perfect present for someone who lived a double life.

A grey, alloy mask stared up from the shelf, its vacant eye slits, and seductively petulant mouth, separated by a petit nose. It was a copy of the mask worn by an unfortunate man who had lived in the late 17th century in France, spending the majority of his life behind bars. Nobody knew what he had done to be imprisoned or why he had been shipped from jail to jail throughout the majority of his life. One of his places of incarceration, only half an hour from the airport, was on the Iles de Lérins - a short boat ride from that ghastly Cannes, home of the rich and wannabe famous. He tut-tutted aloud as he reflected on overpaid actors and their desire for limelight - a blight on the conscience of a caring society.

The prisoner's identity had been a secret throughout his life; and many have conjectured since about whom he might have been. Generations of storytellers, carried away by the romantic pathos of this man, identified him as an abandoned prince, a king forever waiting for a stolen crown. What is true is that he lived among his fellow French prisoners for many years but retained his anonymity throughout. *The Man in the Iron Mask* had captivated generations over the centuries, attaining posthumous celebrity status in novels and cinema.

Considering how his accomplice had helped him escape Barlinnie, Skink hoped he would appreciate the thought he had put into this highly appropriate gift of secrecy, torture, death, and most importantly, everlasting fame. Skink had no doubts that his friend would similarly become a household name by the time he had completed his acts of terror: celebrity and notoriety symbiotically intertwined.

French A&E

The First Minister was lying at a 45-degree angle, his arm in a sling, and head smothered by a bulky white bandage. Two heavily armed gendarmes stood in the corridor on either side of the doorway, hands clasped behind their backs. Wilson appreciated the support of the French police, delivered in their inimitable gruff style. The surly, broody expressions on their chiselled features were enough to deter a stranger from approaching the ward. If Skink had been bent on a second attempt, even he would have thought twice about challenging the two guards.

Wilson's ruminations were interrupted by a groan rising from the bed. She rose lithely from her chair to see the First Minister's eyelids flutter, his tongue protruding through swollen, chapped lips, moistening arid slivers of flaking skin.

"He's coming to!" Wilson shouted through towards the nurse's desk. "Quick, can someone come?"

Within seconds two doctors were at the bedside, checking his vitals, talking to him in gentle, reassuring voices. She could tell that each question was geared towards assessing his degree of concussion. In those few minutes, she learned more about the First Minister than from all the coverage he had received on TV and press; age (he hid it well!), wife's maiden name, first wife's maiden name, favourite football team (*Partick Thistle*, really?) and most enjoyable movie (*Braveheart*, not lost any of his political savvy, then).

The medics spoke another few words of comfort, before leaving him in the hands of a pretty, young nurse, identified by her nametag as Alli. Wilson noticed how efficient Alli was as she adjusted drips and fixed pillows with abilities born of breeding rather than training.

"Hello, First Minister," Wilson said quietly, once Alli had picked up the clipboard at the bottom of the bed and began to update the notes. "How are you feeling?"

"Who are you?" he croaked. "What in God's name happened?"

He tried to sit up but dropped back into his soft pillows at the pain shooting through his collar bone. It is surprising, Wilson thought, just how much a hospital bed could age a person. The politician was in his fifties, and while he carried an extra layer, he was in reasonably good shape. He made great efforts to show the voters that he cycled each day to the Scottish Parliament, while not mentioning he lived a full half mile away. Today, with tubes and bandages and that stale smell of residual perspiration, a passing visitor would have guessed he was closer to 70 years old.

"Sir," Wilson said, as Alli placed a hand gently but firmly on his chest. "Please stay as still as you can. You had a lucky escape."

"There was nothing lucky about it at all," Wilson heard from over her shoulder.

His assistant, Sharon McMonagle, a middle-aged lady with a no-nonsense attitude, carried herself with an air of nobility and pragmatism. She had only gone to the bathroom to powder her nose a few minutes earlier, having spent several hours at his bedside, holding his hand, and speaking to him in a steady tone. She had been told that regular verbal input from a familiar voice could be a positive factor in encouraging a mind to move back to consciousness in circumstances such as these. She clearly did not do anything by halves, reciting, by heart, paragraph after paragraph from the SNP's recently published Constitution for a Free Scotland.

"What... do... you... mean?" he asked. Alli held a glass of water to his lips allowing him to take measured sips between words.

"You have been shot through the collar bone. You've also banged your head giving you some degree of concussion. They are not yet sure how bad it might be. Although the fact you're awake is a good sign, I would assume," Sharon said.

Wilson sensed the assistant had not been hired for her ability to sugar coat her comments. "We have to wait and see how it progresses. Good news is that the bullet has been removed and the bone reset."

"Was anyone else hurt?" he asked. The concern was not a politically tactful question. Wilson could tell he was genuinely concerned.

"No," Sharon answered. "Well, except for DI Wilson here."

The First Minister studied her as if for the first time, noticing a bruised cheek and scratched forehead.

"She dived across the bullet that was most probably aimed for your head or heart. And managed to shift you enough to avoid a fatal injury."

"DI Wilson," the First Minister extended his good arm, trying his best to smile effortlessly. "I can't thank you enough."

She took his hand, and squeezed, before patting and putting it back on top of the covers. For the first time, she saw the vulnerability in this man who had been pushed from pillar to post by the Scottish media. He sported a jovial demeanour, carrying it with apparent ease, more believable because of his rounded girth and friendly countenance.

"I'm happy to see you coming round, we were all worried for a while there." She looked up at the assistant to see Sharon's moist eyes: and knew that she had carried the weight of the unimaginable loss.

"Surely this was not Skink?" he asked, now starting to focus. "He only escaped the day before yesterday."

"We don't know for certain, sir. We didn't catch the gunman. But we're relatively sure it was him - the place and timing were indicated in the clue he left."

"What clue?" he asked with insistence, surprise overcoming his pain. "Should I not have been told about *the clue*?"

"We did advise your security advisers that we thought it would be in Nice and therefore most probably you were the target. Looks like your team did not feel it was a real threat." Wilson took a breath to steady herself for his reaction. "We found out about the timing not long before your speech started. Hence my last second rugby tackle."

"Sharon, find out who got the message, and why I was not informed," he said. "Please."

"And DI Wilson, you can knock off now, I'm in good hands here. You need a rest. Please get those wounds seen to. When I get back home, I'll be in touch with your commanding officers to thank you for saving my life."

He made a significant effort to spread his mouth into a smile but found the exercise too demanding of his frail body. He wearily sunk further into the pillows he was already embedded in. *It was my pleasure, sir*, did not seem like the appropriate response. She stopped herself just in time. She nodded, wished him a speedy recovery, and said goodbye to Sharon. Walking out into the corridor, she focused on holding her nose to avoid inhaling any more disinfectant than she had already. The thought of fresh air and space to think hurried her along towards the elevator. She realised it was already 6 pm; she was hungry and tired. Her flight home was not till the following morning, which meant she had an evening in Nice to rest and get her head straight, before flying back to Skink's next surprise.

Before she could do anything, she had to call Kenny. The elevator had just reached the ground floor and doors opened when she flipped her phone open and pressed speed dial for his number. She could see there was a bunch of missed calls, but she had to talk to him first. For the last few hours, she had chosen not to deal with her sadness at Molly's passing, she had parked it in the *Avoidant* department of her brain, alongside her relationship with Kenny. He would be wondering why she had gone off radar since her messages earlier that morning. At some point he was going to have to accept that was the price you paid for a girlfriend who throws herself in front of a bullet one minute but does not know if she is coming or going emotionally the next.

.

Breaking News

The TV had been on since he had hung up with Wilson. It was the only way he could stay close to the events in Nice - through a filter of lunchtime news, *Loose Women*, umpteen weather forecasts and an excruciatingly painful tabloid talk show.

He recalled the drama of the first piece of coverage to be broadcast barely minutes after the attempted assassination. It had come on the screen as a newsflash, around 1.15 UK time. Grant MacTavish, no less, had been standing on top of a bus stop on the promenade, the only space he could find amongst the pandemonium happening around him. People were running and falling in a desperate rush to escape the madness he was reporting, a cacophony of noise interrupting the news feed.

"Just a few minutes ago, in what was expected to be a happy intro to the festive season, the First Minister was standing on this podium over here."

MacTavish had pointed towards the stage. The police had already cordoned it off and were in the process of searching for clues to identify the trajectory of the bullet. They had found it embedded in the wooden backdrop having exited the First Minister's shoulder. The police were gathered around it, pointing west along the promenade to where they believed it had left the gun, in the direction of Hotel Negresco, one of many hotels and apartment blocks along the walkway. This was not going to be a quick search.

"It had been an eventful morning, a feelgood factor surrounding the trade treaty signings and twin city bonhomie. On the stroke of noon, when Nice's famous '*canon*' boom sounded, all hell broke loose. We have just received the footage from that moment, you can see for yourself."

The news feed had switched to a calm congenial crowd listening to the First Minister in full flow, clearly enjoying the sun, sea and cementing of a new relationship. To his left in the direction of the beach, a disruption started in the crowd - like an invisible snake carving a route through towards the podium, bulldozing anyone in its wake. Some of the audience shouted and gesticulated rudely while others were stunned at the interruption. Kenny saw Wilson burst through the irate spectators, to bound up the steps and launch herself at the First Minister, just as an almighty boom rattled the screen. Kenny had jumped to his feet, hands on his head, stunned at what he was seeing.

In the seconds it took for the security guards to rush up the steps to intervene, there was enough time for the camera to zoom in on the First Minister, to see him smack his head on the stage. And for the blood to burst from his shoulder like the splash of a rock plunging into a tranquil pond. Only a bullet could make that impact, Kenny thought. He could not see if Wilson had been hurt. All he could make out were her legs sticking out from under the First Minister and several gendarmes who had dropped onto their knees around them.

"We will bring you more as soon as we get it," MacTavish had continued as the screen switched back to him. His eyes barely disguised the overpowering concern of realising such a high-profile location on top of a bus stop, with a shooter around, was not the wisest thing to do. "Grant MacTavish, signing off, in Nice." As he spoke the word *Nice*, he was already jumping down.

Time had gone very slowly since MacTavish's first update on the shooting. It was now six o'clock there. He had called her several times, twice as Kenny and once as Kiltman, going straight to the answering machine each time. Throughout the day MacTavish had provided regular updates on the First Minister's condition, although there were only so many ways to say that he was still unconscious and that he had indeed been struck by a bullet. And that the person who crashed into him was DI Wilson, the Scottish detective who had taken down Skink earlier that year, along with Kiltman. MacTavish confirmed that Wilson had not been injured but had been keeping bedside vigil with the First Minister.

The question on everyone's lips, MacTavish teased, was why the *masked superhero* had not been there? Especially if this assassination attempt had anything to do with Cullen Skink's recent escape. Where was Kiltman? After posing all these questions, MacTavish most likely took himself off for a late lunch.

Now he was back on TV, this time standing outside the hospital where the First Minister was in the critical care unit. *Hôpital Saint-Roch* was displayed in faded lettering above MacTavish's shoulder. It was a relatively small building, no bigger than a four-storey block, looking as though it had seen better days. Kenny hoped they would not be saying the same thing about the First Minister in a few hours.

"We are here at the hospital in Nice, awaiting word on the First Minister's condition. His office has been reticent to provide too many details at this stage, although we understand he may be showing signs of consciousness."

Kenny's focus on the TV was interrupted by his phone ringing; it was Wilson. She was calling him, he reminded himself, so he had to be Kenny, not Kiltman. No need for the mask. This was becoming confusing; his dwindling Glentocher 12 collection would testify to that.

"Maggie! Are you okay?"

"Hi Kenny, yes I'm fine. Have you been watching the news?"

She was walking along a recently disinfected corridor towards the exit. The sharp, tangy bleach smell indicated a liberal splashing of the liquid in a haphazard fashion rather than a controlled mopping of the floors. She smiled. Kiltman would have been impressed at the sharpness of her olfactory receptors.

"Yes, that's all I've been doing." He glanced sideways at the whisky bottle. "How's the First Minister? It looks like you saved his life. Did you get hurt in the process?" His voice broke slightly. He was so proud of what she had done but alarmed by her near miss.

"He's going to be okay; it was a close thing. I'm okay. Bit bruised by the First Minister landing on top of me." She stopped in the corridor looking at the signs, trying to identify the nearest exit. "Kenny, how are you doing? I just can't get over the news about your mother. You know I want to be there with you."

"Yes, I know, Maggie. I won't lie. This is so hard." He turned awkwardly in his seat to face the wall. Why did that bottle keep looking at him?

She started to walk again and found the exit on her right along the corridor. "I'm coming back tomorrow. Can I come and see you?"

"Eh, yes, Maggie. I'd like that."

Out of the corner of his eye on TV, he saw MacTavish rushing towards the hospital entrance, his cameraman behind him, the picture jumping and moving, never losing its focus on the hospital's main doorway. By the time he realised what was happening, it was too late. He should have figured it out earlier. If his senses had not been dulled by the whisky, he would have reacted more quickly.

"Maggie, don't walk outsi…," he shouted, watching the screen to see her exit the hospital talking into her phone.

MacTavish, half-turned to the camera, had the microphone under her chin before she could respond. Kenny watched her close the phone and adopt a look of feigned nonchalance normally reserved for their faux poker games with Roddy.

"DI Wilson, how is the First Minister? Was this Cullen Skink's doing?" he panted into her face.

Kenny barely heard his words - he only saw her pretty features, camouflaged by blue bruises and a two-inch cut across her forehead. She had been in hospital all afternoon and did not have a bandage or plaster to show for it.

Evening Times

He walked into the Glasgow Airport terminal after an uneventful flight. The only enjoyable aspect of the trip was the double gin and tonic. He had over-indulged in a variety of salty snacks, now feeling slightly queasy. He had always wondered about pretzels, especially the mini version. They were about as tasteless an object in the food category as one could eat. The fact they needed a massive sprinkling of salt should have been a clue they were under-engineered for human taste buds.

There were several armed policemen standing around the terminal, studying the passengers alighting from the Nice flight. Guns never appeared flattering on a British policeman, he thought - unseemly bulky metal sitting uncomfortably in young hands, in a country that was supposed to be gun-free. He had expected the welcome reception, and had practiced his nonplussed, disinterested look throughout the flight. This did not prevent one of the policemen approaching him. Young, strong, and tall, he reminded Skink of Sean Connery in his early Bond movies.

"Sir, passport please," the policeman said in a neutral tone.

"Sure," Skink answered, wearing a slightly bemused frown. "Is there a problem, officer?"

The policeman did not answer and studied the passport carefully.

"What was the nature of your trip to Nice, Mr. McLeish?"

"Food and wine, officer!" Skink smiled a close-mouthed smile. His teeth had been carefully covered by an artificial layer of enamel, but he did not want to push his luck. "You see, I've been asked to make Christmas dinner for the family this year. I decided to visit the Negresco hotel where its Michelin-starred restaurant, Le Chantecler, does a quite incredible filet d'agneau. I shamelessly convinced them to give me their recipe, and have decided that this year, the turkey will remain on the farm."

"Okay, that's fine, sir." The officer could barely conceal his worn expression, and began to look over his shoulder at the other passengers, in the hope of finding someone who was capable of firing bullets not ovens.

"Merry Christmas," Skink said, taking the passport from the policeman. He smiled inwardly at how easily he could pretend. It helped when the document was genuine, the likeness very close, and that the real Mr. McLeish would be none the wiser - considering his premature encounter with the Grim Reaper. Another reason to be grateful to his new-found friend.

Skink was enjoying his new personality so much that rather than walk briskly out of the airport, he decided to amble along at a slow gait. He was relishing the air of tension generated by the police and the concerned clusters of travellers standing underneath televisions watching the breaking news from Nice. Stepping gingerly through a crowd of passengers waiting to board the flight he had just disembarked from, he noticed a newspaper on one of the Formica-covered tables outside a café.

It was the Evening Times, the newspaper everyone remembers growing up with in Glasgow. An understated tabloid, it dedicated pages to listings of second-hand goods for resale, ranging from household items to cars. It was a one-stop shop for notices of events and social opportunities across the city, guiding many a reveller to pubs with live music late on a weekend. As if these were not enough reasons to buy this quirky newspaper, Skink felt its true value lay in its later production run. Published in the early afternoon, it allowed the reader to be one step ahead of the national newspapers the following morning.

On this particular day, it had missed the First Minister assassination attempt by a couple of hours. However, Skink was pleased to see his picture on the front cover, the full page dedicated to his escape, reminding the Scottish public of *a menace of diabolical cunning and exceptional evil*. The photo was his mug shot from earlier that year when he had been captured in Langbank, coincidentally only a few miles along the river from the airport. It really was not a flattering look considering the picture had been taken when he was grimacing from the pain of a broken arm - and the disappointment of his plans falling through.

He sat down at the table and began to read the article which had clearly been thrown together in a hurry. It focused solely on what they naively called *the twisted mind and evil intentions of a psychopathic maniac*. Really, he thought? They had no idea of what he was all about. His *intentions* were based on purity of purpose, to make the world a better place. He sat down and spent a few more minutes on the front page, before becoming bored reading about himself. He decided to leaf through the rest of the newspaper, enjoying his unabashed disregard for the growing concern of police stopping travellers from his flight. He had not read a newspaper in a long time, relishing the feel of its coarse quality on his fingertips.

On page five there was a short article about a new bar opening in Glasgow on Christmas Eve. *Bringing a taste of Tallinn to Glasgow*, it read, the owner none other than Tommy MacGregor, *the man who had helped Kiltman nail Skink*. He laughed aloud at the gall of this cocksure wheeler and dealer, leveraging the fame he enjoyed at Skink's detriment. He would get his comeuppance. Skink would add MacGregor's fate into the finer detail of his retaliation plan, which was already brimming with victims.

Before long, he was staring at the obituaries. He sniggered quietly, remembering his father's only joke - how people always seemed to die in alphabetical order. No wonder he and his father never got along. He licked his finger and thumb to turn to the sports pages to see whether the two-horse race between Rangers and Celtic was providing any entertainment, when the name Morgan caught his eye. He sat up straight in the chair, forgetting for a moment the importance of remaining nonchalant while armed hunters patrolled the airport terminal. He ignored the guffy religious stuff leading into the detail, focusing on the facts.

Molly Morgan, Widow of Patrick Morgan, much-loved Mother of Kenneth, loving Grandmother to Roderick, passed away peacefully in her sleep in the early hours of December 22nd. Her funeral mass will take place on December 26th at 10 am in St. Stephen's Church; thereafter Old Dalnottar Cemetry, followed by refreshments at Sweeneys Hotel in Duntocher.

"Are you okay, love?" an attractive lady sitting at the next table, reached across to place her hand on his back. "Can I get you something?"

"Eh, what?" he muttered. "No, I'm fine, thanks."

105

He stood up hastily, slipping the newspaper under his arm, tears dropping like jungle raindrops onto his shirt. Poor Kenny, he thought, as he walked through the terminal, working hard to retain his composure. He had always admired his relationship with Molly, envied it in so many ways. They knew each other so well; and seemed to have a bond he could only have dreamt about with either of his parents. He remembered those days when Kenny would bring Molly to the pub for a drink with his friends. Pre-Skink, when he was plain Donald MacKenzie, he would sit at the table trying not to be noticed. He was only there because Kenny had forced him to put his books to the side and come for some *craic*, whatever that was supposed to be. On more than one occasion, Molly had pulled Donald back as they were leaving, slipping a plastic bag under his arm, just as she said goodbye. He recalled rushing to get back to his apartment to light the oven and cook the food she had given him - a combination of various meats, vegetables and her famed, home-made Irish soda bread. He knew he had been losing weight because of an unhealthy lifestyle, but Molly Morgan was the only other person to notice.

He had made it to the ground floor en route to the taxi rank, when he saw the stationers, WH Smith. There was something he had to do before he left the airport.

A Nice Evening

When MacTavish had pounced on her at the hospital, she had to close the phone down and move into contingency mode. Yes, the First Minister was awake and recovering well. No, we were still investigating the shooter. No, we did not know for certain it was Skink. Of course, a full statement would be released as soon as we had more to say. He had quickly run out of questions, wilting under Wilson's steely glare and curt answers; closing the report more quickly than he had wanted.

She had decided to keep walking when she left the hospital. She had called Kenny back to close out their conversation, both agreeing it would be better to talk when she was back home. As she walked through Nice's old town, she was enjoying a breather before going home in the morning to continue the enquiries; and visit Kenny. Her walk had taken her through Nice starting off on the promenade alongside the *old town* area of the city. The salty, fresh air permeated her lungs with ease, allowing her body to release waves of feelgood endorphins. It felt satisfying to have the chance to appreciate such a special place. The south of France appealed to her sense of calm and love of open space. Nice itself would be her kind of break, a city on the beach, lots to do and see in a relatively small area. She was savouring the escapism of vibrantly stocked shops and street entertainment. The caricaturists, jugglers and old town acrobats were a welcome distraction from foiling an assassin's bullet.

She could not fully relax into the evening knowing how sad Kenny was back home. His grief would be all consuming, she just hoped he would hold himself together until she returned. She promised herself she would come back one day for a holiday with Kenny and Roddy.

There was also Skink. He was still at large, but there was nothing more she could do that day. The gendarmes were in the process of searching all locations west of the podium -although the countless number of windows with line of sight made their task Herculean. She did not expect they would find anything, even if they were lucky enough to identify where he had pulled the trigger. She did not remember much from her language classes at school, but bizarrely did remember that French shared the same idiom as in English when 'looking for a needle in a haystack': *chercher une aiguille dans une meule de foin*. She was quite sure the police would find plenty of *foin* and not a single *aiguille*.

And finally, Kiltman; his behaviour had thrown her. His disappearance, then resurgence on the phone, followed by reluctance to join her in Nice, reminded her that she had actually only known him for less than a week. Those days in June had been intense. Kiltman and Wilson had connected on several levels, but she should not presume to understand how he would react in any given situation. There was a mysterious quality to him that went beyond masks and capes, she just could not put her finger on it.

A firm tap on her shoulder stopped her mid-stride and mid-thought. She turned to find MacTavish standing there, the first time she had seen him without a microphone.

"Hey, DI Wilson, small world!" She could see why the public liked him. His boyish charm and floppy, blond hair sat easily with his round, open face.

She did not believe the world was that small, and generally supposed if a coincidental meeting happened like this it was because two people had failed in avoiding each other. Or one of them was following the other. She was quite sure what was going on in this situation.

"Hello. You've finally stopped harassing people, have you?"

"Look. I'm sorry for pouncing on you at the hospital. I've got this producer, and he's constantly in my ear niggling me to get something new to keep folks watching. I saw you walk out of the hospital, and before I knew it, I was running after the cameraman towards the entrance."

Hmm, she thought. She was quite sure the cameraman had been struggling to keep up with MacTavish.

"Oh, well," she shrugged. "I guess we've all got to make a living."

She moved to step past him, when he clasped his hands together, bowing his head slightly. "Please let me make up for it." He waited a moment, feigning deference. "Would you be offended if I offered to buy you dinner?"

Dinner? With MacTavish? She would rather hurl herself head-first into the stomach of a politician. He spotted her impending reaction.

"Look, we don't need to talk about Skink. We have other things to talk about."

"Oh, really?" she smiled, "What exactly might that be?"

"Kenny," he answered.

That threw her. "Kenny?"

"Kenny Morgan," he replied. He was smiling what he regarded as his winning smile. "You weren't aware that we went to university together?"

She slowly shook her head.

"Yes, he studied chemistry, and I studied an interesting degree. Ha! Just joking! No, seriously, we knew each other quite well. Played football in the same team and had a few beers now and then. I know you two are, how shall I say, romantically connected. I'm not a reporter for nothing, you know."

He was grinning at her like the cat that got the cream. If he had licked his lips, she would have given him a ball of string to play with.

This made a difference, she thought. Talking to someone about Kenny. It might be therapeutic - and allow her a chance to understand some of his background. She had become worried about his alcohol intake over the last couple of days. She could tell when she was in the hospital on the phone that he had been drinking during the day. If she could find out more about what made him do this, then maybe she could help him get back on track.

"Okay. I'm hungry. There are supposed to be some good restaurants towards the port area. Fancy a walk?"

She started walking towards the promenade surprised to see Grant had extended his arm in a half loop. He was smiling a broad grin encouraging her to link with him. He waited a few moments while Wilson looked at him, her head at an angle, studying him quizzically.

"Only joking," he said awkwardly when she refused to move a muscle. She knew he had been far from joking.

A couple of hours later she was enjoying a fine steak and local wine in a bustling restaurant close to the harbour, full of yachts of all shapes and sizes, rendered almost divinely white by the full moon hovering above them. In the backdrop, there was a mound of rock around 300 feet high that was the source of the '*canon*' boom - la Colline du Chateau, otherwise known as Castlehill. It definitely sounded much better in French, she thought, as most things did - Colline Noir and Lait du Chateau coming to mind, reflecting areas in Glasgow where she had spent more than a fair share of her career.

It was nearly the perfect evening. The view spectacular, the food exquisite, and the wine caressing her nerve endings with ripples of relaxation pulsating through her tired body. There was only thing – one person - missing.

"Another glass of red?" MacTavish asked, looking into her eyes as if rummaging for hidden treasure.

"Maybe one more," she answered, finding his searching looks increasingly cloying.

They had been talking about Kenny for most of the meal, although it had become clear that MacTavish knew the bare minimum about him. Reading between the lines, she was convinced that Kenny would have chosen to share extraordinarily little of his personal life with the journalism student. His flair for embellishment was the bellwether of someone who enjoyed sharing gossip to acquire information. Fun at a sewing bee or at the hairdressers, but someone you trusted as much as a cracked egg in a boiling pot of water. At least he had not mentioned Kenny's mother, he would not be aware yet of her passing. This suited Wilson - the only person she wanted to talk to about Molly was Kenny.

"Off the record," MacTavish leaned forward conspiratorially, elbows on the table. He deliberately lowered his eyelids a half inch, attempting to make her relax into the change in topic. *Oh dear*, she thought, before he went on. "What about Kiltman? Where was he today?"

She smiled in a manner a parent would use with a child.

"Grant, I think you know; I can't reveal how we work together. But trust me when I say we wouldn't have known about today's attack if it hadn't been for him."

She could say this quite honestly while looking in MacTavish's weirdly half-closed eyes. "I won't be revealing anything else about how we're operating on this case."

He sat back in his seat, awaiting her to move forward, a classic move he had learned from the channel's resident psychologist. Sit forward, then back and the other party will lean forward towards you, giving you a subtle control over the next part of the conversation. Armchair psychology at its best.

She stayed rooted to the back of her seat.

"Eh, right," he said. "I see."

She kept staring at him, without a hint of humour or interest on her face.

"I just need to nip to the gents," he continued after a few moments of awkward silence. "Be back in a sec."

Her own body language trick seemed to work much better than his effort.

As soon as he turned into the washroom, she grabbed his phone. Fortunately, she did not need to guess at a password. He had a frustratingly impolite habit of touching his mobile every few minutes, glancing at messages as they came in. He did it in a way he thought others would not notice. At least it kept the phone live, no need for a password. She went to the messages box and found a stream of communications with '*The Boss*'.

"*MacT. Make sure you drill her on her relationship with Kiltman. Why is he not in Nice? We need to own that story.*"

"*On it, boss. Been following her since the hospital. Will engage now.*"

"*Any updates?*"

"*Yip. We're having dinner. I'm plying her with wine. I'll bleed her dry for Kiltman detail.*"

"*Ok. You know we want to know where he lives and who he is. Anything short of that is failure. Got it?*"

"*Yes sir.*"

She placed the phone beside his plate, a minute before he returned. It gave her enough time to leaf through a Frommer's travel guide, lying idly on top of a cluster of menus. She found what she was looking for as he began to sit down.

111

"One for the road?" he asked. "Remember, the tab's on me tonight." He patted his chest; she assumed that's where he kept his wallet.

"Actually, there's a really fun bar near here. You up for it? After all of today's excitement, I'm ready for some distraction."

She had placed the guidebook back on the menus and was already in the process of grabbing her jacket from the back of the chair.

"Okay." He was not sure whether to be annoyed or excited. He had been halfway through sitting down, and now was on his way back up again watching her stride towards the door. He followed her out onto the sidewalk after paying the bill; not leaving a tip, since he was sure they did not expect one. He had convinced himself it would be an insult to give them money for their impeccable service.

As they walked around the lavish port, she steered the conversation away from Kiltman by asking MacTavish which superstar he thought owned each yacht. He rose to the challenge, convinced he had identified the owners of the three largest: Sean Connery, Elton John and Roger Moore. Whether he was right or not was irrelevant - it kept him from prying any further. They rounded the corner of the port furthest from the restaurant, when she said, "Grant, do you see that pub up there with the lights on?"

He peered up the side street to see a sign, *Skipper Bar*, and nodded, "Sure."

"I need to make a call." She pointed at her mobile. "But I'll see you in there in about ten minutes. Order me a cassis, please."

She sat down on a stone bench facing what MacTavish had thought was Elton John's yacht. She began to push some buttons on her phone.

"Okay, got it," he said turning to walk towards the bar, a spring in his step. He entered a small nondescript doorway into a relatively small space, the bar dominating the room, stretching all the way down the right-hand side to the back wall. He spotted a cluster of wooden stools free at the centre of the bar and clambered up onto the middle one. The bar was cosier than it had seemed from the outside, and darker than it probably needed to be considering it was late evening. He ordered two cassis and a jug of water and leant his elbows on the shiny counter to text an update to his boss. This evening was working out better than he had planned.

He felt a rustle on either side of him and realised the spare stools were no longer free. He turned to his right to advise the customer taking the seat that he was waiting for someone. A man wearing a beret and t-shirt with horizontal stripes was looking directly at him in a manner that was somewhere between friendly and menacing, depending on how he moved the enormous bulk of muscle he had perched on the stool. The horizontal stripes made his pecs look as though they were about to burst.

"Eh, hi!" MacTavish raised his hand to acknowledge the new guy at the bar.

He decided to have the 'please don't take my friend's seat' conversation with the person settling into the stool on his left. He swivelled around to find someone who was the double of the guy on his right, only he had even bigger muscles.

"Bon soir," said the man, barren of expression, a five-day stubble underpinning dark brooding eyes. "Je m'appelle Étienne. Ça va?"

How could somebody introduce themselves in such a chilling way, MacTavish thought?

"Emm, good!"

He snatched a quick look towards the door to see if Wilson was on her way in. She was a policewoman after all, she could help ease the situation. As he waited for his saviour to arrive, he noticed that there was a uniformity to the bar he had not registered on the way in. Nearly everyone wore a striped t-shirt and had a beret. And everyone was male. Most of them were smiling at him.

Wilson walked back to the hotel, feeling slightly tipsy, unable to control the fits of giggles that gripped her every few minutes, wishing she could have been a fly on the wall in *Skipper Bar*.

Christmas Eve

Christmas Eve in Glasgow bordered on magical. Typically a happy go-lucky city, it went into overdrive during the festive season. Kenny alighted from the train at Queen Street station and walked up onto ground level to the breath-taking dazzle of the lights in George Square. Massive, bright snowflakes and reindeer-driven sleds wrapped around lampposts illuminated the vast open space.

It was a cold, damp evening, not a classical Christmas night with billowing snow and snowbanks on pavements. That did not hinder the carefree air of the people hurrying past him to catch the train home to their families - or those spending the evening in the city, walking purposefully to their next oasis of revelry.

Christmas was usually his favourite time of the year, living every moment through Roddy's giggles and gratitude for gifts he would spend the day unwrapping meticulously one by one, savouring each before he moved onto the next. He was not the child to rip off the wrapping to see what he had received, then move on to successive gifts hoping they would be better than the one before.

Kenny was not in the mood this year; his mother's passing had made sure of that. Fiona had invited him round to hers for Christmas dinner. She had insisted, not taking no for an answer, no matter how many excuses he could think of. When he had told her that he and Maggie would not be spending Christmas together, she was genuinely sad. She bounced back in the conversation to say that Maggie was a wonderful person and that she was sure two great people like them could find a way to make it work and deal with their rough spots. Not that simple, Kenny had thought, remembering his discussion with Maggie that afternoon.

Earlier that day, when Maggie had arrived at Glasgow airport from Nice, she had taken a cab directly to Uisge Beatha. They had hugged in the doorway for several minutes before walking into the kitchen holding hands. She had barely got halfway through her cup of tea when she spotted the empty bottles of whisky. From that moment it had not gone well. He became more defensive than a San Marino centre back playing against Brazil, never managing to meet the ball head on, continually looking for a referee to blow the final whistle.

She had only stayed an hour after that, their mutual hurt making conversation difficult. They both realised they were not going to resolve anything, and more than likely would cause even more damage to their fragile relationship. When they parted, she had said, "Please stop drinking, Kenny."

He had quickly replied with, "Please stop running away, Maggie!" in the same manner they had danced around each other's Achilles heels throughout that increasingly awkward conversation.

Fiona had called to ask Maggie over for Christmas, but she had politely refused saying, "Skink won't be waiting around for me to open up presents and finish eggnog. I've got a whole bunch of video footage to study from Nice. Thanks anyway."

Fiona did not push. She knew she should step back and let them sort it out between themselves - the more she got involved, the more complicated it would become.

From Kenny's point of view, he knew he had been spending far too much time alone at Uisge Beatha, in his downward self-destruct spiral. With Christmas Day planned to be at Fiona's with Roddy, and Angus the Oxford rower, he had to make sure Christmas Eve was busy. Tommy's invitation to his pub opening was just what Kenny needed to stop his self-flagellation and recrimination.

He had arrived at the front door of Terviseks not long after eight in the evening. The pub was well-positioned on St. Vincent Street, Glasgow's main road leading west from the city centre, a wide street dotted on either side by pubs and restaurants. Tommy had picked the perfect location. The front was decorated in the blue, black and white of the Estonian flag adding a sense of austerity to the moment of entry. Once inside, Kenny smarted at the noise and chaotic banter scores of people can make in a confined space, especially when fuelled by Russian Champagne, Estonian vodka and Õlu Beer. He was enjoying the afterglow of another half bottle of malt consumed after Wilson had made her uncomfortable exit. He was ready for a top up.

As he approached the busy bar, he saw Tommy waving at him, "Hey, sõber, over here!" Kenny sidled over to the table his friend had reserved to the side of the bar.

"Hello, Tommy. Actually, I'm not that sober to be honest. I need to give you some news."

"Kenny, sõber is the Estonian word for *friend*," Tommy said, a look of seriousness spreading over features far too young for his age. "What's wrong?"

He was holding Kenny's arm firmly, watching tears flow down his friend's cheeks.

"Mum's gone, Tommy."

He wiped his eyes with his shirt sleeve. He had not realised the tears were in freefall when he walked into the bar. Molly would have been there that night taking pleasure and some pride in Tommy's success. His friend took him in his arms and hugged him tightly, crying into his neck. Molly had treated Tommy like a son, allowing him a place to live whenever he was in Glasgow. Tommy brought the world into Molly's kitchen with his stories and adventures, in exchange for a bed, soda bread and a three-course meal.

They unpicked themselves, before walking to the bar to order two large vodkas. Kenny hung his jacket on the 'two-armed octopus hook' underneath the bar. At least that was what Roddy had called it one hot day when they had stopped into Sweeneys for an orange juice. Kenny talked through what he knew of his mother's death, going onto the funeral arrangements, and his fear of having to deliver a eulogy. Tommy nodded along with each comment Kenny made, keeping one arm around his friend's shoulder. They drank the vodkas in Russian style. A toast, *Molly, may God rest her soul*, then a swift necking of the burning liquor. They agreed that Molly was with them in spirit and the last thing she would want was for them to be morose at Tommy's opening.

"Right." Tommy rubbed his hands, working hard to change the mood. "Let's go to the table. I want you to meet my girlfriend, Marsha. We're getting excited about our trip next week."

"What trip?" Kenny asked absent-mindedly. "I don't remember planning to go anywhere."

"No, you daft eejit! Not you." At another time, Tommy would have revelled in Kenny's distraction. Today, he felt his friend's pain. "Marsha and I have been invited to the United Nations meeting on New Year's Eve. You know, the one about countries being able to self-determine their future, what conditions should be in place, and so on. They want to present examples from across the world of countries merging cultures and blending together. Especially small countries that have a leaning towards independence, to show how they can still forge a way in the world whether part of a greater union or not."

He then paused, seeing Kenny drift off into the middle distance. Kenny was remembering George explaining how he had also been invited to what would no doubt be an interesting way to spend New Year's Eve.

"Kenny? Will Maggie be coming tonight?"

Kenny nearly ordered another couple of double vodkas, before shaking his head, realising he had already off-loaded enough on his friend that evening.

"No, Tommy, she's working on the Skink case."

"Yes, I saw that on telly this afternoon," Tommy replied. "She was amazing, she deserves a medal for being able to knock the First Minister over."

They both laughed. Tommy and Wilson had not hit it off when they had crossed paths during the Skink adventure in June, but since then he had endeared himself to her, with his continual banter and cocksure friendliness. She had come to realise that if Tommy had not arranged the kilt night when Kenny had saved her from the thugs in Ashton Lane many years earlier, the outcome would have been much worse.

They squeezed past a few loud customers enjoying boisterous Christmas Eve merriment and reached a small table in the corner of the pub. Tommy pulled out a chair for Kenny.

"Let me introduce my best friend, Kenny Morgan!"

An attractive lady stood up from the table, all blue eyes and sparklingly blond hair, smiling and holding out her hand in a formal manner.

"Hallo. I am Marsha."

They shook hands as Kenny took a sidelong glance at Tommy, whose chest was poking out like a rooster on a cornflakes box.

A tall man with a broad chest and large hands leant forward and spoke in a heavy Russian accent. "And I am Dimitri Grigori, Marsha's brother, but you can call me Digi. It's easier."

He was slightly oriental in appearance, most probably from eastern Russia, Kenny thought. He was what would be considered the strong, silent type. Although he seemed to carry too much tension in his lower jaw, upsetting the balance in the rest of his features, creating an ill at ease disposition

"Cool," Tommy said. "Let's get this party started."

Tommy began to make horizontal, circular movements with his arms extended in front of him. Kenny guessed Tommy was trying to dance. Marsha had already manoeuvred herself in front of his friend and was gyrating to the Estonian folk music blaring out from the speaker above the bar. He realised he had never seen Tommy dancing before. He would like to have said it suited him, but truth was, as the dance continued, Tommy steadily lost the beat to the point his arms and head were moving in jerks and spasms. As Kenny watched, he realised Tommy's dance moves were a vernacular juxtaposition of misplaced confidence meets blissful ignorance. If he were to remember this in the morning, he would text it to him.

The evening did not take long to go from despondency to faux-fun, followed by melancholic bar-leaning in the middle of pushes and shoves Kenny barely registered, the bulk of his anxiety waiting patiently to strike when he was most vulnerable. He stepped back from the bar, shook his head and realised this was not the way to celebrate Tommy's grand opening. It was time to go home. He glanced towards the table where Marsha and Digi sat huddled together, whispering. Why would anyone want to whisper in a raucous bar, Kenny thought, as he lifted a hand to wave, shuffling towards the door? They flickered a glance at him barely registering any acknowledgement that he was leaving.

He put the palm of his hand against the door bracing himself for a blast of fresh air. He felt a tug at his shoulder. Turning as if in slow motion, he saw Tommy sporting a jovial smile. Through his fug Kenny could see his friend was trying hard to appear blasé - he was feeling every twinge of Kenny's pain.

"You'll need this, pal."

He handed Kenny the jacket he had left hanging underneath the bar. He let Tommy place it carefully over his shoulders.

"Cheers, Tommy. Congratulations. You've done well." Kenny ruffled his friend's hair and pinched his cheek.

"See you Boxing Day, Kenny." Tommy placed both hands on Kenny's arms. "You should lay off the booze now. Enough's enough."

"Easy for you to say, Tommy. Over the last couple of days, I've cried buckets and buckets of tears." He could feel a surge of annoyance brewing at Tommy's cheap shot.

"Look, Kenny," Tommy said, waiting a half second longer than normal. "I've told you a million times not to exaggerate!" His smile stopped Kenny in his tracks.

"Ah, the old ones are the best, Tommy!" Kenny laughed between his tears, reaching across to pull him into a tight hug. "I love you, pal."

"Cheers, mate. I always knew how to make you laugh. Anyway, if you want to chat before your mother's funeral, just let me know. It'll give me a chance to get away from Marsha's brother. He's a bit too intense."

"Sure, no bother," Kenny said, somewhere in the recesses of his mind wondering about the story behind this Estonian lady and her Russian brother.

He walked out the door waving a hand distractedly back at Tommy, before tugging the jacket tightly around himself to keep out the damp cold. He gingerly placed one foot in front of the other and walked unsteadily in the direction of the nearest taxi rank, which he remembered was across a lively George Square on the other side of Queen Street station. The few hundred yards walk suddenly felt like a ten-mile hike uphill, his legs weak beneath his unstable frame. If he made it there in one piece without falling over, he fully expected to wait at the rank for an hour, end up in a stramash with someone skipping the queue, then fall asleep when he eventually found a taxi. As he walked he felt a slight jabbing in his shoulder blade each time he took a step. He stopped, steadying himself against the breeze blowing down St. Vincent Street, and brought his jacket round to study it as if it was a long-lost friend. Protruding from the inside pocket was a white envelope. Strange, he thought? He could not remember it being there when he left Uisge Beatha. Although noticing anomalies had not been a skill he had excelled at over the last couple of days.

"Need a cab, mate?" a black hackney had pulled up beside him cutting him a break on the walk to the station rank.

He climbed in, issuing slurred instructions to take him to a house in the middle of nowhere outside Duntocher. He was sure he saw the driver's eyes roll skywards.

"There's a boundary on that, mate, alright?"

There was a time he would have tried to negotiate the inflated boundary charge revered and protected by the Glasgow cab drivers. On this occasion, he just nodded. He would have paid anything to get home, tiredness working its way through every bone in his body. He started to drift off when he remembered the envelope.

He pulled it from the pocket and ripped it open with all the dexterity of someone wearing boxing gloves. There was a card inside, displaying two words in flowery writing *In Memoriam*. He opened it to find the scrawl he had grown to detest but now somehow found oddly comforting.

Dear Kenny,

It's with a heavy heart I send you my commiserations on your loss. My thoughts are with you, and I hope you can take comfort in your memories. Your mother was a wonderful lady, kind to a fault. I remember the times when she shared her love and generosity with me. She was a walking Saint.

I've been wondering why I did not have the pleasure of your company in Nice. Now I know and understand. This will be a very difficult time for you. We will cross paths in the near future, but rest assured I will not do anything over Christmas. I will wait until after your mother's funeral. Out of respect for Molly.

Remember you are who you are because your mother believed in you, and she gave you the strength to believe in yourself... eventually.

Yours in sorrow
Cullen Skink

PS. If ever I am on a permanent downer, please look for the upper, unless too much for you 2 to chew

He stuffed the card back into his pocket, after reading and re-reading until the words began to blur together into one mass of hieroglyphics. He had given up even trying to decipher the PS. Other than the mystery of how Skink had managed to slip the card into his pocket, the conundrum he now faced was how to share the news with Pitt Street that Skink had told Kenny Morgan he was taking a breather over the holidays.

Christmas Morning

Wilson had walked up onto the roof of Pitt Street station to take advantage of its view over the city. She cradled a mug of strong, black coffee in her hands, blowing gently into a spiral of wispy steam. The first cup in the morning stimulated her more quickly than the five or six others she had during the day, more out of habit than desire. There was a long overdue New Year resolution gnawing at her conscience. But maybe not this year.

The sky was cloudy, threatening rain. For a Christmas morning, Glasgow seemed particularly quiet. However, she reflected, today's tranquillity was no different from other Christmases in the past. It was normally the day when she took stock of her life. She had hoped this year was going to be when she could say she was moving in the right direction. With a deep sigh, she realised that Maggie Wilson was as much a lost soul this year as any other.

Her mobile rang. She saw *Tas* on the caller ID. Flipping it open, she made an effort to sound cheerier than she felt. "Morning, Tas. Or rather, Merry Christmas, Brother!".

"Hello, Maggie," he said in a mellow voice. "What are you doing for Christmas? Do I sense a tad of the thespian in your chirpy greeting?"

"Working, I'm afraid," she answered wearily, dropping the pretence.

She wondered if he had seen the news about Nice. She expected not since he was becoming more and more of a hermit in the seclusion of his home in the Highlands. From what she could tell he was happy in splendid isolation cut off from the world. He had abandoned TV and radio years earlier, choosing to read books about various topics most people would eschew. The tomes he invested days and nights studying usually covered famines, disasters, wars, and international conflicts. There was nothing light-hearted on any of his many shelves. On the one occasion she had visited his home, it had been so uncomfortable for him, she chose not to return. Any communication they had since then had been by phone, or the occasional post card, which was always from her on a rare holiday abroad.

She put Tas's anti-societal behaviour down to his early years. Her parents had struggled to have children of their own. After years of trying, in the wake of innumerable disappointments and lots of tears, they eventually decided to adopt. They engaged with an international adoption agency who advised that because of their age - already into their mid-forties - they would be expected to adopt an older child. After some time, they agreed to adopt a fourteen-year-old, Thomas. He later shortened his name to *Tas* when other Thomases in his school were taking the classic Glasgow nickname of *Tam*.

When her mother had become pregnant, her parents could not believe it at first. They went to a second doctor for his opinion, not believing this news they had prayed for on so many occasions. The doctor had laughed when he said he had been asked to give a second opinion on lots of things, but never about whether someone was pregnant. Yes, he had smiled, maybe it was against all the odds, but the fact was she was with child. Considering their luck, the doctor had suggested charmingly, they should also go to the bookies and place a bet.

They had already committed to adopting Thomas, nothing was going to stop them from going through with it. They were not going to turn their good fortune into bad luck for an orphaned child with little hope of finding a caring family. Tas had only been part of the Wilson clan for six months before Maggie was born. Growing up, he had been like a second father, always looking out for her, stepping in to provide protection in squabbles and arguments. He was kept busy considering she had a habit of causing trouble, sticking her nose in when she should have walked away. Her inquisitive nature got her into a lot of scrapes.

Policing became the perfect career path for Wilson. Tas did not approve of her *submission to the establishment*, as he called it. He had tried to talk her out of joining up, by dedicating her life to worthy causes instead. He asked her to help him put a mirror in front of politicians who turned a blind eye to the challenges facing society, economy, and environment. Maggie had generally agreed with his sentiments but had been less inclined to join him in protests, carrying banners or chaining herself to lampposts.

Tas had never met Kenny, and it was not an encounter she was in a hurry to encourage. They were like oil and water; where Tas was thoughtful, intense, and prone to belligerence, Kenny was light-hearted, bordering on happy go lucky. Sometimes she wished Tas could have some of Kenny's devil-may-care attitude to life even if just enough to depressurise his growing angst. And if Kenny could have a smidgeon of Tas's gravity, she wondered? No, Kenny was just fine the way he was.

In one of her more recent conversations with Tas, he had become wildly energised about the importance of finding a way to control political outcomes. He believed that politics should not be allowed to operate in a judicial vacuum, but that certain controls and parameters should be introduced to stop political figures promising outcomes they could not deliver. The effectiveness of the measures he wanted to propose relied on the implementation of penalties for those politicians who gain power on the back of campaign promises that are never fulfilled. When she last saw him, he had written several chapters of a book he had entitled *Po-limit-ics*, laying out the fundamentals of his ideals. She worried continually about Tas, and how reclusive he had become of late. She hoped he would come back to the real world soon.

"You still there, Sister?" he asked.

"Eh, sorry, Tas, got a bit distracted. Well..." She was about to bring the call to a close when he interrupted her.

"Maggie, just be careful, okay?" The concern was evident in the strain of his voice.

"What do you mean?" She was surprised at his tone.

"These politicians are not worth it. If their time is up, then let them pay the price for their pride and false promises."

"Tas, how did you know..."

"Look, I need to go. But please pay heed to my words. Love you, Sis!"

And he was gone.

It left a strange taste in her mouth; she was confused. Maybe he had started to tune in to the news again after all these years.

She decided to look on this as a positive, that he was slowly coming back to the world.

She drifted off again into her thoughts looking over the spires and chimneys of the West End. She had become good at being on her own over the years, spending special days like this alone, usually working on a project or clearing up admin. This holiday was different. How could she feel the absence of someone she had known for less than a year? She had so wanted to spend the day with Kenny and Roddy. Before she left home that morning, she had decided to open the present they had given her a week earlier. It had lain under the Christmas tree they had helped her put up, towering over the presents she had for them: a gym membership for Kenny and a jigsaw for Roddy. Even when she bought it, she had been quite sure Kenny would end up spending more time with Roddy's present than his own.

She put her hand in her pocket and pulled out a phone half the size of the one she had been given by the police. It was a nifty, slim version that slipped into her jeans while leaving space for keys and money. They knew she had to keep her work phone as her primary communication device, but they had made a point of giving her a piece of new technology that she could keep in reserve for an emergency. It was fully charged, already 'chipped' and ready to go.

Whatever happened with Kenny, she would use this phone to keep in touch with Roddy in the future. She could not imagine them not being in her life - the thought of 'friendship' as the definition of her relationship with Kenny did not sit well with her. The phone rested in her hand like a tormenter, cajoling her not to leave the future to chance. She was aware that she had upset their momentum by reacting to Kenny in the way she had. Her timing could not have been worse. Just before Molly died. The two people in Kenny's life he had come to rely on, along with Roddy, had exited his life in less than a day. She felt his pain and would have done anything to help him. Except undo the kiss with Kiltman. She could not rewind and delete that moment of madness. She regretted it, but it had helped her put the brakes on with Kenny. She had lulled herself into thinking she was settling down nicely, when bang, she realised she was not even close.

Her phone rang again. The caller ID was blocked. She answered anyway. "Hello?"

125

"Merry Christmas, Wilson!" The metallic, echoey voice felt comforting. "Well done in Nice."

"Oh, thanks, Merry Christmas to you too, Kiltman," she sighed. "Yes, your clue-solving made the difference. Bit late, but nobody's complaining. Except Skink, I expect."

"That's why I'm calling." He had rehearsed this in front of the mirror.

"Uh-huh?"

"Skink's not going to do anything until after Christmas." He waited a moment. "He found a way to get me this message."

"What? Skink has suddenly found God since he shot the First Minister? And how on earth can he contact you, when none of the rest of us have a scooby how to find you?"

"Let's just say, he has ways, Wilson." He let that sink in, and before she could hit him with another cutting jibe, said, "Well, I better go and put the turkey in the oven. Yo ho ho!"

Click, the line went dead. He could be so infuriating, she thought. She reminded herself it was always better to think about the substance of what he communicated rather than the form. At the end of the day, she was happy to believe that Skink was downing tools for a while. She did not understand it, and Gemmill and Fraser would be highly sceptical, but if Kiltman believed it then that was good enough for her.

Eight miles away, Kenny doffed his mask, and crawled back into bed. He was not due at Fiona's until two o'clock. He was going to focus on sleeping and forgetting. He had barely unblocked his caller ID, texted Maggie, *Merry Xmas x* before he dropped onto his pillow, already snoring. His last thoughts were of Skink, wondering how his nemesis would be spending Christmas.

Thirty miles away, Skink sat across the table from his surly friend. They had argued the previous day, on and off through various calls, about how 'Skink was a great planner but a terrible executioner, pun intended'. The bad feeling had carried through to today, the anger brewing on his face when Skink opened the door to welcome him.

"We have come so far." He was fighting a rising impatience. "Do you have what we agreed?"

"Yes, everything is ready," Skink responded. "Don't worry, I'm going to provide no more clues. All the details are here in this journal, my Christmas gift to you; contacts, details of our weapons, location and codes."

Skink pushed a book towards the other side of the table. Its brown, nondescript cover belied the malevolent content inside, spread over multiple pages of detailed drawings and bulletized instructions. The man picked it up and thumbed through the pages slowly, reading each individually. Skink waited patiently, convinced that his friend would not be disappointed in the terrorist manual prepared to meet his coming needs.

"Hmm, you really have thought of everything. Excellent." His features barely registered any sign of emotion. Skink had not noticed this blandness of expression before and was slightly disappointed at the absence of excitement and appreciation.

"Just one more thing." Skink coyly pushed a duty-free bag across the table. "This is more a thank you than a Christmas gift. Releasing me from Bar L has given us both a chance to realise our dreams. I know how much you risked for me, and I want to give you this small gift as a token of my appreciation of your investment in me."

"Oh!" Finally, Skink noticed his expression change ever so slightly. He watched him tentatively reach across and open the bag, as if a snake were going to jump out and bite him. "I'm sorry. Other than the champagne, I didn't get you anything. I wasn't aware you were into the giving thing."

"No worries," Skink answered, smiling his crooked grin. "My joy will be in your receiving."

Skink lifted the glass to his lips and took a deep draft of his friend's generous bottle of expensive Champagne, enjoying its effervescence and unusually subtle hint of almond.

His accomplice took out the alloy mask and studied it for a few moments. He was well aware of the story of the *Man in the Iron Mask*, a tale of someone born for greatness but whose misfortune resulted in him spending his life in misery and despair. He turned it over in his hands, appreciating its weightiness.

"Very cute," he said. He smiled a smile that barely touched his eyes. He lifted it up and placed it over his face, staring through the eye slits at Skink. "Thank you. I know exactly what I will use this for."

Christmas Dinner

"Chilean reds can be quite exceptional," Angus explained, spinning the wine around the glass after an annoyingly noisy inhalation. Kenny was not sure if that was the fourth or fifth sniff and spin. "Take the wine we are drinking. It's primarily a Carmenère grape with a hint of Syrah."

He swirled and smelled some more. "As a result, the wine can be drunk three or four days after opening. Although," he twirled a bit harder, smiling as if he were about to divulge an extraordinary secret, "it's so moreish I would never let that happen. Hence why I consider it quite a paradoxical onslaught on the taste buds."

He lifted the over-sized glass to his mouth, closed his eyes and let the wine flow gently across his tongue.

"Yes, I see what you mean, Angus." Kenny felt he had to say something.

He was fighting the fear that he might come across as an inverted wine snob, which was exactly how he felt at that point in time. He surveyed his fellow diners at the table: Fiona, Roddy, and Angus. They were all looking at him expectantly, wearing red Santa hats, as was he, in Fiona's attempt to create the perfect Christmas atmosphere. He appreciated the effort she had gone to in helping him survive the most important family day of the year. His emotions had been up and down since he had opened his eyes that morning. Whatever happened that day, he wanted it to be a special one for Fiona and Roddy. His sorrow and wound licking should not bring down Christmas, of that he was determined.

With an air of resolve, he turned to his glass, bending his head to look vertically down into the contents. He took a sniff of the wine that sounded more like an unpleasant snort than a connoisseur's appreciation of grape. He peeked into the glass waiting for inspiration. All he saw was red wine, which he swirled a tad harder than was necessary. A drop of red floated over the rim to land on Fiona's white tablecloth, on practically the only part of the table not covered with food, between the sprouts and mashed potatoes. His coordination had been deteriorating steadily with each drink.

"Eh, sorry, Fiona," he said sheepishly.

"Don't worry, it's an old one," she replied, sighing inwardly at the christening of her thirtieth birthday present from her sister.

"Could you pass the salt, Kenny?" Angus asked, as if he had known his girlfriend's ex-husband all his life.

Kenny studied the saltshaker on the table in front of him. *Does Angus realise how complicated a question he has asked? Is he baiting me?* He could feel the table wine giving him a welcome high after the weight of despair he had felt after his bouts of malt whisky. *It must have been that Carmenère grape after all.* He felt he was back on track, ready to take on the world.

"Salt, did you say, Angus?" Kenny leant back in his seat, with knotted brow.

"Eh, yes," Angus snatched a glance at Fiona, who shrugged with an exaggerated shoulder movement belying the concern building in her stomach.

Kenny continued. "Do you know that if we were in Italy, and I was to do what you ask, I would be stricken with bad luck?"

Angus motioned to speak when Kenny put his hand in the air.

"Indeed, even in our country, it would be bad manners if I gave you the salt without also giving you the pepper. So, for me to be safe from bad luck and accusations of poor etiquette, could you either come and collect the salt, or ask for the pepper too?"

Angus rose from his chair, barely hiding the frustration, and walked past Roddy, to reach across and pick up the salt. "No problem, Kenny. I understand what's going on here. If you've got an issue with me then just say. Don't hide behind the, em, the salt and pepper shakers."

This comment elicited a chuckle from Roddy.

"They'd need to be huge to hide my dad!" Roddy laughed.

Fiona noticed that it was the first time he had laughed since the news of his Gran going to heaven. If that came because of a silly spat between her ex and her new, she would take it. Roddy's chirpy gurgle of a giggle had them all laughing awkwardly, in the spirit of 'moving on'.

The rest of the conversation around the table focused on a smattering of issues, from the various succulent courses Fiona had prepared to the latest Marvel comics and movies Roddy had been watching. Eventually landing on Skink's escape and attempted assassination of the First Minister. Fiona had been avoiding mentioning it at all, but it was the classic elephant in the room rising up on its hind legs and shooting water out of its trunk. Kenny was happy not to talk about it, trying to push Maggie to the back of his mind.

It had become public knowledge that Skink had pulled the trigger - Gemmill had decided it was important to confirm everyone's fears that Skink was the culprit. Christmas Day news reports had been dominated by this information, scenes from Nice played over and over again. Fiona and Roddy could not hide their elation at the role Maggie had played in foiling the assassination attempt. Kenny felt pangs of guilt as they wondered why Kiltman had not been there to support her. Although, Fiona mused, judging by her heroism and success, she may not need the kilted superhero, at least not all the time.

Angus had become visibly bored with the adulation being afforded Kenny's girlfriend, until he lit up like a bonfire. "So, Kenny, where is the damsel in distress turned superheroine?"

When Fiona's eyes switched to look at her Christmas pudding, Kenny could tell that Angus knew about their break-up, and had barely disguised his effort to jerk Kenny's chain. Kenny looked at his plate, reminding himself of his vow to make sure the meal went without a hitch. Fiona had been quiet during most of the afternoon, hoping Kenny would slow down with the wine, and that he and Angus would begin to bond. All she had seen so far was a growing male pride face-off threatening to turn lunch into a cock fight.

"Angus," she said when a lull in the discussion had lasted longer than was comfortable, "tell Kenny how you and Skink are related. Kenny knows him from university."

"Really?" Angus said. Kenny was the only one to notice a slight narrowing of the eyelids. "You were with Donald in uni?"

"Yes," he said. "No biggie. We shared a love of chemistry. I chose to apply it to whisky production, and he chose mayhem and destruction. Amazing that the same course can cover such a wide variety of professions."

"Steady, pal." Angus' voice was tight with a slice of temper. "Donald's still my cousin. His Mum and mine were sisters. You know, not everyone thinks he was completely wrong in what he was trying to do."

"Angus!" Fiona practically barked. "He's a murderer!"

"I know, I know." Angus could not conceal a darkly obstinate shadow crossing his eyes. "But the world has evolved and improved over the years because kings, queens, dictators, explorers and churches took innocent lives. Maybe the world, Scotland at least, needs a wake-up call. Donald was extreme, I give you that, but not unusually passionate when you look at the historical backdrop."

Kenny glanced towards Roddy; whose mouth had drifted open. Roddy had more sense in his little finger than this Oxford rower had between his ears, he thought, before saying, "Everyone's entitled to an opinion, Angus, There's a lot to be said for those who have the guts to say what they believe."

"Look, I didn't say I believed it, but then again... Anyway, I'm just saying, there are two sides to every coin."

Fiona and Roddy were looking at Kenny to say something.

He stayed quiet until Angus said, "Pass me the wine, please. Or do I have to sing an Italian operetta to get it?"

His smile at Kenny carried no hint of charm or endearment. Kenny passed the bottle along the table, before turning to Roddy.

"Hey pal, how do you fancy finishing that thousand-piece jigsaw of Edinburgh castle?"

Maggie had dropped it off that morning on her way to Pitt Street station. The castle esplanade on the box reminded Kenny of when she had stopped his cape from being sucked up into the helicopter blades - the day they prevented Skink's bomb from disrupting the Tattoo and killing the US President.

Roddy nodded, giving them a reason to go to the den and escape an atmosphere laden with questions that would not be discussed that Christmas, at least not when Kenny was around. He stayed for another couple of hours, enjoying the one on one time with his son. They both appreciated the quiet teamwork of doing a jigsaw, not having to talk too much but enjoy the physical contact of passing jagged pieces to each other, nodding their appreciation of the other's ability to spot the correct fit.

131

On leaving, he slung his coat over his shoulder before thanking Fiona for her amazing cooking. As he cuddled Roddy at the door he felt his son squeeze his neck with his tiny fingers to ease his father's tension.

Kenny whispered in his ear, "Just call me if there's anything you need, wee man. Okay?"

Roddy nodded before running back to the den to open some more gifts.

"Well, Angus, enjoy the rest of your Christmas," Kenny tried as neutral a tone as he could muster.

Angus nodded and left for the kitchen before Kenny was even out the door. "Fiona, is everything okay?" he asked.

"Everything's fine," she pushed him gently through the hallway. "Please stop drinking, Kenny. Your mother's funeral is tomorrow, and you've worked so hard to be sober."

"Do you know that means 'friend' in Estonian?" He could not remember where he had heard that but for some reason he thought it would impress her.

"Whatever, Kenny, just go home and have a good sleep. I'll see you tomorrow."

He walked down the stairs and found his growing wooziness was accompanied by a gentle swaying. Hmm, that wine was stronger than he thought. He walked out into the night air and decided to walk the six or so miles to his home. He had made a decision during dinner. He had a eulogy to prepare.

The Final Say

Kenny peered timidly over the top of the pulpit to see benches full all the way to the back of the church. His mother had always said that the number of people at your funeral was a sign of how well you had lived your life. She would have been pleased. St. Stephen's Church had been the rock in Molly's world, *the shelter for her soul*, as she had described it to him. He looked over at the bench halfway down the right hand-side where she used to kneel to pray the rosary, her lips moving swiftly through her favourites, the Joyful Mysteries. On this last day in the church, a bouquet of flowers had been placed on that spot where she had spent many an hour on her knees. Less than ten yards from where her body was now at rest in the newly varnished mahogany coffin in the middle aisle - never leaving Kenny's sight, no matter where his gaze drifted to.

He could feel the nerves churning his stomach. Public speaking was not his thing. Some heads were bowed, others looking at him expectantly. There was no doubting an air of anticipation descending on the church. The delivery of a eulogy had somehow grown over the years from an innocuous speech given by a priest about a person he barely knew, to a close family member bringing their loved one to life.

He was more nervous than he had ever been. He had tried to sleep but had tossed and turned most of the night. Every so often he would get an idea of something to reference in his eulogy, and would sit up, scribble it onto a scrap of paper, then go back to sleep. As the night progressed, he kept finding things to say about his mother, a rush of memories of things she had done and comments she had made coming at him like a welcome shower on a hot summer's day. He eventually had given up trying to sleep, walked to the kitchen and poured a glass of malt, his new late-night companion.

Now here in front of his mother's friends and family - his own friends and family - he saw the faces he had grown to love and cherish looking up at him, praying that he would get through the

133

pain. He was steadily realising that the anguish and sorrow he was feeling were the gateway to acceptance of reality: his mother would not come back.

Towards the front of the church he could see Maggie, Fiona and Roddy; even Angus was there, his face a mixture of boredom meets annoyance. Kenny had no doubts he came along because Fiona had marched him out the door, with words like '*if you want to be part of this family then you need to embrace it...*". Fiona and Maggie were crying, arms linked together. Maggie's bruise covered half her right cheek and seemed to have gone a ripe shade of purple overnight. Her forehead sported the wound he would one day hope to joke to her about as the Minister's Cut. He hoped it would not leave a scar. Roddy was sitting between them leaning forward, his little chin jutted upwards in a defiant thrust. Kenny knew that Roddy sensed how difficult this was.

A few feet to Roddy's left, George sat alone, an air of resignation surrounding him. He always seemed to be on his own, Kenny thought. Molly had become his whole world, his only friend. It was strange that at this stage of his life, he was so isolated. It struck him that he did not even know how George had entered their world a few years back - he just seemed to appear. His comment about being involved in the diplomatic corps had surprised him. His mother had never mentioned his background, maybe she just did not know or really care, happy to have a companion in her later years.

In the row behind them, Tommy sat with Marsha and Digi. Tommy's face was crestfallen. His eyelids were swollen, a combination of bouts of crying and litres of Estonian beer. He had never been good at handling sadness. Fortunately, he rarely felt it, but there was no denying today was not one of those days. Kenny studied him for a few seconds, there was something missing from his friend - the absence of Marsha's hand on his shoulder or her body nestled into his arm. It struck him that Marsha seemed to be sitting a tad closer to Digi than Tommy.

A few rows back were the university friends he had not spent enough time with over the years. Lulu, the elephant-herding tree-hugger with a heart the size of a planet, holding hands with Shuggy. Shuggy, who had been Fr. Hugh until a few months earlier. He had been quietly enjoying the fulfilment of his priestly duties in Rome when it had struck him that he had never stopped loving Lulu. He had spoken to Kenny shortly after he came back to Scotland, in a state of excitement laden with anxiety. Excited to have a new life and be with the woman he loved. Petrified because he had no clue about what he would do and how he would earn an income. He had only just realised the Church was not in the habit of handing out safety nets.

Kenny had advised him not to worry. Anyone with a heart and soul the size of Shuggy's would find plenty of people seeking help. Fortunately, he had recently found a job in bringing social housing to parts of Scotland in need of his caring approach. He was already making his mark on this new world. Lulu, who had given up on love when he had gone off to find his vocation - and seek the oxymoronic gift of celibacy - could not have looked more settled. Today, funerals aside, she was the happiest woman in the church, snuggled up against her 'shnooky bear', a term of endearment remaining from their early, halcyon student days.

Off to Shuggy's left, hunkered into the end of the bench, Grant MacTavish had an air of solitude about him, even though the church was packed. He seemed to be the only person not looking towards the altar waiting for Kenny to start. His eyes appeared focused somewhere around the front row. Watching him, Kenny realised that if the word 'glower' was to be explained, all it would have needed was a photo of Grant at that moment. For some reason, his *glower* seemed to be targeted in Maggie's direction.

Kenny's perusal of the rows of people took a couple of minutes, a long time when a eulogy is awaited. He scanned the pews one by one, seeing his mother's friends from the bingo hall to the members of the Tuesday lunch club. The priest had already coughed a couple of times. One of those unproductive coughs that fall somewhere between impatience and concern. Fr. Hunt was an interesting priest - jovial and friendly - with a hint of saintliness appreciated by the parishioners. During the post-Skink capture and debrief process, it came to light that Fr. Hunt had been in Langbank College studying to be a priest with Skink all those years before. He had been quite reticent to divulge much about Skink's character at that time, citing the importance of confidentiality amongst seminary brothers.

Kenny snapped out of his reverie with a start and noticed a rising level of concern in the eyes fixed on him throughout the congregation. He could not avoid it any longer.

"Good morning, everyone," he announced. His voice trembled with nerves and the recent onslaught of whisky. "What a come down, eh? You've just spent a couple of days giving and receiving presents, enjoying a lovely Christmas, with all the craic and witty banter of your kith n kin. And now here you are at a funeral. Happy days!"

The silence in the church was overpowering. Some people cried or made a sound just to ease the tension. Roddy's chin stuck out even further.

"That was supposed to be a joke." He realised his words could actually ruin his mother's funeral, if there even was such a thing. He pushed the thought to the back of his mind. "Many of you know I am not the best at delivering punch-lines."

Kenny saw Tommy nodding, with his two thumbs in the air, encouraging his friend onwards.

"Mum would not have wanted me to stand up here and make everyone feel sad, especially at this time of the year. Wherever she is, she will be kicking herself at dying on December 22nd, so close to Christmas. I expect she and Michael the Archangel will be having a toe to toe right now. Personally, I don't fancy his chances."

A smattering of chuckles and giggles transformed the atmosphere into a lighter, more hopeful air.

"I miss Mum terribly. I know you all do too. If she had a chance to plan her own funeral, she would have written down what I am supposed to say. She didn't in the end. But one thing I'm sure of is that she would want to say she's happy where she is now. She prayed all her life for many things, one of which was to have a peaceful death. And God granted her that. Also, that all of you, and I, would be content and fulfilled in our lives. I am sure that God will grant that too."

He felt the surge of emotion rising in his chest. Over the last few days, he had let his mother down, losing control and returning to the pathetic shambles he had been years before - the opposite of the person she had brought him up to be. His heart ached to hold and hug her once more, hear her gentle, lilting

136

voice. He felt the silence grip him as the tears broke from his eyes, rolling down his cheeks onto the scratchy notes he had prepared in the wee small hours.

He could not continue. It was all just too much for him. He had tried but failed. Bowing his head and placing his hands on the lectern, he shook his head resignedly and turned to step down from the pulpit. He just wanted to take his seat alongside his mother's coffin and put his head in his hands.

"Come on, Dad!" The high-pitched shout shook him to the core.

He looked up to see Roddy standing on his kneeler, his face beaming up towards the altar, fist held out in front of him. This little boy who bounced when he walked, who fell over himself with excitement when telling a story, had become his father's rock.

Kenny felt the ton of bricks strapped to his shoulders fall away. The tightening in his chest that had been constricting his breathing for days loosened its grip. The realisation that he had been lucky to have been loved by someone so much throughout his life. And now his son was reminding him that the love had not gone, it was still alive and strong.

He rubbed his eyes, took a deep breath, and turned back to the pulpit to tell his mother's life story. Her journey from poverty in Ireland to hardship in Scotland, how she had 'worked her fingers to the bone' and how her purpose in life had been to help others. How she had loved her community and friends in Clydebank and beyond. How she had always found time to sit and talk, or listen, when others would be trying to manage a list of priorities. His mother did not have priority lists; people always came first. No, he said, he would not be putting her forward for sainthood, because she had already become *a walking saint*.

He smiled wryly realising he had just quoted Cullen Skink.

The Letter

Kenny stood at the lounge bar in Sweeneys, chomping on a particularly juicy sausage roll, pastry flakes nestling into creases in his shirt and tie. Maggie would reach across every so often to flick away the next batch of crumbs. She had been at his side since the church. She had hugged him as soon as he had walked back to the bench, to the sound of applause. The atmosphere had changed from sad to marginally buoyant, everyone ready to celebrate a life well-lived.

When he had thought the eulogy would be the hardest part of the day, he had not fully considered the burial process. An hour after the church service, watching his mother being lowered down into a sodden earth, wind and rain pounding them on all sides, he held Roddy tight to him, knees weak with the accumulation of grief. He then felt the security of arms wrapping themselves around his shoulders - Maggie and Fiona, holding him up. The sadness that had descended on him was still there but was outweighed by the shadow of hope and the gift of memories.

Nobody did a funeral lunch like Sweeneys. The lounge had been built as a large open plan square room, allowing full view of all its corners. There was nowhere to hide. In the evenings, this allowed the venue to create a high-spirited party of frivolity and repartee into the wee small hours, disco music blaring into the night sky. In his pre-Kiltman days, Kenny had enjoyed some of his own wild evenings in the midst of partygoers careering off each other - with him in the middle of the floor doing his one hand in the air punch dance. Having not been blessed with rhythm in his legs, he would choose to use his arms instead. The other, significantly younger, dancers would gyrate around him as if he were their collective handbag, while he would be oblivious to the axis of movement surrounding him.

During the day, the lounge hunkered down as a sombre place to visit for a quiet drink, to read the newspaper in solitude. Although the relentless muffled racket from the bar made sure it was never too quiet to completely lose oneself. Kenny had spent many an afternoon sitting there, enjoying the comforting smack of pool balls drifting in from the bar.

Molly's funeral had created a lighter atmosphere than one would expect at a solemn occasion such as this. The pent-up emotions of sadness and grief had been spent, replaced by an air of positivity. The group were enjoying the good fortune of having had Molly in their lives. It was barely the afternoon, and toasts were being made to his mother in various corners of the lounge, spontaneous glass clinking interrupting the buzz of animated conversations.

Kenny surveyed the table in front of him, where five whiskies had been lined up in a row, a tribute act to the Kenny Morgan of old. Locals from the bar next door were ordering drinks for him as a way of expressing their commiserations, and Maureen was bringing them through to the lounge like an airport carousel. Each time she carried one through, she gave him a look of admonition. "Don't you dare!" her eyes were saying as she reluctantly placed the tumblers in front of him. She had seen Kenny take back control of his life – and was saying a silent prayer he would not relapse. She loved him like a brother, having worried about him when he was at his lowest. Kenny smiled back at her reassuringly, knowing their bond was even deeper than she could have imagined.

"Kenny," he heard George whisper in his ear, "can I have a few minutes with you?"

"Sure, George."

He let his mother's friend lead him by the arm to a corner of the lounge.

"I was clearing up some of your mother's things yesterday, going through old photographs." George was looking intensely at Kenny. "I was just enjoying being in her house with the lovely smells and memories of times gone by,"

"It must have been tough, George, to be on your own like that. Especially at Christmas." Kenny rubbed his arm gently. They had invited him to Fiona's for dinner, but he had wanted to spend the day at his mother's.

"It was tough, but it was the only place I wanted to be." George paused, working hard to find the resolve to continue.

"Anyway, that's not what I wanted to talk about. At least not now." He reached into his jacket pocket and extracted an envelope, which he passed to Kenny. "I found this in her top drawer. I wasn't sure whether to call you yesterday or wait until now. But here it is."

He took the white envelope from George focusing on his mother's handwriting on the outside. *For my darling Kenny, only to be opened if I have gone to meet my maker.*

Unable to speak, he looked at George, who slowly shrugged his shoulders, before saying, "I'll leave you for a while, you'll want to be alone."

He turned and walked towards the bar.

Kenny carefully prised open the sealed envelope, more precious than anything he could imagine. His sense of shock outweighed any grief he had been feeling until that moment. He removed the one-page letter his mother had penned in her inimitable handwriting. His mother's writing had narrowed and become practically indecipherable as she had aged - few people would have been able to read it at first look. Not Kenny. Her numerous postcards and letters over the years had helped him keep pace with the deterioration in legibility.

It was dated December 21st, the day before she died.

My dearest Kenny,

If you are reading this, then I have already gone to meet my maker. I hope I go up the way and not downstairs. Ha! I know that you are feeling sad, and the days immediately after my death will be very difficult for you. I only wish I was there to give you a hug, but don't you worry, I will be with you wherever you are, today and every day.

Remember the feathers.

He stopped and smiled, recalling his mother telling him that when someone died they stayed close to the people they loved by leaving a white feather, from their angel wings, in places you would not normally find them. If the feather was more grey than white, it meant you were receiving a warning of something untoward and to stay alert. He loved his mother's superstitions - they were now his superstitions.

There are a couple of reasons I am leaving you this letter. The main reason is that whenever someone dies, those left behind always wish they had said or done something important and had lost the chance. In your case, my son, you should have no regrets. There is nothing more you could have said or done for me. I was always so proud of you. I actually tried to call you tonight to tell you that, since it is always important for a child to be aware of how they have fulfilled a mother's love and expectations. You were probably enjoying a night out with Maggie, such a lovely girl.

There is another thing I want to say, and I hope you are sitting down for this, sonny boy!

He took his mother's posthumous cue, turned to find a seat, and plunged down into it, unaware of anything outside the words on the page.

One of the reasons I am so proud of you is because you became the man you were always destined to be. I am not talking about becoming a chemist, losing it all then bouncing back with lovely Maggie (we can do without any more of those roller-coaster rides, can't we, son?)

No, Kenny, my point is that I know who you are. Yes, I am not talking figuratively. I know about your alter ego. (I won't spell it out just in case, wink, wink!). You will be wondering how is that possible. Let's just say that when a mother sees her son walking and gesticulating, she knows it's her son. She does not need to see his face. And when her son shows up as someone else at the same time as he turns his life around, it all falls into place.

I never wanted to tell you this because it may have made you feel uncomfortable or limited how you did what you've had to do. But now it is important, especially with the sadness you are feeling, to know that I have never been prouder of you. The good people of this world need you. I know you will not let them down.

Lots of love and hugs to you, Kenny, my darling boy. And to gorgeous Roddy, he will continue to make you proud. And Maggie and Fiona, the two lovely ladies in your life. And of course, George, give him a hug from me. Don't forget a hug for Tommy, your brother from a different mother.

Signing off now, keep an eye out for the feathers.

Mum

Xxxx

141

He lifted his head from the letter, stunned and confused. He felt a sense of peace he had not enjoyed in a long time. It washed over him in floods of tears, but this time they were made from joy and relief. He wanted to tell someone, everyone about the letter; but he could not disclose his mother's revelation. She had watched the TV news several times a day - she must have joined the Kenny-Kiltman dots around three years earlier when he had first appeared on screens. Grant MacTavish had certainly helped by embellishing Kiltman's on-screen persona. His mother used to talk about how much she had loved watching Grant, especially knowing his penchant for blagging. He smiled; his mother was still surprising him even at her own funeral.

He lifted his head to search for Maggie, only to see her hurrying through the lounge towards the exit. She had her phone pressed tight against her ear; an index finger plugged in the other. The bar had become noisy, bordering on raucous. Her dash to the door, out of place in light of the festivities building up in the enclosed space, was barely noticed by anyone other than him.

He jumped from his seat and ran across the lounge. He caught her just as she was leaving and placed his hand on the small of her back. "Is everything okay, Maggie?"

She covered the mouthpiece, lifting her head slowly, a look of bewilderment furrowing her brow.

"Skink is dead?" she said, more question than statement. "They found his body at Glasgow Cross."

III

Back on the Wagon

A Terrible Skink

One of the oldest buildings in the city, the Steeple, built in 1636, dominates Glasgow Cross - as impressive today as when it was imprisoning, sentencing, and executing criminals and innocents alike. Its domination lies in its height of over 120 feet, its square girth, several high-ceilinged floors, and a large, blue clock facing in all directions. Over the years, roads had been constructed around it, with apartment blocks and commercial properties on either side - rendering it an innocuous, sometimes annoying, block of stone where an extra lane could have eased the congestion. On a day like this, it seemed to stand erect and strong, like a guard on duty in its perfect juxtaposition between the city centre and its East End.

Only an hour earlier, they had been at the funeral.

Kenny waited until she had made her apologies, then watched her car speed out of the car park onto the dual carriageway to cover the nearly ten-mile journey to the Cross. Once he saw her car disappear, he spoke to Fiona and Roddy saying he needed to take his leave; and would be in touch. Fiona was pleased to see he had left the row of whisky shots untouched. All three of them hugged. Before he left he stood to make a short speech to thank everyone for coming.

"Please make Molly proud! If she were here, she would have enjoyed the party," he said before walking out the door. He heard someone shout, "Don't worry, wee man, she'll never be far away."

By the time he got to the Cross, he had changed into the Kiltman costume, which only that morning he could never have imagined wearing again. He had hidden the car just off an alley near Glasgow's famous, traffic laden Saltmarket before running towards the Cross. Before he walked around the corner into the shadow of the Steeple, he raised the flask to his mouth, then stopped. After the excesses of the last few days, the last thing he needed was the taste of whisky, even though it was non-alcoholic. Yet somehow, Hair o' the Dog's aromatic scent seemed like the only thing he needed at that moment. Pouring a decent sized dram, he felt it ooze into his bloodstream settling into his nerve endings. He grinned wryly realising that he should have known he had the perfect cure in Hair o' the Dog to counteract the crippling hangovers suffered over the last few days. He started to feel better than he had done since before the news of his mother's passing. He took another quick shot for good measure, before placing it back in his sporran.

Wilson was already standing at the entrance when he tapped her on the shoulder.

"Hello, Wilson," he announced with more formality than he had intended. "What's happening?"

"Kiltman!" She nearly hugged him. "How do you do that? I've only just got here myself."

"Ah-hah, a magician never reveals his secrets; a chef never discloses the recipe; and a superhero never..." He stopped not knowing how to end his words of wisdom.

"... explains why he is such a weirdo," she finished for him.

He could see the relief in her eyes. After Nice, he was sure her confidence had grown. He was pleased to recognise the acknowledgement in her smile of the importance of having your partner alongside. He would one day remind her that this did not only apply to professional relationships. But not now.

"So, where's Skink then?" he asked.

"Follow me."

She walked through the entrance - a large wooden door that seemed too heavy to open but moved effortlessly above the worn, grey flagstones. The damp smell of the centuries old building carried with it the scent of the numerous souls who had been locked up and killed there. Torture and death were knitted into every brick and iron bar, creating a claustrophobic intensity ancient prisons convey with ease. Their footsteps echoed throughout the floors above them disappearing into the silence of the Steeple, forever entombed in its walls. Kiltman had passed the ancient prison on hundreds of occasions but had never expected the inside's dank, death-laden air to taste so unpleasant.

There he was.

Dangling upside down from a small window, where he had been attached by his foot using a strong chain locked onto the iron grille, his hands stretching downwards, his face inverted. The body appeared like a dormant pendulum in a broken grandfather clock, not a hint of movement.

Kiltman turned to Wilson. "How do you know he's Skink?"

On the face, there was a mask, a strange wooden object interlaced with strips of metal; it would have seemed at home in the Steeple five centuries earlier.

She walked around and pointed at the body's back, where an A4 sheet of paper had been pinned. The writing was significantly more legible than anything Skink had ever provided.

Dear Kiltman

You should be pleased that I have rid the world of this terrible Skink!

Good riddance. He served his purpose

Mask

PS. You can call me Mask if that suits your silly cat and mouse antics, but the clue-giving game is over. This is the last you will hear from me.

Wilson reached across with her gloved hand, carefully removing the mask. Skink's features were frozen in a shocked rictus. However Mask had killed him, Skink had not been expecting it. Kiltman touched the body, closing his eyes. Memories of his mother rushed back to settle into the back of his mind. He remembered her letter, how with a few words she had freed him from the prison of regret. He turned his attention to Skink, letting his hand fuse with the energy pulses latent in the body, feeling for something alien. Within a minute he could feel the bitter, almond taste at the back of his own throat. He pulled his hand away with a start.

"Well?" she asked.

"Cyanide," Kiltman responded. "Yeuch. I've had cheap tequila that tastes nicer."

"Tequila? I can't imagine you drinking anything other than whatever you've got in that wee flask you pull out of your thingy every so often."

"Wilson, it's not a thingy. It's a sporran. You should know that, for goodness sake, you're Scottish. And as for the tequila, actually when I was younger I was quite the…"

"Nice to see you two chewing the fat." Gemmill had bounded into the small space. "So, this is him, eh?" he asked rhetorically, bending his head awkwardly to look at Skink's upside-down face.

"Yes," Wilson and Kiltman responded in unison. Kiltman nearly said, *now I can see why you're a Chief Constable*. He stopped short of uttering what would certainly have been his last words to Gemmill.

"Cause of death, cyanide poisoning," she continued.

"How on earth do you know that?" he asked, then looked at Kiltman. "Oh, don't tell me, he's now a pathologist too?"

"No, not at all," he answered. "But I can see what's going on inside things, people. Quite a nifty power. Come here and I'll do a quick medical."

"You touch me, and I swear I'll tear that bizarre mask thing off your face." Gemmill really did not have a sense of humour.

"Chief," he said, in the spirit of moving the conversation along. "You made a comment when you came in here. What was it again?"

"What are you on about?" he paused and thought for a second. "I made some comment about you two always chewing the fat. Why?"

Kiltman raised his hand in the air, requesting Gemmill to stay quiet. He was thinking, remembering Skink's *In Memoriam* card.

PS. If ever I am on a permanent downer, please look for the upper, unless too much for you 2 to chew

He studied Skink hanging in front of them. This was certainly *permanent*. Although he could not imagine Skink expected how literal the *downer* would be when it came. He now understood what he had to do next.

"Wilson, can you get me a pair of pliers?"

"Pliers?" Gemmill said. "Wilson, where are you...?"

She was already out the door running to a shop along the road behind the building. She knew not to doubt his instincts. This left a long awkward silence in the Steeple. Kiltman filled it by asking about whether Fraser was still on the case. Gemmill, who had been pretending to read text messages, grumpily informed him that Fraser had been asked to go back to retirement and leave the case to the new team at Pitt Street. It made Kiltman wonder where he and Wilson fit into the 'new team'?

Her return within a few minutes was welcomed by both of them.

"Here you go." She handed Kiltman a small pair of pliers, with red rubber handles, just like he used at home.

"Thanks."

He turned his attention to Skink bending his upper body to get himself into a similar downward pose. He inserted his index finger into his own mouth. He poked it around his teeth, while eliciting a staccato mumbling noise, as if trying to count.

"Ok, got it," he said after a few seconds of grunts and near choking fits.

He reached across to Skink's head and tried to work his fingers into the body's mouth to create space for the pliers. It proved more difficult than he had expected to find enough room to insert them. He pushed a bit harder, squeezing his hand in like an oversized dentist extracting a tooth from a meerkat. Something had to give, he thought, as a brief creak was followed by a loud snap, magnified in the stonewalled steeple.

"Oops!" he whispered, without looking round. Jaws were such delicate things.

He pushed the pliers to the back of the unusually wide gap, looking inside at the same time. "Wilson, can you shine a torch in here?"

She pulled a small flashlight from her hip pocket and shone it into the gaping hole to show two rows of broken teeth, as sharp and disjointed as a Tibetan mountain range. Kiltman put the pliers around one of them towards the back, whispering, "Okay, there is the upper two."

He squeezed the handle and yanked with all his might. He smarted at the overpowering smell as he pulled the tooth from its cradle. The whiff of rotten gums and embedded bacteria released to the air caused all three of them to retch simultaneously in the tight space.

"I love it when we all share a good gag," Kiltman whispered, loud enough for them to hear.

If Gemmill had not been so focused on the tooth, he would have imploded at the inappropriateness of Kiltman's one-liner.

Wilson just groaned. Kiltman stepped back to find a spot that allowed a shade brighter light from the dim bulbs dotted around the walls. He held the tooth out like a marshmallow at a bonfire, its yellowy coat glistening with saliva. They studied the object snared in the pliers. It was a molar, covered in encrusted blood with miniscule crumbs of food nestled in its cracks. He turned the pliers in his hand to show the underside of the tooth. Sticking out of where the nerve used to be was a tiny piece of black plastic.

"Wilson, can you get that?" Kiltman nodded towards it.

She gawped at him with a look of disgust.

"My gloves are too big, otherwise I'd do it myself." He bent his head invitingly towards the tooth.

She was sure she could hear a speck of glee in his voice. She delicately removed the object with her index finger and thumb, to reveal a tightly rolled, inch-long thin strip of plastic.

"What is it?" Gemmill asked.

"It's a microfiche," Kiltman answered. "I would warrant Skink has left a message, probably his last, on there."

Gemmill had stopped asking questions, he was barely keeping up. "Oh, okay. Of course, it is. Well, what now?"

"Wilson, how do you fancy a trip to the library?" Kiltman asked.

She had already guessed what he was going to suggest and was happy to go along with him. The sooner they got away from Gemmill before he exploded, the better.

"Sure. I'd rather be at the library than getting my books here." She smiled coyly at Gemmill, like a child telling her first joke.

"Oh no, not you too!" Gemmill groaned, rubbing the back of his neck wearily.

Mitchell Library

Kiltman sat close to Wilson on the back seat of the police car speeding towards Glasgow's West End. He had decided to leave his vehicle just off the Saltmarket for a later pick up. He had developed a nifty way of changing his parking permit to adjust to whatever area of Glasgow he parked in. If a commuter had a choice between knowing Kiltman's identity or the source of free parking, he knew which one they would choose.

Their vehicle was rushing through the late afternoon throngs of Boxing Day shoppers, some looking for bargains, others returning unwanted Christmas presents. They would be at the Mitchell Library in fifteen minutes; nowhere was ever far away in Glasgow. The city's landscape changed every few streets, and the contradiction of the Steeple to the Mitchell was as extreme as it gets. She knew immediately why he had mentioned the library, and knew he had the Mitchell in mind. It was one of the largest reference libraries in the country, maybe even Europe. Much of its material was stored on microfiches, which meant it had the equipment they needed to unpick Skink's clue. She had studied at the library when she was a student, as had Kenny - it had offered a welcome respite from the chaos of the reading room at the university, ironically where Skink had left his first clue back in June.

"So, Wilson, how was Christmas?" He was working hard to sound nonchalant and chirpy in the back of the speeding car.

"Oh, quite quiet, just looking at Skink videos from Nice and Bar L," she said, then quickly moved on. "Actually, today's been quite rough. I was at a funeral."

She was surprised at herself for disclosing a personal issue; she prided herself in not opening up to others. Although, she mused, Kiltman seemed to have a knack of drawing stuff out of her.

"I'm sorry." He waited a moment. "Someone close?"

"My, em, friend's mother. She was a sweetheart. It was very sad." She felt the tears welling up again despite herself. "Her son made an amazing eulogy that changed the ceremony from, eh, funereal, to one of joy and happiness."

"He must be a very special, 'em, friend'." The metaphorical fishing line was beginning to cramp the space in the police car. She turned round to face him. "Yes, he is." She studied him for a second longer than needed.

"That's us here now," the policeman called from the driver's seat. "I'll wait outside in case you need me."

"Maybe we can finish the conversation later, Wilson," Kiltman grunted as he levered himself through the door.

"What conversation?" she answered. "We've had it, it's done. Now let's figure out what's on this thing." She held up the microfiche, pinched between her thumb and forefinger, still wearing blue, rubber gloves.

"Yes, right." It was beginning to dawn on him just how challenging his girlfriend was. She could close down conversations faster than Sweeneys on a Sunday night.

They approached the main entrance, to be greeted by an elderly guard nervously fidgeting with a massive bunch of keys. "Eh, hello. I've been waiting for you."

Gemmill had already phoned ahead to make sure they had access. The Chief Constable could not be described as an empathetic boss - some would say he had never even been a good detective. But he had a reputation for pulling strings and getting things done, which is all Wilson wanted from him.

"Thank you, Dennis." She nodded, noticing his name tag, followed by the surname Law.

"You've got nothing to worry about, Dennis, with DI Wilson around," Kiltman said.

"Why's that, sir?" he asked.

Dennis was used to people making comments about his name, referencing one of Scotland's most prolific goal scorers. He waited for Kiltman to have his go.

"Because DI Wilson protects the *law*, don't you, Wilson?"

"Sorry, Dennis." She patted the guard's arm. He was not sure how to react. "I think Kiltman's had too much sherry over Christmas."

If only she knew.

They walked into the iconic Mitchell library, barely a century old - it seemed positively youthful compared to the Steeple they had recently exited. As a library, one could be forgiven for thinking its imposing structure had been over-sized and over-engineered, under its copper dome topped with a statue of Minerva, Goddess of Wisdom. However more than a million volumes of important reference points, all in paper or microfiche, required the height of respect – and its architects had ensured this was reflected in the immensity and strength of the building. It took itself very seriously; and required the same from its visitors.

Within minutes they had found and powered up one of the many readers dotted around the room. They carefully placed the 'molar' microfiche on the glass tray underneath the lens and began to scroll. It did not take long before they found a letter.

Dear Kiltman

If you are reading this, then I am dead and will be in the process of explaining to God just why my soul is innately good. Wish me luck ☺

For goodness sake, Kiltman thought, the second posthumous letter within a matter of hours. This was just not normal, by anyone's standards. Wilson slowly scrolled down the page.

The reason for this letter is to allow you a modicum of chance in catching your new nemesis. He is a strange one, quite unusual and more than a little trying. I expect he is the one who bumped me off, nasty blighter! I would normally use stronger language, but you never know who might read this.

Anyway, as I was saying, I want to improve your chances of catching him. But I don't want to make it easy for you. It would make me happy to know I've left you with enough to get you started but then it's up to you, and your cute friend, Wilson.

Rest assured this is not a wild goose chase. Not a hint of Truth Decay in my molars. Ha! Ha!

They glanced at each other before Kiltman whispered in her ear. "I hadn't realised he had such good taste in ladies as well as a sense of humour." She raised her eyes heavenward; and continued to scroll.

So here I go....
Where this means nothing to me
Far from the sea

On the last of five
To be alive
Who sits along-sides of three
(Its cousin lies west in Atlas's sea… call this a freebie ☺)
Movies across the road
Pop inside where the numbers are bold
Find the arty quirk
Which leads to the kirk
Use the Scots key
To find the relic, class three
Two ships sunk, two wars apart,
One the Graf Spee
Above the abbey and brie
That is all from me, see you on the other side, KM
Cullen Skink x
PS. Rules of Riemann hypothesis apply to identities too. My
last gift to you.

She looked at Kiltman, the corners of her mouth pointing downwards, to catch him distractedly scratching the top of his head.

"Oh, great! You're not supposed to look confused."

He hummed quietly while studying the screen, listening to the page being printed on a standalone printer that made an uncannily loud noise in the aula. The only part of the clue that made sense to him was the *PS* at the end, and that he was going to keep to himself.

"Well, bits of it are sort of clear, while other parts are mumbo jumbo at the moment. It's like looking at a dog with fleas."

He waited for her to ask what he was talking about. She did not take the bait, so he continued. "Some are jumping out at me, but it's the ones I can't see that I'm afraid of."

Terviseks

"Kiltman and Wilson, to what do I owe the pleasure?" Tommy shouted, poking his head between the Saku and Õlu beer taps. His voice was raised to compete with the noisy revellers.

The floor was littered with bulky bags from every shop on Glasgow's two main shopping precincts, Argyll Street and Buchanan Street. After parading Glasgow centre for hours, many shoppers had surrendered to swollen ankles and sore hands. They had either taken a break from fighting hordes of shoppers to find that next bargain - or they had overcome their shopping lunacy, to happily experiment with Estonia's finest drinks on display in Scotland.

"Hi Tommy, we need a quiet corner to work through a few things. Would that be okay?" After six months it felt strange for Kiltman to talk to Tommy from behind a mask.

"Sure," Tommy said. "I've got a room at the back you can use."

"Hi, Maggie, how are you?" Tommy asked as he led them through a door behind the bar. "That was rough today, I thought I wasn't going to be able to handle it."

"I know." Her awkwardness was obvious. "Kenny gave Molly a good send off."

It had been Wilson's idea to go to Terviseks to analyse the clue. She had felt bad at missing Tommy's Christmas Eve opening. Kiltman did not argue with her choice of venue.

He felt he should say something, if only to keep up the pretence. "Eh, who's Molly?" Words he never thought he would utter.

Tommy spoke first. "She was our friend's mother. Amazing lady, passed away just before Christmas." He turned to Kiltman before continuing. "Her son is my best friend, Kenny Morgan, and Maggie is his…"

"Okay, Tommy," she interrupted. "We have a clue to work through if you don't mind. This room's perfect."

They settled around a small table covered with invoices and empty bottles. Tommy stepped out to the bar to get them some drinks.

Kiltman studied her for a moment before asking, "Is this Kenny character the 'em, friend' you were talking about?" He was starting to enjoy this.

"What is it with you, Kiltman?" Her face had become redder than the scanty Santa Claus suits the barmaids were wearing. "Do you not know when to back off? It's complicated, okay? Let's leave it at that."

"Okay, fine, Wilson, no problem." He held his palms out in supplication. "But what do you mean by complicated?"

"ENOUGH!" she shouted, her hands pointing at him like shovel heads.

The one thing he had learned about the Skink clues was that they always provided a distraction from whatever else was going on. Within minutes they were both huddled around the sheet of paper she had printed, working through the lines again. She clasped a cup of tea thick with honey, apparently an Estonian winter treat, courtesy of Tommy's generosity. Kiltman had opted for a good old-fashioned coffee. He needed the caffeine hit.

He read the first few lines out loud:

"Where this means nothing to me
Far from the sea
On the last of five
To be alive
Who sits along-sides of three
(Its cousin lies west in Atlas's sea... call this a freebie)

And a wee smiley face for good measure," he added. "Prison must have softened him up a bit, maybe there's something in that Bar L Special Unit rehab programme after all."

Wilson directed a look of incredulity at him.

"Let's not kid ourselves. There was nothing rehab'ed about Skink. He played the system. And with the help of a fictitious priest, a corrupt prison guard and a friendly dentist, he was able to play the system. Oh, by the way, Gemmill dropped me a note to say they picked up the dentist and are interviewing him now. Although I don't think he'll give us much."

"I agree." Kiltman paused. "Trying to get anything out of him will be like pulling teeth."

Wilson grimaced and took a deep breath.

Kiltman returned her stare, shrugged and said, "At least my puns are intended."

"I give up." She shook her head and turned back to look at the paper. "I mean with you, not the clue."

"Okay. Let's pick out the bits we can make sense of. *'sides of three'* could be a reference to a triangle. Agreed?" He made a sign with his fingers of a triangle.

"Yes, makes sense." She nodded.

"*'Its cousin lies west in Atlas's sea'*," he continued. "So, the cousin is not the place he is pointing to, but some sort of a relative. The origin of the word Atlantic is actually *Atlas Sea*. Yes, before you ask, it was another pub quiz question. What do you know of in the west Atlantic that is called a triangle?"

She snapped her fingers, shouting 'Bermuda Triangle'." She rubbed her chin pensively. "But that's weird, why would Mask be doing anything in as desolate a place as hurricane alley in the Atlantic Ocean? They don't need any help there to bring down planes and make ships disappear."

"I agree with all you say. But he's only using the Atlas Sea reference to help us get to the Bermuda Triangle part of the clue. Hence why it's a freebie, probably a bit more than he would normally give us."

Tommy popped into the room. "Any more teas or coffees for my crime-fighting duo?"

"No, we're good, Tommy. Thanks, pal." She winked in a sisterly way. Kiltman enjoyed his best friend and girlfriend (hopefully) getting on so well.

"Tommy, you've done a bit of travelling, haven't you?" he asked.

"I'm not exactly a jetsetter, but yes I've been to a few places. Why?" He put his towel down on the table and pulled up a chair.

"Other than the obvious, what does Bermuda Triangle mean for you?"

Tommy rubbed his chin, thinking for a moment before he said proudly. "A three-day massive hangover and a gorgeous girl called Maria."

"Okay, we do need a bit more than that, Tommy." Wilson rolled her hand to encourage him to open up.

"It was 1996." Tommy settled back into his seat, his hands behind his head, smiling. "Scotland were playing against Austria in the World Cup qualifiers. It was a blast. Game was rubbish, 0-0, but what a laugh we had. It all started when we went out a few hours before the game for some beers and bumped into a bunch of well-known Scottish journalists drinking in a pub. They actually had most of their stories written already, even before the game had started! That's where I met Maria, absolutely gorgeous so she was."

"Okay, Tommy." She waved her hands exaggeratedly. "Come back, come back, planet Earth calling. What has all that got to do with Bermuda Triangle?"

"Oh, sorry, yes, well." He coughed self-consciously. "The area where the pub was situated was called the Bermuda Triangle. It's a fun part of the city where the party goes on all night, loads of bars and clubs. It's been said that some people have never gotten out of there, and just disappeared, hence the nickname. Why?"

"Tommy!" She could not hide the exasperation in her voice. "Where is this place? That's what we need to know!"

"Okay, Maggie. Keep your hair on! It's Vienna. That's what makes the *Triangle* so much fun, because the rest of the city centre is so quiet, like a massive museum of incredible architecture and history. When you walk around you feel that you need to whisper all the time, sort of like a library atmosphere. They definitely need somewhere to go and let their hair down."

She pushed the sheet of paper towards Tommy. "Anything else here ring a bell?"

He considered it for a few moments, running his finger slowly along each line. "Actually, wait a sec." He stood abruptly and left the room.

Within a minute, the music changed from Estonian folk to a strong voice booming out a haunting ballad.

This means nothing to me, Vienna...

Tommy walked back into the room. "Vienna, by Ultravox, Midge Ure, what a voice!" he announced.

157

She darted a glance at Kiltman, a flash of annoyance skirting her pretty features. "That was the tune you were humming in the Mitchell Library! You already knew it was Vienna!"

"Okay, guilty as charged." He put his hands up in a south paw defensive position. "The other part of the clue that made me think it was Vienna, was *Far from the sea*. Austria is landlocked. Although funnily enough, the father of the Von Trapps in the Sound of Music was a navy sea captain. Lots of people thought that was a mistake in the movie since Austria did not have access to the sea. However, when Austria was part of the Austro-Hungarian empire twenty years earlier it did have access and hence had a navy."

She was waiting for him to finish, finding his burst of factoids distracting. "You ready to get started on the *triangle* bit of the clue now?"

"Yes, sure. But to be honest, I really didn't know the *Bermuda Triangle* connection. Thanks, Tommy."

"Tommy, do you have a computer?" She was back on track, trying to ignore the feeling of being a couple of steps behind him.

"Sure, it's the 21ˢᵗ century, Maggie!" he smiled.

She grinned back at Tommy, and for a moment Kiltman wanted to be part of their banter as Kenny, not hidden behind his latex mask. Tommy was feeling pleased with his contributions so far and was not in a hurry to leave the room. He uncovered and booted up the computer and within minutes Wilson was googling a map of Vienna, homing in on the streets around the *Triangle*. She had always wanted to visit this city. She had been a history buff at school and knew just how significant Vienna had been in Europe over the centuries. As she studied the map, her eyes were diverted by the many pinpoints of historical and current interest. The Rathaus parliament building, various luxurious and ornate palaces, and the iconic Opera House, along with a host of museums and art galleries. There was so much history and culture in such a small place.

"Okay, Wilson, here we are." Kiltman pointed towards the *Triangle*. "Got a wee bit distracted, did we?"

She zoomed away from where she was hovering above Stephansdom, the city's centuries old, beautiful, and grand cathedral, before fading right to a vast array of crisscrossing streets reaching towards the river, with the words *Bermuda Triangle* typed in its centre.

"What are we looking for, Kiltman?" she asked glancing at the clue - conscious both Tommy and Kiltman were resting a hand on each of her shoulders.

Kiltman read the lines in the middle of the clue between the Vienna and Bermuda Triangle elements they had solved already:

On the last of five
To be alive

"Okay, looks like we should be searching for the name of a person," she said. They began to scan the streets in and around the *Triangle* to find people's names. They found a Lauren, a Barbara, a Bernhard, a George, and a Julius. None of which gave them reason to think of the *last of five to be alive.*

"Take it out a bit, Wilson," Kiltman said. She pressed the button reducing the size of streets and squares but bringing more onto the screen.

"There's one there." Tommy pointed at a street called Marc-Aurel Strassse.

"Bingo!" She clicked her fingers impressively. "Marcus Aurelius was the last of what were known as the 'Five Good Emperors' of the Roman Empire. He was a renowned philosopher and legislator, and he died in a city called Vindobona."

"Vindobona?" Kiltman asked. "Never heard of it."

"Pub quiz time!" she said sitting back in her chair, a smug grin on her face. "Starter for ten. What modern city was originally known as Vindobona?"

Both he and Tommy shook their heads. Before Tommy eventually said, "Vienna, by any chance?"

Wilson nodded, smiling.

"Touché!" Kiltman clapped his hands slowly. "But honestly…" he spread his hands operatically and sang, "Vindobona means nothing to me."

The hefty cushion Wilson launched at his head missed by an inch.

IV

Vindobona

Vienna

Tommy had been right. During their walk through this majestic city, they found themselves speaking in evermore hushed tones. There could be no other place in the world with such an abundance of grandeur and history knitted into its buildings and streets. The city centre existed within a small circular district, circumvented by the 'Ring', a four-mile long road that limited the central zone of the city from growing any wider. The magical feel around them was amplified by the thick layer of snow underfoot, creating the perfect setting for Vienna's renowned Christmas celebrations.

It was midnight on Boxing Day. Gemmill had managed to arrange for them to catch a late night flight from Glasgow airport. In a brief conversation with Wilson before their flight departed, he had let them know that the dentist had confessed to being compliant with Skink's molar microfiche ploy because he had been frightened. Not because of what he would do to the dentist. Skink had made it clear he knew the names of each of his children, the schools they went to and places they played. Kiltman had felt his skin prickle with anger at how Skink had used a parent's protective instincts to get what he needed. He was not sure how he would have reacted if Roddy's safety had been at stake.

They were now acclimatising to the dry December cold of Vienna, the wind accompanying them as they walked in the direction of Marc-Aurel Strasse. Their approach, from the river east of the centre, allowed them the opportunity to see the infamous *Triangle*, where the young of Vienna could enjoy a night out without having to wander too far from bar to bar. There were still a few straggling revellers out on the streets looking for their next locale before closing time. Although on the whole it was relatively quiet. Vienna was famous for a bustling, happy run up to Christmas but then when the main event arrived, the city settled into a quiet slumber of log fires and quiet reflection.

Barely five minutes after entering the *Triangle*, they climbed a steep set of stairs to cross over towards Marc-Aurel Strasse. At the top they turned to take in the dreamlike atmosphere of the narrow streets twisting and hiding below them, their mood settling into the tranquillity of the evening. They continued their walk and wandered a few blocks to the west to find they were back in the quiet, protected central district, free from the risk of noise. As they stepped carefully in the snow to double back towards Marc-Aurel they walked into a square dominated by a large, bland, concrete and steel structure - it seemed to clash dramatically with the overindulgence of Baroque plushness throughout the city. They realised quickly that they were on Judenplatz, facing the Holocaust Memorial, created in memory of the 65 thousand Austrian Jews killed in the war.

"Oh my!" Wilson said, realising immediately what they were staring at. The austerity and innate strength of the monument was striking. "It might not be the same type of architecture as the rest of this town, but it really does deliver the impact it was meant to."

Kiltman nodded his agreement. They waited a moment and paid their respects before continuing their walk. Within a few minutes of trudging purposefully, they found themselves underneath a street sign.

"Here it is." She pointed at the ornately drawn letters of *Marc-Aurel Strasse* above their heads. The map had not done justice to how long the road was. They could see that it stretched to their right for several hundred yards in the direction of Stephansdom, considered the epicentre of the city. The part they were interested in disappeared into the darkness on their left, towards the river - the section that ran alongside the *Triangle*.

"Kiltman, let's remind ourselves of the clue we're trying to decipher."

She opened up the folded sheet of A4 and read aloud:
"Movies across the road
Pop inside where the numbers are bold
Find the arty quirk
Which leads to the kirk
Use the Scots key
To find the relic, class three

162

Two ships sunk, two wars apart,
One the Graf Spee
Above the abbey and brie

She rubbed the back of her neck. "I'm still baffled."

When she did not get a response, she turned around to see Kiltman running across the road to a group of middle-aged men sitting on a wall. In itself this seemed unusual at this late hour of the evening, a group of five or six men huddled together, congregated around a bench, some sitting, others standing. Kiltman had supposed this would have been part of their evening ritual, judging by how easily they enjoyed their pipes and cigarettes while ambling through a quiet conversation. Until a man in a skirt disturbed their repartee.

"Excuse me," he said.

"Hallo!" the older of the men responded. He had a gentle twinkle in his eye. "Are you having stag here in the *Triangle*?"

"Eh, no." He chose not to explain his regalia. "I'm looking for some information."

"Ja?" the man said. "How can I help? If you're looking for the *Triangle* it's up those stairs and over the top. We may never see you in your skirt again!"

He turned to his friends and translated the conversation. They all laughed in unison.

Kiltman plodded on. "Was there ever a cinema on this street?"

"I have lived here for twenty years." The man spoke with a tone of authority. "I do not remember such a place."

Kiltman's shoulders sagged before he said, "Danke!" and turned to walk away.

"Excuse me." The man had not finished. "There was not a cinema. But there is a video shop. It serves beers and has a café. Just down there."

He pointed along the road beyond a row of tightly parked cars. If they had kept walking, they would have found it in a minute.

"That's great, thanks," Kiltman said, turning to see Wilson already walking past him in the direction the Austrian had indicated. A video shop providing bar facilities seemed like the kind of place she would enjoy, buying a film and having a refreshment at the same time. She had no doubts the place would

163

create a spark for lots of budding romances. At least you could tick the first potential obstacle off the list - *what movies do you like?*

Directly across the road the door number of 99 had been painted in a fluorescent green making it glow brightly at them in the dark of the night. The buildings on Marc-Aurel seemed to stretch far into the sky above them, their grandeur and solidity dwarfing the shops and cars in the street below.

Kiltman whispered the relevant lines from the clue, as Wilson nodded her agreement:

Movies across the road
Pop inside where the numbers are bold

They approached the large metal door underneath the glowing 99, realising it had a distinct absence of locks to pick. While it appeared old, Kiltman sensed that it had been fitted with a state of the art electronically controlled locking system. He laid both palms against it, finding the electronic pulse tut-tutting through the lock. He focused hard on the noise manoeuvring his hand into position. After a few seconds, there was a dull click and the door sprung open.

The group of smokers watched Kiltman and Wilson with interest. Normally they would have called the police to report a break in. However, the person at the back of the group, with his Tirolean hat pulled down over his face, had convinced them not to. He had explained that they were involved in an international treasure hunt that had brought them to Vienna on St. Stephen's Day, an apt location considering Stephansdom characterised their city. He had asked them to go along with the game since he was intending to spring a surprise on the kilted man and his friend. As Kiltman and Wilson entered the building, the man handed around plastic cups which he half-filled with Schnapps.

"Prost!" he shouted!

They all joined in with a dull clunk of their plastic containers, toasting the kilted Scotsman and his schöne frau for bringing some fun to their St. Stephen's Day.

Before they all fell asleep in a heap.

Wilkommen

"How did you do that?" She had given up trying to hide her appreciation of his skills.

"I shorted the circuit. The door defaults to being open when the power stops rather than trap the residents inside."

"Of course. Simple really." He was not sure if her tone was one of admiration or sarcasm.

She regarded the building carefully, assessing the scale of their challenge. "What do we do now? It looks like there are quite a few floors with a few apartments on each."

"Now is when we look for the *arty quirk*," he answered stepping into the hallway.

She nodded and followed him inside. He ambled up the stairs at a gentle pace running his hands against the wall, Wilson behind looking for anything unusual. After what felt like a Himalayan climb, they eventually reached the final floor. Kiltman's laboured breathing had become too obvious for her to ignore any longer. He began to splutter and cough as if he had been thrown into the deep end of a swimming pool.

"Are you alright?" she asked, touching his arm in a maternal fashion.

"Yes, I'm fine. Too much Christmas pudding, I think," he wheezed.

She was also breathing deeply - although her breaths seemed controlled, appropriately intense considering the exertions of their ascent. Kiltman was reminded of how Wilson had been on at his alter ego for months to go to the gym. If he had listened, he would not feel so self-conscious, and older than his years.

Once he had righted himself, they studied each of the doors individually just as they had done on the lower floors. There were three apartments on each floor, and they all had strong wooden doors covered in sterile, brown, industrial paint, lavishly layered to allow them another year or so before re-doing them. With nothing remarkable to note, he lowered his head to look down at the mats. When they were climbing, she had noticed with each

165

floor he was taking longer to inspect the doormats. She was quite sure it had been a delaying tactic to help him progress at a manageable pace - she had pretended to also study the mats carefully, waiting for his cue to continue.

"There you go, Wilson." He indicated a mat with the writing *Wilkommen,* painted into its wiry threads.

"What? It means *Welcome.* You see it on lots of mats everywhere. Just cut to the chase, please."

"There are two 'l's in Willkommen, not one," he said. She studied the mat for a second. She was not convinced it would be that simple, waiting for him to continue.

"It's the kind of detail Skink would have found annoyingly distracting. He suffered from severe OCD and became aggravated if he noticed mistakes in public signs, triggering acute anxiety attacks."

"Really? How would you know that? I didn't see it on his file?"

He winced at his slip. His whisky antics over the previous few days were catching up. He was tired.

"Eh, well, I could see it in his face. Written all over him. Don't need superpowers to pick up on that. Okay, so let's see how to get in here."

"Wait! Should we not knock at least?"

"No need to, there's nobody home." He pointed towards his ears.

Faced with another electronic lock that succumbed to his short-circuitry skills, it took them barely a minute to be inside and walking around. He re-set the circuit when they entered just in case the owner turned up later. It was clear from the dank smell that the windows had not been opened in a few days. The apartment's lounge, if it could be called that, had a table and two chairs, a kettle and two cups, and nothing else.

"Crikey," she said wrinkling her nose. "Home sweet home!"

"There's something wrong here."

He held his hand up requesting a moment of silence. He examined from ceiling to floor and back again, then swivelled focusing on the walls. He stepped out into the kitchen and came back to Wilson. She was biting her lip trying not to interrupt his concentration.

He turned to face her. "This apartment is actually smaller inside than it should be. It's only a one bedroom flat, when it should be a two bedroom. Trust me on this, I've run the calcs in my head based on the size of the block, numbers of apartments, etcetera."

"Okay." She was not going to argue. "So, we're looking for a false wall."

"Correctamundo," he said in a sing-song Italian accent.

She walked around the apartment tapping walls with her knuckles, while he ran his fingers along the grotesque, pastel paper, applying an even pressure. They were in the bedroom when he said, "Here it is!"

He pushed hard against the wall before dropping down onto his knees. He began to trace a line along the paper with his index finger till he reached a knot in the wood in the corner of the floor. He pushed on the knot and a section of the wall opened on the opposite corner of the room flush with the floor. The hole was about three feet by three.

"You've found Vienna's Lilliput, Kiltman!"

She got down onto the floor and started to crawl into the space. Several minutes later, with more than a few grunts and curses, he was beside her inside a room half the size of the one they had just left. He had found a similar knot on the other side of the wall and pressed it closing the hole behind them.

The secret room was intensely dark, until Wilson switched on her torch and lit up the room – to see the same parsimony of furnishings as the lounge. A table and two chairs had been positioned to face a wall porous with pinholes and the remains of Sellotape and glue. At one stage the wall had been much busier than the one they were looking at. There were less than a handful of items stuck there now with the remnants of sticky tape and pins. They studied each of them one by one. The most colourful item was a long list of Italian Serie A soccer fixtures. If that seemed out of place, then *Love Your Planet Society* events scribbled on a scrap of paper seemed even more outlandish. Larger and pinned to the middle of the wall was a map displaying an intricate spider's web of lines spreading in all directions. Finally, dangling from a hook at the far side was a small key, a bronze, metal type with an elaborately designed handle.

167

He grabbed her arm, put his finger against her lips and whispered, "Shh!" She turned the torch off and focused on controlling her breathing.

They heard the unmistakable sound of shuffling footsteps on the other side of the wall. They listened to the kettle being filled, a minute or two before its piercing whistle sounded like a train crashing through a tunnel at top speed in the silence of the apartment. After a clink of a cup and spoon, a loud slurp was followed by a long belch. The owner of the footsteps was not in a hurry to enter the secret room. Their backs flush against the wall, they breathed slowly and quietly.

Wilson was ready to rumble. She had taken self-defence classes during her basic training; and had excelled in the various techniques learned as a *Bobby* on the beat. Since the Skink episode when she had been held captive in an underground shaft, she had realised that while learning to defend yourself was important, there were times when you had to be prepared to attack. Following three months of equally intense, and much more satisfying, training she was ready for an occasion such as this.

After a few minutes that seemed much longer, the cover over the hole in the wall slid to the side. They were poised, ready to jump on whoever crawled through. The silence was broken by a sharp metallic click and a hiss. They stared at each other, the same thought registering simultaneously. They had no time to react before a cannister the size of a travel-sized deodorant tumbled through the hole, white smoke spilling from its tiny nozzle, filling the room. They heard the hole cover slide back into place before they fell unconscious onto the floor.

The Secret Room

Kiltman had not needed any other chemicals in his body, he had already been struggling with the remnants of his recent overindulgence in malt whisky. As he came to, he realised they had been hit with a blast of anaesthetic gas sufficiently measured to knock them out long enough to be tied up. He felt the blood circulation stopping at his wrists, his fingers beginning to numb. The plastic edges of the ties were cutting into his wrists, inflicting sharp stings when he moved his hands. He lifted his eyes slowly from his chair to see Wilson coming to at the same time, shaking her head. The room was now lit by a solitary bulb dangling above their heads.

"Are you okay?" he asked.

"I think so. What was that stuff?"

"Most likely halothane vapour," he said. "We've probably been out for no more than an hour."

They were sitting approximately ten feet apart on the chairs inside the secret room, staring at the wall. The items they had just started to study had been removed, the wall was now bare. A throaty cough indicated someone else was in the small space with them. He was behind their chairs, and not in a hurry to make himself visible.

"Well, well! To what do I owe the pleasure of your company?"

Kiltman was trying to identify the voice. It was annoyingly familiar, but he could not quite place it. He could detect a tiredness in the words, as if their captor were only half interested in what he was saying.

"Who's that?" Wilson asked, while wriggling her hands to assess the tightness of the twines around her wrists.

"Come on," the voice said, now beginning to warm up, "don't you recall our brief meeting only a few days ago?"

Kiltman got there first. "You're either the *lang* or the short of it, aren't you?"

The man walked round to stand in front of them.

"Well done, Kiltman!"

It was Lange, the shorter of the two prison guards at Barlinnie. He was dressed in jeans and polo neck jumper but there was no mistaking him and his peculiarly refined accent.

"What's going on?" Wilson asked. "Don't you know that Skink is dead?" She was trying to think of anything to put him off his stride.

"Of course, I know. Do you think it was not planned? Skink is, or rather was, a very clever man. He provided everything we needed to execute the next stages of our plans. Alas, he had served his purpose. He was really quite the liability, leaving you clues, exposing unnecessarily the plans we have been working on. What an idiot."

He paused for a moment and scratched the side of his neck. He did not seem used to wearing polo neck jumpers, Kiltman thought distractedly.

"Actually, the fact you are here means he must have found a way to leave you an indication of our European HQ. Clever. Although it is a shame for you since it sealed your death warrant. It will take a long time before anyone finds your bodies way up here behind a secret wall." He laughed drawing his gaze towards Kiltman. "Which of you shall I execute first?"

He pulled from his back pocket a knife with a four-inch serrated blade. Long enough to inflict lethal wounds, short enough to be hidden easily. This long and short stuff was beginning to wear on Kiltman.

"Hold on," Kiltman asked, trying to find a sliver of space to think of a way to talk him down. "At least tell us what you are doing here? Is all this violence really necessary?"

"Oh, I see," he laughed again. "This is the bit when you help me see the wrong in my actions, and then I see the light. At this point am I supposed to release you, and all is okay? I think you've watched too many movies." He studied the knife, running his index finger along the blade. "But they don't use real knives in Hollywood." He threw it from hand to hand, looking from Kiltman to Wilson wondering who should be first.

"At least, tell me this, for my own curiosity," Kiltman said.

"Okay, what?" Despite what he had said, Lange was enjoying what could have been the penultimate scene in a Bond movie.

"Your accent, what is it?" he asked.

"That's it? That's your big question?" Lange laughed. "South American is as accurate as I will give you. I spent many years of my life in your not so sunny Glasgow. You can imagine how demeaning it was for someone like me, coming from a superior race of people, to end up in rain-swept Scotland. It took a while, but now I am on top and ready to make the world take notice of who we are and what we are capable of."

Kiltman's mind was racing. South America had amazingly superior football players, of that there was no doubt. However, he was missing the gist of Lange's message. He was struggling to come up with a follow-on question that would keep him engaged. His thoughts were interrupted by a flash of movement. He turned his head to see Wilson hobbling past him running in Lange's direction, bent at an awkward angle still attached to the chair. Somehow, she had managed to get enough space in her ankles to move, her hands still tied behind her. Lange was slower to react than he should have been, surprised at his captor's potential suicide mission. He lifted the knife into the air to plunge it into her back, her body bent at 45-degrees. But he had not counted on her having enough spring in her legs to launch herself into his abdomen. Her head met his lower stomach with such force he doubled up instantly the knife flying through the air to miss Kiltman's cheek by less than the length of the blade.

Lange had been winded and was flat on the floor trying to get up when she shouted, "Kiltman, wake up!"

She was lying on her upturned chair facing the ceiling, trying to roll over onto her front by bumping off the wall. It was proving painstakingly slow giving Lange the time needed to get up on his hands and knees.

Kiltman had been distracted by the knife but now found energy soaring back into his trussed limbs. He hobbled and bumped the chair along the noisy wooden floor towards Lange, who was grunting and cursing, before throwing himself and the chair up into the air in a half spin, to land on top of their captor. Lange's head smacked off the floor, arms akimbo, as Kiltman landed on his back, making sure their captor suffered a couple of broken ribs on top of his sore head. The cracks made quite a pleasing sound.

171

The back of Kiltman's chair rested on Lange's elongated body, there was no movement from either of them - Lange dazed, and Kiltman in no hurry to move. Kiltman heard the noise of Wilson's chair bumping along the floor. Despite her restricted hands and legs, he was impressed at how nimbly she covered the space to where the knife had landed. She rolled the chair at the right trajectory to allow her to fall backwards onto the serrated blade, taking it in the palm of her hand. She found enough traction to cut the rope and snap the remaining threads. Within minutes she had untied herself before starting on Kiltman. He could feel Lange coming to consciousness underneath him as she sawed at the rope on Kiltman's wrists. He threw his head back with a strong jerk and whacked the back of Lange's head. It hurt him, but not as much as it did Lange. He felt Lange's body go limp underneath him.

"Are you okay?" she asked helping Kiltman to his feet.

"Yes, I think so." He looked directly at her. "You were incredible. I didn't expect that Jackie Chan moment." His words belied the surge of respect growing inside his throbbing head.

"Yes, well, sometimes, I can even surprise you, can't I?" She said, with relief that her plan had worked. In truth, it had been half a plan. All she knew was that they had run out of time, and Kiltman's questions, while distracting Lange, were not going to be enough to stop him for long.

Lange began to come to, and shuffled himself into a sitting position, his back against the wall. "Owww!" he groaned.

"Right! We need some answers, pal." Wilson knelt down on one knee, knife in hand, far enough from him that he could not reach her, but close enough that he was in no doubt she could poke him with the blade before he had moved an inch.

"Listen." The look of defiance in his eyes was undeniable. Lange was in pain but it was not going to stop him spewing more words of venom. "You have picked a bigger enemy than you think. Skink was just a pawn in our strategy. He was small fry, a silly Scotsman with a petty gripe on his shoulders about how his country was not what it should be, and so on and so forth. Our movement, on the other hand, has depth and breadth, and most of all, history. If you have ever read Crime and Punishment, you will recognise Skink as what Dostoevsky described as an

172

ordinary person, who never had the right to kill. We on the other hand are *extraordinary*. We are working to create a new future. This enables us to do what is necessary to change the world."

Kiltman waited a moment to digest the literature lesson. In his teens, he had made a valiant effort to be well-read and had attempted this Russian classic. It was only when he was halfway through, he realised why it was so long – to give the reader time to remember the names of the Russian characters. He had enjoyed the 19th century psychological thriller much more than the one playing out in this Vienna apartment.

"Look, Mask… that is, if you want us to use your new pet name. What is it you have planned?"

"Mask?" he asked. "I've no idea what you are talking about. You should consider me as John the Baptist, preparing the way for someone far greater than I. And now, here is my head on a platter."

A strange, resigned smile came over his face. Followed by a crunch and then a grimace. His back arched unnaturally, before he slumped into a heap in front of them.

Kiltman reached across and opened the mouth of the lifeless body lying on the floor. They had to put their hands to their face to protect against the strong, overpowering smell of bitter almonds. Lange had bitten down on a cyanide capsule that must have been implanted in his tooth for an occasion such as this.

He studied their captor's body with a look of bemusement, before shaking his head slowly. He reached across and closed Lange's mouth carefully before whispering, "*Lange, may your gums reek!*"

A Small Café on December 27th

The welcoming smell of strong, freshly brewed coffee embraced them as they walked into the smallest, narrowest café either of them had set foot in. It was 9 am, Kiltman and Wilson had spent the night in the Vienna police station. They had called the police shortly after Lange's demise, and with Austrian efficiency, they were there in minutes. By the time they had entered the apartment building the police knew something was afoot. It was not often they found a group of city elders sleeping on a bench outside their homes in the wee small hours.

Kiltman and Wilson had given a full statement which involved a call to Gemmill in the middle of the night. Kiltman chose that moment to go to the bathroom, saying that Wilson had 'all she needed to explain the situation'. The less confrontation Kiltman had with Gemmill, the higher probability he would be allowed to stay on the case. After a few hours, they had taken the opportunity to cadge a couple of beds in an empty cell for a few hours of slumber.

Kleines Café felt like the perfect place to unravel the remainder of the clue over coffee, with Mozart playing in the background. The locale was positioned discretely, snug in the corner of Franziskanerplatz, a quietly striking square not far off the beaten track in central Vienna. Nestled only a few streets behind Stephansdom, the busiest part of the city, and only a few streets away from Mozart's apartment, the square gave the impression of a country village. If ever a café was created to blend into its surroundings it was this one. Small, inconspicuous, yet immensely characterful inside, it felt like an enchanted tavern of times gone by. They were enjoying the peacefulness and sense of calm after the clanking and banging of the police station.

"Do you know that *klein* means 'small' in German?" he asked.

"Really?" she surveyed the room exaggeratedly. "I'd never have guessed."

"Oh!" He raised his hands defensively. "Sarcasm is the lowest form of wit."

"It was until you came along," she pointed at him with a thumb. "Can we just get on with figuring out a game plan?" She lingered a moment, awaiting a response. But noted Kiltman was distractedly pensive. "We need to crack on. There are a few things Lange mentioned yesterday that we should ponder over."

"Before we do that, Wilson, and all joking aside." Kiltman spoke hesitantly. "For the record, you were amazing last night."

"Kiltman," she smiled at him, nodding her head towards the other customers less than a foot away. "Be careful, people might start talking."

"Emm…" He blushed underneath his mask. And then wondered why he was feeling embarrassed. She was his girlfriend after all! "Very funny, Wilson. You know what I mean."

"I know." She shrugged. "Sometimes I even surprise myself. Anyway, let's get on with our job." She was all business again. "Thinking about Lange's comments, he mentioned a few things that tells us he's not working alone. His reference to European HQ would lead you to believe he is part of a bigger network. As well as his references to *we* and *our*. And then the strange John the Baptist analogy. What do you think?"

"Yes, I agree. They've been powerful and capable enough to free Skink from prison, infiltrate the guards and bribe a dentist in the process. Even the fact Lange had a suicide pill in his tooth talks to an organisation that does not allow capture as an option." He stopped and shrugged his shoulders. "At this point we need to focus on the information we have at hand. They are planning something that has got to do with Italian football, *Love your Planet* gatherings and a detailed map of some technical configuration of cables or pipes of some sort." He stopped and then as if he had just remembered. "Not forgetting a mystery key!"

"It's a pity, we didn't take those objects when we had the chance," she said ruefully. "I was distracted by the Austrian police and their obsession with filling in forms to document every last detail of our encounter. I should have thought about it earlier. I'm sorry. We'll just have to work from memory."

He opened his sporran and one by one placed on the table the items that had been stuck to the wall, including the key. "While you're clearly the brawn in our crime-busting partnership, I see myself as the brains. When you were debriefing with the police in the other room, I took the chance to rifle Lange's pockets. He had cleared these things from the wall when we were unconscious."

"Well done, Kiltman," she laughed despite herself. She had never been known for her physical strength. She was surprised at how happy she felt when he acknowledged the role she had played. "At least one of us was thinking clearly. My head has become more of a hammer recently than a source of ideas."

She touched her forehead where she sported a smooth egg-shaped bump under a tinge of yellow-blue, Lange's contribution to the psychedelic colouring left by the First Minister. He winced with the concern he had been hiding. He wished he could have stopped her picking up these wounds. In fact, he found it odd that when he was Kiltman he accepted her throwing herself around in the line of duty. Yet, when he was just plain old Kenny, he felt nervous when she went out on a case or risked injury. He genuinely believed he was developing a form of emotional schizophrenia. At least he felt relieved to be there at her side, and not over a thousand miles away back in Scotland.

"You're becoming good at those Glasgow kisses, Wilson!" he joked.

She bent her head and considered him reproachfully. While he was thinking Lange and First Minister, she was thinking Parkhead outside O'Kanes.

"Okay." Her discomfiture was becoming obvious. "Let's get back to the clue."

He was relieved to focus on the business at hand. He was finding it easier to be Kiltman with her, putting the Kenny relationship on ice. He sat up straight in his chair in an attempt to show he was ready to change conversation. He pointed to the Italian Serie A fixtures list which showed all the games being played in the month of December in the premier Italian football league. "What do you notice about that list?"

She studied it for a minute or two, realising that in one month alone there was a significant number of contests taking place between Serie A teams in various stadiums throughout Italy - stretching from Naples in the south to Milan in the north. Other than that, nothing jumped out at her.

She turned to look at him. "Go on, spill the beans. What have you spotted?"

"Every Sunday across the month there are league games in each of the cities, except for December 28th in Milan. Inter and Milan, in case you didn't know, are the two Milan teams. They are missing from the list on that day. And their stadium, San Siro, which incidentally they share, is also not there. Doesn't that strike you as odd?"

"Not particularly, but then I'm not a football buff. I guess, if I were a supporter, I'd be a tad aggrieved that our teams were not playing when all the rest were."

"And then if we study the *Love Your Planet* list of events, look at that." He pointed at the date, December 28th. Underneath, written in smaller print, but highlighted in italics, they read: *Location: Milan.* "Any bets, which venue is hosting that event?"

She had already dialled a number and had the phone at her ear. He knew whom she was calling, at least the Kenny side of him knew.

"Hi Lulu! Yes, it's Maggie Wilson here. Yes, Kenny's, em friend." She flashed a look at Kiltman before continuing. "Uh-huh, yes, it was sad. I agree, he did amazingly well, considering." Considering, he thought?

"Just a quick question, if you don't mind. Tomorrow there's a *Love Your Planet* meeting taking place in Milan." She listened and started to nod, relaying her words for Kiltman's benefit. "Yip. Oh, I see, they're having a fund-raising event at the San Siro stadium at noon tomorrow. Both Inter and Milan have agreed to play a local derby, a friendly, with all proceeds going towards saving the planet." She looked at Kiltman, whose thumb was pointed upwards, his head nodding slowly.

"That's great, Lulu, you're a gem. Tha.... Yes, that would be nice... yes, the four of us sometime soon after New Year. For sure. Em..." she snatched a furtive glance towards Kiltman who was rubbing his chin, "I need to go. Love to Shuggy. Bye." She closed the phone slowly.

"Lulu? Shuggy? Who are these folks?" He attempted a show of curiosity.

"Just friends," she answered. "Good people, who care about our planet. Point is, there's an opportunity for Lange to have plotted an attack tomorrow at the stadium. I think we have to assume that even though he's out of the picture, the wheels have already been set in motion."

"Yes, I agree. We still haven't figured out who 'Father' McQueen was. He is still out there somewhere."

He examined the detailed map of what seemed to be pipes and cables. It was a draughtsman's dream; an intricate array of lines, both curved and straight, crisscrossing and dissecting each other, not showing any apparent sense of definition.

He spoke purposefully. "We need to get to Milan to see what's going on. I don't think we've got enough to convince them to cancel the event. If we can get there early enough, we can hunt around."

"I'm with you on that, the sooner we can figure out what the lines mean the closer we will be to an answer," she scratched her head, something Kenny found very endearing but Kiltman had to ignore. "I'll get the station to arrange flights for us." She put the phone to her ear again.

"Not so fast, Wilson," he held his hands up. "We still need to look at the rest of Skink's poem. I wouldn't jump to the conclusion it's all connected to the *Love Your Planet* thingy tomorrow. Before we leave Vienna, let's make sure we feel we've exhausted Skink's clue morsels."

"Fair enough." She placed the sheet, now crumpled and dishevelled, on the table.

"That sheet of paper looks like I feel." He nodded towards it.

"What? Incomprehensible and half-finished?"

"Harsh," he said. "But fair…"

Scotland in Vienna

The church was unusually stunning, classical Baroque architecture identifying its 17th century origins. The original church on this site, built by Irish and Scottish Benedictine monks in the 12th century, had been long gone. Its more recent version, Schottenkirche - a mere four centuries old upgrade - more than made up for its absence. A hidden gem of quiet peacefulness, Kiltman would have liked to spend more time considering its history. He was impressed by how Vienna's original *Scots Church* had been built by Celtic monks wandering through Europe, interested in why they had taken to building a place of worship in the far-flung city of Vienna. While the original church had collapsed and been replaced in later centuries, it was hard not to be impressed by the monks' determination and sense of pioneering spirit. Especially in an historical period when lives were cheap and religious conflicts many.

It was after her second black coffee that Wilson had unravelled the next part of the clue that led them to the Scots church, only fifteen minutes' walk from Kleines Café.

They had spent half an hour on the lines:

Find the arty quirk
Which leads to the kirk
Use the Scots key
To find the relic, class three
Two ships sunk, two wars apart,
One the Graf Spee
Above the abbey and brie

Comfortable the arty quirk was the *Wilkommen* mat that had allowed them to identify the apartment, the kirk reference and Scots key were still a mystery, until she had leafed through a tourist guidebook placed alongside an array of other reading materials on a shelf above her head. It was one of those cafés where people picked up and left books in equal measure. It was their good fortune that an English version had been donated by someone most probably at the end of their trip. It did not take long to connect *the Scots key* to Schottenkirche. Their challenge now was in figuring out where to find the lock that fit this elegantly wrought key.

They walked in through an entrance disproportionately small relative to the size of the church. From the outside, this place of worship appeared compact and strong, quite forbidding in stature – while inside, they were met by a rich onslaught of exquisitely carved pillars and beautiful paintings, dotted along the ceiling high above their heads.

Wilson let out a breath of air when she entered. "My, my, this is how to build a church."

He nodded.

As soon as they had adjusted to the sullen light of the place of worship, and while enjoying the magnificence of its design, their eyes were drawn to the altar at the top of the aisle. He clicked his fingers. "I think I've got it!" The echo of his finger-clicking resounded through the arched pillars and back again.

They walked slowly, and somewhat reverently, to the altar. He turned to her and whispered, "The things I have to do to get you down the aisle, Wilson."

"Funny." She barely registered his comment, while surprised at how her stomach had flipped. "Where do you think the key goes?"

"*To find the relic, class three,*" he repeated from the clue. "I've just remembered some of my Religious Education training from primary school. Altars in Catholic churches are required to have a relic somewhere inside them. There are three classes of relics." He began counting along his fingers. "The first will be part of a saint's body, usually a bone." She scrunched her nose up. "I know. The second class will be something the saint used, for example, clothing. The third class, and the one we are looking for according to Skink's poem, is something that has touched a saint, whether he was alive or dead."

"I'm impressed, Kiltman. You may have missed your true vocation," she whispered.

They were now at the altar, a strong marble structure gloriously beautiful and timeless, the perfect table on which to remember the ultimate sacrifice of body and blood. He looked over the top of the altar and scanned the church as many a priest would have done over the centuries. Fortunately, on this occasion they were on their own. They both knew the exercise they were performing would not be happening if even one local Viennese parishioner was in attendance. They were on borrowed time and had to be quick. He lifted the cloth covering the altar and saw a marble slab with a metal box embedded in its middle.

"Here we go."

He pushed the key deep into a hole in the centre of the box, finding a lock. He had expected the mechanism to be sticky and rigid. After all, this was a centuries old church in a city that wore age like a fashionable necklace. It turned first time with barely a whimper of noise. The top of the box proved to be more resistant, opening slightly. He inserted his fingers to prise it further. While the lock had been effortless, the box itself was proving more defiant. Eventually he was able to reach in and remove an object.

He held it out above the altar to allow them both to inspect it. "What do you think it is, Wilson?"

She studied the narrow, four-inch long item with sharp edges. "If I was to hazard a guess, it's either part of a femur or a wrist bone."

"Yeuch," he said placing it on the altar. He inserted his fingers again towards the back of the box and extracted a metal object - another key. "This looks more like it." He placed the bone back inside. "If that scraggly bone is the Church's view of first class, I can't imagine what they think of economy."

"I agree," she said without laughing. "So, what about the key?"

It was bigger than the one from the apartment and even more ornate.

"This is like one of those babushka dolls you get at Russian markets." He turned it in his hand. "One key leads to another, but in this case they are getting bigger not smaller."

She took it from his hand and studied it carefully. "It definitely looks like it would fit a modern lock. We just have to figure out where that is."

"Yes, makes sense," he said, and recited from memory the remainder of the clue.

"Two ships sunk, two wars apart,
One the Graf Spee

181

Above the abbey and brie"

They stood for another minute hoping for some inspiration. Eventually she said, "I know we need to spend time on the clue, but we have to get to Milan and figure out what Lange had planned. Time is not our friend. We'll have to figure this one out on the hoof. On the way you can tell me everything you know about San Siro and Italian football."

"Sure," he responded, as they walked back out onto the streets of Vienna.

They enjoyed the December cold air on their cheeks for a few minutes, both taking deep breaths before the next stage of their adventure. He already had an idea of what was planned for the San Siro but had chosen not to share it with his partner. At least not at this stage. He had guessed what the apparently haphazard drawing of crisscrossing lines represented. If he was correct, then they were looking at a potentially horrific outcome. No, if he had told her then she would have been obliged to notify Gemmill, and ultimately create a disruption that would play into Mask's hands. It may not be classic teamwork, but he was going to have to dribble the ball on his own for a while with this particular clue. He just had to avoid scoring an own goal in the process.

V

Milan

Matricola

Their flight to Milan took just over an hour, fortunately to Linate rather than the city's other airport, Malpensa – for some reason built closer to Switzerland than Milan. Linate put them within half an hour of the centre, avoiding the city's infamous traffic jams building up around its external *Tangenziale* ring road. As they walked through the Arrivals hall, Wilson called Gemmill to brief him on the latest from Vienna, although she had to confess they still did not know what the most recent key was meant to open. They were under no illusion that whatever was on the other side of its lock would present a host of worries and potential danger. For the time being they were directing all their efforts towards Milan and the risk of an attack there. Gemmill advised that his office had been in touch with both the *Love Your Planet* organization and the San Siro stadium. Neither were in the mood to let a Scottish Detective Inspector and a kilted man with a mask walk around the venue.

When she updated Kiltman on the conversation with Gemmill, he asked, "Which part did they think was far-fetched? The microfiche in the tooth; or the secret room in Vienna; or the third-class relic in the altar? I can't imagine why they won't let us into the stadium to poke our noses around."

Wilson shrugged, even she was finding this adventure stranger than fiction.

Gemmill had made it clear that whatever plans they followed in Milan, they had to make sure to be discrete. The Scottish police force's reputation was at stake, they could not afford to make them appear in a bad light.

While she had been on her call to Gemmill, Kiltman had taken himself off to another part of the Arrivals lounge to call Roddy and Fiona to check in. They could tell from his chirpy tone he had continued to improve emotionally since his mother's funeral. He was happy to hear Roddy's news that Angie's father had been selected to go to the United Nations for the December 31st assembly on self-determination. The First Minister's prolonged

184

stay in hospital meant he had to select someone to replace him on the trip. It certainly seemed like the place to be this New Year – Omar, Tommy and George, who did not know each other, were destined to enjoy Hogmanay together.

What made Roddy even more excited was that Angie - her father now scheduled to be out of town - would be spending New Year with him. They had been hoping to persuade Fiona to let them stay up until midnight to celebrate. When Kenny had asked Fiona to thank Angus for coming to the funeral, she became less comfortable with the conversation.

"Look, Kenny. Angus has decided to take a bit of time away from us. I haven't seen him since your mother's funeral, and he's not been answering my calls. Please don't keep asking about him. I just find it too awkward. Okay?"

They had agreed not to continue talking. He had wished her well while quietly hoping that whenever Angus came back, he would be a bit more congenial. Angus had work to do to be a role model for his son. Before he hung up he suggested that Angie and Roddy might make good New Year companions for her. He read her barely audible pensive murmurs as a positive sign she would appreciate their company in bringing in a new year with fresh opportunities.

It had been Wilson's idea to stop at the first eatery they spotted as they approached Milan town centre. The biscuit and cold tea on the plane had not satisfied their hunger. She knew she did not need to spend time convincing Kiltman - she had heard his stomach rumbling, barely concealed by the plane's steady hum. They were looking for somewhere close enough to the centre for them to arrange a meeting with the local police, and far enough away from the throngs of tourists to remain relatively incognito.

He had been enjoying the banter of the taxi driver, a relatively squat, handsome man from southern Italy. He was clearly taken by Wilson, telling her his life story, major events punctuated by the many traffic lights he stopped at, each time uttering a curse at their frequency. His broken English and flamboyant arm gestures added to the drama of what should have been a simple journey. Whenever he became excited about a particular event in his life, he would speed up and career around a corner or overtake dangerously. She kept looking at Kiltman for support, while his attention was drawn to the tassels of his sporran, playing with them distractedly.

She eventually shouted, "Here's perfect! Thanks, please, enough. I mean, stop!"

They watched the taxi speed off into the distance, just after she had politely refused to give her telephone number to the driver. In a strange way Kiltman had felt sorry for him as he kissed her hand effusively before he left. He seemed to be comfortable with rejection.

They turned to take in their surroundings. The street sign above their head showed Viale Romagna, the name of a long wide road with trundling trams that stretched back towards where they had come from. On the intersection with a smaller road feeding onto Romagna, was an inconspicuous bistro pub, with the letters *Bar Matricola* artfully crafted onto the wood above the door. The drinking aspect of the establishment was reflected in the subtly Irish graphical lettering, and the Guinness sign in the window - they hoped the bistro offerings were Italian.

They gave each other a considered glance to see if either of them was objecting. There was nothing else in the vicinity, and the bar appeared welcoming. There were tables outside, but the idea of eating al fresco did not appeal to them with the temperature hovering around five degrees. They entered the bar to find it surprisingly busy for lunchtime on December 27th, most of the tables occupied by couples. The liveliness of the atmosphere and the thriving bar with a wide selection of drinks and meals boosted Kiltman's spirits.

"Wilson, can I buy you a drink?"

"Does your *sporran* have any Euros in it?" she asked, adding a few *R*'s to the word to achieve an exaggerated Highland accent.

"Romance is never far away with you." He stopped and began to rifle through the contents of his sporran. "Eh, no, actually I don't."

"And do you have a debit or credit card?" Before he could answer, she said, "No, of course you don't. Because if you did, then we might know how to identify our masked crusader, wouldn't we?" She laughed and turned to look at the gantry behind the bar with an abundant array of spirits and wines. "I'm tempted to have a glass of wine. I've not been in a pub for ages."

He thought about that for a moment. He had not realised she missed the pub atmosphere back home. His drinking issues had meant he had avoided taking her to pubs for a night out, opting for evenings at home or meals in *nice* restaurants. She had never mentioned this gap in her life, probably not wanting to put Kenny in a difficult situation. He touched her on the shoulder, more of a caress than a prompt. She noticed it and turned to look at him.

"Kiltman, all I said was that I'd like a vino. It obviously brings out your caring side." She grinned goofily. He yearned to tell her right then, without further delay, who he was and how much he loved her and that he could not live without her. This bizarre schizoid behaviour was becoming too much for him, and for her, even though she did not realise it.

"Hey, Kiltman!" A broad Scottish accent boomed across the bar.

They both turned to see a smattering of bright jerseys at the far end of the pub. There was a group of around ten men, of all shapes and sizes, waving at them. They seemed somehow unified by a sea of red-coloured football tops; *Coca-Cola* emblazoned across the front. One of them, a dead ringer for Robbie Coltrane, sported a wide grin and a powerful physique that came from generations of good breeding, topped off with more than the occasional beer and cheeseburger.

He called, "Over here, come and join us."

Kiltman and Wilson resigned themselves to the moment before walking to the table conscious they were being studied by the group.

The Robbie Coltrane lookalike extended his hand, "Hi, I'm Wee Donald!"

His accent carried the educated notes of an Edinburgh upbringing polished off with a soft baritone quality. Wilson found the timbre quite pleasant.

"*WEE* Donald!" She extended her arms as if demonstrating a snared salmon. "I'd hate to see *BIG* Donald." Kiltman was not sure but he saw a flicker of a twinkle in her eyes that had not been there a minute earlier.

"That would be me." One of the red top wearers rose to his full 6-foot 3 stature, sporting an affable smile. While his size would dominate any gathering, his Scottish accent was spoken with a distinct, welcoming softness. He reached across the table to shake hands with each of them.

"What's going on here?" Kiltman asked. "A gathering of *Clan Donald?*"

"We're Matricola Rovers," said Wee Donald. "Been representing this pub for quite a few years already in a local Milan football league. We had a game this morning, and actually won for a change." He stepped back and sized Kiltman up and down. "We're looking for a goalkeeper, how do you fancy signing up?"

Kiltman laughed. "I'm seriously tempted but I don't think my diving around the penalty box in a kilt would go down well with the censorship folks."

"You're in Milan now, Kiltman, anything goes," said one of the other players. A tad older than the others, he walked around the table towards them with a swagger that matched his eyes - the space in between appearing half an inch closer than would be considered normal, adding a congenial feature that invited conversation. "I'm Russell, the team captain. Have a seat. What you having?"

"That's very kind of you." Wilson was smiling. "I'll have a prosecco, and my friend here…" she gestured with her hand to Kiltman.

"I'll have a Coke, and, eh, a straw too, please." He pointed at his mask.

The Rovers laughed in unison, with another member of the team pulling up a couple of chairs for them to sit down. As they sat, the man, with greying hair and pleasant blue eyes, introduced himself. "Hi, I'm Andy. Technically not Scottish."

He sported an open smile and landed a friendly pat on Kiltman's back. His accent had twinges of northern England, overlaid with the clear articulation that comes when Brits attune their brogue to a more communicable level on the international circuit.

An hour later, they were sitting at a table strewn with leftover pizza and baguette toasties, chips, and breadsticks, intermingled with glasses of beer and wine. And Kiltman's Coke, which he regretted ordering. Every time he took a drink through the straw feeding up through the bottom of his mask, someone at the table would shout, "Kiltman's having a drink!" They proceeded to slap their hands on the table in a drum roll, as he lifted the straw into his mouth and sipped. He wondered if Scotland was the only country where a superhero had to be prepared to be one of the boys. For once, he thanked his lucky stars for the years he had spent in Sweeneys where he had developed a layer of skin thick enough for moments such as these.

They met the rest of the group over the course of munching and sipping to find a couple more Scots and Irish, including a friendly Belfast man called Robert Burns. Equally as engaging with a twinkle in his eye, Kiltman imagined Robert's quick wit was in no small measure due to a lifetime of comparisons with the famous Scottish bard. He made a point of buying Kiltman and Wilson a drink to welcome them to Milan, while mentioning that he believed they would have a future in academia if ever they were short on criminals to chase. "The young need to believe in superheroes and strong women in equal measure," he said. "It would be great if both of you found a way to tell them about your exploits. One of you could talk about the international adventures of a world-famous crime fighter - and the other can explain why wearing national *dress* is so important." He wandered off into the back of the bar smiling, while Wilson chose to study the beer mats. And Kiltman sighed.

The others were mostly Italian, a sign that the Celts and English had extended their bonhomie to the locals. While this brought the obvious benefit of an integrated ex-pat community, the added upside most probably lay in the additional advantage of Italian flair, enhancing their chances of success. As he observed the group, Kiltman was convinced winning games would always be second to enjoying each other's company.

Eventually, Big Donald asked the question they were all wondering, "So what brings you to Milan, Kiltman and DI Wilson? We were all enthralled watching your adventures from afar last summer. Is it because Skink has escaped?"

Interesting, Kiltman thought. Gemmill had chosen not to publicise Skink's demise in the Steeple at Glasgow Cross. He had managed to keep the lid closed on that for the time being. Once again, while he did not agree with Gemmill's style, he was aligned to holding back this piece of information. Better to keep Mask and his compatriots in the dark in terms of where they were in the investigation. Although if they were to be honest with each other, they were feeling anxious about Mask's plans for the San Siro. Kiltman was growing increasingly frustrated at having to waste precious time in a pub, when they would have been more effective searching the stadium.

"Hang on a minute." Wee Donald pointed at Wilson. "Are you not the detective that headbutted the First Minister's belly on Christmas Eve?"

She nodded, rubbing her bruised cheek. "Yes, and I got a '*Nice*' trophy to show for it," she spoke in a mock French accent. She was taken aback when everyone laughed. She was not used to cracking jokes, especially ones that made others chuckle.

"'Nice' one, Wilson," Kiltman offered in his version of a French accent. Nobody laughed.

"Hey!" Andy sported a faux scowl on his face. "You can't recycle DI Wilson's joke. Kiltman or no Kiltman."

"To answer your question," Wilson nodded towards Big Donald, "we are following up on a piece of information that leads us to Milan. Before you ask, we have to limit what we tell you for obvious reasons." This caused a hush to descend on the table, an air of expectation pulling them into a collaborative lean forward. "We have to get into the San Siro tomorrow to follow up on, em, a particular clue we've been given."

She glanced at Kiltman, who made a gentle downwards movement with his hand. Slow down, he was thinking. One prosecco and you've suddenly become the life and soul of the party. He had not realised she was such a cheap date.

"Problem is that the local authorities aren't as excited about the clue as we are, so they're not allowing us access to the stadium." She turned to Kiltman. "In fact, I've just received a note from Gemmill. He advised we're not allowed near the event in case we create some sort of diversion and disrupt the *Love Your Planet* gig."

Russell had been quietly enjoying the banter and energy generated by the Rovers and their new friends, appearing quite pensive in the midst of the hustle and bustle. He spoke up for the first time in a while.

"I can get you into the San Siro. But only if you promise to do something for us first."

Fund-Raising

"I've just come down from the Isle of Skye,
I'm no' very big, and I'm awfy shy,
The lassies shout when I go by,
Donald where's your troosers"

If he did not have a mask, he would not have agreed to Russell's unusual proposal. He had to take Wilson to the side to confer. The fact of the matter, they had agreed, was that Gemmill had not been able to pull enough weight to get them access to the stadium. They had no other option but to accept Russell's offer.

It was now evening of December 27th and they were back in Bar Matricola, after a visit to the police station in the afternoon to make one final plea for their support at the event the following day. Working with the local authorities was their best chance of addressing the threat as quickly as possible - giving them the chance to explain in person the risks the spectators at the stadium faced. Believing it to be a strong negotiation tactic, Wilson had cited the Cullen Skink attempt to destroy the Church's think-tank earlier that year in Rome. The policemen looked at each other with an expression of exaggerated tedium; it was clear they had minimal respect for the Roman police. Rather than bolstering their request, it gave the police even more reason to ask them to leave the station. They had been snubbed in the same way Gemmill had. While there was more than a little politeness in their rebuttal, Kiltman and Wilson were in no doubt that their priority lay in making sure such an important event - focused on saving the planet - would not be denigrated by the ridiculous '*brutta figura*' flamboyance of a Scottish superhero.

Kiltman had been left with no alternative.

Standing on a small, raised dais where the television usually took up space in the bar, Kiltman had been nervous to hold the microphone in front of a group that had started off with around twenty people. By the time he had reached *Donald, Where's Your Troosers*, after having already sung *Flower of Scotland* and

191

Scotland the Brave, the bar was full. Italian families and couples who had been walking along *Viale Romagna* enjoying a quiet *passeggiata* before dinner had not expected to be distracted by the metallic crooning emanating from the pub. With a natural curiosity, they had entered to find a man in a skirt, with a cape and mask, singing his heart out. The slapstick comedic element of this show appealed to their sense of humour, probably more so than most countries. Italian TV is strewn with the absurd; the more ludicrous and flamboyant, the more popular the programme. Within half an hour the customers had ordered drinks and squeezed into tables and chairs dotted throughout the bar.

Russell's request had been quite simple. That evening, Matricola Rovers were having a pre-arranged, fund-raising event to collect money to pay for an upgrade to their kit, which Kiltman acknowledged had seen better days. The faded red *Coca-Cola* tops were apparently already five years old - a sponsorship deal orchestrated by a gracious Scot who had lived there a few years earlier. They needed two thousand Euros to buy a replacement kit and a couple of new footballs.

His side of the bargain was to sing songs requested by the audience, with the choice of song determined by a bidding process. *Donald Where's Your Troosers* had been auctioned at 100 Euros, and those of the crowd who knew it, or parts of it, were enjoying every cent of the experience, cheering along, and singing the chorus raucously. After every few lines, he would look towards Wilson. She was laughing more openly and effortlessly than he could remember seeing in any of their times together. This environment, surrounded by innocent fun and friendship, suited her so much more than he would have imagined.

While he was singing, she had hooked up with some of the better halves of the Rovers' players, who had come to the bar an hour earlier. It was quite an international gathering of elegant and pretty ladies. Wilson felt relaxed with them and was finding it easy to let her hair down. They had taken to her in ways she had rarely experienced back home, asking her questions about what it was like to be a Detective Inspector. Once the girls realised she had upended the First Minister a few days earlier, and nearly took a bullet for him, they were practically falling over every word she uttered. If she had not been looking for an international maniac and his band of followers, she would have asked Gemmill for a few days holiday before New Year. She was enjoying the banter with the jolly, eclectic group: Gina, an English lady, who had a beautiful wide smile; complimented by Michelle's French flair and style, Hilda's German sassiness and Carina's Italian warmth.

Wilson turned to the group, working hard to have a conversation above the noise of the bar and the increasingly irritating grind of Kiltman's voice changer turning well known songs into the equivalent of a tuneless, robotic answering machine.

"So!" Wilson was enjoying her third prosecco of the day. "I've got a puzzle for you."

"Sure," Michelle, Big Donald's girlfriend, purred in her sultry French accent, "what is it?" Her enchanting green eyes expressed a genuine desire for some fun.

"Let's go over there away from the noise." Carina, Russell's Italian wife, had a refined Scottish accent, courtesy of many years spent with her man and his Edinburgh twang. She pointed at her ears with both hands, the first of the group to admit to feeling acoustically pummelled by Kiltman's increasingly energetic efforts to reach unachievable high notes.

They sat down at a large circular table in the corner far enough away from the speakers for Kiltman's singing to become more muzac than conversation-inhibiting. The table was available courtesy of Russell labelling it with a handwritten sheet of paper - *Rovers WAGs*. The girls raised their eyes in unison, before removing and tearing it up, barely hiding their mutual exasperation at Russell's awkwardly sexist effort to be organised.

Carina groaned resignedly. "Yes, that's my man," she said, encouraging the others to laugh.

Hilda made a mock sad expression and sighed. "Aww, *poveraccia!*" Poor lass.

Gina arrived with a tray of drinks, finding enough melody in Kiltman's rendition of Gloria Gaynor's *I Will Survive*, to encourage her to dance as she approached the table. The others were impressed with her ability to only spill half the drinks despite her hip gyrations and shoulder swings. She even managed to fit in an overhead ninja kick to knock Wee Donald's hat off just as Kiltman hit the line *Walk Out the Door*. Wee Donald was in the process of tuning a guitar, and barely noticed his locks of wavy brown hair falling down around his ears.

"So, what's the clue?" Hilda, Wee Donald's girlfriend, asked with typical German efficiency as Gina sat down at the table and distributed the drinks.

"Okay." Wilson mustered an air of seriousness. "It's quite odd but goes like this:

Two ships sunk, two wars apart,
One the Graf Spee
Above the abbey and brie

"Is that it?" Michelle asked, her quizzical expression strangely entrancing. "Are you looking for the name of a place, or the names of ships? It is a bit confusing."

Wilson smiled. "Welcome to my world. Criminals don't hand us solutions on a plate, you know!" A silence descended on the table as they began to realise this was not a party game; they were being asked to help in an inquiry.

"Let's see what we come up with and then take it from there." Wilson suggested, enjoying the seriousness settling on the table.

"Actually, I should go first since there's a German connection," said Hilda with gusto. She coughed, pleased with her chance to impress. Her face took on a look of solemnity, which Wilson guessed did not happen very often - she had a light-hearted, jovial air about her, reflected in her soft, attractive features. "Graf Spee, which was actually called Admiral Graf Spee, was a German ship from World War II. It was a bit of a pocket battleship, known for its small size and aggressive tactics. How would Wee Donald put it? Yes, got it."

She stopped, concentrated for a moment, pushed her chin closer to her chest and then said in a deep Scottish accent, "*Aye, it punched above its weight, so it did!*" They all cheered in unison, laughing at the almost perfect imitation of her boyfriend. She then resorted to her Bavarian drawl again. "Yes, several British ships were sunk by it, I think, somewhere off South America in the Atlantic. After that I'm not sure."

She sat back in her chair and took a long sip of her white wine trying to recall more information about the *Admiral Graf Spee*.

"That's a good start." Wilson scribbled notes onto the back of a Matricola napkin. She wrote *South America!!* and drew a circle around it. Less than 24 hours earlier Lange had mentioned the same continent.

Gina spoke up, "I know, Detective, you might think I am some sort of Ninja warrior, but I'm actually a history teacher. I can add some more clarity to the puzzle." She smiled a pearly white smile, further enhancing her prettiness. She had the air and poise of an English woman but the passionate expression of someone at home in the Mediterranean. "It's true, the Graf Spee was powerful and took out quite a few British ships at the beginning of the war. But it didn't get very far because it had been badly damaged in those early battles. The Captain decided to scuttle the ship just off Montevideo in Uruguay rather than let it get into British hands. He then killed himself. All very tragic when you think about it." She pushed out her bottom lip in a sympathetic pout.

"What happened to the crew?" Michelle asked, genuinely concerned. "Did they escape?"

"The data's fragmented from that time," Gina said pensively, "but apparently quite a few were sent to prisoner of war camps. Although some escaped and made their way into Argentina and headed for the hills."

"All makes sense so far." Wilson nodded affirmatively, although she was not sure how it would help them. "But then what about the other ship '*wars apart*'?"

"The only other ship I know of that's famous from that part of the world was the General Belgrano," Gina said thinking aloud.

"Go on." Wilson could see from the perplexed looks of the others at the table that she was not the only person who did not recognise the reference.

"It was an Argentine ship sunk by the British navy in the Falklands War in 1982. It was a defining moment in that conflict, and one of the main reasons Britain won." Gina paused, a genuine look of angst crossing her pretty features. "The war itself was a bit of a farce, most people believing that the leaders of the

195

two countries were using their acts of aggression to grow their popularity at home. Too many people died, and not much was gained in the end."

"Okay, thanks. Something's starting to build here." Wilson felt they had answered the '*two wars apart*' comment - World War II and Falklands ironically linked by Skink's poem.

In the background, she could hear Kiltman destroying the third verse of *American Pie*. The dissonant harshness of his vocal limitations was lost on the crowd, who appeared happy to ignore the lack of harmony as long as they could see a man in a skirt singing. They joined in on every song, continually bidding at auction prices increasingly higher than the one before. Russell, Robert, the two Donalds and Andy leant against the bar, grinning from ear to ear, imagining how professional they would look in their new team strips.

"Since you girls are on a roll," Wilson encouraged, "what about *Above the abbey and brie?*"

The five of them sat for a few minutes before Michelle offered, "The only thing I can think about is an Abbey in northern France called Bec. It's a very famous Benedictine Abbey. We used to go there as a family when I was younger. It was quite a drive from where we lived in Bordeaux, but worth it in the end." Michelle paused and enjoyed a drink of her red wine. She studied the glass carefully. "Funnily enough," she continued, "if you think about it, Bec also appears in the name of the wine, Malbec. This was originally a French wine known for its purple grapes, but what might be relevant here is that Malbec grapes were not at their best in France. In fact, the climate they performed better in was South America, Argentina to be exact."

Wilson lifted her head from where she had been scribbling, "Another Argentina connection, Michelle. It's starting to come together for me."

They had at least narrowed it down from a continent to a country, albeit the second largest in South America.

Carina, whose strong, appealingly lovely face lit up like a beacon, clapped her hands together. "Abbey and brie would then become Bec and brie. Then Malbec and brie... Whatever you are looking for, DI Wilson, is above a *bec and brie* shop which of course sells…"

She waited a moment, before the girls all shouted at the same time, "CHEESE AND WINE!" Caught up in the euphoria of the moment, they began to clap energetically in unison at their team problem-solving skills - realising they had more or less cracked the clue. Just as Kiltman arrived back at the table. A relaxed hush seemed to have descended on the pub.

"Thanks, girls, I appreciate the recognition." He bowed his head and extended his hands in a feigned effort at humility. He knew the first couple of songs had been shaky but was pleased when he remembered all the verses of *American Pie*. He was happy to see the girls acknowledging it. "I think I was getting into my stride by the end there."

They looked at each other before a ripple of laughter broke free from them one at a time like a Mexican wave.

"Kiltman, while you've been serenading the pub, we've been working." Wilson tried hard to maintain a serious face. "Did you hear about the English, Italian, French and German who walked into a bar?"

"Don't forget the Scot!" Gina shouted pointing at Wilson, spilling half her prosecco in the process.

"Eh, no." He played along.

"They figured out the clue. At least the bulk of it." Wilson pointed towards her smiling helpers. "All we're looking for is a cheese and wine shop in Argentina!" As soon as she had uttered the words, she realised the concept was less powerful when verbalized.

Before he could react, he heard Russell approach the table. "Kiltman, great job! You've certainly delivered your side of the bargain. We've made enough money to get our new strips and the footballs." He stopped for a moment, then laid his hand on Kiltman's shoulder. "Just don't give up your day job!"

Kiltman nodded his acknowledgement of the thanks, sighing at Russell's scorn for his singing.

"On a serious note, we're all set for you two at the San Siro tomorrow. The game starts at 12, but we'll get you there for 11.30. Okay?"

"Sounds good to me," Kiltman replied, and Wilson nodded.

"By the way, this is Jimmy." Russell stepped back to let a taller, dark-haired man - with boyish features younger than his years - through to the table.

"Hello, folks." Jimmy put his arm around Kiltman's shoulder. "Now that the big fella here has entertained us all night, it's only fair we do the same for you. So, sit back and enjoy the *Rovers Rockers!*"

Jimmy turned and walked over to the stage where Andy was tuning an electric guitar, with Big Donald gently tapping a set of drums, bobbing his head to an imaginary song. Wee Donald had grabbed the microphone and was running a hand through his wavy dark hair, now more Robbie Williams than Coltrane, observing the crowd settling into their seats to enjoy the show. Once he felt a gentle expectant hush descend on the pub, he announced, "We are the Rovers and we are going to rock this joint tonight!"

With the noise of shouts and clapping increasing across the bar, he cast his eyes towards Kiltman and raised his thumb in appreciation. "And if anyone wants a dance with our Scottish superhero, it will cost you five Euro a go! Cheers, Kiltman!"

Russell began to massage the back of Kiltman's neck. "You're welcome back any time, Kiltman!"

He enjoyed the feel of the thumbs kneading his upper body. At any other time or place he would have politely asked Russell to refrain from the back rub but considering how many firsts he had achieved that evening, he succumbed to the pleasant, languid pressure applied effortlessly to his weary muscles. He was beginning to feel exhausted with his efforts to raise money for the Rovers. In the last few years, he had worked hard to create his Kiltman persona - he felt he had built a strong degree of credibility in a Scottish superhero. This evening his brand of crusader had taken a different turn, rendering him more human than super. He resignedly sat back into his seat with the dawning realisation he was actually not bothered.

He closed his eyes and spoke over his shoulder. "Russell, just up to the left and over a wee bit. That's it. Ahh, you got it, right there."

He squinted over towards Wilson who was taking a break from her bantering with the girls. She was looking back at him, slowly shaking her head, before she elicited a long sigh and mimed, "We've got work to do tomorrow!"

He wondered whether this was directed more at herself than at him.

San Siro

Football stadiums are not built to be aesthetically beautiful. Fans are not attracted by a stunning building; they are there to appreciate the skill, talent and entertainment displayed on the pitch. The San Siro, situated in a north-western suburb of Milan, could not be described as visually stunning, yet there was something strikingly handsome about the enormous construct reaching high above them. The corners at the top of the stadium were punctuated by large, protruding rust-coloured, metallic arms which appeared curiously triffid. The main section, the seating area, rested on a number of large, coiled walkways from ground level to the floors above, giving a caricaturist's impression that the building could easily bounce into the distance and take up home somewhere else.

The roads leading to this mecca of Northern Italian football were chaotic with the frenetic bustle of thousands of supporters of Inter and Milan. There seemed to be an endless onslaught of fans dressed in equal measure of blue and red - united by black, the collective colour conjoining the rival teams. Horns blared, songs were chanted, and shouts and screams rose from the crowd, who had clearly been cooped up with their families for days eating and drinking. They were desperately in need of space, people and football and were soaking up the atmosphere, excited by the prospect of 90 minutes of top-class entertainment.

Unusual for a Milan derby day, the fans were diluted by a large, colourful group of young, energetic people wearing t-shirts, carrying colourful balloons, and wearing flowers in their hair. The *Love Your Planet* environmentalists were every bit as jubilant as the supporters and were bringing their own version of fun and merriment to the occasion. Fortunately for Wilson and Kiltman, who were hemmed in on all sides by the throngs of characters, the spirited party atmosphere made it easier for a kilted superhero to blend in. He was just one more person in colourful regalia, finding his own way to express his love for the planet. Every so often, he would feel a slap on one of his buttocks and turn around to catch whoever had the audacity to do so. After a while he realised the hordes of people made it impossible to identify the culprits and gave up trying - even when a hand slipped up the back of his kilt and pinched his bottom. He resigned himself to accepting that this was the price he had to pay for the role he performed. Could be a lot worse, he considered quietly to himself.

The journey from central Milan had taken them an hour, including an underground metro, a crammed bus and a twenty-minute walk to the stadium. Kiltman had slept the night on Russell's couch. The cost of the free lodgings was to endure what felt like a homage to the 80's, Russell and Carina taking turns to play a host of songs he had not heard since the beer bar in university. Wilson on the other hand, enjoyed an uninterrupted sleep in Wee Donald and Hilda's spare room. They had left Bar Matricola at 1 am barely able to stay awake, becoming increasingly apprehensive as to what lay ahead.

By the time they stood outside San Siro, Russell and the two Donalds had brought them up to speed with the clandestine access plan. Their opportunity to gain covert entry resulted from a decision made a quarter of a century earlier. In preparation for the 1990 World Cup tournament being played in Italy that year, a decision had been taken to increase the stadium's capacity to around 85 thousand, an increase of 10 thousand. To accommodate this substantial escalation in spectators, an extra tier was built contributing a third layer to the building. Considered quite an ambitious architectural feat at the time, there was only one downside to this new seating capacity, which did not become evident until afterwards.

Apparently one of the challenges of adding an extra level to such a large structure was that the increasingly vertical design prevented the sun from reaching the grass. As a result, it became difficult to maintain a playing surface of the quality required for some of the best footballers in the world. Without the heat and rays of the sun, the grass began to die prematurely.

As Russell and the Donalds explained the background, they went to great lengths to make it clear Russell was a Milan fan, Big Donald an Inter supporter and Wee Donald a Hearts lifer, as if this helped the picture Kiltman and Wilson were trying to comprehend. This resulted in them engaging in distracting banter and jokes, which Wilson found particularly infuriating. Kiltman had to take her to the side to explain that if you hung out with football fans this is the conversation you should expect.

"Thank goodness I'm not into football!" she had answered. Before turning to their hosts and saying, "Okay, guys, can we cut to the chase. This is driving me a tad demented. How does all this relate to us getting into the stadium?"

"Well," Russell said enjoying her discomfiture. "The grass was dying, and they needed help. They advertised for greenkeepers to sort it out, and one of our friends is now working there. He had a good pedigree working in North England, fighting against the elements. Based on how the grass is looking, those skills seem to be transferrable to working in North Italy."

While they considered the international aspects of grass maintenance, as if on cue, a tall, wiry man with a green helmet and orange overalls walked towards them. He boomed in a Northern English accent, "Hello, folks! How did the fund-raiser go last night?"

"Great!" Big Donald declared. "All thanks to Kiltman here!"

"Pleasure to meet you, Kiltman, and you too, DI Wilson. They call me Herb around here. Sort of goes with the job!" He paused to let the comment sink before he looked directly at Wilson and said. "Your fame precedes you!" He made a shimmy move as if he was going to dive headfirst into the middle of Russell, who jumped back in alarm. "Seriously, DI Wilson, you are a real hero. I'm honoured to be able to help you guys."

Wilson felt her cheeks tinge with the heat of self-consciousness. She wondered whether one day she would get used to such off the cuff compliments.

Herb was carrying a large canvas bag, which he dropped on the ground between them. He reached deep into it and extracted orange overalls and green helmets identical to his own. He handed them to Wilson and Kiltman.

"I got you an extra-large set, Kiltman."

Kiltman rubbed his tummy, feeling a tad aggrieved that his growing bulk had preceded him. Quickly realising what he had said, Herb put an arm around shoulders that had slumped visibly. "Oh, no. Not for that reason. You see, I expected we would need to cover your costume and cape; and would need a larger helmet to go over your mask."

"And the rest, Herb," Wee Donald threw in, patting Kiltman's tummy - incurring a seriously malicious look from him, perfectly concealed by the mask. Pots were calling kettles black, even in Milan, Kiltman mused.

"Thanks, Herb, but why do we need to wear the overalls?"

"Oh, sorry, I should explain." Herb folded his arms, clearly enjoying his role in the exploit. "At the end of the first half, sometimes the grass can be chunked up quite badly. All to do with the lack of sun; I am sure the lads have explained. Anyway, it can be quite fragile especially during the winter months. The overalls show that your role is to go on at half time and replace the divots. You know, stand on them and push them back down into the pitch. You're being allowed to enter as part of the *divot-replacement* team."

Wilson laughed. "Oh, Herb, I don't know if Kiltman can do this." She waited for comedic effect. "You see, he has become an overnight cabaret star. Replacing divots is probably beneath him at this stage."

"Very funny," Kiltman said, as Russell and the two Donalds joined in with Wilson's laughter. Even Herb was laughing, and he had not even been in Bar Matricola to witness the kilted cabaret. "Look, can we go, we're running out of time?"

After some awkward hugs for Kiltman and far too many kisses for Wilson, they bade their goodbyes and thanks, mutually appreciative of how they had helped each other. It would be much later when Kiltman and Wilson realised their Matricola Rovers friends had selflessly forfeited their own chance to 'replace the divots', missing a Milan derby. The Rovers were not as *wild* as their name suggested.

Below Siro

Their brisk walk to keep up with Herb seemed somewhat ceremonial as he casually swiped a plastic card at turnstiles and electronic doors along a set of corridors on the ground floor. Halfway along the route Kiltman was able to step back a pace behind Wilson to take a hefty swig of Hair o' the Dog. He knew he would need to be fully alert to assess what lay in store for them. He thought he had got away with it until Herb - who must have had extraordinary peripheral vision - whispered, "I know the feeling, Kiltman. You can't beat a curer next morning. I've been out with the Rovers too. They know how to throw a party." Kiltman chose not to argue.

After what seemed a labyrinthian maze of passageways, they found themselves standing pitch-side in one of the world's most iconic and impressive soccer stadiums. The seats around them and far into the sky overhead were filling up quickly. The surreal nature of the extra layer sitting atop the already huge stadium was breath-taking. It gave the image of a structure spiralling up into the heavens, where fans seemed to practically sit on top of one another the higher up they were seated. The game had been sold out, not surprisingly considering Inter and Milan were two of the best teams in Italy and Europe. There was a growing sense of anticipation that the players would introduce a high degree of flair into the friendly match to turn it into a classic football spectacle. Without the worry of losing points against their arch-rivals they had the opportunity to dazzle and impress and add some fun to help the spectators feel their ticket donations had been worth it.

Especially, Kiltman thought, when the money was to be directed towards a critically important campaign to save the planet. The movement's main focus was to raise awareness that the Earth was heating up faster than ever before, evidenced by the polar ice caps melting. High levels of carbon dioxide emissions were building up in the atmosphere creating a greenhouse effect, throwing the planet dangerously off balance.

Kiltman personally understood how easy it was to lose balance when he had abandoned self-respect and focused on excess. When humans lost respect for their planet and gorged on the activities and industries that fed the greenhouse above their heads, the impact became cataclysmic. The human race needed a wake-up call to realise the damage they were doing. Ironic, he thought, that when our planet needed *harmony*, its custodians fell short by delivering only its first four letters.

As he scanned the stadium filling up he was not surprised that a large number of seats were occupied by colourfully-dressed, kind-hearted, responsible people - desperately trying to awaken the realisation in others that our generation's legacy should not be one of infamy for irreversibly damaging our world.

He was awakened from his reverie by the anxiety in her voice.

"So, Kiltman. I can't stand the suspense any longer. What do we do now?" Wilson asked as Herb took himself off to discuss grass-related topics with his colleagues, leaving them standing on the side-lines of the playing field.

"Show me the page with all the lines, Wilson, please." She pulled it from her satchel and placed it on a chair beside them, hoping for some direction.

"All these lines are related to the grass conditions and the problems Russell explained, caused by the extra layer of seating. This is one of the ways they keep the grass fresh and as lush as it is." They both examined the pitch to see an effervescent green colour, unnaturally fresh for late December.

She turned back to look at him, "Yes, the grass is lovely. But I am not following you, Kiltman. It's always better to give me a bit more detail." She found his way of drip-feeding information more and more frustrating.

He pointed towards the pitch.

"Underneath the turf a myriad of pipes has been installed, to allow hot water to reach all corners of the pitch and generate heat to keep the grass healthy. This maintains the necessary temperature and allows them a way to avoid some of the challenges of the absence of sunlight, resulting from the extra layer. This detailed design that was stuck to the wall in Vienna is actually a map of where the pipes have been placed under the pitch."

"And?" She put her hands out to her sides. "What can they possible do with that? Heat the pitch up so that the players burn their toes?"

"Well that's what we have to figure out," he answered, ignoring her edginess. "Here is an access point where the water flows into the piping system." He pointed to a large black dot manually scribbled onto the bottom of the sheet. "We find this, and I believe we will know what Lange and his pals have planned to upset today's game."

Without waiting for her to answer he continue, "The match is about to start; we need to find the access point."

He marched off around the outside of the pitch towards the halfway line. He kept his head bowed as he passed police and ball-boys dotted around the area between the spectators and the grass. They arrived at the tunnel to find the players from both sides had already lined up and were waiting to be escorted onto the pitch.

Big Donald, an accountant to trade, had explained to Kiltman that the value of the two teams was more than £1 billion - which had elicited a comment from Wilson about 'a waste of money for grown men to chase a ball around a field'. Big Donald and Kiltman had exchanged a glance, shook their heads slightly and sighed. Where should they begin to explain?

Up close facing over £1 billion of human flesh, Kiltman was struck by the visual impact of the players in such a confined space. While it was not his bag to go around admiring men, he was taken aback by how powerful these players were, sinews and muscles bulging from taut, tanned legs. Yet it was their faces that struck him more than their physicality. They were truly handsome in ways that he had only guessed at or assumed existed in the same species he belonged to. He turned to Wilson to suggest they wait until the players had started to run onto the pitch before they explore. He saw a look on her face he had never seen before. He would realise later that she had the look of a five-year old who had walked into a sweet shop for the first time in her life.

"Wilson. Hello, are you there?"

"Eh sorry, Kiltman, yes." She wiped her brow dreamily with the back of her hand.

With the players shaking their legs and cracking their necks, he realised they were standing at the centre of all the attention, scores of cameras flashing with the intensity that comes just before a game begins. He had been keeping his helmeted head bowed and collar pulled up high around his face, and quickly realised that this may not be enough. He hastily bent down to tie his shoelaces.

As the players walked out to the screams and shouts of the crowds, Kiltman and Wilson, heads down, walked obsequiously along the side of the tunnel in the opposite direction, searching for the route towards the pipes' access point. It took them twenty minutes of wandering through corridors and underground walkways to access one layer down in the stadium where the pipes had been installed. They heard the muffled sound of the referee's whistle signalling the start of the game, followed by the noise of the fans further energised by what sounded like a fast-flowing start to the match.

They turned a corner to find themselves in a wide room with a large number of round pipes stretching across the walls. They were occasionally interrupted by an intricate system of iron handles and levers.

"Okay, Kiltman, looks like we've found the access point." Wilson pointed at the pipes.

"Something's not quite right." He itched the corner of his mask where it kept snagging with the hood. The temperature was much hotter so close to the heating system, the heavy overalls inhibiting his concentration. Looking around, he felt comfortable they would not be disturbed with the game already started, and yanked off the orange boiler suit and helmet, throwing them down in a corner.

He looked up and down, then along the walls counting the number of pipes, assessing their length and width, mentally comparing to the drawing he had committed to memory. Suddenly he punched one of the pipes and let out a loud scream. "Aaggghhhh!"

"What is it?" she asked, surprised at his exaggerated show of pain. He had not hit the pipe that hard.

"Give me the diagram," he said.

She handed it to him cautiously. It made her uneasy when he acted stranger than normal. He took it from her and made a point of turning it around in a dramatic fashion.

"I had memorised the diagram upside down! What an idiot, I am! How on earth could I have done something so stupid!"

"Okay, it's not the end of the world, Kiltman. Let's just go to the correct access point."

He shook his head and raised the palm of his hand towards her. His mind was racing with the enormity of the error he had made. He cursed under his breath. Bending down to study an inconspicuous pipe closer to the floor, he laid his hands on either side and gripped it tightly. After several long minutes he stood up and swivelled round to face her.

"We need to hurry! We're definitely in the wrong place," he shouted, before sprinting back along the corridor.

A Kilted Streaker

Wilson was surprised at how quickly he covered the first ten yards. She caught up to run shoulder to shoulder. They were nearing the pitch, the roar of screaming fans intensifying with each step. She shouted, "Okay, tell me! I'm getting worried, what is it?"

He was already panting. "Look, I just checked the contents of the pipes, through the touch thing I do now and then." He took a few deep breaths before continuing. "The water in the pipes is laced with hydrogen cyanide. Yes, more cyanide. Seems to be this guy's favourite tipple of death. I could also sense a timer device at the other end, on the access point. It is set to trigger an explosion through the pipes. The whole heating network will blow at the same time with enough force to rupture the pitch."

"Seriously?" she asked, speeding up to encourage him to run faster.

"You should know that I don't joke about things like this, Wilson." They were now back upstairs in the tunnel, sixty feet from the pitch. "If the pipes blow with that toxic gas inside, you can be sure that you won't get much change out of the wealth of football talent running around 'chasing a ball around a field'." His attempt to copy her voice was lost on Wilson.

"Then there is the impact the gas will have on all the officials, support staff and fans. I was able to sense how much time was left before it goes off. My guess is that we have less than ten minutes. It's set to detonate in the middle of the first half when the stadium is at maximum capacity and players are at full pelt. Tens of thousands of people could be dead within the next few minutes."

They were now standing a few steps from the grass, looking out towards a sea of Inter's blue and black competing with Milan's red and black. He peeked at his watch; the minutes were counting down before detonation. He realised there was only one action open to them.

"You ever watched American football, Wilson?" he asked.

"Sure! I prefer it to this version." She pointed at the pitch. "What's your point?"

"I'll be the Quarterback and you are the Tight End... which suits you, by the way!"

She squinted at him quizzically. "Funny. I get it. I just make sure nobody gets near you. Ready when you are."

Without another word, he sprinted out of the tunnel, past the police, ball boys, managers and substitutes and ran directly onto the pitch. He focused on running along the halfway line towards the entrance at the other side. The sound of her steps crunching behind him felt reassuring.

The shouts and screams from the crowds increased a few notches, reverberating around the stadium in support of the kilted streaker, believing this was some sort of protest run. It was one of those days when the spectators were happy to support any means of publicising their worthy cause. It could not get much better than a masked, kilted man, with his cape billowing in the air behind him, running through the middle of San Siro - followed by a pretty woman, chasing him as if he had stolen her purse. The players stopped passing and running, several of them pausing to applaud and join in the whoops and shouts rippling across the thousands of fans.

As he neared the centre spot, he started to feel this was going much better than he had expected, when he saw two policemen running directly at him. It was clear they did not see the funny side of the pitch invasion. Their trajectory was aimed straight at Kiltman. Until Wilson ran past him, finding an extra notch of pace. She sprinted towards the surprised policemen, her hands waving in the air as if she were trying to stop a car from going over a cliff.

It proved just enough of a distraction for her to achieve maximum impact when she launched herself into the air, dropping into a horizontal shape about three feet off the ground. She took them both out at the same time, her arms hitting one and her legs the other. They crumpled onto the grass in a heap with her landing on top. She saw Kiltman jumping over them awkwardly before turning to see if she was okay.

"Run for goodness sake! Go!" she shouted. The policemen were scrambling to get up, more focused on redeeming their faltering self-esteem than catching Kiltman.

She had just thrown herself at someone else, Kiltman thought, as he ran across the pitch. How many times she could do that and not break a bone was a discussion he could have with her later - if they had a later. He only had a few more yards to get to the other entrance; he was beginning to believe he would get to the access point in time. Until another Italian policeman jumped over the advertising boards and sprinted towards him, pistol in hand - wearing the burden of avenging his two fallen colleagues on his chiselled face. Kiltman sensed that this particular cop would be an insurmountable obstacle until someone stepped out of the shadows to put a surreptitious leg in the policeman's way. He fell forward into a spectacular somersault crashing onto San Siro's perfectly nurtured grass. Kiltman side-stepped the policeman and dashed into the darkness of the entrance receiving a wink and cheeky grin from Herb on his way in. As a greenkeeper at San Siro watching Italian football week in, week out, he had obviously learned more than how to look after the turf.

He ran in the direction of where he believed he would find stairs leading down under the pitch. Wrong turnings were a luxury he could ill afford. He focused in on the sickly aroma of hydrogen cyanide only he could detect, barely sensing it as he ran along the tunnel underneath the rows of spectators who seconds earlier had been encouraging his mazy run. It would not have occurred to them that they were in mortal danger.

He took a sharp left, before descending a metal staircase to the lower level. The darkness engulfed him. There was no time to search for a light switch. He automatically kicked into his own infra-red vision. Half-running, half-stumbling, he rushed towards the poison. The dampness and heat of the lower floor grew increasingly intense as the pipes worked to offset the stadium's winter chill. His heart was pumping harder than he remembered it ever having to do in the past. He wheeled around a corner to find himself staring at row upon row of pipes. The harshness of his gasping and physical exertions made it difficult to concentrate on where the hydrogen cyanide had been planted. He rested his hands on his knees, trying to focus and absorb his surroundings, ignoring the increasing clamour of footfall cascading towards him.

It took only a few seconds to know where he had to direct his attention. He ran towards the far wall where a large, bulbous pipe sat underneath a scarlet-red, circular handle. To the side of the handle a cannister had been awkwardly welded into a small opening in the pipe. It was the only alien object in the room. Attached to the cannister was a square box with a clock which appeared no more threatening than a travel alarm. An array of loose wires dangled underneath - the trigger that would send cyanide and explosives shooting down through the pipes to erupt on Milan's San Siro pitch like sprinklers in a Chelsea garden, spraying a callous shower of death.

He studied the device for a moment to make sure there were no booby traps. The digits on the clock were counting down in a steady, unremitting pulse of doom: 30, 29, 28... The clatter and screams of what felt like a small army descending on him invaded his hearing and added unnecessary pressure to an action that would ultimately be half guess and half wish. There was a circular switch on the side of the clock designed to move either up or down. It was a binary decision.

Assuming that upwards was always a good thing, whether at work, in a football league, or when dead, he placed his thumb underneath and flicked it upwards - just as he felt the air escape from his body with the weight of two policemen charging him simultaneously. He had already steadied himself for the expected crash, his legs spread wide enough to mitigate the impact. It was the thud of his head smashing off the edge of the pipe that he had not bargained for.

As he succumbed to the darkness of unconsciousness, he prayed for the sake of 80,000 spectators and Milan's finest footballers that he had guessed right.

Respect

"Kiltman, wake up! Kiltman!" the urgency in the sweet, Glasgow accent he had grown to love washed over him like a crashing wave of cold, salty ocean. The panic in the voice combined with the bottom of his mask being lifted up over his chin forced him to raise himself jerkily onto his haunches, arms thrashing to push away a policeman's hands. He lurched into a standing position quickly taking in the scenario around him.

Wilson was staring at him with genuine concern in her eyes. "Are you okay?"

Several policemen were attempting to put his arms in cuffs while he frantically shook and jolted his hands up and down to stop them. He thrashed his head from side to side to prevent an inquisitive policeman from removing his mask. In any other scenario it would have been comical.

"Stop!" he shouted. "Stop!"

Whether it was the sound of his voice or the exasperation they felt at not being able to lock his wrists, he managed to claim back a few seconds of calm, before he spoke, "Wait, please! I can explain."

"Okay!" The tallest of the policemen held his hands in the air to calm the growing impatience of his colleagues. He was dressed in the uniform of a senior officer judging by the three rows of medals and stripes decorating his jacket. At his hip, Kiltman could see a leather flap dangling over a black, shiny pistol; it was open and ready to be used. "You have one minute to explain what is happening here."

Kiltman realised that his unconscious state had lasted barely a minute or two. He had awakened just in time to stop the policeman revealing his identity. That would have been an extraordinarily awkward moment, trying to explain to Wilson why Kenny was in a Kiltman costume. The Italian police would have become spectators at an operatic quarrel more at home in Milan's La Scala than San Siro.

Kiltman hobbled towards the cannister and clock and pointed at the wires. "Sir. You need to get someone to come and dismantle this device very carefully. It contains a deadly gas that would have exploded throughout the pitch's heating system. The clock is a timer and was set to go off a few minutes ago."

He stepped back and let the policeman lean forward to peer closely at the mechanism. The officer was tall with a shaved head and piercing blue eyes. Italians, Kiltman reflected, carried baldness better than any other nation. His own tresses had largely disappeared years before, and while he was not conceited, he did spend more time now trying to rearrange his sparse locks to cover the gaps. At that moment he decided to take a leaf out of the Italian's book about not trying to hide the inevitable but welcome and celebrate it.

"Madonna!" The policeman stepped back quickly from the device. He could see that the cannister had been manually inserted into the pipe and that the clock was not a standard heating fixture. "Are you sure of what is inside here?" He was looking at Kiltman, a hint of respect finally showing through.

"Yes, I am," he answered. "Hydrogen cyanide, a killer gas. The heating system has been laced with explosives too which would have blown each and every pipe under the pitch releasing an almighty belch of poison." He saw Wilson scrunch her nose. He had probably gone a bit too far with the metaphor.

He paused for a moment and then suggested, "I would not clear the stadium now. You should wait until the game is over. There's no indication that this will self-detonate now. I've run my fingers over the connections and wires. The trigger is dead. We need to avoid creating mass panic when it will achieve nothing."

"I understand," the policeman said. "I agree with your recommendation but will need to make some calls now." He stopped for a moment, and extended his hand, taking off his black glove. "On behalf of everyone in this stadium, I want to thank you for your courage." He turned to Wilson and kissed her on both cheeks. "And to you too, *cara signora*, for your bravery and, eh, athleticism."

Why did everyone in Italy want to kiss Wilson, Kiltman thought? He then noticed that she had a bruise on her left cheek, virtually symmetrical with the discolouration on the other side of her face, caused by the First Minister's midriff butt. With the Lange bump sitting squarely in the middle of her forehead, she was running out of places to bruise. He was quite sure that underneath her sweater and jeans, she was sporting several similar black, blue and yellow colourings, courtesy of her enthusiasm for throwing herself at people. He hoped one day soon they might be in a more agreeable place that he could suggest applying some soothing arnica cream to her wounds. That day felt further away with every minute they spent on this zany, mysterious journey they had found themselves on - not knowing who they were chasing and what was coming next. He sensed they were only at the beginning of their adventure.

Gemmill's expenses budget, he realised, would need to stretch to a transatlantic trip for a Detective Inspector who did all her own stunts, and her kilted partner.

Il Duomo

"I'm finding this quite frustrating." She could barely hide her annoyance. "How long does it take Gemmill to get us clearance to make a trip?"

Kiltman took a deep draught of his Diet Coke, satisfied at the sharp tingle of bubbles on the back of his throat, where a hint of hydrogen cyanide had nestled earlier that day. At a corner table outside a bar at the foot of Piazza del Duomo, they were enjoying a welcome break from crime-fighting and fund-raising.

Once Kiltman had advised of the contents of the cannister, it did not take long for the under-pitch area to be inundated with investigators and chemical experts. They had provided statements to several different investigative bodies assigned to unpick the available evidence and remove the device to a laboratory far out of Milan in the direction of Turin. It took several hours, but eventually the *Capo della Polizia*, (the Police Chief), arrived at the scene taking a no-nonsense approach to the findings and potentially devastating outcomes. He embraced both Kiltman and Wilson, launching into a glowing speech on the importance of true detective work and collaboration across borders.

After some time, it became clear that no further clues were going to surface. They bade their farewells and jumped a metro into the centre of Milan to escape the photographers and TV crews heading towards the stadium. News of the near disaster had been leaked, and an air of tension had descended on the underground, with the *Capo della Polizia* having barely enough time to comb his hair and straighten his uniform before he went on air. When Wilson remarked to Kiltman that Gemmill could take a leaf out of the Milan Police Chief's book in how to appreciate their officers, he could not argue.

Now with the first chance to relax since Bar Matricola, which in hindsight had not been particularly relaxing for Kiltman, they feasted their eyes on one of the world's grandest cathedrals, Milan's Duomo. From their vantage point at a short distance, the front's triangular façade appeared to look like a bar-chart chronicling the rise then fall of a business venture. The image reminded him of the one whisky they had produced at Wallace Distillers which promised so much, then died a quick death. It was called *Hold the Alliance*, a play on words related to the special bond between Scotland and France - known as the *Auld Alliance*, a friendship nurtured by their shared history fighting against England.

The brand's launch had coincided with Scotland's much vaunted upcoming performance in the 1998 football World Cup in France. The whisky had been layered with the added complexity of grain from the Normandy region, imported specially for this unique blend, giving it a gentle fragrance. Kenny had felt this was a fitting way to celebrate Scotland's ancient relationship with France - and to capitalise on the French being the world's highest per capita consumers of Scottish whisky. A special formulation for a special nation.

Four minutes into the first game, a stolen Brazilian goal rang the death knell of Scotland's chances. And also meant their special whisky went from *Hold the Alliance* to *Halted Dalliance* – in tandem with Scotland's increasingly languid and uneventful performances. Kenny had taken three days off work to travel to Bordeaux for the Norway match. While it was never going to be a classic demonstration of soccer skills, a fizzled out 1-1 draw was much less than the travelling fans deserved. The highlight of the event, which he did not remember much about, was how the Scotland fans had been lauded for their exemplary behaviour - receiving an open invitation to come back to the city of Bordeaux whenever they were in the neighbourhood. The Tartan Army had become experts at not letting a result get in the way of a good party. That night proved to be a triumphant gathering in the face of a disappointing tournament - where they came bottom of their group, the draw with Norway proving to be the best of the three games. Those days seemed a long way off, he mused.

"Hello? Earth calling Kiltman, come in!"

He could hear the humour in her voice. She knew he was tired and recovering from the exertions of the San Siro earlier that day, but that did not mean she would not jerk his chain now and then, all the same.

216

"I'm assuming you don't expect a response," he answered, before removing his gaze from the Duomo. He cracked his neck a couple of times. "Where's Russell with his back rubs, when you need him?"

They both smiled. She was becoming good at knowing when he was grinning despite the mask.

"Do you want another drink?" she asked.

"No, I'm fine. Would be good to walk though. No point in waiting around here for Gemmill to untie the purse strings."

He stood as she nodded her agreement. She left a ten Euro note, which allowed for a couple of Euros tip, before they walked towards the cathedral. They needed a distraction while they waited for approval for the next stage in the investigation. At the table they had taken a moment to distractedly review some tourist pamphlets explaining the Duomo and its history.

The cathedral's magnificence did not come from its outward appearance, or not only from its outward appearance. Its true splendour came from the uniquely Milanese history of how it was built. From beginning to end, the construction took nearly six centuries - including various architectural styles mongrelised into its quirky and distinct features. The façade had been completed by Napoleon Bonaparte, which allowed him pride of place enshrined in a statue on one of its 135 spires. Hard as it was to believe, Da Vinci had put forward a proposed design for the cupola, which was not accepted, the honour going to a lesser known architect. This building encapsulated huge swathes of European history, knitted into its busily flamboyant opulence. It was definitely worth a visit, as Wilson had suggested. Kiltman nodded, although reluctantly.

They entered through its large, bronze door to step into the grandeur and majesty of Italy's largest church. When Kiltman informed her of this, she tut-tutted, waving her finger, and asked him not to forget St. Peter's Basilica in the Vatican.

"Ha! St. Peter's." He waited a moment for dramatic effect. "How could I forget our adventures there during the summer?" He then tut-tutted and wagged his finger nearly exactly as she had done. "I hate to correct you but St. Peter's is not in Italy, DI Wilson. It's in the Vatican, which is the smallest country in the world."

She punched him on the arm, and walked ahead into the church, remembering why she found him so annoying. They stood behind the benches at the back of the cathedral for a couple of minutes taking in the vastness enveloping them. Where they had been overwhelmed by the magnificence of Schottenkirche, they were overpowered by the clamorous carvings and extravagant excesses of the Duomo. Rather than encouraging the visitor to settle into a prayerful mindset, it created an edginess, not knowing what to feel at this sensory overload.

His reluctance to enter was due to his memories from when he was there six years earlier.

Wilson stopped and gazed at the altar, recalling a conversation with Kenny a couple of months before. They were having a coffee outside an Italian café in central Glasgow whiling away the afternoon watching people go about their lives. Whilst sipping on their *macchiatos*, they found themselves sharing views on the royal family. While not the first conversation to materialise in a Scottish relationship, it was never far behind the topic of independence, which they had discussed many times before – they both saw the pros and cons of the argument for a 'free' Scotland.

She recalled how despondent he had been when he talked about Gianni Versace's funeral several years earlier, which had taken place in Milan's Duomo. Kenny had never known the fashion guru, but he had been deeply saddened by his killing. By chance Kenny had been invited to attend the funeral, courtesy of Wallace Distillers providing some of the high end whiskies consumed at the reception. He had nearly cried when he explained how he saw the sadness in the tears breaking from Lady Di's eyes. She had sat in a bench near the front of the cathedral, her grief and sense of loss evident for the world to see.

Only for the Princess to become a tragic victim herself forty days later. Wilson recalled Kenny's words clearly, "there was something unbelievably heart-breaking about the biblical connotations of Lady Di in mourning forty days before her own untimely end." Kenny's telling of the story had made Wilson shed some tears at the café - she had felt the sense of good lives lost for nothing.

Kiltman snapped out of his own reminiscing, remembering the same event Wilson was struggling with. He reached across and handed her a paper napkin he had taken from the bar.

"Thank you," she said, wiping away the cascade of tears that had burst from her eyes. Her sorrow was layered with complexity she could not begin to explain to him. And she did not attempt to do so. Some things had to remain secret between them.

He put an arm around her shoulders and squeezed gently. She did not shrug him away. She leaned into his comforting touch, feeling as though somehow he knew what and why she was feeling so sad. She wondered, could his special powers really reach that far into someone's soul?

She did not see him slip a hand below the mask to stem the flow of his own brackish blues.

Not so Innocent

"Had enough?" Wilson asked, half-turning to face the door to leave the Duomo. Kiltman nodded. He was already finding the cathedral's oddly extravagant architecture - his memories of death and tragedy, and their mutual melancholy - overwhelming.

They stepped out through the entrance and down the steps back onto the piazza, which was half-full of tourists, some idling around while others posed for photos feeding the multitude of pigeons at home in the Duomo's shadow. She checked her phone to see that Gemmill had still not been in touch. She made an impatient harrumphing cough that startled a nearby flock of pigeons, who scarpered into the sky, only to descend on another group a few yards away. She did not want to harass him, but it was already 6 pm and they did not know if they were coming or going that night. Literally. She was tempted to call or even drop a text, but she prevented herself with the thought that Gemmill would probably not be thinking about anything else at that moment. She decided to wait. Her boss would need clearance to send her and Kiltman to a far-off continent. Their reasons to support this trip were the equivalent of Blu Tack and Sellotape holding up a loose shelf - a strange key stolen from an altar in Vienna on top of a clue from a dead man's molar which was *'solved'* in the middle of a raucous Milan pub with a bunch of well-meaning strangers. She was trying not to place too much hope on this request coming through. But it was their only option. Even then, once they got to Argentina, what next? She just hoped Kiltman had something special to move this case forward because she had run out of ideas.

They walked along the Corso Vittorio Emanuele II, a wide pedestrianised street running alongside the Duomo. The Corso's exquisite combination of designer shops and high-priced cafés and restaurants enticed throngs of people to settle into the tables and chairs scattered sporadically on either side of the broad walkway. After barely a minute's stroll, Kiltman stopped and touched her arm. He pointed towards a flag hanging outside a window on Via Agnello, a small street off to the left of the Corso. The flag was unusually vibrant in the evening glare - light blue and white stripes as bright as a summer's day, with a yellow sun in its middle. There was no mistaking the country it represented.

"Oh my! It's the Embassy for Argentina. How weird is that?" She paused for a moment, before asking, "Kiltman, is this another one of your tricks, where you pretend not to be aware of something and then, hey presto, you knew it all the time? Did you know this place was here?"

"Wilson, while I appreciate your admiration of my intelligence - and have noted your scorn for my duplicitous ways - I can assure you, I had no idea this was here." He studied the building. "Actually, this is not the embassy. Embassies are usually in capital cities, and I expect Argentina's is in Rome. No, this is the Consulate General, also important, but its purpose is mainly to look after the needs of its citizens abroad."

"Well, whatever it is, "she replied, "it's probably closed at this time. Although no harm in having a look."

She walked towards the entrance, a relatively inconspicuous doorway within view of the Corso. Surprisingly, inside one of the ground floor windows, they could see a large group of people talking and laughing, each with a cocktail or beer in hand.

He turned to her. "How do you fancy going to a party?"

"I don't think so, Kiltman." She was surprised at even the hint of gate-crashing a diplomatic event. "Can you imagine Gemmill's reaction?" She paused, took a deep breath and said in a deep, broad Glasgow accent, "Aye, Wilson, you and your comic book partner. All you had to do was wait a wee while before I got back to you. But oh, no, you decide to get yourselves arrested for breaking into the consulate of a country we were at war with, twenty years ago!"

They both laughed at the half-decent attempt to mimic her boss, when they noticed some people at the consulate's window pointing at them, talking animatedly. He expected it was kilt-surprise, which happened whether he was in full Kiltman regalia or not. The kilt was a magnet for comments and stares - which happened at home just as often as abroad. Nobody ever tired of looking at a kilt; or took its wearing for granted. He felt it was his duty as a kilt-wearer to acknowledge their attention. He raised both hands and waved with all the energy of someone valeting a car.

A couple of minutes passed with them discussing what they should do next, when the consulate's door opened. Two young, uniformed soldiers stepped out and walked quickly towards them. They were handsome lads, one around six foot and the other a little shorter. Both gave the impression they could easily survive ten rounds with Mike Tyson, arm and chest muscles bulging in their uniform.

The taller spoke first. "Sir and Madam. We have been ordered to ask you to come inside for some questions."

"Questions?" Wilson struggled to hide her incredulity. "What on earth for?"

"Please do not make a scene here outside the consulate. We will have to use physical force if you do not comply," the taller spoke, seriousness etched in his young features. The smaller soldier, while not talking, was even more intimidating than his colleague, looking at Kiltman as if sizing him up for a punch.

"Look, Wilson. Let's just do it. There may have been a misunderstanding, and I'm sure we can clear it up."

She nodded, although not convinced. If Kiltman had not been there, she would have reacted differently.

The soldiers stepped aside and let them pass through and up the stairs into the building. Once inside, they were guided along a couple of freshly waxed corridors to a meeting room. The room was spartan, comprised of a table and four wooden chairs in the middle. On the far wall there was a large mirror, which she knew from experience was what they called 'reciprocal' - a one-way mirror to surreptitiously observe interviews being conducted.

"Please wait," the taller spoke in a clipped tone, before leaving with the other soldier, closing the door behind them with a clunk.

"This is weird, Kiltman. I feel as if I've been taken to the headmaster's office, and I don't even know what I'm supposed to have done." Wilson's tiredness was beginning to show in dark circles under her hazel-brown eyes.

"Probably kissing the boys behind the bike shed," he said, hands raised as if expecting a flying punch.

Before she could react, the door opened and a woman entered along with the two soldiers, who seemed to get broader each time they stood to attention. The lady carried an air about her of someone who was used to confrontation, ready to engage or desist, depending on what the circumstances required.

"Hallo," she declared, no hint of her mood apparent in her olive-green eyes, nor in her compact jawline. "My name is Alessandra Santiago."

Tall, with long, flowing blonde hair, she did not extend a hand, nor acknowledge that the giving of her name was less an introduction than a statement of fact. She sat at the table, the soldiers standing to attention on either side of her, hovering over Kiltman and Wilson like vultures on the Argentine pampas awaiting a carcass, or two.

"Well, I am..." Wilson began.

"Yes, yes," Santiago fluttered her hand as if waving away a nuisance fly. "You are Wilson, and this is, em, the ostentatious Scottish superhero, Kiltman. We know all about both of you and your trips around Europe."

Wilson raised her eyes to the ceiling and took a deep breath. "Okay, fine then. But why have we been marched in here like two common criminals? We are only complying out of decency, but I can speak for both of us." She squinted at Kiltman. "We are one step away from calling our own embassy contacts."

"Well, Ms. Wilson, I will, as you say, cut to the chase. You have broken International Law, article 18.75 subsection 89, and this carries harsh penalties."

Kiltman was bemused by the confrontation, finding it mildly enjoyable, but increasingly irritating in the context of their pending approval from Gemmill for their flights.

"18.75, 89! What on earth is that?" Wilson stood up with such speed that her chair fell back behind her onto the floor with a loud clatter. It appeared much more aggressive than she had intended, but she was not going to apologise. The two soldiers stepped forward. Santiago was in no doubt as to how well she was protected against a diminutive Scottish policewoman and a man in a kilt.

"Article 18.75 subsection 89," Santiago repeated, as if reading from a book, "is the international law that applies after countries have been at war together. For a period of 50 years after the war

223

ends, anyone seen loitering outside the other country's embassy or consulate with an air of intent can be arrested and kept on remand for 48 hours." She paused, letting the words settle in.

"This is outrageous!" Wilson was shouting now. "I am going to call my boss in Scotland to let him know what's going on here."

"Your phone will not work, Ms. Wilson. All phone signals are blocked in this room, which is our interrogation area. Now please sit down and stop making a fuss."

Wilson picked her chair up from the floor and sat down, exasperated, looking at Kiltman, who shrugged.

"We have to go with this, Wilson. Let's be patient." He was becoming just as anxious but felt that a position of neutrality was their best option.

"Okay, we have to ask you some questions." Santiago's stern face became even more sombre. Her face had bordered on sardonic since she had entered the room, barely a hint of emotion betrayed by her richly coloured eyes.

"The first is very important. You have to answer with absolute truthfulness." She waited several moments until the tension in the air became intolerable.

"What does Kiltman wear under his kilt?"

The silence was deafening as Wilson and Kiltman looked at each other. Before Santiago and the two soldiers burst into loud laughter. Their guffaws slipped into uncontrollable cackling and howling, growing louder by the second, their hands reaching out to each other to steady Santiago from slipping off her chair. She banged the table with the palm of her free hand, snorting and throwing her head back. The absurdity of the scene playing out in front of the Scottish crimefighters could not possibly get any more surreal.

Until the door burst open and two men and a lady entered, also laughing hysterically, falling over each other on their way into the room. They must have been watching though the reciprocal mirror. One of the men slapped Santiago on the back, the other hugged Wilson, while the lady grabbed Kiltman and squeezed him into a strong embrace, his arms still at his sides.

"What the…?" Wilson started to speak - trapped in the arms of a chortling stranger.

She was interrupted by Santiago, who was barely regaining her composure. "Happy Holy Innocents Day, detective and Kiltman!" She again fell into a fit of cackles, once again slapping the table.

"Sorry?" Wilson asked.

Santiago scanned them both, tears running down her cheeks, "Today is December 28th, Holy Innocents Day. The day we remember the children who were killed by King Herod on the birth of Jesus."

She eyeballed Kiltman and Wilson as if this powerfully tragic date in the Church's calendar suddenly made the picture any clearer. They were stunned, barely able to speak, or even find the right question to ask. On all sides, grown-ups were acting like kids, laughing, and patting each other on backs. It took a few moments, but eventually the room seemed to get back to a semblance of normality. Santiago wiped tears from her eyes before she introduced herself as head of the consulate's security. The older of the two men who had barged into the room had been an Ambassador several years earlier. He and his assistant were in Milan to celebrate the consulate's pre-New Year party. The lady who had entered with them was tall and imperious. She extended her hand and presented herself formally as Cristina, the Consul General from the same era as the former Ambassador. She then realised that she had enjoyed her hug with Kiltman so much, she decided to do it again, this time tweaking his masked cheek with her thumb and forefinger. Kiltman felt it was better not to resist until he had a better sense of what was going on.

"Okay, okay!" Wilson lifted her hands in the air in a simulation of surrender. "Can someone explain what has just happened here?"

Cristina, unwrapping herself from her embrace with Kiltman, spoke up, "Ah, Ms. Wilson. You are now incredibly famous, after your acrobatics in Nice last week. And now here in Milan., where you have been launching yourself at policemen in the San Siro. When we saw you and your cute partner standing outside our consulate, we could not resist." She winked at Kiltman then stopped for a moment before beaming an engaging and friendly smile that would have melted butter.

"Let me complete the picture for you. Holy Innocents Day, December 28th, is the Argentina equivalent of your celebration, April Fool's Day. We perform pranks that those children killed by

Herod would have enjoyed if they had been allowed to fulfil their childhood.

"The combination of Holy Innocents Day, a few glasses of Malbec and the sight of you both standing outside the window gave us the idea. We also know that the Scottish have a great sense of humour."

Wilson and Kiltman looked disbelievingly at each other, then back at Cristina, before they realised the comic absurdity of the prank - one they would have been proud to have concocted on any day of the year. They began to laugh self-consciously, which only encouraged the Argentines in the room to start guffawing again. The smaller of the two soldiers left for a moment to come back with a Jeroboam sized bottle of Malbec and a handful of glasses, which he placed gently on the table. He promptly poured the wine and handed the glasses around the room. Kiltman politely refused while Wilson could not grab her drink quick enough.

"Salud!" Santiago announced ceremoniously, glass in the air. "What is even more ironic is that our consulate is situated on Via *Agnello*." She emphasized *Agnello*. "This is Italian for 'the way of sheep'. Today, my friends, you have been, how do you say in English, '*innocent as lambs*'."

Everyone raised their glass - while Kiltman grabbed a sparkling water from a nearby drinks trolley - shouting in unison, "Salud!"

Cristina cleared her throat ceremoniously before she spoke, "Ms. Wilson and Kiltman, we hope you were not offended by our behaviour this evening. It was all in good fun. Let's just say that this was our way of building a good relationship with our British friends."

"Actually, Cristina," Kiltman responded, "I think you have been particularly, em, 'diplomatic' in how you have handled the sensitivities between our nations."

There was a moment's silence, before the Argentines groaned their understanding that somewhere in his comment there was an overworked grasp at humour. They turned to look at Wilson for her reaction.

"Welcome to my world," was all she could say.

Anger in the Trossachs

The loch was still, not a ripple of the clear, cold water to indicate an inquisitive fish or a roaming bird. The peacefulness and serenity of the crisp afternoon contrasted sharply with the anger raging inside the remote cottage halfway up Ben A'an. The glass smashed off the wall with such force, the shards splattered in all directions bouncing off the window, table, and chairs. The impact barely smudged the writing painstakingly scratched onto the white board over months of preparation. It had all been going according to plan until Vienna.

Mask would not carry any remorse for the First Minister fiasco in Nice - that fell apart because of Skink's shambolic homage to his inflated ego. Vienna was different. He had racked his brain, trying to understand how they had identified the Marc-Aurel Strasse cell. He was quite sure he had left no clue to lead them there. Other than himself, Skink and Lange, no-one knew of their covert operation. He could not see how Skink would have been able to communicate from beyond the grave. Skink had not seen his downfall coming, even when he had handed over the plans and details needed for the next stage of their operation. Despite his evil intent, Skink had been unusually trusting of a fellow fiend. Six months in solitary confinement had softened him, which had become clear when he escaped. He had lost his edge. His death had become inevitable when it became apparent he still wanted to leave his cuckoo clues for the police and Kiltman.

Kiltman, he pondered - what kind of power did he have over Skink? There was something in their relationship that seemed bigger, somehow more intimate – much more than superhero-nemesis shenanigans. Skink would never open up on that front, no matter how many questions were put his way. If he could unearth that mystery, Mask might have a chance of disposing of this weird, kilted freak.

Lange on the other hand had been a different kettle of fish. Pun intended, he thought as he sported a crooked grin. Lange had been a zealot from an early age, believing in a greater world, with their race in control. They had been friends since grade school, growing together in their hatred, feeding off each other's negativity. Strange, he did not feel remorse for his friend's suicide. One day, maybe he would, but at the moment, he felt empowered in the knowledge that he had sacrificed himself so that their mission could be completed. Lange's death gave power to the cause and emboldened Mask's strength of belief in what they were doing.

The one thing that had irked Mask above all was that Lange must have left something around the cell in Vienna for them to realise San Siro was the target. Lange had been sloppy and had paid a price for that amateurish error. Mask took a deep breath and picked up the hand-held hoover looking for rogue shards on the floor. The suction sound and crackle of the glass clinking down the pipe felt somehow relaxing in the quiet of the cottage. Self-absorption and emotional outbursts were qualities he despised in other people. If he let himself give in to these weaknesses, then others in his life might be able to see his dark side. He had found living a parallel life easier than he thought it would be, he could not afford to blow it now. He was already regretting breaking the crystal tumbler in his anger. He had to remind himself that San Siro was merely a warm-up for the main event, only days away.

He had targeted the stadium and the Love Your Planet Society to send a message to the world leaders that nothing was sacred to him. Yes, he was willing to go that low to show his scorn for the world. Only acts like that would attract the attention he needed to force more like-minded people to follow him and rise up out of their comfortable lives to change the world order.

His worry now was whether there had been anything lying around the Vienna flat to lead them to his South American bunker. He had made a point of keeping both sides of his organisation separate. Lange was not informed of what the South America team were working on, just like they were blissfully unaware of what Lange was doing. But one never knew. And he was learning from Kiltman that he should not underestimate him. To be safe he would create an unexpected treat, just in case this kilted man was cleverer than he had given him credit for.

He picked up his phone and called his comrade in Argentina. The conversation was short and to the point. Nothing would disrupt their plans. His friend challenged him, as friends should, to assess whether he was ready to resort to the final solution for anyone who got in their way. He did not have to think about his answer before he closed his phone down. "Eliminate those who prevent you from accomplishing your task, no matter who they are."

The glass continued to clatter through the metal tube, rattling like maracas at a Samba party. The sound made him feel homesick for his childhood and the merging of cultural ambiguities. The environment he had grown up in, he was quite sure, had allowed him to develop both sides of his personality, both fully formed and equally credible. He consciously switched from one to the other with ease, so expert at being duplicitous he never made mistakes.

He thought about Milan some more, how the Italian press had made a meal of the near miss in the stadium – embellished with flair and flamboyance the national RAI news channels were famous for. In doing so, they had created the publicity he wanted in creating an atmosphere of terror. He recalled the day he and Lange had sat planning the San Siro event. He pushed a twinge of melancholy away, Lange was gone. End of.

In some ways, the fact the detonation had not happened - and nobody had been injured, apart from a few bruises on a couple of clumsy police officers - meant there was an even greater fear of the unknown. No-one liked the thought of a frustrated terrorist, he reminded himself. After emptying the contents of the hoover in the kitchen bin, he walked back towards his drinks' cabinet. He took a fresh crystal glass from the shelf and poured himself another malt whisky, adding the slightest drop of water. He settled down in his rocking chair and surveyed Loch Achray to see a kingfisher hover patiently above the glassy surface. Before it dived recklessly into the loch to pull a flapping pink salmon up into the sky and off to dry ground.

Mask raised his glass to the bird and spoke aloud, "Kiltman, you have just strayed into the wrong loch."

VI

Argentina

Cheese and Wine Airlines

Kiltman was jolted awake by the jerk of the wheels touching tarmac, combined with the pressure of the thrust reversers pulling him back into his cramped seat. Fortunately, there was plenty of space in front, allowing him to stretch his legs out with his bottom half-on, half-off the seat. His lower back ached from the awkward angle, and he had lost feeling in his buttocks, but it had allowed him to get some shut eye during the 16-hour flight. The real challenge on the journey had been his thoughts about his mother. Over the days since the funeral he had found distractions and reasons not to deal with his grief. On the flight, between tosses and turns, he could not think about anything else. He had to keep reminding himself that she had given him her posthumous blessing. While he wanted to believe with every sinew of his being that she was always at his side, it did not come naturally to him - he realised he would have to work at the whole belief thing.

He swivelled to see Wilson behind and to his left, reading a magazine, looking as if she had slept like a baby, soaked in a bath, and enjoyed a relaxing walk in the hills.

"Morning, Kiltman! How did you sleep?" she asked. Bugs Bunny could not have been more bright eyed and bushy tailed.

"Okay, I suppose, all things considered," he answered, twisting, and cracking his spine. "Although I've flown in more comfort - and in significantly less smelly planes - to be honest."

"I can't argue there." She turned to look at their surroundings.

They were the only passengers on the plane, accompanying four pilots, who had worked a two-on, two-off rotation during the flight. Behind them, there were scores of pallets of produce ranging from Italian wines to fresh pasta. Further to the back, a large, cold storage unit was filled with Italian cheeses and meat products.

When the phone had buzzed in the middle of the consulate gathering the previous evening, Wilson was already on her third glass of Malbec enjoying her newfound fame as the Scottish detective who floored anyone who got in her way. It took Gemmill a few minutes to be heard against the cacophony of voices and laughter, and even longer for him to absorb and understand where they were. In truth Kiltman did not expect him to understand the Holy Innocents explanation, Wilson had lost some of her clarity at that stage. The important thing was Gemmill had given them the all-clear to go to Argentina and get to the bottom of whatever Skink had been pointing them to. They now had enough experiences from Vienna and Milan to know that something major was afoot - Skink's posthumous molar message was their only chance of finding out.

Their evening in the consulate had proven to be enriching in several ways. Not just in increasing Wilson's appreciation of Malbec. It gave them the opportunity to put the remnants of their clue to a new audience. Kiltman had smiled ruefully considering the pub quiz excuse he used for some of his inspirational ideas. They now had their own format which they were shipping from one social event to another. Wilson had read it aloud:

Two ships sunk, two wars apart,
One the Graf Spee
Above the abbey and brie

They had explained to their new Argentine friends that they felt the ships were the Admiral Graf Spee and the infamous General Belgrano from the Falklands War. The Ambassador and Consul General moved quickly over that point. It may have been Holy Innocents Day, but the bitterness felt at the UK for that war - particularly the sinking of the Belgrano - had not disappeared.

It was Santiago who had said, "Look, maybe it is referring to General Belgrano. If it is then it might be using the ship to point you to something else." She had paused for a moment, collecting her thoughts while taking a long sip of her wine. "General Manuel Belgrano was famous for many things. He is a legendary hero in our country. He played a key role in liberating Argentina from Spain 200 years ago. In fact, the Argentina flag that caught your attention this evening was designed by him."

She paused again before adding, "Hmm, I think I may have your connection. In the mountains not far from Córdoba in the centre region of our country, there is a town called Villa General

Belgrano. It's a beautiful village in the hills. Do you know who were included in its early inhabitants?"

When Kiltman and Wilson had shaken their heads, Santiago had spread her hands wide and proclaimed as if it was obvious, "German sailors who fled from the scuttled Admiral Graf Spee. Many of them escaped to the mountains and settled in Villa General Belgrano."

Wilson recalled pretty Gina's history lesson the previous evening in Matricola, which she had relayed word for word to Kiltman on the way to San Siro earlier that day. It was falling into place. This was the missing link in the puzzle, that allowed them to justify the trip to South America. But more importantly, give them a chance of finding out what Skink was directing them to.

The added bonus was when the smaller of the two soldiers, who had stood to attention all evening, broke ranks and coughed self-consciously. "May I make a suggestion?"

When he was given the nod to continue, he continued, "We have the monthly Italian food and drink supplies cargo plane leaving tonight for Buenos Aires. They might be able to take Ms. Wilson and Kiltman."

This was nearly worth as much as the Villa General Belgrano titbit. Normally there were no direct flights from Milan to BA (they had learned to shorten *Buenos Aires*, in the course of the evening, and took great pleasure in sounding 'in the know' when they said *BA*). If they did not mind travelling in a clunky, wind-tunnel of a cargo plane then they had 90 minutes to get to Malpensa airport. Without further discussion, they had rushed to their feet and Wilson had necked her wine. The opportunity was too good to miss. The soldier quickly took their passport details and confirmed he would call it into the flight for them to update the manifest. They had gone from sitting around talking and drinking to suddenly being in a rush. It had reminded Kiltman of when he had lived with Fiona. He would find himself either waiting or rushing out to the car after her.

It had been impressive how speedily they had got to the front door. For all of their alacrity to be used up with hugging and kissing and *hasta la vistas*, their consulate friends barely able to let them leave the building. Standing at the front door in view of

233

the spot where Kiltman and Wilson had been *snared* earlier that evening seemed to give the Argentines fresh impetus to recount the evening's events. Punctuated with more laughter and jocularity. Kiltman was in no doubt the two Scots had become part of Holy Innocents Day folklore

They had made it to the airport with five minutes to spare courtesy of the consulate's chauffeur-driven Alfa Romeo.

Shortly after touching down in BA, they found themselves being escorted through the airport by a policeman and policewoman. They had not expected the welcome committee, but apparently it was another gift from the consulate that just kept on giving. The policewoman, petite and nimble, carried an air of importance as she manoeuvred them through the crowds in the transit area. She helped them clear immigration without waiting in the long, snaking queue of tired travellers coming from all over the world to be in BA for New Year with family and friends. They were able to cope admirably with Kiltman's one fear of flying - having to take his mask off. Their faxed letter from the Milan consulate proved sufficient to convince the immigration officials of the necessity for his anonymity - in the spirit of national interest.

She explained along the way that she was taking them to a commercial flight bound for Córdoba, which should take a little over an hour. They had already purchased the tickets on their behalf, which she handed to Wilson during their walk. As she did so, she stopped for a moment, barely hiding the hint of a smile, before asking, "We have assumed you would take a commercial flight, or would you like to fly on a plane full of smelly foodstuffs?"

It was at that moment, Kiltman and Wilson realised they probably could have manoeuvred their own way through the airport. The cheese and meats they had sat close to for many hours had permeated their clothing, providing an exotic blend of stale parmesan and ham, very crude.

They made it to the Aerolíneas Argentinas plane ten minutes before take-off. Prior to boarding, they thanked their escorts and proceeded to walk up the steps to the flight.

"Wait!" called the policeman, a handsome lad, barely beyond his teenage years. He produced from his pocket a map of central

Argentina indicating Córdoba, and just under 70 miles to its south west, a small dot representing Villa General Belgrano. "I hope this helps. It will take you about an hour and a half to get there. Adios!"

"Thank you!" Kiltman and Wilson shouted in unison and waved their farewells. They climbed the remainder of the steps, before settling into their seats and buckling up. They had not spoken to each other during the march through the airport. Wilson had a clawing sense of foreboding in her midriff, which she could not seem to shake off. Kiltman could sense it even though she tried to smile when they sat down. He felt it too. There was something in Villa General Belgrano, waiting for them, that made him anxious. The angst felt like the type he would have during a nightmare when he was falling off a building or running around naked trying to find somewhere to hide. He was beginning to realise he would not be able to wake from this one, punch the pillow and turn back to sleep. Whatever awaited them in the centre region of Argentina, he thought, as he closed his eyes before take-off, would require them to be on their A game.

As he dosed off with the change in cabin pressure, he remembered another time when a famous group of Scots had visited Córdoba, around 25 years earlier. They most certainly had not brought their A game.

We're on the March
with Ally's Army

"Hola!" an attractive red-haired girl called to them as she leaned against her yellow cab – first in a row of airport taxis. She seemed relaxed, hands resting in the front pockets of her jeans, her short-sleeved yellow blouse open a couple of buttons. Her hair was the crinkly kind that if not tied back would explode into a wild hedge of lively curls. She had tamed it with a tartan scrunchy, not too dissimilar to the black and blue in Kiltman's kilt. She was in the company of three men, the owners of the other cabs. The men were smoking casually and laughing boisterously, with no apparent care in the world to disturb the warm, sunny morning. While she was not smoking, the girl was producing much of the merriment, firing off one liners, punctuating their lively comments.

"Hello!" Wilson said as Kiltman lifted his hand to acknowledge the drivers.

"Hey," one of them called. "Come on, Scotland!" He turned to his driver colleagues, encouraging them to burst into a tuneless song:

"We arra marching with Allys Ammy
We gonna go to Argentine... "

"Okay, okay!" Kiltman remembered the song he himself had tempted fate with alongside five million other brainwashed Scots 25 years earlier. "Enough! Very cute, guys!"

Wilson was obviously confused. He would have explained it to her, but he could tell from her look that she really did not want to know.

"We remember the Scots in 1978." The man who had started the singing was clearly enjoying the trip down world cup memory lane. "They were incredible. Every night, drinking and dancing with women. Those guys knew how to party. Crazy!"

"Yes," Kiltman acknowledged reluctantly. "The Scots fans, our very own Tartan Army, are famous for a good-old knees up." He should know, he had joined them on many an occasion.

"No, Mr. Man of Kilt!" The man smiled broadly. "Not zee fans. I talk about zee players! Every night before a game, drinking and dancing! They not perform well in games, but they perform well at night!"

The group fell into a fit of laughter, enjoying their memories of the 1978 World Cup, which Argentina had won with a powerful, disciplined performance. In sharp contrast to Scotland's woes of late-night revelry, which were well-documented and hard to argue with. Scotland had gone to Argentina believing they had a strong chance of winning the World Cup, whipped up into a frenzy of Hare Krishna self-belief by a manager who had let his heart exploit his brain. Never had so much optimism turned to depression so quickly.

Where Scotland had hoped to see photos of thirty-yard goals and successive victories, they left the tournament after a hammering by Peru and an ignominious draw with Iran - before winning against the Netherlands, which had proved to be too little too late. The Scottish team and supporters had been based in Córdoba, playing two of the games there. They had to endure a barrage of reports focused on the players excesses off the field rather than on it. Scotland even had a player banned for allegedly taking performance-enhancing drugs. In an era when drug-taking was rarer than a Penny Black, it was unconscionable they would not accept the fact he was taking hay-fever medication. It had become a raw lesson in the crippling power of the media. When the tournament had ended and the fans had forgotten about the humiliations, they celebrated the wizardry of Archie Gemmill's goal against Holland. That one piece of magic made the whole shambles bearable. And that is what makes a Scotland fan, Kiltman thought.

To dampen the drivers' enthusiastic Scotland-beating, Kiltman was tempted to inform them of the origin of football in Argentina - that a man from Glasgow had created their first national football league. He chose to save that line for when he met a group bemoaning the 1986 Maradona Hand of God. He would have more fun with it then.

237

While she had been listening to the discussion with interest, the redhead was not joining in the laughter. Either it did not appeal to her sense of humour, or more likely she was not even alive in 1978. She was at least thirty years younger than the others and seemed to have a quiet intensity beyond her youthfulness.

"Do you want a ride?" she asked. She could see they were desperate to escape what seemed like the beginning of an onslaught of well-rehearsed jokes about Scottish football.

"You bet," Wilson clambered in a door the girl had already opened. Kiltman was not far behind, squeezing into the back seat alongside her.

"My name is Ana," the girl said in perfect English before strapping herself into her seat. As she drove out onto the main road, she snatched regular glances at Kiltman through the rear-view mirror, allowing him to notice her green, almost hypnotically penetrating eyes, sitting above a freckled nose. "Where are we going?"

They had been walking to the bus station to find a coach going to their destination when they had stumbled upon the taxi rank. They had not considered a cab as an option, but Wilson had obviously felt there was no contest between listening to old men talk about failed World Cup ventures or overspending Gemmill's sparse budget.

"Villa General Belgrano, please," Wilson requested.

"Cool!" Ana's joy was palpable – this was the best fare she could have hoped for. There had been many times in the past when she had waited for hours, only for a passenger to be going to a nearby suburb – easily within walking distance, were it not for an abundance of heavy bags. It would be a pleasant journey to Villa General Belgrano, nestled in the sedate, rural Calamuchita valley. "That's a nice bonus for my New Year celebrations!"

New Year, Wilson thought. The concept had nearly passed her by. It was already December 29th, she had not considered any plans for bringing in the new year. She turned to look at Kiltman as he rested his head against the seat humming Ultravox's *Vienna*, a tune he could not get out of his head since the Mitchell Library. She could not see him being much of a New Year party goer either. Just as well - at this point Cullen Skink was posthumously dictating their end of year activities.

"So, what's taking you up there then? Are you going to their New Year's party?" Ana asked.

"No," Wilson answered. "We'll be gone by then, I expect. We're em, just fans of German beer and sausage, and we've heard the Villa is the place to be." Kiltman groaned quietly at Wilson's clumsy effort.

"Seriously?" Ana asked.

"Yes, seriously," Wilson answered, her voice less sure this time.

"No, I mean, do you seriously expect me to believe that Kiltman and his acrobatic detective friend are here to drink *brunnen* beer and eat *wurst*?" Wilson and Kiltman shifted in their seats. "We do have TVs here in Argentina, you know. I've seen all the coverage of Nice and Milan. You guys are having quite an impact. You were already famous here on the news after your adventures from last winter."

Last winter, he thought? Then realised that they had just flown into the southern hemisphere's summer months. It was around 25 degrees outside - he had barely noticed the change in temperature, his mind distracted by their task at hand.

"Thanks," Wilson answered, not sure if it had been a compliment but erring on the side of caution.

"What I meant," Ana continued, flashing Kiltman a look in the mirror, "is that wherever you go, people believe there's going to be an assassination attempt or a bomb. So that means, when you get to Villa, where they also have TVs," she laughed, "they'll be petrified!"

"So, Ana," he asked, realising she had a point, "what would you recommend we do to become more incognito?"

"Ah-hah!" She winked at him, "I've already had an idea. We just need to make a slight detour en route if that's okay."

Wilson and Kiltman exchanged looks, as Kiltman shrugged. "We're in your hands, Ana!" He hoped he would not regret his trust in their green-eyed driver.

Wise Disguise

"SPLSHSHSH!" Wilson spat the brown liquid onto Kiltman's arms and legs, before she groaned, "Yeucchhhh! What in God's name is that stuff?"

"Maté," Ana said. "It's the Argentina national drink, made from maté leaves. It takes a bit of getting used to, I admit. But it's our version of tea."

"I'm sorry." Wilson was picking pieces of leaf from her teeth, directing her apology to Ana rather than Kiltman, who seemed to be the only person concerned as to whether the splattered, soggy leaves would stain his kilt. Wilson had barely noticed that she had doused him in regurgitated maté. "I usually take to different drinks in other countries, but I've honestly never tasted anything like that. I guess it's an acquired taste."

Ana laughed, "Don't worry. Most people don't like it the first time." She passed a cup and metal straw to Kiltman.

"Eh, no, thanks, Ana." He put his hands up. "When we go on international trips, Wilson is my taster - she always goes first. If she doesn't take to it then I'll give it a miss."

"Okay!" Ana shrugged. Before she took a long, noisy sip and finished its contents. "Maybe next time."

They were sitting in the back room of a store on the outskirts of Córdoba. Ana had introduced them to her Uncle Jorge. A pleasant, affable man, he owned a small warehouse providing industrial and protective clothing to workers in the factories dotted around the hills. He came into the room holding an array of orange, yellow and dark blue overalls. "Take your pick, Kiltman!"

Jorge had jumped at the opportunity to support the Scottish crime-fighting duo. Before he had disappeared into the walk-in cupboard, he had spent a few minutes entertaining them with his William Wallace impersonation. His favourite movie was Braveheart, and his Australian-Scots accent was perfect when he spoke dramatically, "Ah luv you, ah always have and ah always wull!"

Strange, Kiltman thought, how a national identity could be remembered through movie soundbites and football tournaments. This made it even more important for him, in these far-flung corners of the world, to wear the kilt well and encourage respect for the history and resilience it represented. Before he looked in the mirror at himself in a yellow helmet with a peak and flaps and a deep blue version of the boiler suit he had worn at the San Siro.

Kiltman had spent twenty minutes trying on the overalls, looking for something that would allow him space to manoeuvre, while covering his mask and costume. He knew that Wilson just wanted to get on with the drive to Villa and was becoming steadily impatient at his yearning for secrecy. If he were not so damned good at what he did, she thought, she would have left him in the warehouse. Despite her unease she was not complaining at having to spend more time with Ana and her uncle, pleasantly humble people her mother would have described as 'guileless'.

Within half an hour they were speeding towards the hills - Kiltman in his overalls with his helmet and a hefty toolbox resting on the seat beside him. Wilson wore a blonde wig Jorge's wife had been only too happy to offload. Kiltman was working hard to avoid looking at her, finding it difficult not to laugh at how much she appeared like someone trying to look like Marilyn Monroe.

"Villa's really only one street," Ana said. "About six thousand people live there. When we arrive, we need to find a quiet place to park so that you can sneak out of the car and go about your business."

Wilson affectionately rubbed their driver's shoulder. "Thanks, Ana, you've been amazing. I don't need to say this, I know, but you have to keep this very quiet, tell no-one."

"Yes, I know," Ana nodded. "When you get back to Scotland, drop me a note and let me know how you're doing. One day, you never know, I might make it over there to see you!" She passed Wilson a card with her number and address written on the back.

"You can count on it, Ana!" Wilson slipped the card into her blouse pocket. She felt a tinge of remorse that she could not spend more time with their Argentine escort. She could tell there was a lot she wanted to talk about; it felt like they had only just started the beginning of a friendship that distance would not thwart.

Kiltman was seeing a side of Wilson he had never seen before. Not just in Argentina, but in the consulate and in Bar Matricola. He loved his Maggie; he knew he always would. Yet he was only now realising the person he had fallen for was only a small part of the woman sitting beside him. There was so much more of Wilson for him to fall in love with.

It was not long before they were stepping out of the car saying *Adios* to Ana. She waved them off after a significant amount of toing and froing when Wilson pulled a batch of pesos from her pocket. She had made a point of cashing in a few hundred pounds for eventualities such as this. She was not going to take no for an answer when Ana tried to stop her paying. Yes, she would buy Ana dinner in Scotland and yes, she would let Ana stay with her when she was there, but that was no reason for her not to spend Gemmill's budget. After some cheek kissing, and hugging, Wilson tapped Kiltman on the shoulder and said, "Excuse me, Romeo! It's my turn!" He realised he also had a soft spot for their driver and reluctantly stepped aside to let Wilson embrace her.

Ana drove off, her arm extended out the window waving animatedly at an over-dressed builder and blonde lady waving back from the shadow of a quiet cul de sac. If anyone had been watching, they would have wondered how much of a tip had been given to warrant that degree of fondness.

"Okay, let's see if we can find what's *Above the abbey and brie.*" Wilson's words sounded oddly weary.

He realised her jaw was tighter than usual. In fact, the closer he studied her, the more he realised her chin was scrunched up, in an effort not to show a hint of the emotion she was feeling. He wanted to hold her at that moment. He could sense her sadness. Back in Scotland she lived a quiet life, spending any free time she could carve out of a crazily busy job with her weird boyfriend and his gorgeous son. She rarely if ever spent time with friends. Yet on this trip she had blended and clicked with so many people, it had awakened something in her that made her feel life at home was less than a life should be. Kiltman recognised he was watching a caterpillar grow into a butterfly. Any sadness, he realised, should be directed at himself, watching her become a happier, more enriched version of herself. He hoped that this newly awakened butterfly would not fly off.

Above Bec y Brie

Walking along the narrow road, they enjoyed the anonymity of a tributary to the town centre's high street. They absorbed the tranquillity, the gentle flow of pace common to hillside towns the world over. They were smack in the middle of Argentina, but it felt more like a village somewhere in Bavaria. The town was nestled in the middle of a range of hills small enough to encourage a hill-walk and large enough to give an Alpine foothill feel. The houses and shops sat under slanted rooves, lavishly designed with ornate wooden beams dotted and crisscrossed around their façade. Large, strong verandas made from dark brown wood underneath squat roofs gave a Walt Disney feel to the place, as if something magical might happen at any moment.

The smell of spicy sausage and cabbage drifting from kitchen windows reminded them that they were approaching noon. Kiltman felt his tummy rumbling, they had eaten bits and pieces of whatever was on offer for the last three days. For some reason, the lingering bitter smell of the maté had accentuated his hunger pangs, which he had been working hard to ignore.

The sun was now splitting the sky - they could feel its glare beating down on them. He was heating up in his overalls and Wilson's head was itching. She had never worn a wig and was worried if she scratched, she would move it to an unnatural angle that gave the game away.

They walked onto Avenida Roca, the town's main street, to see a shop across the road with bright yellow writing across its large window: *Bec y Brie*.

"Bingo!" Wilson said quietly, remembering her conversation with the girls in Matricola.

Behind the glass, there was as fine an array of cheeses either of them had seen before. They were lined up in rows of slices alongside large cheese blocks waiting for a sharp knife. Dotted generously across the display were various types of German sausage and meats. Higher up, sitting on shelves to the sides, there was a multitude of wines, both white and red; but mainly red, largely bottles of the Malbec grape Wilson had been enjoying in the consulate.

"Wilson, don't be tempted to go in and drink the wine, you had enough last night!"

"Funny, Kiltman," she replied. "It's more like you being tempted by the cheese and sausage based on all that grumbling your tummy's doing." She waited a moment then added. "You never know, in a *Wurst Käse* scenario we might end up spending longer in the shop than we wanted."

She did not wait for his reaction. How had she managed to crack a joke he would have given his right arm to have thought about, let alone expressed with such perfect timing. Wilson was surprising him on several levels on this trip.

Unaware of her partner's ruminations she pointed to above *Bec y Brie*, where they could see a one floor apartment with two windows overlooking Avenida Roca.

"Let's go round the back," she whispered. "But listen, we need to keep a distance between us. Individually we are a tad conspicuous in a town where we don't know anyone. A builder and a blonde stranger walking about together will be a complete giveaway. Stay twenty yards or so behind me. From this moment I am the happy go lucky tourist, and…"

"I am Bob the Builder," Kiltman finished. "Got it."

She set off walking purposefully across the street towards the alley running down the side of *Bec y Brie*. She stopped and peered in the shop window for a few seconds with an air of nonchalance, as if whiling away her lunch break before going back to her desk. After a minute of browsing, she turned to casually wander down the alley, towards the rear of the shop.

The Avenida was busier than they had expected, many of the town's six thousand taking the opportunity to do some shopping before lunch. This suited them, providing a degree of hustle and bustle camouflage. He had waited a moment before following her, choosing to take a circuitous route to the alley. He walked up the Avenida to his right and inspected the bottom of a lamppost before taking his hammer out and tapping the joint where it met the pavement. Convinced that the lamppost would not fall over, he stood up and crossed the road, before cutting left towards the alley Wilson had disappeared into. As he was about to turn down towards the back of the *Bec y Brie*, the shop door opened with a noisy creak and two policemen stepped out. They appeared particularly officious in their uniforms with medals and coloured ribbons dotted across their chests.

He dropped down onto his knee, beside a drain at the side of the pavement. He rumbled around inside his toolbox and found an oily rag, which he extracted and used to polish the metal covering. He hoped the policemen were not looking at him - their feet were in his line of vision, the polished black shoes shining in the sun. They stepped back to allow someone to walk past. A pair of black suede shoes with yellow flowers on the sides nimbly skipped past the policemen, distracting them from focusing on him. He continued to rub the drain cover, inserting the rag between its rusted iron bars. They waited at the shop door for a minute talking animatedly in Spanish before marching up the Avenida in the other direction. He stood quickly after a brief glance back at the cover shining more brightly than a manhole should ever glow. Before hustling down the side of the shop to find Wilson standing at the corner looking upwards.

There were two back windows to the apartment, approximately fifteen feet from ground level. The backyard was tidy, organised into defined sections with a parking spot, and a large bin, for each of the homes dotted along the alley.

"I've got an idea," she said. They surveyed the area, studying the windows to see if anyone was looking at them. They were about to burgle someone's house in a foreign country. No number of consulates and kilts were going to make this palatable to the local constabulary.

She took up position beside a large green bin, close to six-foot-tall, and pushed it to a position alongside a white, box van that had *AVIS* stamped along its side. He realised what she was doing and made a move to help her. Stopping himself he remembered there was something he had to do before they entered the apartment to confront whatever was waiting for them.

He turned to look towards the lush, inviting hills, slipping his hand down the front of his overalls. He quickly entered the code 1402 to open his sporran before popping the flask. The deep chug of Hair o' the Dog stirred an immediate warmth and strength in his veins. It had reacted faster than normal, another indication, as if he needed one, that he needed to eat. He slipped it back before turning to face Wilson. She was standing, leaning against the bin, arms folded.

"Really?"

When he did not answer and just spread his hands to his sides, she cocked her head and continued, "Don't you dare give me a hard time about my Malbec consumption. I've seen you having your wee snifties on this trip. Just as well I don't drink whisky, otherwise I'd be tapping into your secret supply."

She shook her head and turned back to the bin, "Well, you going to help me, 'Flaskman'?"

"Might as well," he sighed. "But I thought it was your turn to take the rubbish out this week." He ran over, settled in beside her and helped push the bin over to the van.

"Okay, Kiltman, plan is you get up on top, reach down, pull me up and then we do the same with the van. And then we can climb in the window. Simple?"

It made sense for him to go up first. With all the best intentions in the world, she would not be able to help him up. The challenge they faced, and they were realising this at the same time, was how to get him up to the top of the bin. He had an idea, but he was reticent to suggest it.

"I know," she acknowledged, "how do we get you up there?" She waited a moment before saying, "Nothing else for it. On you go, get on board."

She bent down into a 90-degree angle and waved her hand to invite him to step up onto her slim back. She placed her hands on her knees, quietly grimacing as she awaited impact. He searched around the carpark and found a sheet of cardboard that had seen better days. Placing it on her lower back, he lifted his foot up onto it. He wrapped his fingers round a bar on the side of the bin to take the weight off his legs, before lifting himself up on her back. While it helped to some degree, her grunt as he climbed up with his other leg told him that she would not be able to hold him for long. He quickly threw his arms over the top of the bin lid and scrambled up as gracefully as an elephant on a mudslide.

"You okay, Wilson?" he called down. She was still bent over rubbing her back with both hands. She picked up the cardboard and flipped it up to him.

"Yes, I'm okay," she answered, quite obviously far from okay. He bent down, extending his hand towards her. Straightening up to her full 5 foot 2, she reached up and grabbed his hand with both of hers. He yanked her up onto the lid so quickly that she whacked her stomach off the side of the bin. "Ooof!" she groaned as she winced with the pain of a new blow that would result in another layer of bruising.

They took a moment on top of the bin before they repeated the same procedure to climb the van. This time seemed to go much more smoothly. As they caught their breath under the window, Kiltman whispered, "Imagine we had to do that, and I wasn't wearing overalls? Could have been a wee bit embarrassing."

"Stomach-churning, more like," she answered before leaning in closer to whisper. "Have you used your super-duper hearing to see if anyone's home?"

"Actually, I have. Nobody's inside. Also, no alarm system. I guess when you live in the back of beyond, you can afford to feel safe." He hoped these were not famous last words.

They studied the window directly in front of them and saw that it had an electronic lock. He sensed it was not particularly complicated before he employed the same technique he had used in Vienna to short the circuit. They heard the click of the mechanism spring open before they gently prised the window.

"Age before beauty," he said as he crawled in through the window. His mother had drilled into him that he should always let women go first. She had never added 'except when there's a threat of imminent danger' - he knew she would cut him some slack on this occasion.

He had already scanned the apartment before entering and had a sense of the layout. They had entered through one of its two bedrooms. There was also a decent sized lounge, a roomy kitchen and a bathroom. It took them ten minutes of walking around inspecting the rooms, opening drawers and looking under beds to complete their survey, finding nothing untoward.

In terms of inhabitants, they were sure the apartment was more a pied-à-terre than a lived-in home. The drawers had no clothes, the bathroom absent of soaps and brushes and the lounge bereft of any form of entertainment other than a small television.

The kitchen had the usual mishmash of utensils, cutlery, and crockery but otherwise it felt as barren as a student flat. There was a mirror in the bathroom and one in the bedroom. In the lounge, a striking, full-sized copy of a Gustav Klimt painting adorned the wall facing the TV, dominating the room. It was what Kiltman, with his limited appreciation of art, would have called a *typical* Klimt painting. It portrayed a woman's head practically submerged in an overpowering blanket of yellow interspersed with blue peacock feathers. She was being kissed on the cheek by a man, whose half of the quilt was identified by square patterns. He was sure art lovers would spend time trying to understand the hidden meaning between the squares and circles, but it was just a reminder for him that art was not his thing. The only thing he found interesting about the artwork was that the breadth of the painting seemed shorter than the height. Yet he knew it was a perfect square, six foot by six. A good example, he thought, of how things were not always as they appeared.

The painting had been wall-mounted, surrounded by a metal frame. Wilson pointed at its bottom corner where written in small, tidy lettering were the words *The Belvedere Art Gallery, Vienna.* For an apartment with only one piece of art, they had certainly made the most of it.

While they accepted the Vienna reference was a decent indication they were in the correct apartment, they were not able to see anything remotely connected to Marc-Aurel Strasse or to a potential target. There was no indication as to what Skink was pointing them to. As wild goose chases went, they were hoping this would not become one of the most expensive to be funded by Gemmill's tightly controlled purse strings. They stepped out into a small hall barely bigger than a yard in either direction. Kiltman lifted his head up and pointed to the ceiling, at a wooden panel indicating access to the attic.

"I can't see any ladders around to get up there." Wilson walked around the apartment popping her head into each room in case she had missed them.

"No, there are no ladders." Kiltman was running his hands along the wall, searching for an electronic current leading towards the ceiling. He continued to move his fingers until they took him back into the lounge. He had already guessed where it would lead but followed it all the same until his fingertips moved over the Klimt painting. She had followed him knowing not to interrupt his concentration.

He grabbed a nearby chair and hefted himself up onto it to inspect the painting in more detail. He focused on where the man with curly hair planted a smacker on the woman's cheek. He rubbed his hand gently over the surface of *The Kiss*. He eventually realised that under the canvas there was some sort of a control box with a keypad, positioned under the face of the sleeping woman, blissfully unaware of *The Kiss*.

He ran his fingers over her face, detecting four buttons underneath, one behind each eye, one under the nose and the other the mouth. He left his hand on her face for a minute, with Wilson behind him considering this a particularly bizarre way to appreciate a painting. If he had been in the Belvedere Gallery in Vienna, he would have been thrown out on his ear. After a moment, he pressed her right eye twice, then her nose, followed by her mouth and then three times on her left eye. Nothing happened. Then he remembered.

"Wilson, do you have the key from the Schottenkirche?"

They had both forgotten the key in their haste to enter the apartment. She dug deep into her pocket and pulled it out. Before handing it up to him, she turned it in her fingers as if it would provide a clue as to the lock it would fit. She carefully placed it in the palm of his extended hand.

She was standing back from the painting, allowing her a better view of the intricacies of a piece of art she did not consider engaging. Garish and tacky were words that came to mind, but then she recognised she was far from an art afficionado. She scanned from top to bottom trying to see if there was something unusual, other than the painting itself. It took a few minutes but eventually she noticed a small indentation beside the woman's pinkie. "Kiltman, the pinkie!"

He had been so close to the face he missed the advantage of distance. Looking up he saw a thin hole running alongside the small finger, where her hand was flopped around her lover's neck. Kiltman slipped the key inside and turned it clockwise. He waited a moment before they heard the mechanical whirr from the hall, a gentle high-pitched whine similar to a soft-top car roof opening. He jumped down from the chair and followed her out into the small space to see the ceiling panel had opened and a set of steps were dropping slowly towards them.

"How on earth did you know the code that went with the key?" she asked, immediately regretting it, expecting him to provide a corny answer about knowing how to press a woman's buttons.

"That's why we're a team, Wilson. I guessed the pin and you had the key." He waited for a moment, genuinely believing this time she would laugh. Her bemused expression encouraged him to explain. "Pin and key. Don't you get it? *Pinkie!*"

"Oh God," she rubbed her head wearily. "Your humour just gets more infantile by the day, by the minute even."

In an effort to recover, he said, "Okay, I get it. What if instead I had declared something more magnanimous like, *great things are done by a series of small things brought together?*"

"Yes, that would have been more appropriate," she answered, now wishing she had never asked.

"Actually, it was Van Gogh who said that, not me." He placed his foot on the ladder and boomed, "Up, up and away!" feeling pleased with himself.

She watched him climb up ahead of her, wondering if Kiltman in the real world had ever had a wife or partner. Heaven help whoever ended up with him, she thought, he could not be an easy man to live with.

Villa General Belgrano

"Hello, yes, it's me. I'm watching them now."

"Where are they?"

"They've just climbed up into the apartment. They are a farcical couple. I can't believe we're even considering them as a serious threat to our plans."

"What do you mean?"

"He's walking around pretending to be a builder, in overalls that are far too big for him, and she's wearing a peroxide blonde wig, pretending to be God knows what."

"Look, don't underestimate them, they're not as amateur as they look. Once they're inside the attic, and trust me, Kiltman will figure out how to gain access, take them down. I want them out of our lives for good. We have invested too much time, money, and energy in our mission. Is that clear?"

"Abundantly," the man answered before closing his phone and crossing Avenida Roca.

Mask placed the phone on the table beside his empty whisky glass. During the conversation he had not let his gaze drift from the beautiful day that had descended on the Trossachs and Loch Achray. He sighed wishing he could continue to feast in the glory of this spectacularly glorious landscape. One of the many things he loved about Scotland was how every scenic snapshot was like the perfect picture postcard. There were no massive Alps to dominate a single view, or a lolling lake that seemed to never end. Scotland's diminutive proportions meant breath-taking views could fit easily in a 6 by 4-inch frame - mountains, lochs and glens perfectly visible across the terrain. He could have stood appreciating the view for longer, reminding him of the home he had not seen for many years.

"Enough," Mask said to himself, picking up his passport. "I have a plane to catch."

The Secret Attic

Kiltman was surprised at how much space there was. From outside they had barely noticed the attic was a feature, most likely because they had been focused on the apartment itself rather than the angular roof. They had enough room to stand and walk around the central area, although they had to bend at the sides to avoid clashing with the sloping walls.

Wilson was already stepping methodically around the space, not touching anything, sizing up where to start first. He had seen that she meant business when she popped her head up through the entrance. She had already taken her wig off and donned her blue gloves, ready for action. It inspired him to unzip his overalls and take off his helmet, the heat in the attic quite overpowering, the tiles absorbing the noon day sun's glare.

Where the walls in their last burglary in Vienna had been sparse, the attic was full of pictures and drawings, lacking any logical connection. It was as if someone had found a software to download all their thoughts onto pictures before placing them in no particular structure on the wall. To the left of the hatch, the vast majority of the images were black and white, showing scenes from a period that appeared to be at least a few decades earlier. If there were less than a hundred, Wilson would have been surprised. At a time when photographs were only starting to become more commonplace, she would have expected the subjects to be austere and sombre in the face of the camera. However many of these black and whites captured happy moments. They were mostly of children, many in uniform at school, while a large number were in what appeared to be Calamuchita Valley, sitting on carts, haybales, tractors and farm fences. They were full of smiles and tomfoolery, kids jostling for pole position.

To the right of the black and whites, there were rows of colour photos depicting a myriad of anonymous streets and buildings from a host of aerial vantage points. They gave a bleak view of a city they could not at first decipher. Chunky office blocks and apartment complexes separated by the occasional splash of green, with tiny pixeled dots showing cars streaming down long, straight avenues. Kiltman turned up his vision a few notches and was able to identify some of the cars as New York cabs. He could not identify exactly where in the city it was, but he would store the photos in his memory for later processing. He began to recognise that feeling when something was niggling him. Just gnawing at the recesses of his subconscious. It would surface eventually but for the time being he had to be patient and let it meander its way to the front of his mind.

They stepped slowly along the floorboards looking at each of the snapshots trying to find a clue of something or someone. It surprised him that the floor did not creak, not even a slight noise. Back at home in Uisge Beatha - a house not much more than ten years old - he could have used his attic as a percussion instrument, knowing exactly which boards to stand on to get a different tonal creak. He was impressed by the craftmanship of whoever had built the Villa attic. This was not the work of a builder who tried to copy a Bavarian style, this was done by someone who had a pedigree in such construction, an artisan who had grown up in southern German and had spent many years learning his trade.

"Look, Kiltman, over here." Wilson was less concerned about the absence of creaks and more focused on the jumble of wires and boxes lying on top of a table in the middle of the room. She had opened a drawer and had begun to extract large sheets of paper placing them on the table.

He knew before he got there what she was looking at. He took the pages from her and spread them out onto the floor. They studied them for a few minutes, trying to decipher page after page of plans and diagrams. From what they could tell they were looking at a series of interconnected rooms and pipes spread over several floors. He was conscious of her looking over his shoulder, enjoying the closeness of her breath on his neck. Reluctantly he stood and walked back to the table. He carefully lifted a mess of wires and an obscure, nondescript metal box from the table. He ran his fingers along each of them carefully.

"Well, Kiltman," she whispered. "What is it?"

He took a deep breath before he started.

"Wilson, if you studied these drawings for a while, you would be able to make a bomb. But not just any bomb. The wiring and configuration of the device that this relates to would leave a crater half the size of San Siro." Until a day earlier, this was not a metaphor he would ever have expected to use with her.

"What type of explosive would it use?" she asked.

"The design is what they call a 'layer cake'. He pointed at the middle of the drawing on the floor, at a series of square blocks sitting one on top of the other, similar to a step pyramid. "Each of these blocks is an increasingly potent explosive, interconnected with the others in an organism that magnifies its potency to a level far beyond their individual capability. It's like a new virus unleashed on a community. The impact it has extrapolates exponentially to create an effect far beyond the sum of the single cases. By my reckoning this particular bomb is designed to have ten layers - all connected in an intricate matrix - magnifying its explosive power a hundredfold. The explosive content itself will be relatively small, its impact coming from the layering, not its size. This makes it easier to conceal, dressed up as individual books or inconspicuous boxes, to be later plugged together like Lego pieces."

She did not respond immediately. After a moment, she said, "No shortage of dramatic overkill when you're around, Kiltman." She waited a moment lost in thought. "But I get it, don't worry. The question is, where's it going to happen and when?"

Nothing they had seen other than the pictures of New York gave a clue as to the location. He thought for a moment and walked across to the wall. Wilson watched as he ran his hand across the pictures touching them gently, sometimes pausing longer on some for no apparent reason. He halted for a second longer on a photo of an inconspicuous high rise. Taking it in his hand he prised it from the wall where it had been attached by a safety pin. Underneath it, there was a small tack, embedded so deeply it was impossible to remove with a fingernail. He pushed his thumb against it with a degree of force, feeling it give way slightly. As he felt the release of pressure, they heard a noise from the other wall. Where there had been scores of photos, the panels were inverting, going through a 180-degree rotation. The next version of the wall taking shape in front of their eyes was of a building and its foundations. The top half showed the building by floor, while the lower half showed a dissected cut, from top floor to the basement.

Above ground the top half of the enlarged photo depicted a flat-fronted façade underneath a pyramid shape. The roof had been layered in a pagoda style decreasing in size until it reached a pinnacle in the centre. The underground section had been painstakingly drawn in miniscule detail to show basements and corridors with an array of piping and wiring sketched in a darker colour than the rest. The top half of the photo had not been touched or scribbled on, while the foundations were full of added lines and pen marks, with smudges and rubbings out. All of the attention seemed to be focused below ground in bringing to life the network of infrastructure that made this building operate; electrics, plumbing and ventilation.

There were aerial shots too of the building taken from a helicopter or plane close enough to the ground to allow a clear view of its shape. It was perfectly hexagonal with one side facing out onto water, the other sides dotted with trees or facing nondescript office buildings.

"I know this building." She was clearly pleased at her power of recall. "It's in lower Manhattan, not too far from where the World Trade Centre used to be." She stopped and took a deep breath, the horror of 9/11 still fresh in her mind. "It's the Museum of Jewish Heritage. My brother visited there a few years back when it was opened. He showed me some photos at the time."

She chose not to talk about how difficult that afternoon had been. Tas had been off grid for several years, at least from the point of view of people contacting him. He would pop up every so often and say hello or share an experience, but otherwise nobody knew how to reach him. His visit to New York and to the museum had been one of those moments where he had made a point of sharing his photos and talking animatedly about the visit - he had met many like-minded people.

She remembered his words. "Listen, Maggie, New York is amazing. Way beyond anything you might imagine it's like. In fact, it's actually a living caricature of a city; so unnaturally regulated, it's like a pressure cooker."

255

She had thought about those comments and her brother on several occasions since then, not least because they were not the typical things someone said when they visited a city. Most people talked about the museums, the night life, the food, or the vibe. It was unusual for someone to try and psychoanalyse the place. That was her brother, she mused.

"Well done, Wilson. I've never been there but I remember hearing about its opening. It was quite an eventful day in New York, with a large crowd at the initiation ceremony. Apparently it was built to remember those who had perished in the Holocaust, and also to celebrate the Jewish way of life - the many incredible gifts they have brought to the world."

"Well," she said, "there's someone out there who doesn't share our appreciation of this museum and what it represents."

He nodded. "Now we've identified the target, we need to figure out when this is expected to happen. I just hope we're not too late already."

They spent the next half hour lifting and moving objects to see if there were any other secret panels or information to help them put the picture together even further. The niggle he had felt earlier when looking at the photos had not gone away. He could not identify what it was, but before the wall had morphed into the picture of the museum, something had nipped his subconscious. Just like when a mosquito inserts its proboscis into flesh inflicting that initial twinge. It is only later when you understand the consequences of the bite, when its saliva inflames the skin and it begins to itch. He was hoping that his subliminal mozzy bite would start to prickle soon and help him realise what he was missing.

"Okay, we need to go." She turned towards the steps.

"Yes, let's try and leave the place as we found it," he replied before folding the drawing and placing it in the drawer. Next, he pressed his thumb against the tack to reverse the panel back into place. Before he left he took a moment to scan the pictures to see if he could identify what had been bothering him. There were too many photos and it was too far away, too deep in the recesses of his mind. It may have been nothing, he had to remind himself as he donned the overalls and helmet.

They climbed down the ladders, which felt much steeper on the way down. Wilson walked towards the bedroom where they had climbed through the window.

"Just a sec," he called, before running into the lounge to press a few facial features on the Klimt painting and use the pinkie key one more time. He then checked the ladders had disappeared back into the attic and the panel had closed before following her.

"Wilson?" he called when he entered the bedroom with the open window. She had gone already, which he thought strange since in his mind he would have had to lower her down onto the box van's roof. Maybe she had enough spring in her step to drop down on her own, he supposed. He walked to the window to see the box van driving into the distance. He watched it turn a corner at speed and disappear.

He lent out the window a tad further to check if she was obscured from view below the window, hoping to see her there putting her blonde wig back in place. The quick shuffle of steps behind him alerted him to what was coming. The two hands that rammed against his back had only one thing in mind, to push him into a fall he most probably would never recover from. From the height of the first-floor window, a landing onto concrete would be at a minimum life-changing, but most likely fatal. He had no chance of avoiding the fall at that stage. He had to concentrate on where to land. As he fell through the window, he saw to his right that the green bin was still there. It was not directly below but over to the side about a yard or so. Someone had opened the lid, most likely to throw in leftover lunch rather than have it rotting in the heat inside the house. With an almighty effort he remembered the diving event at the 2000 Olympics and threw all his energy into twisting his body in a combination of a half-pike, a tuck then a somersault. The combination of jerks and twists gave him enough lateral momentum to land squarely in the middle of the bin.

He felt the explosion of air evacuate his lungs just as the whiff of cabbage and sausage invaded his nostrils. Thankfully, there were enough bags of rubbish and food waste inside to absorb some of the shock of his fall. The impact of his bulk crashing into the bin propelled it onto its side, Kiltman and the contents spilling out across the concrete. He jumped to his feet, ignoring the food and rubbish stuck to his clothing. He looked up at the window as he pulled off the stained overalls, to see that it had been closed already. Whoever had pushed him would not be far away. That was not his main concern as he swivelled on his heels to examine all around him, out to the hills and across the carpark. There was no clue as to where Wilson had been taken. She had been kidnapped. He had that same sinking feeling as half a year earlier when Skink had taken her to his lair.

Scottish Burglars

"Look, I'm not a burglar!" Kiltman was unable to quell his rising concern. "I'm investigating an international terrorist and his cell is up there. We were trying to find a clue to a potential terror threat."

He pointed up towards the apartment. With each word of his explanation, he felt his credibility crumbling. The two policemen he had avoided outside *Bec y Brie* were standing a yard away from him, studying this kilted man with a mask and cape. They had not taken their pistols from their holsters, but he was sure they were only one flinch away from doing so. Several people had gathered behind them, a mixture of men and women who had been at home a few minutes earlier. He was sure they had rushed out when they heard the clatter of the bin crashing on the concrete. It was still there on its side, its contents spilled on the ground, a couple of stray dogs sniffing around dollops of food, not believing their luck.

"Mr. Kiltman, we know who you are," one of the policemen said. He had his hat under an arm, notebook, and pencil in his hands, making him look much younger than the 22 years Kiltman estimated him at. "Your presence here is a concern in itself. We need to know what you were doing inside that apartment."

"I've told you already. The fact is I was pushed out of the window and was lucky the bin broke my fall. But what's worrying me is that my partner has been kidnapped. The best use of your time now would be spent helping me find her." He was not trying to hide his growing worry, anxiety knitted into each of his words.

The voices of the group behind the policemen were getting louder, becoming more agitated. He did not expect they understood much of the conversation in English – their attention focused on a costumed stranger breaking into an apartment in their block. Their ire was becoming all too evident in their gesticulations and shouts. Kiltman could not blame them – this reaction would be the same in any country.

259

"Sir?" said the other policeman, around the same age as the first, but with a gravitas that gave Kiltman some confidence they could make progress. He had been on his phone for the first few minutes of their on-street interview. Every second was vital to finding Wilson, who had been out of his sight for around ten minutes now. "I've just called our HQ in Córdoba; they have asked us to take you there. Apparently, someone called Gemmill has been in touch with them to let them know you are, what can we say, bona fide?"

Gemmill was proving to be quite the ally throughout this trip, it was as if he was one step ahead of them at every juncture. He would have called the Córdoba police just in case he and Wilson ended up in a situation just like this one. He wondered if he should see this as foresight or foreboding?

"Normally, I would jump at that," Kiltman answered. "but right now, we need to find Wilson, my partner."

As the policemen turned to look at each other, beginning to feel out of their depth, a large man barged aggressively between them. Before Kiltman could react, a punch landed squarely in his midriff. While he saw it coming, he was not quick enough to avoid the blow. It caught him in the solar plexus knocking the wind out of lungs that had recently just filled up after his fall. He dropped to his knees, bent over double, gasping for breath, holding his stomach with one hand, the other resting on the ground stopping him from falling over.

The policemen had grabbed the man and held him in a vice like grip, each of them holding an arm, shouting at him to calm down. It was clear that they knew who he was. Not surprising in such a small community, Kiltman mused. He was big and strong, with a face like thunder. He seemed like he could have shaken off the policemen with a shrug of his shoulders, although seemed to be more concerned about pointing with his head towards the apartment.

Kiltman forced himself to his feet oblivious to the queasy pain of the gut punch. "Hey, what's he saying about the apartment?"

The policeman with the notebook translated. "He is angry because the apartment you broke into belongs to his friend. Well, actually his friend died a few years ago, it had never been sold."

"Really?" Kiltman asked. "How did he die?

The policeman spoke to the man in Spanish before replying, "He was in a car accident. It seems it happened because he was quite elderly and missed the bend in one of the roads."

"Did he have any children?" His mind was racing.

Again, a discussion between the man and the policeman.

"Yes," the policeman confirmed. "He had a son, but he ran away from home when he was a teenager. He was never heard of again."

"What were the father and son's names?" Kiltman asked.

Some more discussion then the policeman said, "Father was Juergen Mann and the son was Alois."

He had heard enough, he had to quickly change tack. "Right, officer, get your car and take me to Córdoba. But first we have to take a detour." The officer was nodding, writing something in his notebook. "QUICKLY!" shouted Kiltman.

Shouting at a police officer in the UK would not get you very far, he thought, but somehow it sprung the catch on the Villa policemen. They turned and ran to their car which had been parked on Avenida Boca.

Once in the vehicle, Kiltman directed them back towards the road where he had seen the Avis box van disappearing into the distance. Sitting in the back seat, he was able to sneak his flask from his pocket and take a healthy sip without the officers in the front noticing. He was going to need every ounce of his sensory processing skills to figure out where Wilson had been taken.

He quickly rolled the window down and revved his olfactory receptors to max. While humans have only around two percent of the nose power of dogs with their 200 million plus receptors, Kiltman had previously tested his smell when it was fully charged by Hair o' the Dog. He was pleased to see that it was ten times more powerful than that of the average dog, which he could affirm with empirical evidence. Sweeneys had a pub dog, a beautiful long-haired Collie called Sam, who was owned by no-one but cared for by everyone. She had been a stray and happened to chance upon the pub one evening in the dead of winter when the snow was several inches deep outside. Maureen had seen an emaciated Sam shivering and snivelling outside the pub doors and brought him in for the night, giving him food and water. From that moment, he had become part of the Sweeneys

261

family. Maureen created a rota for walking him, which was attached to the wall beside the dart board. While it was full of holes due to errant darts players drinking and darting, it was the one schedule everybody adhered to. Kenny had put his name on it a few years earlier when he was trying to understand what his senses were capable of. He regularly took Sam up into the Old Kilpatrick hills behind his house testing his smell against the dog's, until he realised his smell was not just superhuman, but was superdog.

He took a deep sniff as they passed along the road in the midst of green fields and plush trees. Every olfactory receptor he possessed was employed in their search for Wilson. He gazed out over the flat grasslands of Calamuchita Valley, looking for potential hideaways. His head was fully extended through the car window like a dog on holiday with the family. He did not want to think about what the policemen or people in passing cars thought of this strange masked man sniffing his way across the countryside.

He could sense Wilson's scent ever so slightly as they drove along the road towards Córdoba. Whoever had kidnapped her had so far stayed on the main road - they were heading towards the city, and by the fading of her smell, they were travelling fast. Kiltman had been working hard to exclude the many flowery perfumes interrupting his receptors. The rich nectar scent of the red-leaved, cockspur coral tree seemed to be everywhere. At any other time, he would have breathed deeply of Argentina's national tree and flower but right now it was fast becoming an encumbrance, interfering with Wilson's natural odour.

Twenty miles along the road, her scent disappeared. It was there one second and gone the next. It had just disappeared, as if her body's apocrine glands had stopped producing the fluid his receptors had come to know and cherish. Her lovely, sweet smell had gone.

Lost the Scent

The car had pulled up to stop on the verge of an embankment, alongside a field busy with cows meandering towards a trough at the far end. The sleepy feel of the rural setting belied the tensions building up in Kiltman. How could her scent just disappear, he thought frantically? For the last five minutes he had been running up and down the road sniffing at the gravel one minute, the foliage the next. He was desperate to find a trace of the one person that would make him whole. The policemen were walking up and down the road looking for signs of anything that would indicate where she had gone.

Finding no trace of her on the road, he climbed into the field to his right and started to run across the soft, lush grass towards the increasingly steep gradient sloping up into the surrounding hills. They had been on the road for forty minutes, nearly an hour since she had disappeared. He knew that her kidnappers had no reason to keep her alive. He was quite sure their plan was to drive as far from Villa as possible to find a quiet spot, then dispose of her. He stopped in the middle of the field, raised his hands in the air, and shouted, "Wilson! Maggie! Wilson! Maggie!" He shouted for ten minutes, running towards the hills continually screaming and shouting - hoping upon hope that she was somewhere nearby listening, and would take courage from his presence.

He sat down on a tree stump and put his head in his hands, tears spilling inside his mask. He had not given up; he would never lose hope in finding her. The thought was not something he would allow himself to entertain. He was concentrating on the smells around him, trying to block out the sweet, tangy cow manure, the fresh grass interspersed with fragrant flowers and billowing trees. He looked up towards the hill above him to see a radio mast towering above the summit, the only sign of human existence in such an ostensibly quiet, practically remote, region in Argentina.

He caught a slight whiff then it was gone. It was definitely her. He took a deep breath sucking hard through his nose. It was undeniable. She was somewhere close by. Somehow the huge antenna dominating the landscape had interfered with his sense of smell, limiting the sensitivity of his olfactory receptors. He realised for the first time how his powerful ability to smell operated. It was not only the olfactory receptors in his nose doing the work, but rather he was able to smell by connecting to surges of scent transmitted through the air in a similar way to how sound moves in waves.

He focused on tapping into this realisation forcing his senses to reach out for the waves pulsating subtly through the air towards him. He could sense the radio waves drifting back and forth smashing the inside of his skull like huge, wayward Atlantic breakers crashing down on the beach. The massive buzz of radio activity he was opening his mind to was draining him. But he had to do it. He had a glimmer of her scent and could not afford to let go.

Below him along the perimeter of the field, there was a rough path leading up towards the top of the hill, one of those country lanes that reminded him of his holidays in Ireland as a child - rough stones and grit on either side of a green tuft of grass running through the middle. The path stretched as far as the antenna, and no doubt beyond the hill on the other side.

Without warning, a thunderous noise invaded his ears, interrupting the silence of the sleepy afternoon. He had to put his hands up to block it out. He had become so used to the quiet he had increased his hearing capacity to max, not expecting to pick up anything louder than a cow moo or a bird squawk. Even that seemed an impossibility, the cows lazing in the afternoon sun and the birds sheltering from its powerful rays. He turned to stare at the main road and saw a cloud of dust billowing along the path towards him. In its centre, there was a car, a flash of yellow. A taxi. He saw Ana at the wheel, and even from where he was sitting and despite the cloud of dust, he could see the anger and determination in her freckly features. She was on a mission.

Trapped

Her hands had been trussed so tightly behind her back she had lost all sensation in her fingertips. A plastic cord was stretched around her wrists before reaching down to her ankles, which seemed to have been crushed together with the tightness of more plastic ties cutting into her flesh. She had given up trying to shout for help, her mouth scrunched underneath an industrial grey tape that tasted like *Bec y Brie*'s foulest gorgonzola.

She was annoyed at herself for letting her guard down in the apartment at Villa. She had leaned out the window to assess the scale of jump needed to land on top of the box van. As she studied the distance, she had let herself become distracted by the top of the van. The roof was opening up like a concertina. She had not noticed that aspect of the Avis van when they had climbed onto it earlier. In hindsight she should have called to Kiltman immediately to give him a warning that something was not right.

The hands that connected with her buttocks and pushed her out the window felt small in size. They were either a child's or a small woman's. Considering the strength of the shove, she decided they belonged to an adult female. Her fall from the window through the van's open roof onto its splintered, wooden floor had seemed to happen in slow motion, her mind understanding what was happening before the impact of the fall knocked her out. She was not sure how long she had been unconscious, but by the time she had regained consciousness her limbs had already been tied. She expected the driver had rushed from the scene and parked for a moment in a safe place to render her immobile before continuing the journey.

She could feel the van moving quickly careering around corners, jerking her from side to side. The accumulation of bruises strewn across her body were becoming kaleidoscopic. The impact of the van's bumping and jerking was most likely joining them up into one mass of blue and black. Not too dissimilar in shade to Kiltman's kilt, she thought, as she struggled to loosen her wrists.

Kiltman would not be able to get her out of this trap, she had to do it on her own. He had no way of tracking her or even had a vehicle to follow them in. She was on her own, but rather than being panicked by the thought, she moved into survival mode. On this venture she had been feeling more empowered with every event that occurred, whether dangerous or sociable. She was becoming a whole person again and it felt good. The adrenaline rushing through her body provided the welcome jolt of motivation she needed to deal with what lay ahead.

On one of her tumbles when the van took a corner too quickly, she noticed on the wall a jagged piece of metal jutting out from the woodwork. It had most likely been disturbed from the van's framed structure during the transportation of an object large enough to distort the metal joints. The jagged edge was barely noticeable, and unless one was desperate to find a way out of a life-threatening situation, it would have remained unnoticed. Wilson rolled over towards it, fighting against the buffeting of the van, eventually landing in the position she wanted underneath the metal's edge. From her horizontal position on the floor, she managed to pull her legs underneath to leverage herself up into an awkward crouch. She was close enough to the wall of the van to fall back onto it and let it absorb her weight. Navigating her wrists until they were touching the sharp corners of the metal, she took a deep breath and began a steady sawing motion. It took five or six goes of running the plastic along the metal's edge until it sprung open releasing her wrists.

"Hmmmmm," she murmured under the tape, as the blood rushed into her fingers bringing with it a burst of pins and needles, which felt painfully refreshing.

She quickly rubbed her wrists, before pulling the tape from her mouth, providing more exfoliation than a month's worth of Immac. Dropping down onto her back she lifted her legs up onto the metal edge, employing the same sawing motion she had performed on her wrists. It took only a few seconds for the plastic ties to break open. Above the piece of metal, she noticed a small hole barely half an inch wide, which allowed her to peak through and study the passing landscape. The van was speeding through a countryside lush with meadows and bordered by hills, without a marker in sight to pinpoint her location.

She crouched down into the corner of the van and searched for her police phone. It had gone. Her pockets had been emptied of her passport, credit cards and money. She cursed quietly. She prided herself on not using bad language, but on this occasion she felt she could cut herself some slack. Stuck in the back of a van in the middle of a foreign country, in a different continent, with a maniac driving her to God knows where to kill her - she felt she could allow herself the odd cuss word. Then she remembered.

Lifting her foot, she pulled off her heeled shoe, three-inches high. Just enough heel to give her a bit more height, but not too lofty to result in her breaking an ankle in a run. She levered the sole of the shoe open to see the phone that Kenny and Roddy had given her as a Christmas present. Roddy had mentioned to her many times that if she had a phone on the day Skink had taken her to his lair, then she could have let everyone know where she was. She did not have the heart to tell him that she had been paralysed from the neck down and not able to scratch her nose, let alone use a phone. Nevertheless, she had taken his advice and made a special place for it in her shoe.

She pressed the ON button to see that there was 3% battery remaining. It had not been charged since she had opened it on Christmas morning. The bars on its display indicated that it was picking up a signal, giving her one last chance. She could not call Kiltman to tell him what was going on, for the simple reason he had never let her know his number. Not very helpful or even perceptive considering the types of situations they seemed to get themselves into. She could call Kenny but what good would that do? In another country thousands of miles away with no way of helping her, it would feel more like a *goodbye I loved you call* than an SOS. She realised there was barely enough battery to make one call, she had to dial wisely.

In their emptying of her pockets, she was relieved to see they had not checked the blouse above her right breast, where she had placed Ana's card. It was a shot in the dark, but she did not have any other option. She plugged the number in looking up every so often to squint through the tiny hole. Just as Ana's number began to ring, the van turned a corner to bring a large radio antenna into view at the top of a hill about a mile off the road. It seemed significant enough for it to be noticeable from a distance. The van turned sharply throwing her onto the floor, knocking the phone from her hand. She crawled over towards it trying not to make a sound. She picked it up.

"Hola! Hola!" she heard Ana's pleasant voice crackling through the phone.

"Ana, it's Wilson," she whispered.

"Hey, I didn't expect to hear from you so…"

"I've been kidnapped. I'm in a white Avis van. They're taking me towards a large antenna about half an hour from Villa General Belgrano. Get me help, please!"

The phone went dead. The battery display read 0% in the top corner of the screen.

The van pulled up to a hard stop. She heard the engine being turned off and the handbrake engaged. Judging by the angle of the floor it had been parked on a gradient, with the nose of the van pointing upwards. Heavy footsteps walking purposefully on gravel permeated the thunderous silence she felt around her. The steps moved from the driver's door towards the back. She realised she only had one chance to turn the tables. She grabbed the masking tape and reapplied it to her mouth then thrust the remnants of the plastic ties in her pockets. Dropping down onto her knees in the middle of the floor, she tucked her hands and legs neatly behind her out of view.

A key was placed slowly into the lock and turned quietly. The doors opened allowing a burst of sunlight into the back of the van temporarily blinding her. She nearly threw her hands up to block the light, which would have gone down as one of the greatest mistakes made by anyone in a mortally dangerous situation.

A slim man stood outside the door facing her. His face was nondescript, not a blemish or remarkable feature she could have pointed to in an identikit. The absence of personality made him ominously more frightening than any scar or eye-patch would have done. A billiard ball bald head and piercing blue eyes rendered him somehow mechanical, as if pre-programmed for evil acts. What was worrying her more than his facial blandness was the large pistol he was pointing at her.

"Shuffle over here towards me. Be careful and do not try anything stupid. When you get to the edge of the van lie down on your side. I will help you onto the ground." He spoke in what she had learned would be considered a Teutonic accent, more than a hint of German intonation.

A few yards behind him, she could see a deep hole recently created in the ground, with a fresh, damp mound of earth on either side. She had no doubts what that was for, and that it would have been dug even before they had entered the apartment. She found it even more disconcerting to know that they had probably been followed from the minute they had arrived in Villa.

She hobbled towards him, working hard to keep her hands and ankles from his view. He stepped back from the van, moving out of arms' length of a woman who had a reputation for ramming into people. Behind him into the distance she could see a flurry of dust coming in their direction. It seemed to be a car, but she could not let herself get distracted from what she had to do.

Then the strangest thing happened. Where his focus had been singularly directed down the barrel of his gun at her, he unexpectedly threw his hand into the air to flap at something white that had floated into his line of vision. He let out an impatient grunt as he waved his hand around to swat away the source of the irritation, while twisting his head an inch to the side taking his eyes from her for a brief second. In a situation where he was confident that a tethered Wilson was helpless and restrained, he could be forgiven for taking a millisecond to swat away whatever had distracted him.

That moment was all she needed to spring onto her feet, rush forward and using the edge of the van's doorway, launch herself at the man. Her forehead cracked his nose with a loud smack which she hoped was his nose and not her head. She had never delivered a *Glasgow Kiss* before. She had not even intended to do it on this occasion. It had just come naturally as if in-bred in her through years of intervening in fights and disagreements outside pubs late on a Friday night. She wrapped one hand around his neck to pull him into a headlock, while grabbing the pistol with the other. His neck was so slippery with sweat, she did not gain the traction she had hoped for; his strong, wiry frame

269

remained upright, although off balance. The momentum of her other hand grasping the pistol forced his finger to squeeze the trigger. The bullet whistled by her ear and exploded with a crack against the back of the van.

As she landed on the ground with a jolt, she fully expected a bullet to pierce the back of her head. She had missed her moment to pull him to the ground with her, and fully expected to pay the price. When it did not happen, she looked up, to see him topple backwards, stunned by the headbutt, blood pouring from his nose. The more he tried to regain his balance, the less coordinated he became. Until ultimately, as if auditioning for a stuntman role in a B movie, he fell with a flourish of limbs into the freshly dug hole. As his feet disappeared after him, she heard the crack of the pistol.

She scrambled over to the hole to see him lying motionless at an awkward angle, blood oozing from his chest. She read the situation immediately - the gun had gone off on impact and by chance, or by his bad luck, it had been pointed at him. Struggling to get her breathing back under control, she sat down on the ground her hands inserted into her matted hair tresses rubbing gently. She was starting to feel another lump coming to join the Vienna egg-shaped mound already taking up a portion of her forehead.

The car screeched to a halt a few yards down the road from the hole, a burst of dust ballooning towards her. In the middle of the cloud she saw Kiltman running in her direction, followed by Ana. She was surprised by the way Kiltman launched himself at her throwing his cape over her shoulders as if it provided a form of protection. He squeezed her harder than she had ever been squeezed before, feeling a surge of energy rushing from him to her. Later she would explain it as the feeling one gets when pumped full of vitamins. An explosion of inexplicable feelgood. Somehow in that moment he had imbued in her a surge of power that had permeated every muscle and nerve in her body.

"Hey, Kiltman, it's okay." She nestled her head into his neck. Rubbing his back with her hands, she felt that she should be comforting him. She thought she could hear him snivelling slightly but was not sure if she was hearing things. Another pair of arms wrapped around her and Kiltman. She realised Ana had joined in for a group hug.

"Maggie Wilson. You're my hero!" Ana declared through tears and laughter, before giving each of them a body crush.

He stepped back and spoke with a crackle in his voice. "How on earth did you do all this?" He pointed to the prostrate man in the hole, staring up at them in a blank stare.

"Good question!" She turned to walk towards the van. She bent down to pick something up and then came back to Kiltman and Ana. "This fell at just the right time to put him off his stride."

She held up a gloriously white feather with a grey streak through its middle, shining in the brilliance of the afternoon sun.

"Thanks, Mum!" Kiltman thought, his eyes closed and his legs quivering.

En Route to Buenos Aires

"How did you get to me so quickly, Ana?" Wilson asked from the back seat of the car as they sped towards the airport. They had a booking on a flight leaving for Buenos Aires in just over an hour. It would get them there for early evening allowing them several hours to kill before an overnight flight to New York. Gemmill had given up arguing with her; he had succumbed to her request without discussion. He had come to realise how close he had been to losing a uniquely gifted detective inspector. Despite himself he was developing a strong respect for Wilson and valuing her policing skills with each additional stage in this reckless adventure of a chase. While he was not sure of the additional value Kiltman was bringing at this stage, he knew that whatever they were pursuing seemed to be several steps ahead of them. They were in catch up mode and needed all the help they could get.

"I was dropping off at a small village, literally just around the corner from the antenna," Ana answered, clearly relishing her role in this international escapade. "It's called Alta Gracia, which means *Grace from on High* in English."

Kiltman touched his sporran, where he had placed the feather that had saved Wilson's life. It certainly was grace of the highest brand, he thought, convinced his mother had chosen that moment to show she was with them on every step of this journey. It gave him a sense of calm beyond anything he had felt before. Coincidences happen, he thought - even flukes that appear beyond the ordinary can have a rational explanation. There was no other reason in his mind for the feather, falling from the sky without a bird in sight. If birds had been nearby, they would have been hidden in the shade of the woods half a mile from that spot, not hovering around a metal mast bristling with mid-day searing heat.

He had been noticeably quiet during the journey, and he knew Wilson would be wondering what was wrong. It was not possible at that moment, even if Ana had not been in the car, to explain all the feelings rushing through his head and heart. He was not sure when he would find the moment for that discussion - how her boyfriend back in Scotland was actually in disguise and with her every minute of each day. He realised now more than ever the depth of love he held for this person who had taken her life in her hands - and threw it with apparent carefree abandon into the barrel of a loaded gun.

The two policemen from Villa had proved helpful in calling the case into the Córdoba HQ and getting reinforcements out to the radio mast. They had already sent a team to Villa to search the apartment and look for the person who had pushed them from the window. She - and they were assuming 'she' based on how small her hands had felt - would have disappeared into the Argentine pampas. Whoever she was, they did not expect to see her any time soon.

Ana pulled up at the airport in record time. After another round of hugs and kisses, Wilson had pushed a wad of pesos into her pocket, while hugging her round the neck. It was more money than Ana made in a week of picking up and dropping off. She had again protested trying to explain that she should not make money and have so much fun at the same time. It just did not feel right. In the end she pocketed the cash, murmuring to herself that she knew exactly how she would spend it. She sped off into the distance, her hand waving back to them just as she had done in Villa General Belgrano.

Kiltman and Wilson rushed through the terminal and cleared immigration with the help of Andrea, a tall, friendly policeman Córdoba HQ had arranged to meet them. Andrea had briefed the appropriate officials in advance, facilitating the Scottish crime-fighters' rush through the airport to catch a Buenos Aires flight.

They had barely sat down in their seats - weary with the exertions of running through the airport, ready to settle into an hour of calm - when Andrea joined them on the plane. The stewards tried to push him back out the door, creating a human barrier to block him. He flashed an ID in their faces and barged past with more strength than his thin frame appeared to contain. He ran towards Kiltman and Wilson, who were sitting halfway down the plane on either side of the aisle.

"I've just had a call from Córdoba HQ," he panted. "There's a man waiting for you in Buenos Aires. He will meet you under the tree in Recoleta. He can explain some things to you, that's all I know." The stewards had caught up and now had a hold of Andrea's shoulders, yanking him back towards the entrance, shouting at him in Spanish - something like *get yourself off our plane, we're going to miss our take off slot*, Kiltman assumed. As he was being heckled out the door by three stewards, Andrea popped his head back and shouted, "Buena suerte!" before disappearing from view.

"Under a tree?" Wilson whispered, as the doors closed, and the plane immediately taxied to the runway. "That has to go down as *the* vaguest meeting spot in the history of vague meeting spots."

"That's why you're a detective, Wilson. Because you figure those kinds of things out." He had genuinely meant it as a compliment. Whether it was the tiredness in his voice or the stress of the events over the last few hours, she turned to look at him.

"Sarcasm is not particularly attractive, Kiltman. No matter what mask you're wearing." She turned her head back to look straight ahead, and not knowing what to do with her hands, yanked a magazine from the pouch touching her knees. She barely glanced at it, but pretended to turn the pages, the anger bristling under her skin. Why did Kiltman have this impact, she thought? Why was she feeling as if she was having a domestic with someone she knew nothing about other than that he had incredibly powerful senses, but the sensitivity of a barn door? It took most of the journey to BA for her to calm down and realise they had a job to do. This was not personal.

He was annoyed at himself for being inconsiderate with her. She had been kidnapped and shot at, coming within an inch of losing her life. All he could do was throw flippant comments at her, when he knew all she needed was a cuddle, a cup of tea (or maybe a Malbec) and a few Danny O'Donnell songs.

The BA Gum Tree

Kiltman had never seen a tree sprawl so much, shading hundreds of diners and drinkers from the evening sun. The cafés and restaurants dotted around the area seemed to take comfort in its wide shadow. From a short, stocky trunk, its thick branches stretched out far across the square as if looking to close out any chink of sun threatening to break through onto the pavement. On the way into BA, the taxi driver had known immediately which tree they were looking for. A gum tree, planted by Franciscan monks, known as 'Recoletos', two hundred years earlier, it was one of the most famous landmarks in BA. There was no doubting how old it was, its long, sturdy limbs supported by wooden poles to keep them upright. Lots of diners were relying on those poles being strong enough to bear the strain.

"Hey, Wilson!" Kiltman was starting to feel he was back on her good side, pointing at a table of lads drinking Quilmes beer. "The last thing those drinkers need is to be crushed by a two-hundred-year-old branch. Imagine the headlines. Their love of *Quilmes* killed them!"

"Jeez," she answered, "don't go into marketing whatever you do."

Before he could explain that actually he did have some experience in the drinks' world in a previous life - which was feeling like a long time ago - he felt a tap on his shoulder. He turned to see a man walking away from him. His "Follow me!" sounded more like an order than a request.

The man, wearing a cream-coloured fedora with a brown band, was dressed in a blue, short-sleeved t-shirt, and white slacks. At a height of no less than six feet, he walked at pace bending underneath the tree, striding past a table of patrons. He kept walking, with Kiltman and Wilson skipping in pursuit, as far as a large iron gate supported by four strong pillars. They could see through the bars that they were approaching a cemetery. It felt weird but was not the weirdest thing that had happened to them that day, not by a long chalk.

He stepped inside, and they followed. The cemetery was breath-taking, jam-packed with grandiose and resplendent mausoleums telling the stories of prominent Argentinian families. It struck Kiltman how different this was to the rows of humble headstones he was used to - recognising specific individuals rather than dynasties. After a hundred-yard walk down an alley of tombs, the man stopped at a quiet corner and turned around, extending his hand.

"My name is Joseph Abram." He spoke in a pleasant accent tinged with a melodic hum. There was something very deliberate about how he carried himself and spoke in a deep, slow voice.

"Welcome to Recoleta Cemetery. This is where the most important and famous Argentines over the centuries are buried."

He pointed at a tomb with a plaque showing a woman's head inclined to the side, with her hair bunched just above her neck. The face bordered on religious, Kiltman mused, similar to many depictions of the Virgin Mary adorning churches all over the world. The name on the tomb was *Familia Duarte*.

"Do you recognize her?" he asked. He waited for a second. "Your country made an opera about this lady. Evita, also known as Eva Péron."

"Oh, wow!" For a moment Wilson appeared to be on a South American backpacking trip. "Is she buried here?"

"Yes." Joseph stretched his arms wide. "Just like many of Argentina's most powerful people, including presidents and influential diplomats." He paused for a second and scratched his chin. "Okay, enough of the tourist stuff, follow me."

He turned on his heel and walked down a couple of alleys towards the centre of the cemetery. He stopped at a tomb and pointed at the inscription. The grave itself was relatively inconspicuous compared to many of the resplendently ornate vaults they had walked past. Some of them, Kiltman supposed, could have been used as a small apartment if necessary, considering their breadth and depth.

They both read the inscription:

Adam Abram
3 October 1895 – 22 May 1986
His mission will never end

Joseph touched the tomb. "This is where my father is buried." His voice choked slightly. "Mum never made it out of the camps, and he never remarried. He brought me up singlehandedly."

Wilson, without thinking, placed her hand on his back. "I'm sorry."

"Thank you," he acknowledged.

Kiltman nodded and touched his arm, which encouraged Joseph to bow his head slightly. This man seemed to exude trust and integrity from every pore of his being.

"What was your father's *mission*?" Kiltman asked.

"That's the right question," he answered, rubbing his eyes. "And that's why we're here. After the war, he dedicated himself to finding as many of the perpetrators of the holocaust and related crimes as possible. He spent all of his energy bringing runaway Nazis to justice and was considered to be successful. But he was never satisfied. He would not be content until every last Nazi had been caught and punished. Despite his dedication, he went to his grave frustrated by what he considered a failed task." He stopped for a moment and took a breath. "He brought 34 of them to justice. But there was one man who evaded him. His name was Adalbert Schmidt. At least that is what he was called in Germany. He was seen boarding a ship for Argentina but was never seen again."

He stopped for a moment regaining his composure.

"Your find in Villa General Belgrano today was the missing link in the case."

"Really? You've been able to work this through already?" Wilson's surprise was tinged with scepticism.

"Yes, we have people everywhere. One of our colleagues checked for fingerprints in the attic, and many of them matched Schmidt. He had become Juergen Mann, the owner of the house, settling into the town after the war. He pretended to have been a foot soldier in the German army. I won't go into the details of the tortures and horrors he was responsible for - you can imagine, I expect.

"Mann died a few years ago, but we now want to find his son, Alois. We believe he can point us towards others who have escaped justice. I know that many of them have already died, but as the tomb says, the mission will never end." He stopped and studied the tomb, touching the inscribed words.

"At an early age, he showed many of the same traits as his father, no doubt ingrained in him from birth. Ironically, or more like, deliberately, he was named Alois, after Hitler's father. A subtle way for his father to retain a connection to their Führer. Alois would have been born around the early sixties. For some reason, we don't know why, he left home in the mid-seventies. It was the talk of the town at the time. Alois had been gifted in many ways. A higher level of natural intelligence than anyone had seen in his school before. But he was recognised even more for his ability to quickly learn how to play any sport; a naturally gifted athlete, with an unnaturally aggressive speed and tenacity to win. It came as a shock to the community when he ran away with a friend, someone from school, Helmut Bach."

Kiltman clicked his fingers. "I've got it!"

Before they could ask, he continued. "On the wall in the apartment, there were lots of photos. But something niggled me, I couldn't quite figure it out at the time. Actually, now that I think about it there were two things. First is that somewhere in the recesses of my memory I recognised one of the faces in the photos. There was a boy with a serious face, he seemed to be taking less pleasure from the moment than the others. It felt like he was the child that had to be coaxed to pose for the camera."

He spread his hands wide. "It was Lange! A much younger version, I admit, but it was definitely him. It makes sense. I bet you Lange was actually Helmut Bach. On the occasions we spoke with him at Barlinnie and in Vienna, I remember trying to place his accent. It wasn't quite Scottish, there was an inflection of something else in there." He turned to Wilson. "And before you say it, I know the same thing could be said about some folks in Kelvinside, Glasgow, but this was different."

"Okay, go on." Joseph was not in the mood to understand the linguistic nuances of *Kelvinside*. His eyes encouraged Kiltman to proceed with the explanation.

"The other thing was that in every photo where there were groups of children, one of them was always looking away from the camera. It didn't strike me as odd at the time, because there are always one or two kids who are too boisterous to focus. But this was different, in each photo there was a boy deliberately looking down or to the side."

"That was Alois Mann, Kiltman. Very observant." Joseph nodded. "From an early age, he feared the camera. He hated having his photo taken. We actually don't have any images of him."

"What about the guy that kidnapped me?" she asked. "Do you know who he was?"

"Yes, we have identified him as Rolf Müller. He was a friend of Mann and Bach. He would have been in some of the photos you saw on the wall. Back then he had a head of thick red hair, barely recognisable as the man with the gun."

"I see." Wilson had one more question. "Would you have any idea who the person was that might have pushed us out of the window?"

"Only one person comes to mind." Joseph rubbed his chin thoughtfully. "Müller's daughter, Sophia. She and her father were inseparable, feeding off each other's bigotry. We lost track of them both a year or so ago but seems she may have resurfaced, just like her father did. We already have our team out there looking for her. She should not be too hard to find. It is unfortunate for the good, honest people of Villa General Belgrano that these fanatics used their beautiful, proud, and noble town for their camouflage. Its people are kind and generous of spirit. The people we are looking for are not representative of this special place."

Kiltman and Wilson nodded their recognition of Joseph's comments. It would not be the first time, people with evil intent hid behind decent, respectable people.

They decided not to ask who Joseph's 'team' might be. They were quite sure he was the thin edge of a wide wedge of investigations and pursuits. As time passed, their search for Nazis would accelerate rather than dissipate. They would be determined to bring them to justice before nature beat them to it.

Kiltman and Wilson were trying to make sense of the story that seemed to be burgeoning into a saga with every sentence their cemetery guide uttered. He continued.

"Let me lay it out for you. You are looking for a terrorist who is connected to the Nazis. The clue that led you there was

279

discovered in an apartment just off the *Bermuda Triangle* in Vienna." He put his hand up. "Don't ask me how I know, I just do.

"While today the *Triangle* is known for its parties and nights out, at the start of the war it was the Jewish quarter in Vienna. In fact, there is a still a synagogue there today, the only one to have survived in German-speaking Europe. And that was only because it was embedded in a built-up area. They couldn't burn it down without causing widespread damage.

"That clue leads you here to Argentina, where you find plans and photos of the Museum of Jewish Heritage in a house we know belonged to Mann, or as we know him, Schmidt."

He placed a hand on each of them, touching their shoulders. "Tomorrow, December 30th, there's an event taking place in New York, at the museum, at three o'clock in the afternoon to remember the six million killed in the holocaust. While there are regular memorial events to mark the tragedy of all those lives, tomorrow's event has a special audience.

"Many international leaders will be there on this occasion. On the following day, they are attending the United Nation's special New Year's Eve discussion on the importance of countries being able to self-determine their future. Since they will be in the city already, they have been invited to the memorial event at the museum. They have of course all accepted. Presidents, Prime Ministers and Royalty from all over the world will be there.

"They will not cancel the event just because of what you've uncovered in an attic somewhere in Argentina. While security is already very formidable for such a service, you can be assured tomorrow will be stricter than ever, but the event will still go ahead. Thanks to you they are searching every nook and cranny of the museum, and surrounding areas, looking for rogue devices. If something's there, they should find it."

He stared at each of them, moving his gaze from one to the other. "Having said that, you need to be there. You need to use your skills." He turned to Kiltman. "You must stop them."

He directed his scrutiny to Wilson, before kissing her on both cheeks. "DI Wilson, please give us some more of that tenacity and drive for righteousness you are becoming famous for. I believe we are close to catching Alois and his comrades, but we are against the clock. They have one more trick up their sleeves, yet it could be the most devastating of all."

She smiled back at Joseph in what appeared more like a grimace, while thinking '*when did my chosen career path incorporate standing in graveyards in Argentina talking about doomsday scenarios?*"

Then she realised. It was when she met Kiltman.

No Such Thing as Failure

"He's dead!" she cried. "He's dead!"

"Calm down," Mask declared with measured authority. "That's enough!"

The sobs were ricocheting down the phone towards him, the helplessness of her self-pity irritating him with each whimper. He waited, allowing her some time to regain her poise.

"Now, tell me what happened. Don't spare me any details."

"It was all going according to plan. They went up into the attic as you said they would. The woman came down first, giving me the chance to shove her out the window into the van. Just as Father drove off with her, Kiltman walked over to the window." She took a deep breath, beginning to get herself back under control. "I did the same thing to him, hoping he would land on the ground. My plan was for it to look like an accident. Father wanted to shoot them in the apartment, but that would have been problematic clearing up afterwards and moving the bodies.

"The fall should have killed him. But somehow he did a sort of sideways somersault that landed him in a bin, breaking his fall. It should have been impossible. But I saw it with my own eyes."

"And your father, what happened?" There was no hint of emotion in Mask's voice to indicate the extreme annoyance he was feeling towards this incompetent girl. All she had to do was take a pistol to the apartment and finish it there - but there was little point in scolding her when he still needed her for his plans.

"I drove to the mast, but by the time I got there the woman had escaped and father was dead." This started another fit of sobs, before he could hear her working hard to get back onto the story. "Kiltman had also managed to get there before I did. I think he convinced the police to take him."

"Okay, listen carefully to me. The plan is still on, do you understand?"

"Yes, sir." Her breathing was steadying.

"The chances of them convincing anyone to stop the event is small to zero. Make sure you are in New York tomorrow. Is that clear?"

"Yes, I have my ticket already."

"Make no mistakes this time." That comment hurt. It was the first he had made to indicate he held her responsible. She had lost her father, and it felt like he did not care, not even a few words of comfort.

"There will be no mistakes, I promise."

"Look, Sophia, I know you're hurting. But there's nothing we can do to bring your father back. Your only chance of feeling better is to make his sacrifice worth something." He waited a few moments before saying, "New York is your way to avenge him."

She sniffled quietly, trying to regain her composure and lift her spirits. He was right. He always was. "Don't worry, New York will go according to plan. I hope to see you there."

"Yes, I will be there. Stay strong."

Mask closed the phone and shook his head. She was finished, he thought, barely enough left in her to complete the next mission. He would have to move to the contingency plan created for a scenario such as this. It was not ideal, but he realised it was his only option.

VII

New York

Murphy's

The subway train rumbled noisily along the tracks eventually shaking the tiredness from their weary bones. Wilson could not remember ever feeling so sore and tender to touch. The jarring of the train shook and jolted her, inflaming her bruises. She realised she was beginning to anthropomorphise her wounds, each contusion belonging to an international event with its own unique identity.

Gemmill's team had managed to get them a couple of seats towards the back of the plane - crunched into a corner - where they had squeezed themselves into their seats. During the flight they tried hard to respect each other's elbow space. In the end the eleven-hour journey to New York's Newark airport, saw them poking, shoving and clasping each other's limbs time and again in an effort to find mutual comfort. Their immigration process into the United States had been simple and routine, guided by Officer McDermott who seemed to carry rank over the men and women dotted throughout the immigration hall steadily checking thousands of visas and passports. He led them quickly through the various checkpoints and questionnaires they had to complete on entry. The only thing worth declaring was the substance in Kiltman's sporran flask. Considering it was minimal in volume and could always be passed as *Scotch*, Kiltman chose not to declare his Hair o' the Dog.

When McDermott had bade them farewell at the taxi rank, he whispered into Wilson's ear, "Tell Gemmill he owes me a Guinness! Otherwise I may have to tell people about his nights out in New York!"

McDermott had winked knowingly at Wilson as if she had been meant to understand the comment. Although she was quite sure she would never bring this up with Gemmill unless he pushed her too far.

It was 11 am and they were en route to midtown Manhattan, having decided that they needed to eat before going to the museum. The New York Police Department had issued a communication that nobody would be allowed into the building until 2 pm. They did not say why, but Kiltman was in no doubt it was to allow them the time needed to conduct a thorough search. If that was the case, he thought, then at least their efforts to warn them had resulted in some action. They did not yet have a game plan to access it themselves, once again they were relying on the wizardry of Gemmill. One thing they were both learning on this trip was to be patient and wait.

They were both standing on the subway train on the 6 line, holding tight to the overheard bar. Next stop was 53rd on 3rd, which Kiltman remembered from the Rod Stewart ballad about the tragic ending of a man named Georgie. It had been a reminder to him when he first came to New York in his early twenties that he needed to be careful. In the pre-Giuliani days New York had been a grittier city - and some would argue, more fun. Many people felt that the mid-'90s Mayor's zero tolerance clean-up had sterilised New York to the point of being a shadow of its formal self.

They had already taken three trains to get to this point. The 6 train hurtling northwards through the east side of Manhattan seemed to be going faster than any underground ride either of them had been on in London or Glasgow. Kiltman smiled, when he realised the only time he had taken Glasgow's one line underground with its 15 stops was on a 'sub-crawl'. It had been during university freshers' week, when one of the students, nicknamed Scratchy, an enterprising lad, game for a laugh and social event, had arranged the trip as a welcome for the first years. At every stop, Scratchy would lead the party out of the underground, walk upstairs for a beer and then back down again. By the time they had completed the crawl, they had become acquainted with the city centre, West End and suburbs of Glasgow. The only problem was remembering them the next day. Kiltman made a mental note to introduce Scratchy to Tommy, they would get on well.

Wilson pointed at the advertising stripes above their heads. She beamed a smile he had not seen in what seemed an age.

"Just in case," she whispered, giving him a nudge in the ribs.

He looked up to see an advert that read:

Anal warts? Fissures? Hemorrhoids? Call 1 800 MD TUSCH

"Ouch!" he answered, instinctively squeezing his buttocks together. He could see Wilson would love a trip to New York when they were not chasing villains. She had that peculiarly Scottish trait of looking for humour and a reason to laugh when faced with the intensity of an overwhelming city.

The train screeched to a stop - the noise of the tracks replaced by the high-pitched squeal of the brakes being engaged at the last minute. Kiltman wondered if the train driver had ever driven a bus in Glasgow.

They stepped off the train and made their way upstairs into the daylight. The cold hit them like a tsunami of sharp knives bayoneting their faces. Fortunately, his mask gave him some respite, but Wilson's sharp intake of breath showed she had not been expecting the fiercely aggressive winter wind. They had noticed the cold when they had walked through the airport, it was December after all. They were back in the northern hemisphere now. While it felt quite brisk in the terminal it seemed manageable, barely worthy of comment. In the middle of the city, it was downright paralysing. Third avenue was acting like a wind tunnel driving the accelerated sharpness of the cold along its perfectly straight road, dropping degrees every few blocks it passed. By the time it hit mid-town it was lethal.

Above a shop across the road from the subway exit, they squinted up at a digitised clock switching between the time and temperature. The time was 11.05 am, and the temperature 14 degrees.

He shouted against the noise of the wind, "Wilson, 14 Fahrenheit is minus 10 centigrade. Officially that's what a weather forecaster would call *Really Cold*! And with a wind chill factor of goodness knows what, it'll be a lot colder than that. We need to find somewhere indoors fast!"

She nodded, wrapping her arms around herself. "It's so cold I can hardly breathe. I've never been anywhere so bitterly freezing, yet there isn't even a smidgeon of snow."

"Too cold for snow, Wilson," Kiltman answered. "Snow needs moisture, and there's none at this temperature."

He noticed her small frame was shivering, her chin tucked into her chest in a vain attempt to prevent the wind stabbing her face. He wrapped his arm around her shoulders to share their body heat, while thinking, *at least you're wearing underwear.* His knees were knocking together uncontrollably trying to create some circulation around his nether regions.

"Let's head down there." She pointed to a cross street a block or two east.

"Works for me." He was looking up at skyscrapers stretching high into the sky. The one directly overhead was the Citicorp building which he recognised from many of the New York movies and shows he surfed on television at home. It was one of the tallest high rises in the city, identified by its slanted roof, but never seemed to attain the distinction of the Empire State or Chrysler buildings. A group of young men exited through its swing doors, carrying small, identical backpacks. They walked quickly towards the cross streets she had indicated.

"Let's follow them, Wilson, they seem to be on a mission to eat lunch."

They stepped in behind the six fleet of foot men, clearly accustomed to the New York chill. They quickly covered a two-block walk to arrive at a spot on Second Avenue. Kiltman and Wilson were hot on their heels and followed them inside a barely lit pub identified by a neon sign, *Murphy's*. At the entrance two men, who appeared to come from a different breed of humanity, were checking out the customers to make sure they were suitable for their establishment.

The doormen were at least 6 foot 8, Kiltman thought. They had bulk to go with the height, while sporting flowing red hair and freckles. Considering they had just walked into an Irish pub, he wondered whether they had stumbled upon the two largest leprechauns of all time. Their nameplates read: Patrick Sean and Michael Brian.

"Sorry, sir, no fancy dress parties or singing telegrams allowed in here," said Michael Brian, the taller of the two by an inch, but who was counting? "We are expecting large crowds in here today as businesses close for the New Year, and we can't have cheap entertainment like you upset the vibe."

Kiltman was unsure how to react. His pride had been dented - he would normally have turned around and asked Wilson to follow him to another eatery. But it was cold outside. Pride or no pride, he was not leaving.

"Look…" he began.

"He's only jerking your chain," laughed Patrick Sean. "Come on in. Welcome to Murphy's!" As they stepped into the pub, Michael Brian grabbed Kiltman and gave him a tight hug. "Man, you're a hero! I was only having a laugh. We've seen you on TV lots. I hope your being here isn't an omen of trouble on the horizon."

Kiltman was struggling to speak with the tightness of the hug, "Eh, no. We're just here to eat. Thanks for the hug, just what I needed."

"Well," said Patrick Sean, "If we're doing the customer hugging thing, then come here you! Bring it in, baby!" He reached out and wrapped his arms around Wilson before she realised what was happening. She quickly appreciated that being hugged by such a tall man felt strangely satisfying, bringing her a sense of well-being and security. And warmth. She was happy to remain in the arms of this strange Irishman for as long as it took for the circulation to come back to her limbs.

"On you go in. Enjoy yourselves," Michael Brian unlocked his arms from Kiltman, before rubbing his head as if he was a schoolboy. Patrick Sean took a moment longer to release Wilson, but eventually did so, giving her a last second peck on the cheek.

They walked over to the bar and placed an order for that traditional New York staple, cheeseburgers and fries. They saw a table in the back of the bar far enough from the door for them not to be frozen every time it opened. Carrying their two mugs of coffee, they wandered to the back, surprised at how busy it was for late morning. The sound of Shane MacGowan and Kirsty MacColl singing their haunting, edgy *Fairytale of New York* in the background caught Kiltman's attention:

You took my dreams from me when I first found you
I kept them with me babe. I put them with my own

He looked to see if Wilson was registering the irony in the words – a portent of the conversation she and Kenny would need to have soon. He smiled when he watched her trying not to spill her coffee as she navigated between tables. At that point, those lyrics were the furthest thing from her mind.

The pub had a long, narrow bar stretching from the entrance all the way into the back, where a few tables had been placed closer together than would normally satisfy a private conversation. But somehow it worked in this small, cosy pub. Coincidentally, they found themselves sitting beside the men they had followed, who were engrossed in animated discussion, a variety of beers of different shades scattered around the table. By the time Wilson and Kiltman had sat down, the men had nearly finished their first round.

Kiltman felt his phone vibrate in his sporran.

"I'm off to the loo, Wilson. Be back in a jiff." She barely noticed as she flicked through her own phone looking for messages from Gemmill.

Walking into the dark bathroom he saw it had the luxury of one urinal and one cubicle, with a sliver of light sneaking in over the top of the door. Which was useful since the overhead fluorescent bulb was broken. He opted for the cubicle, flipping the phone open before lifting the bottom of his facemask to deactivate the voice changer.

"Hello," he whispered, looking at the display to see Tommy's name shining in the darkness of the cubicle.

"Hi, Kenny!" Tommy sounded chirpy. "How you doing, mate? I was worried I hadn't heard from you. Your mother's funeral seems so long ago now."

Tell me about it, Kiltman thought.

"All okay, Tommy. I had a rough patch for a few days. But I'm genuinely in a much better place now." He took the feather from his sporran and kissed it gently, admiring its beatific whiteness, and the tinge of grey warning of danger. "How are you?"

"I'm in New York! What an amazing place. Can't believe I left it so long before I came here." Of course, Kenny remembered, he and Marsha had been invited to participate in the UN discussion on New Year's Eve.

"Marsha and I arrived this morning. Her brother, Digi, came too but on a separate flight. It's the first time I've had her to myself in weeks. Something strange is going on with them." The concern was etched in his voice. "Anyway, I'm not going to let that put me off a wee session in the Big Apple."

"What you got planned other than the UN meeting tomorrow?" Kiltman asked.

"We've just checked into a hotel near Grand Central Station. Cheap and cheerful. Not as bad as your stag in Rome. Ha! We're a bit more upmarket now. We're going to go for a walk, a short walk I may add. It's so cold here. I thought I had got used to it in Estonia, but the wind here makes it feel 20 degrees worse. Even Marsha's struggling."

Tell me about it, Kiltman thought again.

"There's a pub on the Upper East Side called Elaine's," Tommy continued. "Billy Joel's hit *Big Shot* mentions it. It used to be one of his haunts back in the seventies apparently. Lots of famous folks in New York hang out there. We're going be there for early dinner and then after a wee swally, we've been invited to a fashion event downtown. One of those catwalk things with beautiful women from all over the world. Marsha's sister is one of the models, she got us tickets. Should be a laugh. Anyway, better go, Marsha needs a hand zipping up. Bye, pal."

"Okay, cheers, Tommy!" Kiltman closed the phone, feeling the envy rise in his chest. He could take or leave the models and catwalk, not his cup of tea, he thought. But Elaine's, Billy Joel's haunt! He hoped that one day he would bring his own *uptown girl* back to enjoy it with him.

New York, New York

"Kiltman!" Wilson spread her arms exaggeratedly. "Meet the lads."

He had barely been to the bathroom for five minutes, yet when he came back she was sitting at a different table along with the group of men they had followed from the Citicorp building. They did look like a lively bunch, chatting excitedly amongst themselves, waving arms and hands to punctuate whatever stories they were telling. They barely nodded their acknowledgement of Kiltman as he pulled up a chair. They appeared so unaware of a masked man in a kilt, he really wondered at their attention to detail.

"Guess what they do?" she asked.

"I don't know, tell me." He was wondering if they were Broadway actors or a band who had been up partying all night.

"They're accountants!" She giggled like a teenager. "Four Irishmen and two Scotsmen walk into a bar in New York of all places! That's a joke waiting to happen."

Kiltman noticed their various disjointed discussions calming down, as they took it in turn to introduce themselves. Without further ado, they launched into a series of questions directed at him and Wilson to garner information about the exciting exploits and adventures they were involved in. They made a point of interrupting every so often to wind each other up about an innocuous comment one of them had made. It seemed - and this was not dissimilar to pubs back home - that this banter was the way they let each other know they were best of friends.

Kiltman had found that as his superpowers developed, he was becoming better at reading people and understanding their characters from a look or glance. It did not work in all cases but was developing in a way that provided him a form of entertainment. He surveyed the lads surrounding, and enjoying, Wilson.

Dominic and Crawford were the two Scots. Dominic had a cheeky-chappy air, contradicting his short back and sides, slickly oiled, black hair. Crawford had the look of a highlander ready for the next Jacobite rising. A hint of mutiny brightened his eyes, letting the world know he was more interesting than he first appeared. They were in an animated dialogue about whose turn it was to go to the bar, talking so quickly that he was sure none of the Americans at the surrounding tables would understand a word.

The Irish lads were Aiden, a fair-haired fellow who had the air of a parish priest; Braz, tall with the presence of an absent-minded inventor who is about to make his world-changing discovery; Shayne, a twinkle-eyed lad who seemed to be a couple of steps ahead of the pace encouraging the banter; and Huggy, a canny Belfast lad who had learned to know whom to trust from a very early age. Aiden and Braz wore their Dublin accents well while Shayne and Huggy displayed their Northern Ireland roots through their booming voices.

Kiltman had expected the Dubliners to be railing on the Northern lads, but in fact Shayne and Huggy sat back and enjoyed the air of the untouchable; while Aiden and Braz poked fun at each other for coming from opposites side of the River Liffy running through the centre of their city. An anthropologist would have had a field day as an observer watching these individuals interact on foreign soil.

Kiltman and Wilson's food arrived in record time. They barely spoke for the next five minutes, as they devoured their substantial cheeseburgers and fries. Kiltman was surprisingly adept at squashing food into his mouth through the small space he created by lifting the corner of his mask at his chin. The rush of calories sparked a welcome blast of energy. Wilson realised if they were going to make progress and deal with whatever the afternoon had in store, they would need to confide in their new friends. She had already called Gemmill, who had informed her that there was absolutely no chance of them gaining access to the museum before the event. He was working on getting them passes to the memorial ceremony but even that was in doubt. He made a point of emphasising that foreign cities did not take too kindly to police from other countries coming to tell them what to do. Especially those police - and she heard him take joy from this comment - who travel with a kilted partner in a mask.

293

"We can't tell you everything." She scanned the faces at the table. "But we're trying to get into the Museum of Jewish Heritage for an event that's taking place this afternoon at three."

"Sure," Shayne acknowledged, "that's the big downtown shindig where they're closing off roads for several blocks around. Apparently, they increased the level of security just this morning. I saw it on the news, seems like there's been a heightened level of risk."

Wilson and Kiltman shot each other a brief glance.

"It's already creating chaos with the traffic, especially with lots of people trying to get away for Hogmanay tomorrow." Shayne smiled at Kiltman and Wilson, pleased that he had used the Scottish name for New Year's Eve.

"The thing is…" Kiltman paused wondering when Shayne would stop smiling at Wilson. "The thing is, we are trying to get into the venue, how can I say, incognito."

"Incognito!" laughed Braz, the northside Dubliner. "A Celtic fan wearing the hoops at an Orange Lodge would be more incognito than you!" That elicited a laugh from his fellow accountants, reminding Kiltman of how low the comedy bar was in that profession.

"I've an idea," Aiden announced. He turned his head to Huggy. "Remember that guy who worked on the financial services audit with us last year up in Boston. What was his name?"

"Yes," Huggy sat up. "Saul. I remember him, great character."

"Well," Aiden turned to Kiltman and Wilson, "Saul was involved in the creation of the museum, which was only a few years ago. He and his wife are well-connected and, from what I understand, esteemed members of the Jewish community here in New York."

Before they could respond, Aiden had flipped his phone open and was pressing buttons.

"Hello, Saul?" He paused. "Yes, Aiden here. How you doing?"

Everyone had waited to listen in on the conversation but after a few minutes, when Aiden in his typically Irish fashion was still telling Saul about what he was doing for New Year, how his family were keeping and which girl he was dating, they all tuned out one by one. It gave Kiltman the chance to find out that Dominic originally came from close to Duntocher back in Scotland. Small world. he thought. He felt that he may have recognised him, potentially from Sweeneys, at some point in his past - although his pre-Kiltman memories were quite a bit fuzzier than they should be for a man his age.

"Okay, all sorted!" Aiden closed the phone.

"Get the drinks in, Crawford!" Dominic shouted, as if it were the most important thing anyone had communicated throughout lunch. Crawford pushed his chair back from the table and made his way to the bar, as if the weight of the world were on his shoulders. When he got to the counter, the barman with the nametag, Ryan, spoke loud enough for everyone to hear. "Hey, Crawford, I haven't seen you up here for a while!"

The rest burst into exaggerated hoots of laughter. Even the barman was in on the act. Kiltman had seen similar moments in Sweeneys over the years. The reluctant buyer of beers had probably only missed his round once in decades of visiting the pub with friends. But that was enough to seal his fate. Must be a Celtic thing, he mused.

Wilson interrupted his thoughts. "Aiden, what happened? What's 'all sorted'?"

"Okay." Aiden was pleased to be the object of Wilson's attention. "Saul will meet you at the Tribeca Grill at 2.30. His table is on the right as you walk in. Yes, he has his own table!" Aiden turned to the others. "Apparently, he and Robert are connected."

"Robert?" Wilson asked, frustrated at losing the thread.

"De Niro," Aiden said as if she should have known the owner of the restaurant was the world's most famous actor. "Anyway, Saul will be with his wife, Sarah. They're actually going to the memorial and, as luck would have it, have got two extra tickets. Tribeca is about fifteen minutes away from the museum."

Crawford arrived back at the table carrying a tray laden with pints of beer, plopping it down in the middle.

"That's the last drink I'm buying this year," he announced with a twinkle in his eye. Kiltman was sure he would have been working on that comment all the while he was at the bar.

Wilson stood up. "Kiltman, we need to go. It's already 1.45, and Tribeca is at the other end of Manhattan." She was pointing towards the lower end of the city on a tourist map she had taken from the edge of the bar where a host of tourist magazines and brochures had been crushed into a box. "I just need to go to the ladies, but let's leave when I get back."

He nodded. He was already bracing himself for the cold outside.

Barely a minute after she left the table, he felt a familiarly pleasant vibration in his sporran. "Sorry, guys, I need to take this."

As he stood, he flipped open his sporran and grabbed his phone. He was thankful Wilson was not there to rail on him for his secret mobile. Walking towards the entrance, he glanced at the display. *Maggie!*

He squeezed past Patrick Sean and Michael Brian, who were busy checking IDs from two girls wrapped from head to toe in wool and leather, reminding him of how underdressed he was for December in New York. He walked out into a blast of freezing cold wind howling up Second Avenue that made him shudder. He walked to the corner of the avenue where it met 52nd street seeking some shelter from the gale. He lifted his face mask to speak, "Hi Maggie!"

"Hello, Kenny!" She spoke warmly. "So nice to hear your voice."

"You too, Maggie. Where are you?" He was sure he could hear the toilet roll being torn in the background.

"I'm in New York. Long story, and I'll tell you all when I get home. I just wanted to say hello and hear you. I've really been missing you. I can't believe the last time we spoke was at your mother's funeral. Are you doing okay?"

"Yes, all good. I've turned a corner, I really have. Not something we need to get into now." His bottom lip quivered with the fierce cold numbing his extremities.

"Okay, I know," she said, hearing the emotion in his frail voice.

That was definitely a flushing sound, he thought.

"I'm not sure when I'll be back but I would love to meet you as soon as I return."

"That… would… be… great," he answered, his vocal cords constricting.

"Are you okay? You sound as if you're upset."

"Eh, yes, I'm f-f-fine. Just walking up a h-h-hill here behind the house. Hope to s-s-see you tomorrow." He had to go back inside; this was becoming dangerously cold. He squeezed his knees tight together.

"Yes, great, love you!" she managed to say before the line went dead. She hoped he had heard her. He sounded distracted, as if he had other things to do that were more important. He had not even bothered to ask what she was doing in New York. Fine, if he was trying to make her suffer then it was not going to work. She had plenty of other important things to keep her occupied.

He pulled his mask back down over his chin, shivering uncontrollably, before slipping the phone into his sporran and running back to the pub door. The two Irish giants were trussed up in woollen hats and overcoats shouting at him as he ran down the street towards them.

"Get yourself in here, Jock! Not even superheroes should be out in a cold like this." Michael Brian's strong brogue was beginning to sound more mid-west than middle Ireland. He had a sneaky feeling that the two bouncers belonged to the notorious FBI – Foreign Born Irish. Although he was not going to challenge them with this observation.

"Aye," Patrick Sean chimed in. "The question is, how true a Scotsman are you on a day like this?"

"Cheers, guys," Kiltman muttered as he ran into the bar, wondering why everyone wanted to be a comedian when he was around. He had barely crossed the threshold when the light suddenly disappeared. He felt himself being crushed under the colossal weight of the two bouncers hugging him tightly between them.

"Body heat." Michael Brian spoke knowingly. "Best thing to warm you up, wee man!"

Patrick Sean did not speak, but Kiltman was sure he heard him make a gentle purr-like sound, settling into the moment. By the time he had extricated himself, he got to the table just when Wilson came back from the bathroom. "Where were you?" she asked, looking towards the entrance.

"I felt a wave of jet lag, so nipped out for some fresh air." He was struggling to get his breathing under control.

"Right, you two are taking these and there are no arguments." Huggy called from over his shoulder. His strong, booming Northern Ireland accent made it more of an announcement than a comment. He was holding two green sweatshirts and woollen hats with *Murphys* emblazoned across them. "They're left over from St. Patrick's Day, and Ryan has kindly given them to you to keep you warm."

Kiltman and Wilson looked towards the bar, where Ryan was saluting. "Sure, if I can't help the Scots, I wouldn't be a proper celt! Food and drink are on the house too, no arguments!" He smiled in a collegiate manner as if he had a sense of what they had been through. He saw the faces of the six Celts light up and he said, "No, not for you toe rags, you need to pay. Cheeky monkeys!"

"Thanks, Ryan," Kiltman and Wilson spoke in unison. They turned back to the table and Wilson exclaimed cheerfully, "Guys, you've been so helpful. Whenever you're in Glasgow, look me up." She pointed to Kiltman with her thumb. "This guy might be harder to find, but I'd love to see you all."

"Don't worry. I'll definitely be there too." Kiltman waited a moment before adding. "Especially if Crawford is buying."

The uproar from the table, and Ryan clapping his hands behind them, confirmed he had maintained some of his comedic timing despite the cold embedded in too many important parts of his body. The group rose in unison from the table and hugged them both, saving their kisses for Wilson. After what had now become a customary goodbye ritual, they stepped out into the bracing chill of New York city, dressed as if they were looking for a Paddy's day party.

Wilson, apparently oblivious to the cold, crossed to the edge of the sidewalk, as she had seen in nearly every movie she had watched set in Manhattan. She put her fingers in her mouth and whistled at a pitch that interrupted Kiltman's exchange of goodbyes with the two Irish bouncers. All three turned to see her standing with a yellow cab's door open.

"Come on, Kiltman! No time to waste." She blew a kiss to the bouncers and jumped in the back of the cab.

Kiltman snuggled in beside her in seconds. "Don't get the wrong idea, Wilson, I just need the body heat." He squeezed up closer to Wilson. She was surprised at how much he was shivering.

They waved through the back window at Patrick Sean, who was puckering up and blowing a kiss. She smiled at Kiltman, "I think that's for you!" Michael Brian was making an exaggeratedly religious sign of the cross with his right arm.

"I think we both need the blessing!" Kiltman said, a wave of angst raising his heart rate a notch.

Regrets I've Had a Few

The entrance to the Tribeca Grill was busy. A horde of diners were shedding clothes in the cloakroom on the righthand side of the doorway. They all seemed in a hurry to find a table and an aperitif in the warmth of a busy lunchtime. Jostling for space in a crowded foyer, there were just as many people putting their heavy coats on to brace themselves for the outside. The cloakroom assistants were handling the jackets with ease, not the first time they had to manage such large numbers.

It was proving difficult for Kiltman and Wilson to navigate through to find someone to ask where Saul's table was. It had crossed his mind to wander around the tables on their right enquiring if anyone was called 'Saul''. She had put this idea out of his mind as they walked in, reminding him that as a caped Kiltman, anything he did would be seen as a *'harbinger of doom'*.

Eventually they saw a group of men huddling around a glamorous maître d', who was standing behind a wooden workstation. They seemed to be engrossed, sharing a computer screen depicting a planogram of the tables in the restaurant - most likely working out whether they could squeeze a few more places in.

"Excuse me!" Kiltman approached the group, "we're looking for a guy called Saul, who's dining here."

One of the men with his back to them, slightly taller than Kiltman, with greying hair, half turned to him and said, "You talking to me?"

"Eh, no, I don't know." Kiltman's tone was more apologetic than he had intended. "Sorry to interrupt, but em, I just need to speak to someone who knows Saul."

"Yes, but are you talking to me?" the man asked, this time slightly more insistent in tone. He had still not had the courtesy to turn and address him directly. Kiltman was surprised that the maître d' did not intervene and point to Saul's table. She seemed to be holding back, enjoying the conversation, while the other men, who were mostly waiters, appeared to be stifling giggles at some mutual joke.

"Look, what's going on here?" Wilson intervened looking at the maître d'. "We're looking for…"

"Hi, guys," a voice came from behind them. They turned to see a strikingly beautiful couple standing with their hands extended. "It's probably easier for us to find you than for you to find us." The man was pointing at the kilt. "I'm Saul, and this is my wife, Sarah."

Kiltman and Wilson shook hands with a couple who could have been on the front of any glamour magazine the world over. In many ways they were quite similar in their looks, with darkly enchanting features and thick black hair. Saul's broad smile melted Wilson - Kiltman could see it happening and did not mind. A guy as good looking as Saul deserved women to melt in front of him. He seemed completely unaware, adding to his charisma. She put her hand out to say hello, but words did not escape her mouth.

"Hi!" Sarah said, with a broad smile. She was working hard not to show any hint of the amusement she was feeling at the kilted superhero.

"Let's go!" Saul turned to walk out the door. He had an air about him of someone who gave instructions regularly and reassuringly. As he walked, he half-turned to Kiltman and said, "I see you've already had your brush with acting royalty. Not bad for someone who only arrived in Manhattan a few hours ago."

"Sorry?" he asked.

"At the workstation, the guy you were chatting to." Saul was smiling.

Kiltman stopped in his tracks. For a moment he had forgotten the bitter cold, that seemed even worse in lower Manhattan where there were fewer buildings to break the wind coming in from the Hudson River. "You mean, that was…"

"The very man - the Godfather, Raging Bull, Deerhunter," Saul said, before lifting his hand and shouting to a cab hurtling towards them, "Taxi!"

"…Driver!" Kiltman slapped his head with a gloved hand.

The cab pulled up alongside the kerb, with Sarah and Wilson jumping in the back, Saul in the front. Wilson stuck her head out the door, "Kiltman, are you coming?"

He realised he may have just spoken to his all-time hero, whom he held in an esteem far beyond a mere superhero. He had spent his life wondering if ever he met him, what he would say, how cool he would be in the moment. He had even practiced in front of the mirror, not too dissimilar to Taxi Driver.

And then, all he could say was *Eh, no, I don't know*. He could already see himself needing to take a call during that future dinner conversation, when he was asked what his greatest regret was.

"Kiltman, come on!" Wilson's impatience was now reaching the high-pitched stage.

He had barely crushed into the back seat and closed the door when it sped off south towards the Battery Park area of Manhattan. In a few minutes they would be at the museum. Sarah was leaning forward into the front section of the cab explaining to the driver, a dead ringer for George Clooney, how to get close to the museum despite the blockades created around the park.

Wilson leaned in close to Kiltman, and whispered, "Is it just me, or are the people in New York incredibly beautiful?"

He looked at her, and whispered back, "Wilson, whatever room, or cab, you walk into, you will always be the prettiest."

She turned her head to him, trying to discern whether he was joking. His mask made it an impossible task. She sighed, giving up attempting to read him, before also leaning forward into the front of the cab, enjoying the *Clooney* driver's natural cologne. Kiltman also sighed realising that delivering heartfelt compliments in a mask was becoming increasingly frustrating.

After a series of skidding around corners and amber gambling with the lights at various junctions, they screeched to a halt five blocks from the museum.

"This is as close as we can get," the driver said. The Manhattan grid system had been designed with 20 blocks to a mile - they had quarter of mile to go. It was now 2.45. Fifteen minutes before the event started.

"Okay, thanks." Saul squeezed the driver's shoulder in gratitude for his sense of urgency. Wilson also clutched his shoulder, just because it seemed to be inviting her, right there under her nose.

They clambered out onto the sidewalk, steam billowing up from a nearby underground ventilator, adding a paradoxical sense of warmth to the cold surrounding them. Thank goodness I am not wearing the Marilyn Monroe wig, Wilson thought.

"Come on," Sarah shouted back towards them as she began to jog. "Last one there's a rotten egg!"

Saul and Wilson dropped into a fast-paced run behind her, Kiltman taking up the rear, feeling more hard-boiled than rotten. Sarah moved at a fast clip, taking them past crowds of people increasing in density the closer they came to the museum. Not surprisingly there were also growing numbers of police, lined up behind large wooden barricades emblazoned with the letters NYPD. They were running down the embankment looking onto the Hudson River, barely noticing the haunting swells of the water lapping up against Manhattan. At any other time, this would have been a moment to stop and take in the breath-taking power of this great city.

In taking up the rear of the group, Kiltman was able to inconspicuously slip his hand into his sporran and extract the flask. On this trip, he had noticed how deft he was becoming at that action. He lifted it to his mouth and poured a robust dram while concentrating on not stumbling. He felt the warmth flow through his body instantly. Hair o' the Dog seemed to be aware of the coldness in his limbs and immediately created an internal warmth he had not experienced before. He would analyse this later when he was back home, but he was sure he had found another functionality in this special drink. It did not just imbue special sensory powers but searched out and protected the vulnerable parts of his body.

As he put it back in his sporran he could already feel it reaching parts other drinks did not reach.

303

The Museum

"Hi, Sarah and Saul!" The burly security guard in a tailored suit spoke affectionately. "So, are you going to let me know why you wanted to meet round here?"

He quickly took the tickets Sarah was holding out. "These look fine. Why don't you just go through the main entrance like everyone else?" He handed them back but could not take his eyes off Kiltman. "Is it something to do with your kilted friend here?"

"Abel, I know this is going to sound weird." There was enough anxiety in Sarah's tone to encourage his attention. "Can you let us in through this door? We don't have time to explain, but my Scottish friends here need to check out some of the security aspects of the venue."

Abel paused for a few moments. There really was not a question he could ask that would allow him to break the rules in this way. His job was to stop people doing what Sarah was asking him to do. He either trusted her or not, it was as simple as that. He sighed, shook his head resignedly, then pushed the door inwards.

"Okay, just keep it discrete," he whispered, as Sarah kissed him on the cheek and Saul patted his back. Sarah's powers of persuasion started with her dreamy brown eyes; friendliness and integrity took care of the rest. It helped that she had chosen to meet Abel at an entrance at the side of the building allowing them access away from the security services and police.

Before entering, Kiltman peeked around the corner of one of the hexagonal walls to see the square facing the building. It was filled with close to thirty rows of dignitaries sitting in padded, metal chairs in front of a makeshift stage erected specially for the event. It was a Who's Who of world leaders, with the first row full already and the other seats filling up quickly.

At the front there was an overly jolly UK Prime Minister trying to encourage conversation with a surly Russian President. Ireland's Taoiseach was cracking a joke with the German Chancellor, whose face was creased up in a smile long before the punch line had been delivered just in case he missed it. The US President sat in the middle of the front row, reading the order of service, working hard to appear solemn. To his left, there were several Rabbis and religious leaders looking up towards the podium waiting for the memorial to be delivered. Behind them and dotted throughout the rows he could see the majority of European countries represented, as well as leaders from Asia, Africa, the Middle East, and South America.

He was initially surprised how at ease the dignitaries and religious leaders were despite the sub-zero conditions. Then realised that they would not be wearing second-hand St. Paddy's Day gear from a midtown pub. They would have been dressed that morning in designer thermals and meticulously planned layers of wool and cashmere. The large heaters dotted generously around the rows of seats also meant they were shielded from the fierce cold.

He realised that if the UN meeting had not been taking place the next day, the turnout may have been less. Although he expected that many of those leaders would have been there anyway to recognize such a tragic loss of innocent lives sixty years earlier. He whispered a silent prayer he would be able to find a way to stop more deaths happening that afternoon.

"Kiltman, down here," Wilson called as she walked through the door.

Saul and Sarah had bid them goodbye and good luck, before walking confidently to their seats in the middle of the audience. He found it odd that they were so willing to participate in an event that had been targeted by a terrorist. He then realised it was not odd. It was their sense of determination and obstinacy in the face of evil. In fact, he thought, that was exactly why they were there at the museum in the first place.

They had descended a floor into a large basement area below the museum. It felt less cold the lower they went, protected from the harsh gales blowing in over the Hudson.

"Over to you now. What do you feel?" She looked at him, the anxiety registering on her face more than he had noticed before. She was tired, operating on adrenaline, willing herself on to close down Mask's acts of aggression.

His sensory inputs had been working hard since he had entered the square, trying to see, hear, smell, and feel every strange out of place nuance. In an acre full of world leaders, this had nearly overloaded his senses. Now that they were underground, in the quiet of the basement, he was able to offload those distorting inputs and concentrate on the immediate vicinity. Part of the technique with his sensory superpowers was knowing what to exclude, allowing him maximum focus on what remained.

He concentrated hard, pressing his hands against the basement wall facing towards the square, trying to find a hint of the unusual. It took a few minutes; it was now 3.05. He knew he was on borrowed time. There it was, just a glimmer of a pulse but enough for him to hear a clock ticking down towards a detonation point. It was through the wall on the other side.

"Wilson, there must be a way round beyond this wall. Did you see anything?"

"Yes, as we walked down here, we passed a staircase. Quick, follow me."

She started sprinting back the way they came. Soon they were hurrying down a dark, damp set of stairs that spiralled around behind the wall into a corridor. The overhead light was flashing erratically, its bulb needed replacing. It barely gave enough cover for them to run along the walkway taking them underneath the square. The further they ran the louder the pulse became, till Kiltman put his hand up. She nearly bumped into him, having the presence of mind to bring herself up short just in time.

"It's here!" He pointed at an innocuously bland, off-white wall. "Placing his hand against the texture he leaned into it and pressed gently then with more force, gently, then again with more power. To the side of the wall, there was a light switch, a simple white flip on, flip off version.

"Wilson, this wall should be damp after years down here below sea level. But it's as dry as a bone. That tells me, it's been replaced recently. Do you have any keys?"

She did not question his request. She pulled her house yale key from her pocket and passed it to him. Slipping it underneath the edge of the switch with enough force to get traction, he twisted until the switch popped off the wall and fell to the floor.

306

Underneath they could see a metal clock counting down. 4:43, 4:42, 4:41...

They exchanged a quick glance; they had less than five minutes. No time to warn the security teams to evacuate. They would not have believed them even if they had been able to make it upstairs on time. He tapped the wall around the hole left by the switch. The plaster gave way a little bit more on each tap. The more he tapped, the more evident it became that the wall was a fragile new addition to the basement. He stuck three fingers into the hole where the switch used to be and pulled hard. A foot-long piece of plaster gave way, immediately spilling onto their shoes and creating a cloud of white, chalky dust. She did not need to be instructed. She quickly grabbed the wall and began to strip away the plaster along with him, dust spiralling around the corridor making them cough as they continued to tear large strips.

After hauling and tugging, and when the dust had settled somewhat, they faced a gaping hole. In its middle, there was a metal box about three feet square, attached by wires leading up to the clock, which hung loosely from a wooden support beam. He remembered the designs they had found in Villa General Belgrano. This was the 'layer cake' bomb he expected, although had hoped he would never see.

4:05, 4:04, 4:03...

He ran his fingers along the wire and onto the box, feeling and kneading its sides. It had been laced with PETN, which contained those explosive elements normally found in TNT and dynamite. There was enough nitro in the box to create a hole in the square large enough for the dignitaries and religious leaders to disappear into.

2:01, 2:00, 1:59...

"Come on, Kiltman!" she urged. "Think! How do we defuse it!"

He bent down and placed his ear against the box, trying to hear where the pulse was leading. As he listened, he traced the sound with his fingers, tracking all the way down underneath. He waited a moment before stepping back an inch or two. He wrapped his arms around the metal and yanked hard, dislocating the box from a concrete slab where it had been placed to provide an even surface. It was lighter than he had expected. He pushed it over onto its side to reveal an intricate series of coloured wires connected to various screws and joints leading back up into the bomb. There must have been ten of them, all different colours, strangely menacing in the flickering fluorescent light.

1:01, 1:00, 0:59...

He knew one of the wires would trip the mechanism to explode the bomb, another to defuse, and the rest were camouflage to confuse anyone who found themselves where he was at that moment. He did not have a clue as to which was which. Without seeing inside the device, where the wires connected, he had no way of knowing.

0:20, 0:19, 0:18...

He put one hand in his sporran, and put his other on the wires, taking a deep breath and waiting. He felt his fingers wander across the mesh of cabling, touching each of them individually. Finally, they landed on the green wire, embedded in the middle of the mass of electrics.

0:10, 0:09, 0:08...

"Do it, Kiltman! For God's sake, do it!" Wilson screamed.

He tugged the green cable with all his might, feeling it detach itself from the inside of the box, with a soft metallic click.

0:02, 0:01, 0:00

Nothing happened.

She threw herself on him, wrapping her arms around his neck, and kissed him hard on his latex cheek. He could feel her heart beating against his chest.

"How on earth were you able to do that?" she asked gripping him tightly.

He exhaled a long, slow breath, his hand still in his sporran, wrapped around the white feather.

Shoes

She was beginning to feel uncomfortable at how long the embrace had been going on. She had held him for a long minute after the bomb was meant to detonate, enjoying his strong arms around her and his slow breathing in her ear. In a matter of seconds, they had gone from impending devastation and death to warmth and security.

He was not complaining, happy to have his girl in his arms again after so long. Not being able to tell her his thoughts and feelings was much more difficult. At least now he was not entertaining the idea of breaking the news that he was Kenny. That would have been madness, making her relationship with Kiltman much more complicated at this point in their adventure. He was happy to wait until they were back home. He had also reconciled himself to how affectionate she was being with him. It was not a form of cheating, he thought. She really was attracted to Kiltman because he was Kenny, she had just not realised it.

She gently stepped back from him loosening her arms from his neck. "Sorry, I just got caught up in the moment."

"No need to apologise, Wilson. I think you know I enjoy those moments with you," he answered in a warm, gentle voice.

She gazed at where she thought his eyes were behind the mask. "Look, Kiltman, I really don't want to give you the wrong impression. Yes, I like you. We have a connection. But the truth is, I'm in love with someone back home. It's taken me a while to fully realise it."

She stopped, feeling her rising annoyance at saying more than she intended to.

"Let me guess. Is it, *em, Kenny*?"

"Yes," she answered. "Kenny, an amazing guy. I hope you get to meet him one day." She broke into a broad smile as if a weight had been lifted from her.

"I would like that, Wilson. But to be honest, I will probably be jealous of him. If he has you in love with him, then he must be a good-looking, big-hearted guy."

She moved her head to the side slightly, considering how to answer. "Yes, he is big-hearted. I wouldn't say he's classically good-looking. His appeal comes from something inside him, not from how he looks."

"Yes, but he must be pretty handsome, no?"

She thought again, "No, not really. I mean, he's handsome to me. But he's not the guy who would turn heads walking down the street."

"I find it hard to believe a girl as pretty as you would end up with someone that wasn't attractive, at least to some degree."

"Enough, Kiltman! This is becoming weird. We need to get upstairs and tell the security team that they've got an unexploded bomb underneath the world leaders. I think that trumps the conversation about whether my *em, Kenny* as you call him, is a looker."

She barged past him on her way back along the corridor shaking her head. He knew how to push her buttons, she thought. He sighed, not quite sure how to handle the discussion about his looks. He knew that he was no oil painting, but did she have to be so convinced about it?

They surfaced towards the end of the memorial service, catching the last few words of the ceremony. A six-minute silence was being held to remember the six million killed during the war. It gave them a chance to compose themselves, out of sight behind the hexagonal wall. They looked at the ground, the energy of emotion and unity in the square revitalising them. Their thoughts were with the Jewish community and the history of those despicable acts of horror. Individually they felt their resolution strengthen as they absorbed the silence, appreciating the importance of the role they had played in averting a disaster. They could not take the pleasure they wanted in that thought, realising they were now out of clues - literally clueless. Mask and his compatriots had a blank canvas; not knowing what would be painted was worse than knowing.

The silence ended. The dignitaries shook hands and embraced one another before being joined by their security detail and led off towards their cars dotted around the inside of the police blockade.

Saul and Sarah rushed over to them. "How did it go?" Saul asked.

"Yes, there was a bomb, and yes, it's now defused," Kiltman responded. "We need to advise the NYPD. They will need to bring in bomb disposal experts. They will also need to keep the blockade in place until they've properly investigated this area. The perpetrators may still be here somewhere."

He scanned the mass of people swarming to their cars and onto their next appointment, as Saul ran over to one of the more senior police officers to explain the situation. The dignitaries were ready to go onto their next appointment, having had enough of the New York wind. He was impressed at how they knew which black, anodyne sedan belonged to them. The rows of cars and people hurrying in-between gave a sense of a chapter closed, the next one starting soon.

His scan of the crowd triggered something at the back of his mind. It was nothing he could specifically identify, but there was something once again niggling at him.

"What is it?" Wilson asked detecting a mood change.

He scanned the square again looking at each person individually trying to find a hint of a clue. Yellow. Something yellow had flickered in the corner of his eye. Most people were wearing black, very few had chosen to branch out into more lively colours, partially due to the solemnity of the ceremony and also because people tended to choose dark clothes in cold conditions. He painstakingly searched for yellow, where was it he thought? Why was it even important?

It took him a minute or two but there it was again, over to the side crossing his line of vision. A pair of black shoes embossed with yellow flowers.

"Quick, Wilson, let's go. Now!" He started running towards the shoes, with Wilson following behind him. She had not questioned his command; she knew not to now. As they ran, he shouted, "You won't be able to see her yet, but there's a woman in the crowd. She was in Villa General Belgrano. I think it's Rolf Müller's daughter."

Running was difficult for him at the best of times. Talking while running was nigh on impossible. He decided to point instead. As they approached the yellow flowered shoes, the owner turned around to look at them. There was no doubting the look of anger and hatred painted across a face that would normally have been quite appealing. Wilson could see her icy blue eyes were the same shape and colour as her assailant in Villa General Belgrano. The woman turned and ran into the crowd losing herself in the melee of cold people heading to wherever they could find a warm beverage.

Wilson had kept her eyes on Rolf Müller's daughter, remembering her conversation with Joseph Abram in the Recoleta graveyard. Her name was Sophia. Knowing her name and realising she and her father had tried to kill her, made Wilson even more determined. She increased her acceleration to overtake Kiltman, disappearing into the thickening crowds. He chose to take a circuitous route around the edge of the people working hard to avoid bumping into the hordes trying to squeeze through police barriers. It took a couple of minutes, but he ran out onto the street at the same time as Wilson a hundred yards or so down the road. She was pointing in two different directions at the same time. One arm gesticulating to Sophia climbing into the driver's seat of a small, black car. The other was pointing at a row of taxis beside him.

He understood immediately what she was telegraphing to him. Turning to the first cab in the rank, a yellow car more dishevelled and scratched than usual, he jumped into the back seat. "Follow that black car. But first pick up that lady on the corner."

The driver could tell that Kiltman was not in the mood for small talk. The driver's ruggedly handsome face epitomized Wilson's earlier comments, which stung even more. The driver's name plate identified him as Rocco Garcia.

"You gotta be kiddin, man?" Rocco smiled two rows of pearly white teeth. "I live for these moments!"

"I've never been more serious," Kiltman answered already liking the driver, despite his swarthy good looks.

When they pulled up alongside Wilson, he had the door open for her to jump in. Rocco did not stop. He crushed the accelerator squealing his tyres in pursuit of the black car, which was disappearing into the distance a block and a half away, heading north. The vehicle was nipping in and out of traffic taking advantage of available spaces between cars and buses. The lights seemed to stay green for her, while Rocco had to hurtle through several ambers and one red with horn blaring to keep her in sight. No matter how hard he tried he could not get closer than a block and a half which was barely close enough to maintain visibility. Kiltman had become the navigator block by block as he directed Rocco through the maze of mid-afternoon Manhattan traffic. He had found a way to assess the depths of cars beyond their line of sight and could direct the driver to the available spaces.

"Are you for real, man?" Rocco said barely hiding his incredulity at Kiltman's talents.

They tore up through SoHo into the famous Greenwich Village before they hit midtown. The lights were in their favour as they sped through the chaos of Times Square. Rocco was feeling pleased with himself as he exited onto Avenue of the Americas, until a group of pedestrians distracted by the buzz of the most famous square in the world walked out in front of his car. He had to swerve hard to the left bumping up onto the pavement.

They hurtled towards a group of men gathered around a makeshift table. The table flew through the air, money and objects of their trade scattering across the sidewalk. The men dived to the side to avoid the car's impact. From their cab, they could see one man bash his head on a garbage can and another smack his back on one of New York's ubiquitous fire hydrants.

Rocco opened his window and spat onto the street beside the shaken group.

"Three card monty scum!" he shouted, without a hint of remorse.

Kiltman nodded his appreciation, having lost $100 many years earlier to a group just like the one Rocco had mercilessly disrupted. Not far from Times Square, they had set up a table made from cardboard to allow them a quick escape if the police approached. He had not realised they were all in on the scam encouraging him to believe in his uncanny ability to guess which card was the red queen. The money he lost was due to a combination of overinflated self-belief and a St Patrick's Day hangover. Justice will always win in the end, he thought, enjoying the sight of a similar group flat on the sidewalk with two cops approaching.

"There she is," Wilson shouted, when they had lost concentration for the briefest of moments. The black car was speeding towards Central Park, looming ahead of them, the greenery a welcome respite after the claustrophobia of the built-up lower half of the city.

The car disappeared in a blur into the park, just missing a horse and carriage that had turned down into its entrance. The horse barely noticed, nonchalantly trotting along, chewing grass, having lived most of its life in the city. The driver was similarly nonplussed sighing at another hothead screeching around a city that did not know how to slow down.

Rocco pointed his yellow cab towards the entrance to the park, pressed the accelerator to the floor and narrowly missed a bus turning towards a busy Fifth Avenue. They had her in sight and were now gaining quickly through the lower end of the park, no traffic lights to hold them back. He skidded his cab around a wide bend encircling Central Park Zoo working hard to keep from swivelling out of control. As he came out of the bend he slammed on the brakes when he saw the black car embedded in a metal barrier. Wilson had been wondering if she would have been able to take the curve at the speed she was going. Obviously not. Her passenger door was open, and she was not in sight.

Wilson threw a bunch of twenty-dollar bills in the window to Rocco, shouting, "Thanks, Rocco, you're a star."

He was already pulling up beside the black car clearly disappointed the chase was over. "Cheers, mate!" Kiltman added, clambering out clumsily.

He was scanning the woods to their left where he was sure she would have dashed for cover. His heat-seeking radar picked her up sprinting north on a parallel road. He sensed she was one of quite a number of runners and walkers, but her erratic style gave her away. She was swerving and bumping into the other joggers, her desperation evident in Kiltman's inner eye.

"Let's go," he shouted.

They ran through a smattering of woods onto a gravelly, pedestrianised area to see her a short distance ahead, zigzagging between innocent New Yorkers swathed in layers of Nike and

Adidas nylon and polyester. He and Wilson set off with a spring in their step that felt good after the exhausting and unnerving car chase. They were heading north on Central Park's Mall, a testament to some of the world's best-known poets and writers, represented in the large, strong statues of Rabbie Burns, Sir Walter Scott and William Shakespeare.

"Wilson, do you think you can catch her? I'm struggling," Kiltman panted after a few minutes.

"You bet," she answered, visibly stepping up a gear.

"Okay, I'll see you at the northwest corner of the park whatever happens," he shouted as she kicked up dust in her wake. As he slowed up, he could see Wilson gaining on her - they were approaching the reservoir made famous by Dustin Hoffman. Unlike Hoffman, he felt his heart pounding uncomfortably, his legs becoming heavier with every step, the gnawing ache of a muscle spasm in his right calf reminding him he was more a Snickers Man than a Marathon Man.

Escaping

Sophia was angry. With every step she ran from the Scottish detective and her kilted partner, the madder she became. She wanted to turn, stop, and put a bullet in each of them, ending it right there alongside the statues of their famous countrymen. While it may have felt good, she knew that it would mean certain capture for her. Police were dotted throughout the woods and roads in the park, she would never escape. For the moment, she seemed to be a quirkily overdressed jogger. In New York, quirky was the norm. Even Kiltman blended into Central Park and its scores of funkily dressed runners and walkers.

She took a look back over her shoulder. Kiltman was giving up, but the woman was gaining on her. Sophia prided herself on keeping fit, running up the hills around Villa General Belgrano. It irked her to see she was losing ground. She ran up the steps to the path surrounding the reservoir dominating the middle of the park, named after one of its most famous joggers, Jacqueline Kennedy Onassis. Instinctively she chose to run along its west side. Her focus was on getting to her apartment in Harlem, 25 blocks north, just over a mile away. Clockwise allowed her to take advantage of some degree of obstruction from her pursuers, with the majority of the joggers following the traditional anti-clockwise route around the water. There were enough people out exercising to make it difficult for Kiltman and his partner to run in a straight line.

At the top end of the reservoir, she headed out of the park onto Central Park West, finding an additional kick in her legs. She looked back briefly but could not see her pursuers. The tactic to take the reservoir had most likely worked, creating the confusion needed to allow her to exit the park with some cover.

Now that she had lost them, she was beginning to think about her conversation with their leader. He would have no sympathy, no words of comfort at the failure of the plan. He would find a way to punish her, of that she was in no doubt. She had tremendous respect for him, for his devotion to their cause and the passion with which he had led them. But without her father to comfort her, she felt alone, terribly alone. It was important for her to find the next project where she could prove herself as a faithful, loyal soldier.

She remembered the words oft quoted to her by her father when he was making her harder and tougher each day - words that their ultimate leader had announced gloriously shaking his hands above the lectern: *Life doesn't forgive weakness*. She found another gear she did not know she had, increasing her speed, a smile spreading across her pixy features as she found the energy to go on.

Just before she was crushed by a flying detective.

Finally

Wilson knew immediately what Sophia was doing. Running into the middle of a group of joggers coming in the opposite direction was one of the oldest tricks in the fugitive's book as far as she was concerned. Rather than compete with the head-on runners, Wilson found a line on the outside of the path and stuck to it all the way around to the top end of the reservoir. She saw Sophia slip down into a snicket of woods heading towards the upper west side of the city. The fugitive ducked and weaved through bushes and trees before leaving the park to continue her escape along Central Park West. Rather than follow too closely, Wilson stayed within the park on West Drive running parallel with Central Park West. She could see Sophia running alongside the wall, her pace not slowing down, a look of determination settling into her features.

When West Drive began to curve east, Wilson knew it was time to leave the road and snake through the sparse woods. She hoped she had got her timing right as her legs led her through the bushes, the crush of dried twigs and crackle of dead leaves masked by the horns and engines from the traffic beyond the wall. Jumping onto a wooden bench snug against the perimeter of the park, she sprung with both feet over the wall, not quite sure where she would land. She did not care, learning how to break her fall in such a scenario had been drilled into her throughout years of training.

Wilson did not need to worry because she fell squarely on top of Sophia, flattening her like a burger on a bun. Anyone else would have been winded, or even concussed, but Sophia frantically punched and kicked like a wild animal caught in a trap, disorientating Wilson with a whack to the side of her head. She managed to struggle free and scramble to her feet, giving her pursuer another kick, this time in the ribs, to keep her immobile long enough to get away. She turned to run up the busy road and find an escape route through an increasingly erratic bedlam of cars rattling noisily towards downtown. Scurrying up the avenue towards Harlem she searched frantically for a gap between the vehicles to disappear into.

The barricade surrounding the hole had been placed only a few hours earlier. The construction team had been asked to investigate the increasingly pungent smell spilling from the drains. Soon after they had opened the hole, they realised that someone had poured poisonous sludge into a deep pit below ground. With nowhere to go the sludge had festered and putrefied. If the barrier had been higher, it would have prevented Sophia from crashing into and falling over the top of the wooden, makeshift obstacle. When she made impact forty feet below, her days of terrorising were over. The enquiry into the dangers inherent in such low barriers would take place weeks later – it was accepted that Sophia's accident would have been avoidable if she had been looking where she was going. Nevertheless, a decision was taken to increase the height of barriers employed in future maintenance around the city. When the decision was reached, the official made a point of noting the irony of a terrorist - intent on killing – ultimately savings lives.

CNN

The television had been on all afternoon in the New York hotel room. Mask had been watching, waiting for news of devastation at the museum. He expected it to come on stream around 3.30. When nothing was reported he checked his phone to see if Sophia had sent a message. This went on until after four o'clock when he gave up waiting and called her. There was no answer, a signal that the plan had failed.

In his mind's eye he had imagined the explosion playing out like a tragic opera, wails of grief interrupted by police sirens as the camera scanned the square outside the museum. Instead his TV demonstrated what the absence of a tragedy looks like. Innocuous news reports about the New Year parties taking place across the city - how the policing would be conducted the following night at Times Square to manage the midnight revellers.

All those dignitaries had been sitting there like ducks waiting to be annihilated. Sophia had the straightforward task of starting the timer on the bomb in the basement. It could not have been simpler. Her father had done all the hard work before he had died, arranging the passes to the event, and building and placing the bomb. If Rolf had not needed to go back to Argentina to confront Kiltman and his detective friend, he would have been able to see the act all the way through to the end.

The NBC and CNN news reports had been relatively light on the actual ceremony at the museum, focusing more on the relationship between the leaders ahead of the UN meeting the following day. They explained that many of the politicians, from Scotland, parts of Spain and Italy among others, had an agenda in terms of self-determination. It would be their moment to stake their claim to the right of autonomy on a world stage. The other countries were showing up to be part of the spectacle, paying lip service to what they saw as a relatively trite agenda item. They would use the meeting to schmooze with those nations where they wanted to build relationships. The New Year party laid on by the assembly would be an added bonus, a chance to show just how human they were, capable of letting their hair down.

A newsflash interrupted the CNN reporter, with breaking news about an accidental death on the Upper West side of Manhattan. This was not unusual, Mask thought, they were in New York after all. Accidental deaths happened all the time in such a populous city, alongside large numbers of murders and gangland killings. This one seemed to be different. He turned up the volume with his remote.

"Today, shortly before four o'clock, a woman was killed when she fell into a deep hole on Central Park West. Bystanders described the scene as horrific. Witnesses claimed the lady, as yet unknown, tried to cross the busy road. She did not see the barricade around a hole that had been the source of a smell neighbours had been complaining about for days."

The female reporter's dark brown eyes threatened to crinkle into a smile, her warm demeanour belying the seriousness of the message she was communicating. Behind her right shoulder, the camera scanned across the street showing the hole and its orange, wooden barriers, with several police cars and an ambulance dotted around the area, lights flashing. The sidewalk was busy with police officers interviewing witnesses, who were animatedly describing the woman's last seconds.

"Apparently the woman was being chased by a Scottish police officer, Detective Inspector Wilson, from the Glasgow police in Scotland. If you recall in our international segment last week, we showed footage of her in the south of France, knocking Scotland's First Minister over. We later found out that she had saved his life from an assassin's bullet.

"And then earlier this week, we saw her taking out two policemen in the San Siro soccer stadium in Milan, Italy. It later transpired that she and her accomplice, the famous Kiltman, were in a hurry to defuse a device set to explode under the pitch." She paused to let the weight of her words settle with the listeners.

"Today, we find this Scottish heroine on the streets of New York chasing an unknown woman."

She lifted her finger to her ear to help shut out some of the background traffic noise, lifting her other hand to the camera. "Wait! Yes, we are getting further information that this chase

321

started all the way down Manhattan at Battery Park, where earlier today there was a memorial ceremony at the Museum of Jewish Heritage. We have a witness on the other camera, let me switch you across to him."

Rocco's designer stubbled face appeared on screen. "Yeah, it was Kiltman and that cute Scottish detective. They asked me to follow this dame's car all the way up the island to the park. They then chased her on foot. It was awesome. That Kilt guy was amazing, he seemed to know how to direct me through traffic and catch up on her. Em, I mean, not that I was speeding, he helped me by working within the speed limit." It cut back to the female reporter.

"Amazing action and drama in New York - it seems a scene from a movie has played out in real life today on the second last day of the year in Manhattan. But ultimately it has ended in tragedy.

"This has been Anna O' Boyle reporting from CNN in New York city."

Mask pushed the remote to turn the television off, before slumping into his seat, resting his head back against the satin feel of the red cloth covering. Not only had Sophia messed up the operation they had been planning for months, dreaming about for years. She had also made sure that her death was the news leader across New York, which would filter out to channels throughout the country and internationally. It would not be long before they made the connection to her home in Villa General Belgrano. How could one person mess up so badly, he mused?

Well, he thought, placing a miniature whisky bottle to his lips, courtesy of the mini-bar, tomorrow is a new day.

A Harlem Bar

Kiltman was sipping a Diet Coke through a paper straw, up through the bottom of his mask. He was watching CNN, on a TV high up above rows of liquor bottles, in a bar buzzing with pre-New Year revelry. They had played the report a few times now about Wilson and the unknown lady who fell into a hole. He did not feel any pity for her knowing the horror she had tried to unleash a few hours earlier. He knew exactly where it had happened but decided not to go there. Wilson did not need Kiltman showing up to cause even more fuss. He could see her on TV, she was doing just fine. The pub was a local tavern just off the North West corner of the park where Central Park West met Central Park North. He sat at the edge of the bar, one eye on the TV, the other on the junction outside.

He was pleased to be able to sit in public in his kilt, his cape dropping down to the floor behind his stool. Nobody was bothering him, allowing him a sense of peace and space for the first time in a long time. The bar was busy, a growing sense of excitement building before New Year's Eve. Many folks had started early. The sense of bonhomie was tangible, Aretha Franklin songs belting out from a juke box in the corner. Spontaneous dancing, glass-tapping and headshaking filled the room, the sense of fun tantalising.

Through the misty window, he saw the green sweater and woollen hat moving briskly along Central Park West, her arms wrapped around her petite frame. The Paddy's Day accoutrements were proving a lot less effective as the temperature dropped with the arrival of evening. He ran out onto the sidewalk and put his arm around her shoulders. She slipped her arm around his waist and put her head on his shoulder. "Please tell me you've found somewhere warm for us to talk."

"You bet!" He led her into the bar and ordered a Malbec. They nurtured a few moments of silence as they waited for the wine to be poured. The barista, a tall man who carried the air and posture of a young Denzel Washington, placed the drink on the counter and winked at her. "This one's on the house. Not every day we have a real-life celebrity hero in here."

He pointed at the TV which was showing the incident from earlier with Wilson in the background talking to the police.

"Oh, thanks!" She was genuinely surprised. She turned to Kiltman as they walked over to a table in the corner near the jukebox. "I hope you don't think I'm stealing your thunder."

"Wilson, you can steal my thunder any time you want. You were incredible today. I really thought we had lost her. Do you know how many lives have been saved by her not being around anymore? I know that you'll be feeling it," he leant across and took her hand in both of his, "but please keep that in mind if you feel yourself getting down."

"Thanks, Kiltman." Her eyes welled up with big thick tears, one spilling down her cheek, before she brushed it away with the back of her hand. "I really don't want to talk about it now. I think it's over, at least for a while. NYPD are looking for her apartment, where I'm hoping they'll surface some more evidence that may lead us back to Mask."

"I agree." He sipped his drink. "Mask will be feeling disorientated. He's probably running for his life. It's going to take time for him to retrench."

Her phone rang, interrupting a quiet moment in their conversation. She whispered, "Sorry."

He nodded and put his thumb in the air.

"Hello? Tommy? Yes, hi. How are you?

"What, you're in New York?

"Oh, yes the UN assembly meeting, I'd forgotten you were going to that tomorrow.

"You saw me on TV? Ugghh, I'd rather not talk about it, I'm still recovering."

She waited a moment, listening.

"Well, you know I'm here with Kiltman. Are you sure?"

She put her hand over the mouthpiece, lifting her eyes to him. "How do you fancy going to a catwalk tonight? You remember Tommy MacGregor. He's inviting us to a modelling show this evening."

"Really?" Kiltman answered. He waited a moment. "How could I forget Tommy! Yes, that would be the kind of distraction we need after the last few days. It should be fun."

"Okay, Tommy, we're in. Where is it? Carnegie Hall? Yes, we'll find it. See you there at nine."

"Carnegie Hall?" Kiltman said as she closed the phone down. "Now that's appropriate. One of the most well-known concert venues in New York, if not the world. But the best bit is its construction was funded by Andrew Carnegie, from Dunfermline in Scotland. As a philanthropist, in today's money, he gave away close to $100 billion of his fortune to worthy causes."

"Amazing." She was genuinely impressed. "So, are you going?"

"Is it a date?" he asked, swirling the last of his Diet Coke around his glass, watching the ice melt slowly.

"Look!" She grinned at the blue and white masked face gawping back at her. "I made a decision a long time ago not to date two types of men."

"Oh, yes, and who would they be?"

"Superheroes…"

"And?" he asked.

"Total numpties like you," she laughed, throwing her napkin at him.

The New Yorker

They exited the bar into a chilly, dark New York, the bright lights of the cars adding a dreamy quality to what had already been a surreal day. It was only seven in the evening, but the absence of light made it feel much later. They turned left out of the bar into lower Harlem.

"Let's walk along here to one of the main roads going south. We'll get a cab going in our direction." Kiltman was already a couple of steps ahead, eager to get to their destination and relax into an evening free from danger.

Wilson nodded her agreement, happy to breathe in the city air, feeling its cold sharpness in her throat. They were both feeling tired, their bodies finally submitting to the tempestuous storm of minimal sleep, physical exertion, and adrenaline rushes. If someone had pushed a bed out onto the road, they would have fallen down into it. They had already trudged a couple of blocks west away from the park. She was beginning to wonder whether the Carnegie Hall event was a good idea.

"Hey, Kiltman! Over here!" A voice floated over towards them from across the street.

They looked around to see on their right a full block dedicated to basketball - one of those play areas made famous by West Side Story in the sixties. A large open space layered with flattened tarmac, a number of basketball nets along each side of the spacious square. Underneath each net, there were small groups of youths spinning and twisting, throwing balls back and forth and now and then towards the net, invariably passing through the hoop. They seemed oblivious to the cold, their misty breath adding a magical feel to the evening.

Behind its fence there was a young, fresh-faced man, wearing a New York Yankees baseball cap round the wrong way. He could not have been more than thirty - slim, with darkly exotic features and a broad, welcoming smile. He was the only white person in the area, very much at ease hanging out with the local lads.

They walked over towards him.

"Hi!" Kiltman said. Wilson lifted her hand in a guarded greeting, not quite sure what was coming next.

"Listen, please don't say no, but would you come in here and play some hoops? You and me, against a couple of the lads."

"But I haven't played basketball before, let alone the hoops version." Kiltman was surprised at how apprehensive he was feeling considering the day they had already survived.

"Ha!" the New Yorker laughed. "You really haven't, have you? Hoops is basketball, it's one and the same thing. Come on."

Kiltman and Wilson both shrugged at the same time. The day could not get any more surreal. They walked down to the end of the fence to a rickety, wire gate and stepped into an arena of kids rushing, ducking, diving, feinting, slam-dunking. They barely stopped for a second, running nonstop, throwing balls from one to another with alacrity and accuracy neither Wilson nor Kiltman would have imagined possible. The New Yorker approached with two tall lads behind him, around 16 years old. One of them, wearing an LA Lakers top, had a ball balanced on his head, keeping it in place with slight twitches of the neck. The other, wearing a New York Knicks jersey, was spinning a ball on his index finger.

"Okay, two on two," he spoke in a refined New York accent. "Kiltman and me against you guys. Let's go."

The lads tossed their balls along the tarmac to nestle against the wire mesh surrounding the area, close to Wilson's feet. The friendly New Yorker threw his ball at the boy wearing the Lakers top before backing off him, legs spread and arms pointing forwards. He started wiggling and jerking each time the Lakers guy moved. Kiltman thought it looked like some sort of strange ritual dance.

"Kiltman, get the other guy, quick!" the New Yorker shouted continuing to back off the player with the ball.

It was only at that moment Kiltman realised he was standing under a net. He turned on his heel to run after the opponent who was already passing him, a brief flash of NY Knicks catching his eye. At least he did not have the ball, he thought, settling into a false sense of security. He continued to watch the opponent until he leapt up into the air twisting 180 degrees in the process. He

327

heard Wilson shout, "Wow!" The guy seemed to float upwards as if he was weightless. Just as he reached the top end of his jump, the ball came floating over Kiltman's head into the player's hands. He slam-dunked into the net in a casually gifted manner that had Wilson clapping and whistling. Kiltman put his hands high in the air and applauded, shouting, "Well done, son!"

The NY Knicks guy moved to the centre of the play area and threw the ball at Kiltman, which he found very generous of his opponent. He then realised he was supposed to do something with it. Turning on his heel he started to bounce the ball quickly off the surface concentrating on not letting it slip, in a manner he thought was typical basketball bouncing. His teammate shouted words of encouragement, clearly enjoying what was become a farcical contest. One of the opponents sauntered past Kiltman, inserting his hand into the bounce, robbing him of the ball, before throwing a three-pointer, all net.

Kiltman was never going to come close to scoring, it was becoming more evident every time he was dummied or dropped the ball. His team-mate was able to scramble a few points through some of his own ingenuity and flair, managing to save some of their blushes. He was as natural an athlete as Kiltman had seen, with an added spring in his step and ability to duck and weave. He was giving as good as he was getting, twisting and turning, throwing and dunking. Each time he scored, he walked up to Kiltman and casually high fived, one time patting him on the bottom. Out of the dark of a Harlem night, this stranger had created a massive feelgood factor Kiltman was relishing and Wilson delighting in.

The local lads had realised quite soon after the 'two on two' got going, that Kiltman, while looking every bit the Scottish superhero, did not know one end of a basketball from the other. Whether out of pity or in an effort to teach, they began to throw the ball to him. If he dropped it, they picked it up and gave it back. They practically escorted him to the net before giving him a leg up to drop the ball into the ring. Finally, he scored.

At that point, pouring with sweat and panting like a horse after the derby, he gasped, "Enough! I'm done."

The three other players approached him smiling and laughing. They each gave him a hug in turn before the two local lads walked over to Wilson, who was holding their basketballs in each hand. They hugged her, dwarfing her in their large, athletic frames before sauntering out the gate. The New Yorker, who was so obviously at ease in Harlem, grinned and put his arm around Kiltman's shoulders.

"Kiltman, you did great. I wish you lived here in the city. I'd teach you how to play. You've got some good moves."

Kiltman laughed, sensing a sincere generosity of spirit emanating from this man. "Trust me, if I lived here, I would let you teach me. You're a good man." They hugged and bade their goodbyes, walking off on their separate journeys.

Wilson turned to Kiltman. "That was cute, you did well."

He laughed. "Not bad, considering..."

"Did you get that guy's name?" she asked.

"Actually, no I didn't." Kiltman looked back but he could no longer see him in the play area. He had ghosted out of sight into the welcoming bustle of a New York city evening.

"Okay, let's just remember him as the New Yorker, the kind, gentle, fun-loving New York man we met when we needed our spirits lifted," Wilson offered.

"Works for me," Kiltman replied, wondering whether their paths would ever cross again.

Carnegie Catwalk

"Over here, Maggie!" Tommy shouted from the front row, just underneath the edge of the catwalk.

From the outside, Carnegie Hall had seemed quite unexceptional dominating the corner of 57[Th] Street and Seventh Avenue. Its midtown location had meant less than a three-mile walk for Kiltman and Wilson. They were already feeling revitalised by the basketball scrimmage, beginning to get the measure of the cold. Fortunately, the harsh wind had slowed up to a gentle breeze, icy but manageable

Once inside, they understood what all the fuss was about. The hall was normally used as a concert venue, many of Kiltman's all-time greats having played there over the decades, including Duke Ellington, James Taylor and Simon & Garfunkel. Its exquisitely designed gold trim and red edging softened the immensity of the wedding cake structure, tier upon tier stretching up high towards the roof.

The venue was brimming with an animated audience, fully expectant to be awed and inspired by the latest summer collection from the new up and coming Milan designer, Anto Bruni. Wilson had read the billboard outside on 57th Street before they entered - apparently Bruni had become the most exciting designer since Versace. She found it hard to believe that only two days earlier they had been in the Duomo, Versace's funeral front of mind.

They crept along the front row trying to avoid toes and handbags, to find two seats free where Tommy had left a scribbled note on each saying: *Don't dare touch Kiltman and Wilson's seats!* To Tommy's right Marsha and Digi sat quietly looking at the programme. They barely acknowledged the new arrivals as they squeezed into their seats on the other side of Tommy. "You've had quite a day!" Tommy was smiling at Wilson. "I bet you need a drink."

"Actually, I'm okay," she replied. "Just happy to be here and have a chance to de-stress."

"Me too," Kiltman added, still feeling the exertions of the basketball lesson in his legs and arms.

"Excuse me," Kiltman heard a deep melodic voice pronounce carefully from behind him. He turned to find a rather solemn man in black tie and tails.

"Yes? Can I help you?" Kiltman asked, fully expecting someone to comment on the dress code of the Carnegie Hall not stretching to accommodate capes, masks and kilts.

"Don't worry, sir, nothing to be overly concerned about. However, the manager has asked to have a word with you."

Kiltman shook his head and rose from his seat. It surprised him just how difficult it was to shake off an inferiority complex born of years of catholic guilt topped off with a predisposition to self-destruction.

"I'll hopefully be back in a minute." He looked at Wilson and Tommy, who both shrugged.

He had barely left his seat when the first group of models began to step softly along the catwalk. Cameras flashed, women squealed, men shouted, as an impressive, dark-haired lady, no smaller than six-foot tall with an extraordinarily slender body, shimmied along the floor. Her costume comprised four strategically placed coconuts, preserving her honour, but not much more. She was oblivious to the noise and clamour rebounding off the hall's walls.

Walking behind her was another tall lady, blonde hair reaching down to her midriff. Tommy turned to Wilson. "That's Marsha's sister."

She was wearing four large coconut leaves, providing just enough covering to have the men in the audience straining their necks to focus. Wilson was starting to understand the reason why the evening had been named *Parody of Paradise*, displayed in a large banner stretched across the stage behind the models. It was incredible, she thought, that as long as the name fit, then people would buy into the concept.

They sat through around ten models wearing all sorts of objects from coconuts to pineapples. One wore nothing but a covering of sand similar to Helena Christensen in that famous Chris Isaac video. Wilson looked over her shoulder, she was becoming worried about Kiltman. It must have taken something serious for him to miss out on this show. She scanned the hall as far back as the entrance to see if he had met someone and had settled into another seat. He was nowhere to be seen.

She nearly jumped out of her skin when shrieks and shouts escalated all around her. It had been noisy already, but suddenly the place erupted. The Carnegie Hall was large and spacious, but it was still a confined space when thousands of people were screaming and whistling. She turned to the stage to see what had caused the uproar.

Kiltman was walking down the catwalk, wearing his customary mask, cape and kilt. He had his head bent backwards at a slight tilt, his arms swinging, hips wiggling as he strode towards the end of the stage. He stopped at the end, paused for a moment throwing a look out into the audience with a flick of his head, then turned with a curl in his shoulders to begin his walk back along the catwalk. The shouts grew even louder when the audience saw strapped to the back of his kilt a large martini glass with umbrellas, straws and cocktail sticks poking through several large green olives. As he passed Wilson and Tommy, he gave an extra shimmy before twisting into a 360-degree spiral, arms extended like a whirling dervish, kilt spinning. He proceeded to walk out through to the back of the stage, where the models surrounded him, practically lining up to hug and kiss their kilted model.

Wilson and Tommy glanced at each other. Words were in short supply. Wilson was slowly moving her head from side to side, wondering whether her world and the people in it could get any more peculiar. Tommy was looking at the floor, regretfully, wishing he had worn his kilt that evening.

Kiltman was back at his seat a few minutes later, red and pink lipstick marks smattered across his blue and white mask. He sat down sheepishly between Wilson and Tommy, putting his hands in the air. "Look. We're not going to talk about what happened. All I'll say is that a famous person in the audience offered to donate $100,000 to a charity of choice if I would walk down the catwalk." He paused for a moment and put his hands out palms facing upwards. "Someone made me an offer I could not refuse. I asked them to donate it to *Love Your Planet* research."

He pointed up towards the first tier to see a man, who had acted as a vast array of gangsters, waving, and blowing faux kisses. Kiltman's one regret was that he would never be able to tell anyone about how he had interacted twice in the same day with his hero. Wilson and Tommy were nodding. In the circumstances, they could not argue with Kiltman's decision.

There was a break for twenty minutes before the next parade of beach beauties, allowing Kiltman a chance to read the programme to assess how much more they had to endure. Lots of people would have wanted to be in his seat, directly underneath gorgeous, long-limbed, scantily clad models. But for him this was as far from entertainment as he could imagine. To distract himself from the rising tedium, he began to tune into the conversations taking place around him, one of the benefits of his super-hearing. Some people did people-watching - he amused himself with people-listening. Sometimes it was hard for him to shut out all the chitter-chatter on buses and in large rooms, especially if he had recently slugged at Hair o' the Dog, which he had done before they had entered the Carnegie. There was potential danger around every corner on this venture, he had mused, better to be safe than sorry.

He heard the elderly couple behind him discussing whether they had paid their Park Avenue doorman his Christmas bonus this year, since he had been particularly surly over the last few days. Another couple, younger, their voices animated by all the excitement, were trying to whisper:

"Hey, Ague, they really are Kiltman and Wilson, aren't they? Ask them for their autographs."

"No, you do it. I'm always the guinea pig, Julie. It's your turn. The last time I was near someone so famous was in 1985 when Peter Rose beat Ty Cobb's hit record. The greatest day in the Cincinnati Reds history." Kiltman could tell Ague was from the mid-west by his pleasantly refined accent and love of this iconic baseball team that compelled loyalty in its fans.

Julie sighed, "I'll leave them alone. They probably don't want to be disturbed. Celebrities just want to be allowed to do their own thing."

Kiltman picked up the programme and passed it to Wilson. "Can you sign that?" he requested.

"Sure." She decided not to ask.

She pulled a pen from her jacket pocket and wrote *Maggie Wilson* in flowery writing before turning back to continue talking to Tommy. He had never autographed anything before. He had, for obvious reasons, never signed *Kiltman* on a document. On this occasion he decided to concoct his first ever autograph, writing a large *K* and an *l* and *t* of similar height. The other letters he made quite flat, barely indecipherable. Finally, when he crossed the *t*, he extended the line all the way to the right and underneath *Kiltman*. He looked at it, nodding his appreciation of the nifty artwork, before adding at the top: *for Julie and Ague, Happy New Year! Go Reds!*

Turning round to see an attractive young couple holding champagne flutes in their hand, he handed across the program. "There you go, folks. Enjoy your evening."

He turned back to face the catwalk, smiling inside his mask, hearing Julie say excitedly, "Awesome! He must have read our minds! Who knew Kiltman was a Reds fan!"

Kiltman felt a sharp pain in his side and turned to see Wilson looking at him. "Did you do what I think you did?"

"I'm not a mind-reader. What do you mean?"

She shook her head, turning back to Tommy, muttering, "No, but you are a strange one sometimes."

He went back to listening in on conversations, choosing Marsha and Digi this time. They were talking quietly in Russian, their heads barely inches apart. He decided to test a power he had been experimenting with back home a few months earlier. An extra-large drink of Hair o' the Dog had been consumed that day, before he read, cover to cover, a series of Russian language tutorials and grammar lessons. He found he was able to spend 20 hours straight just studying and absorbing, although since then he had not tested whether he had been able to properly digest the language in a meaningful manner. Sitting in the Carnegie Hall alongside two strangers who had inserted themselves into his best friend's life, people he did not trust an inch, would be the perfect opportunity for him to test his Russian. He tuned his ears up to the level required and sat back to listen.

"You have the papers?" Digi asked.

"Yes," Marsha answered. "They are in my bag."

"He needs to sign them tonight; we've waited too long. I need to scan them back to the leaseholder in Estonia tomorrow so that the deal is closed before the end of the year. He has to sign the assets and lease over to me now so that I can renew the new contract under our name, starting January 1."

"I know all the details, sweetheart," she whispered. "I fully understand the importance of the date. I waited until tonight to get him distracted. He has already drunk too much. We will have our own business on the first of the year. You can rest assured, my love."

"Okay, good. I look forward to it just being us again. I miss being close to you. If this idiot tries to follow us home, he will be putting his life in danger."

"He will not be that stupid," she answered. "But if he is, then he pays the price."

Kiltman could feel the anger rising within him. His friend was naïve, Tommy would be the first to admit that. Trusting people is how Tommy lived his life. He put himself out there regularly to help others and support those in need. With that mindset, when people walked into his life, he immediately believed that they had the same good intentions. Tommy needed to be made aware of this betrayal and deceit. If he signed the documents, he would lose the bar in Estonia, for which he had worked tirelessly over a decade building a business he was proud of. There was also a chance of him franchising the *Terviseks* brand globally if Glasgow was successful too. Kiltman was sure that if he signed over the bar to Marsha and Digi, the brand would go with it and his dreams would crumble. He had to tell Tommy. The only question in his mind was whether he should wait until after the show before breaking the news. When he considered that over the last week he had not been able to plan ten minutes ahead without something happening, he leant over and tapped Tommy on the knee.

"Tommy, do you have a minute?" he asked, breaking into his debate with Wilson as to whether coconuts and palm leaves will ever take off as a beach clothing accessory.

He stood and led Tommy out towards the foyer, where people were milling around discussing haute couture. Some of them shook hands with Kiltman, which he reciprocated with an

335

increasing sense of awkwardness. He managed to find a relatively quiet spot to the side of the cloakroom.

"Tommy, I've got a question for you," he asked.

"Sure, go ahead. But I am definitely not getting up on that catwalk... without a kilt."

"No, it's more serious than that." Kiltman realised there would never ever be anything less serious than his catwalk debut. "Is Marsha expecting you to sign something?"

"Yes," Tommy answered, surprised. "How did you know? She's brought some papers along to do with building an extension in the pub in Estonia. The business is booming so we are going to scale up."

"What language is it in?"

"Estonian, of course," Tommy said. "Why?"

"You don't speak Estonian, so how do you know what you're signing?"

"Kiltman, I trust Marsha." Tommy's voice was shaking.

"Don't trust her. She and Digi are an item. They are going to rip you off and get you to sign the bar over to them." He put his hands on Tommy's shoulders. "Believe me!"

"Crikey! I had thought something was going on with them, but just in a sort of closely knit sibling kind of way. Are you sure?"

Kiltman nodded.

Tommy muttered out loud, although really talking to himself. "I have been in Estonia for years now and I love the people of that country so much. They have taken me into their hearts and helped me build my business. My best friends are Estonians. They are the salt of the earth. I can't believe Marsha would betray me so badly."

Tommy examined the floor and kicked a stray plastic cup, contemplating the middle distance for a few seconds. He knew this was how Tommy made decisions. He blanked out for a few moments and then...

"Right, that's it." Tommy nodded his head resolutely, tears glistening in his trusting eyes. He turned on his heel and shouted back to Kiltman, "Thanks, mate. I owe you one."

"No, you don't, pal!" He remembered Tommy saving his and Roddy's lives six months earlier. And recalled the many good times he had shared with his lifelong friend.

He watched Tommy stride up to Marsha and Digi. He tuned his hearing up a notch to hear him say politely and calmly, "It's all over, you two. Get your sorry asses out of this place and crawl back into the hole you came from. But you're not going to trick me with your false contract. I'll know where to find you. Hurry!"

Marsha and Digi quickly gathered their coats and bags and rushed along the aisle tripping over the front row audience in their haste. They had chosen not to argue, expert enough in the art of scam to know when they had been rumbled. The sooner they could get back to the anonymity of the former eastern bloc the better. Running past Kiltman on their way out the door, they saw him wave before shouting, "Where are you 'russian' to? I guess you 'moscow'! Do svidaniya!" He laughed inside his mask, feeling good that despite his tiredness, he had lost none of the razor-sharp wit he was so proud of.

United Nations

"Kiltman, you're in the habit of throwing out little titbits of knowledge, factoids as you call them. Well, I've got one of my own." Wilson was enjoying the walk along 5th Avenue, looking in shop windows - appreciating the merchandise, avoiding the prices.

"Okay, shoot," he said.

He was happy to engage in the conversation, becoming increasingly self-conscious at the whistles and shouts following him down the street. He was used to being in public with his costume on, it had become normal. Somehow doing so in New York City prompted a significantly more vocal reaction. He put it down to Americans always looking for that next superhero to fight against spider, super or batman, before reconciling with each other, the world a better place, a few villains captured in the process. He sighed, if only life was that simple.

Tommy had found them a small hotel near Grand Central station below midtown, allowing them some privacy with the luxury of a room each, a decent mattress, and a shower. Despite the sleep Kiltman was feeling less optimistic than Wilson - it had prevented him from falling into a relaxed slumber. Mask was still out there somewhere. There was no doubting that wherever he was hiding, it was in full view of everyone, as an ordinary member of society, maybe even married with children. He would have worked hard over the years to create a sense of normalcy around himself. Now that his plans for creating mayhem had been thwarted, he would fall back into the normal routines of that person he had created out of the people and circumstances surrounding him. Most likely waiting for the noise to calm down, before instigating his next act of terror.

"Okay." She waited a moment. "Do you know that I am related to Uncle Sam?"

"What? How does that work?" Kiltman recalled the picture of the man with the American top hat and the long, white goatee, pointing accusingly, saying *I want you*.

"His actual name was Sam Wilson and his parents came from the West of Scotland, Greenock to be precise. He had a business in New York during the 1812 war – his company distributed meat to the army. The meat crates had US stamped on them, as in United States, but the soldiers changed it to Uncle Sam because they relied so much on these food deliveries. His name then became synonymous with whenever the US was at war, finally resulting in the *Uncle Sam* recruitment posters we've all seen. Anyway, my point is that my, wait for it, great, great, great, great grandfather was his uncle, which would make him my first cousin six times removed." She turned to look at Kiltman, pride etched in her face, in a 'beat that' defiance.

"Wow! Now that you come to mention it, he does look a bit like you." He made a point of scratching his chin theatrically. He had not seen the punch coming, but he felt it. For a pint-sized Scottish detective, Wilson could deliver a powerful thump, landing on his arm just above the elbow.

"That wasn't called for," she said with a fake pout, as he rubbed his arm, trying not to groan.

They had spent the afternoon walking around the city, enjoying a temperature now at freezing point, ten degrees warmer than a day earlier. With the absence of a windchill, it felt closer to twenty degrees hotter. They had been soaking up the electric atmosphere of New Year's Eve for a few hours now, although the city was a tad less busy than they had expected. Initially they were surprised at Manhattan being so quiet; but then realised that the vast majority of residents came from somewhere else. Most people had gone to spend the festive season with their families. It was now after six in the evening and they were on their way to the United Nations assembly on 42nd street on the east side of the city. After Marsha and Digi's sudden departure, Tommy had given their passes to Kiltman and Wilson. Tommy had to call the UN offices that morning to ensure a transfer would be allowed. When they realised who they were being reallocated to, they became excited, saying it would be their honour to have the famed, Scottish crimefighters at the event.

They turned the corner onto 42nd street to see a large crowd of people gathered around the entrance to the UN building. It seemed every continent was represented in the group somewhere. There must have been three or four hundred of them carrying homemade banners and wearing sweat-tops and jackets with whatever slogan matched their territory's claim for independence. The atmosphere was generally quite jolly although some factions were taking it very seriously. The Spanish, Kiltman noted, were tending to be more belligerent in their chanting, while the rest of the groups seemed happy just to have the chance to claim the right to self-determine.

"Kiltman!" rose up from the edge of the group.

He turned to see Grant MacTavish running towards them, microphone in hand. When he saw Wilson standing beside Kiltman, Grant started to slow up, a crestfallen look shadowing his face. Behind him, they could see around twenty or so Scots in kilts singing:

My future lies over the ocean
My future lies over the sea
My future lies in the UN
Bring back my decision to me

Cute, Kiltman thought, hoping they got what they were looking for.

"Hi, Grant!" She failed to conceal her smile. "Did you get home okay from Nice?"

"Very funny, Maggie," he answered, before chortling in a self-conscious manner. "You got me! No hard feelings." He surrendered, his hands in the air.

Kiltman looked at her. "Am I missing something here?"

She shook her head - MacTavish had been embarrassed enough.

"Let's just say Grant and I had a date in Nice that wasn't very *nice* for him," she said, dropping into an exaggerated Charles Aznavour accent for the last few words.

"We're running late, Grant." Kiltman saw him talk to his cameraman. It was clear he was aiming to orchestrate a shot of Kiltman and Wilson outside the UN building.

"We'll have a chat after the event if you want," Kiltman continued.

"But, Kiltman…" he started to push the microphone under his chin.

Wilson placed her hand on it and pushed it away, shaking her head and wagging her finger from side to side. "Why don't you go and wait for us in a pub, and we can have a drink together later? There's one a few blocks away called *Skipper Bar*."

She linked arms with Kiltman and walked away laughing. Kiltman decided not to ask. She was becoming more of an enigma every day, and he was enjoying it.

They approached the building made famous by its countless resolutions over the years, flags from countries across the world bringing a welcome splash of colour to an otherwise nondescript high-rise structure. Security checks seemed quite routine, the guards prepared for the arrival of people from all over the world carrying bags of all shapes and sizes. Kiltman hoped the security teams were not a tad relaxed believing the threat had gone thanks to them foiling the museum attempt. It was not as simple as that - there was still an unfulfilled terrorist out there.

As they walked through the aula they enjoyed the immense presence of the internal design of the UN building. The bland exterior gave no indication of the sumptuous layout waiting for them on the inside. There were around two thousand seats for the near 200 member states – yet this capacity was dwarfed by the vast empty space rising over 150 feet to the highest ceiling either of them had stood under. Long, vertical, golden bars stretched from the roof towards the floor like sun's rays shining on the leaders. Above the podium, the UN world map symbol dominated the room, nestled inside a vast, golden wall. While the UN assembly was a traditionally secular organisation, there was something disturbingly religious about its design.

Kiltman could see nametags placed on each desk identifying where the world leaders were expected to sit. They did not seem in a hurry to take their seats, wandering around shaking hands and acknowledging each other in the carefree manner of old friends who had not met in years. They had all been made aware of the prior day's bomb in the museum, which seemed to have added a spring to their step. He was impressed by how they had apparently put that behind them and had moved onto the UN agenda. Politicians had layers of resilience, he thought, that either made them or broke them. It was usually when the resilience morphed into thick skin that they let themselves down.

He felt a buzz in his sporran. He extracted his phone to see a call coming in from Roddy. It was 7pm, midnight in Scotland. He found a discrete corner and opened the phone to hear Roddy shouting, "Happy New Year, Dad!"

He turned to face the wall and lifted the bottom of his mask. "Hi, Roddy, Happy New Year to you too. Are you all having a good time?"

"Yes, Dad, I'm with Mum and Angie. Her father is in New York, remember I told you?"

"Oh, yes, I forgot."

Kiltman examined the aula to see Omar settling into a seat towards the front row. They had prioritized the countries with self-determination issues, allowing them the opportunity to present their concerns and reasons for independence. He seemed calm and pleasantly confident, shaking hands with the leaders around him from Spain, Italy, and north-east Africa. He was in the process of placing his papers on the desk ready for his speech.

"Hey, are you guys staying up much longer?" Kiltman asked.

"No, Mum said we have to go to bed after watching ten more minutes of TV," Roddy answered dejectedly. Kiltman heard the bagpipe and accordion music in the background, smiling at his memory of Fiona enjoying the more traditional New Year celebrations rather than the comedies and chat shows that seemed to dominate New Year TV. They had disagreed on many things, particularly towards the end of their relationship, but that was one thing they agreed on. They would rather enjoy New Year themselves than watch people talking to each other in a pre-recorded show.

"Bye, Dad. Here's Mum!" Roddy blew a long, wet kiss down the phone.

"Bye, son. Love you." He felt the emotion break in his voice, before Fiona came on the phone shouting, "Happy New Year, Kenny!" She sounded tipsy. She rarely drank alcohol; he reckoned she had probably consumed two glasses of wine.

"Happy New Year, Fiona! How are things?"

"Okay, Kenny. Angus has got up and disappeared. That's fine, he was getting on my nerves anyway." He heard her fighting back the tears before she started again. "He was so pretentious, as if he was above it all. Well, I'm better off without him. So how are you?"

She was hurting, he felt for her. She was a good person with high standards. He did not want her to be sad and lonely, but he also had his own misgivings about Angus. "Well, Fiona, it's a New Year with new opportunities. I think this will be your year. You deserve to be happy."

"Thanks. I need to go and put them to bed. Oh, by the way, where are you? Sounds like you're at a party. I forgot to mention... must be the wine! Maggie's in New York. She's quite famous now, have you been watching her?"

"Oh, yes," he answered looking across the hall. Her profile was illuminated by a wall light, silhouetting her against the backdrop of rows of world leaders. He noticed her reaching hurriedly for her pocket to pull out her phone, then opening up to read a message.

"I'm not sure if she'll want to wholeheartedly take me back into her life," he said more to himself than Fiona.

"Oh, she will, Kenny. She adores you. It took her a while to realise it, but she's all in now, I'm sure." She waited a moment before saying with genuine concern, "Please don't mess it up."

"I won't, Fiona. Take care."

They hung up just in time for him to hear the president of the UN announcing that they all had to take their seats, the meeting would start in 15 minutes. He saw Tommy settling into a seat close to Omar, his face beaming. He was one of ten people invited along with the Scottish representative to bring to life the impact Scotland was having on the world - how it was able to forge its own path without need of a maternal overseer. He noticed George sitting further to the left, talking to, of all people, the Argentinian president. They seemed to be old friends, leaning in close to each other, smiling and joking. George seemed a different person from the man that had been crying uncontrollably at his mother's funeral a few days earlier.

Kiltman was sure Tommy had already put Marsha behind him. It was one of the things he had always admired about Tommy, how quickly he bounced back from a setback that would have put others off stride for months.

Before he moved to his own seat in the back row alongside Wilson, Kiltman hoped that Mask did not bounce back as quickly as Tommy. His partner barely noticed him settling in beside her. She kept reading the text from her brother trying to decipher the hidden message in the parsimony of his words, "*Happy New Year, sister. Whatever happens, I hope you will always love me. XX*"

The Speech

"It's a great honour for me to stand here before you today, representing a country that has played a huge role in shaping the way our planet operates," Omar spoke carefully, his soft accent adding a subtle lilt to the words, encouraging the auditorium to listen. Scotland was last in the line of speeches, following representatives from Northern Italy, Catalonia, Chechnya, Hong Kong, Kashmir and Quebec. It struck Kiltman that there was a lot more unease across the world than he had considered before. Significant swathes of populations were unhappy in their constitutional skin, wanting to shed and start again as the same animal in a different covering.

"First of all, I want to send the First Minister's apologies. He would have wanted to deliver this speech himself. Unfortunately, as you are all aware, he is recovering in hospital from a failed assassination attempt.

"It would be remiss of me not to stop for a moment to recognize the bravery of Detective Inspector Wilson in saving our First Minister from certain death. And also, to recognize her and Scotland's very own superhero, Kiltman, in preventing many of you from being targeted yesterday at the museum.

"DI Wilson and Kiltman, please stand up, wherever you are." Omar put his hand above his eyes to shield the glare of the lights as he scanned the rows of world leaders. A few cheers and a smattering of applause started across various corners of the auditorium.

"Oh, God," Kiltman heard Wilson mutter under her breath. "At least you're wearing a mask."

"I'm not that bad-looking, you know," he responded.

"You know what I mean." She stood up, trying to smile naturally. Her pretty face was contorted into an uncomfortable expression only Kiltman noticed. He rose alongside her to an increasing wave of clapping. Shouts rose up from various corners of the room. He recognised one of them as belonging to Tommy, reminding him of his graduation day when Tommy had whooped while others clapped. The room warmed to the moment, to a person, each on their feet turning to look at them in the back row. Rarely had the United Nations assembly ever been so united, Kiltman thought.

As the applause subsided, Omar said, "Thank you, DI Wilson and Kiltman!"

He put his hands in the air motioning downwards for them all to take their seats. Kiltman and Wilson were the first to sit down. What kind of investigators were they, if they could not have seen that coming, Wilson mused?

"Scotland has not just been helping the world in the last few days, you know," Omar spoke clearly, his warm, brown eyes scanning the room. His eloquence and relaxed manner had the audience listening to his every word.

"Scots have been travelling the world for many years - the city we are in today was practically built by this great race. It was only 200 years ago that nearly ten percent of New York was comprised of bona fide Scots who had emigrated to build this fledgling country."

He paused and let his words settle in.

"Let's also remember that the Scots have invented many of the objects we use today to live our lives to the full. Please indulge me for a moment but here are a few things you might recognise – let's start with your home comforts." He began to count along his fingers one after the other. "Television, fridge, telephone and, believe it or not, the electric toaster, which many people say is the best thing since sliced bread. In fact, it was invented before sliced bread."

Those in the audience who understood the idiomatic humour laughed and clapped.

"And of course, the two blockbuster inventions that triggered change on our planet like no other: the steam engine and penicillin." He paused again for effect. He had everyone waiting expectantly for his next comment.

"There are many more, but you don't have time to listen to them all. The last I leave you with is that while Scotland cannot take credit for the invention of the wheel, we can at least claim the tyre. Thank you, Mr. Dunlop!"

A ripple of laughter passed along the rows like a Mexican wave.

"The reason I mention some of the many contributions Scotland has created for our world is to reinforce that Scotland in its own right is a great nation. Independence of thought and spirit are knitted into how Scots operate. Every sinew of Scottish being is the product of years of self-determination. For many centuries they may not have called it that. But it has always been what they wanted and believed they deserved. Some people would call that their birth right.

"Scotland as a nation is still to this day full of the energy and drive that makes our world more integrated and connected. Not long ago the Iron Curtain came down, recognising the rights of many of you to sit in the seats you occupy today. Scotland was one of the world's first countries to seize on the opportunity to help get those nations back on their feet. One example is Tommy MacGregor, who gave up everything in Scotland and moved to Estonia to start a business. This is the essence of pioneering. Taking what is great at home and exporting it to another country for the betterment of that place. Tommy has a small business, with twenty Estonian employees, but the point is that grassroots economy-building starts with those enterprises. Tommy embodies the spirit of Scotland, by helping others to be stronger. That, my friends, is the sign of a country that should not be held back but be allowed to grow on its own terms without being prohibited by another layer of government."

Omar pointed to Tommy, who stood up with his arms raised in acknowledgement of the applause he was receiving, particularly from the former soviet republic nations. Tommy had worked hard to build something from nothing and took a number of personal risks in the process. It was a thrill to see this being recognised on a world platform such as this. As he turned to sit down, George extended a hand to congratulate him. Kiltman noticed a haunted look in his mother's friend's face; he now seemed worried, somewhat apprehensive. He hoped that George was doing okay, it was peculiar to see him in such a globally powerful environment. Even more so when he appeared increasingly distraught. He had seemed relaxed at the beginning but as the event progressed, his demeanour had darkened.

"I am not going to give you a history lesson on the 17th and 18th centuries and the political machinations that resulted in the Act of Union bringing Scotland and England together. Many much wiser people than me have dissected that part of history a hundredfold.

"I am focused on today. When as an assembly you meet to place your vote in a few minutes, the question in front of you is *Should a country or state be allowed to unilaterally self-determine its constitutional future and secede from the superordinate union it has been assigned to?*

"That is not, my friends, a simple YES or NO question. Many of you will not say YES, in fear that riots and coups will start all over the world. It is therefore easy for you to default to NO and protect world order. Whether by default or design, the question is one that leads you to a comfortable NO or a very uncomfortable YES.

"Today I say to you, let's add a condition to the YES vote. If you vote YES, then YES should recognise that self-determination is automatically triggered in exceptional circumstances. Such circumstances should reflect a change in the status of the superordinate body. If this body creates a new normal, where its substance fundamentally changes in a way that impacts the underlying nations, then that should be considered a trigger for a vote of self-determination.

"For example, to bring this point to life, let's imagine the following scenario. While it is not common, in fact exceedingly rare, it can happen that the government responsible for managing a union of states can choose to change that union's membership of highly significant organisations. In a situation close to me and many of my European friends, if Westminster were ever to decide - based on a national referendum - that we leave the European Union, then that should allow an automatic referendum in Scotland. The purpose of the automatic referendum would be to determine whether Scotland should stay in the UK in these new constitutional circumstances. Of course, we may decide to stay with the UK. But the choice should be ours. In those conditions, the UK should not have the power to choose whether or not to gift a referendum to Scotland. Our birth right as a nation demands that we decide."

Omar surveyed the room for a few seconds, allowing the importance of his words to settle. Many leaders were listening through translators, he did not want them to miss the substance of his message. He continued with a glimmer of a smile at the corners of his mouth.

"It would be like Santa shaving off his beard, going on a diet and wearing an Elvis suit, while still trying to give us presents as if he still owned Christmas. Yes, it would be just as ridiculous if the UK left Europe and then tried to dictate Scotland's future.

"There may be other conditions you want to add to the ballot paper, but that is definitely one that should be there. So, let's not make this a binary ballot, a simple YES or NO decision. Let's put the question in a pragmatic context where political landscapes and constitutional commitments change. This must be recognised.

"Thank you for listening. I look forward to the results of the vote and to our New Year celebrations later."

Omar turned to step down from the podium. The leaders clapped loudly, some knocking tables with their knuckles. A couple of whoops and shouts rose up around him as he walked back to his seat. Tommy was on his feet applauding exaggeratedly alongside George who patted Omar on the back as he sat down.

Kiltman and Wilson both shouted their appreciation. Omar's speech had been a quietly triumphant plea for the right to take your future in your own hands when the conditions dictated it was necessary. Umbrella governing bodies would face the consequences if they changed their constitutional allegiances.

It was 9.30 pm and the evening was about to change shape. The votes had to be submitted by 10.30 pm - the UN President had made it clear that if the ballots had not been cast by then, they would not be accepted. After half an hour of collation, the results were to be announced at 11 pm. The announcement would make some people in the hall happy, and others concerned. It was an inevitable consequence of the motion on the table. Drinks would follow soon after to encourage congratulations and smother commiserations, leading to a countdown at midnight to bring in the New Year.

Lots to look forward to, Kiltman thought, so why was he feeling nervous?

The Result

"Ladies and gentlemen," the President of the UN announced at 11pm on the dot. "It's with great pleasure that I am able to announce the results of the vote. I am pleased to see that everyone has cast their ballot here today. I am not sure if that conveys a deep desire to address the question of self-determination, or you are in a hurry to start your New Year celebrations." He laughed and beamed a smile across the auditorium. No-one else seemed to find his comment humorous, there was too much at stake for them to take this vote light-heartedly.

Kiltman looked at Wilson to see if she had registered a modicum of humour - even if not at the joke, at least at the absence of laughter, which in itself was quite amusing. Her face registered a look of distress.

"What's wrong," he whispered.

"Look," she said. "It's from my brother. I've tried to call him a few times, but he's not answering. I'm really worried. He's fragile emotionally."

She showed him the message. It did read like someone at their wit's end, sending a message of pending calamity. Wilson had never mentioned her brother to Kiltman before, and she had rarely talked to Kenny about him. Yet there was no doubt she loved and worried about him in equal measure. If Kiltman had received a similar message from a close one, he would have been just as anxious.

In the absence of something more soothing to say, Kiltman whispered, "Don't worry, I'm sure it will be okay. He might just have gone to bed, it's late back home."

He immediately realised the inadequacy of his words. Words that a total stranger would say to another. Not someone who shared such an intimate relationship – whether Kenny or Kiltman.

He did not know what else to say given the confines of secrecy barricading his emotions into a superhero identity. He reached across to her hand to take it in his. She did not resist. He squeezed her fingers gently, applying a firm but gentle pressure to each of her fingers in turn to ease her tension. She closed her eyes and submitted to the soothing hand massage. Her breathing began to regulate into a soft, slow rhythm. Her eyes remained full of worry.

"He has never sent wishes like this before. He avoids the whole New Year thing, thinks it's a waste of money, tainted by hypocrisy. People pretending to like each other."

He had never met Tas. Whenever she had talked about him it was as a passenger in another story, more as a reference point than as subject matter. He had chosen not to pry, sensing her discomfort. He squeezed her hand hoping Tas would not upset the new Wilson who had mushroomed over the last week into someone who receives, and deserves, a standing ovation at the UN.

Silence had descended over the auditorium in an awkward hush. The only sound came from the grumbling hum of heaters and ventilators, keeping the temperature of the room at a steady 18 Celsius - not too warm for the leaders to drift into somnolence, while cool enough to keep them engaged.

The President placed an A4 page on the table in front of him, pressing carefully down on the corners that had curled up slightly when he held the document in his hand. He turned his gaze to the audience, looking across the rows and allowing an appropriate build-up of tension for the announcement of results.

"As I said, everyone has voted, nobody has abstained. 191 nations have cast their vote. The question before you all today is *Should a country or state be allowed to unilaterally self-determine its constitutional future and secede from the superordinate union it has been assigned to?*

"Interestingly, many of you have reacted to the words of Scotland's delegate today, where he articulately explained the importance of avoiding binary choices and recognising how we should consider the catalyst of valid conditional changes. Therefore, without further ado, I present our summary of the votes.

"173 have voted NO to the question of unilateral self-determination, with the remaining 18 voting YES."

351

A murmur of spontaneous reaction and chatter rumbled through the hall, nobody particularly surprised at the outcome. There was a rising sense of expectation, many of them awaiting recognition of exactly how the countries had positioned their votes.

"However, nearly everyone has reflected a condition on the ballot paper, which we have hurriedly worked to incorporate in the assessment of the message you wanted to send today, and the decision you wanted to be taken. Of the 171 NO votes, 120 of them have noted that where a superordinate body changes its allegiances fundamentally to a larger body critical to its economic outcomes then this automatically triggers a country or state's right to self-determine their future. In this case, if this condition is accepted, then their vote would be YES.

Therefore 120 out of 191, in addition to the 18 YES votes, means that there is a majority for an amended resolution for countries to self-determine. The following resolution will encapsulate the UN expectations of how sovereign states fulfil their responsibilities." He paused and waited for silence to descend on the leaders.

He continued. "*Where a country or state belongs to a political and constitutional union, and the government of that union chooses to leave a fundamental framework underpinning its economic security, the individual country or state should be allowed to unilaterally self-determine its constitutional future.*"

The spontaneous applause and shouts rising across the hall demonstrated overwhelming support for the majority vote the President had just articulated. In reality, nothing had changed in terms of self-determination, but Kiltman felt a good outcome had been achieved. Omar should be pleased with the massive contribution he had made to the debate and ultimately the vote. The final resolution confirmed the expectations of the assembly that self-determination, as a unilateral right, was not to be encouraged. However, it would be a valid entitlement in an extreme situation of economic suicide carried out by the overarching, governing union the country belonged to. Fair do's, Kiltman thought.

New Year

"Well, Kiltman, there are ten minutes before midnight. Do you have any New Year resolutions you want to share?" Wilson asked, holding her second glass of champagne. She had wolfed the first one down immediately after snatching it from the tray. Her nerves were on edge. A combination of concerns about Tas as well as having to stand in front of nearly 200 world leaders had neutralised her earlier laid-back mood. He could sense her need for distraction. The hall had erupted into a cacophony of noise, as many as a hundred different conversations taking place at the same time. The atmosphere had probably never been so collegiate in this room, the personal interactions a welcome respite from the tensions created by countries competing on the world stage.

"You mean, apart from catching Mask?" he asked.

She nodded, encouraging him to open up.

"Actually, I've decided to do more exercise this year." He rubbed his belly. She waited a moment, the silence drifting between them.

"Is that it?" she asked. "Are you telling me the only thing you are going to focus on is your belly?"

"I didn't say the only thing," he answered. "There are other things I need to sort out, but I'm not telling you, Detective! A superhero needs some secrecy in his life."

"Fair enough," she said putting the glass to her lips. She hesitated for a few seconds. When he did not say anything, she added, "Well, whether you want to know or not, I'm going to tell you my resolution."

"Oh, okay then," he answered.

"I'm going to tell my 'em, friend' Kenny," she did the inverted comma sign with her hands spilling some of her Moet on Kiltman's arm, "how much I love him and how much I want to be with him." She glanced at Kiltman, a glimmer of expectant acknowledgement in her eyes.

"'em Kenny' is one very lucky man." He was finding it difficult to contain his rising euphoria.

"Hey, Kiltman and Maggie, how are you guys?" Tommy had arrived beside them with George walking slowly alongside. "Kiltman, have you met George?"

George stepped forward, his face carrying that same crestfallen look Kiltman had seen earlier. He was not at ease. "Hi Maggie, you have done us all very proud," George said courteously giving a short bow to Wilson. He turned to Kiltman and extended his hand. "It's my honour to meet you, Kiltman."

Kiltman shook his hand. "Likewise, George."

An awkward silence floated up between them, Kiltman not knowing how to engage with George in this context - flooded by memories of how he and his mother had spent so many moments together.

They both realised they were looking in the direction of the podium, where Omar was talking to the UN President, who was openly appreciating Omar's intervention in the debate and ultimately the resolution. They were surrounded by a large cluster of leaders, enjoying the limelight, and basking in the camera flashes snatching them in their jovial mood of banter and repartee. The US President huddled together with the UK Prime Minister, talking to each other while looking towards the photographers. They appeared like an elderly couple at a wedding, trying to make their way to the end, hoping nobody would ask them to dance.

He was not sure what to say to George as it was all just a bit too difficult at that moment - pretending not to be Kenny Morgan in the face of his mother's special friend. He could hear George talking to him, but Kiltman continued to focus on the podium.

"Yes, Kiltman, this is a difficult time for me this year. You see, I lost my best friend last week. She meant the world to me. We were going to spend New Year together in the Highlands, walking and talking like we always did." George continued to express his sadness, his voice breaking slightly - but Kiltman had started to become distracted.

He saw Omar puffing on an inhaler as he spoke to the UN President. It was one of those inhalers asthma sufferers keep in their pocket for emergencies. He had turned his head to the side

354

and was sucking hard on the mouthpiece. Kiltman felt a pang of concern, wondering how severe this asthma attack might be. Nobody else seemed to have noticed Omar's apparent distress. They were too busy interacting and feigning respect for each other to worry about the Scottish delegate, great speech, or no great speech.

Kiltman walked away from George leaving him speaking into space. "Eh, sorry, George, I need to go. I hope you have a great New Year."

His mother would have been horrified at his show of bad manners. Although George had already forgotten Kiltman was there, talking more to himself, tears wetting his eyes.

Omar was at the other end of the auditorium, sucking harder and harder on his inhaler. His shoulders were heaving with the effort. The noise of the room was too loud for Kiltman's shouts to be heard above the clamour of clinking glasses and deep-chested guffaws. Kiltman hurried towards the podium, jostling through the crowds of world leaders and their secretaries. Instinctively he put his hand in his pocket to withdraw his phone. He hit the block caller ID button and pushed the speed dial for Roddy. It rang for a few seconds before a sleepy voice murmured, "Eh, hello. Who's that?"

"Roddy, it's Kiltman here. Is Angie with you?" He was pushing harder against the mass of bodies, increasingly dense the closer he neared the podium. He was surprised that no-one made a fuss of his robust pushes and clumsy apologies. The auditorium had been designed for leaders to sit in their seats and debate. The aisles were only supposed to be a conduit to their positions, rather than a social area to accommodate hundreds of people drinking and chatting.

Roddy could not contain his excitement.

"Kiltman, this is so cool! How did you get my number? Are you working on something exciting? How can I help? She's sleeping in the next room."

"Please put her on the phone, this is urgent. Hurry!"

He heard Roddy skip from the bed, his small footsteps pounding along the carpeted floor to the guest room.

"Angie! Angie! It's Kiltman, he wants to speak to you?"

A few moments passed. Kiltman had given up trying to navigate through the density of people occupying every available square inch of aisle. He could see Omar labouring to take deep inhalations. Kiltman began to clamber over the rows of seats and tables knocking papers and objects to the floor, holding the phone to his ear.

"Eh, hello," Angie's sleepy voice murmured. "Is this some kind of a wind up?"

"Angie, what kind of respiratory disorder does your father have? Is it asthma?"

There was a silence on the other end of the phone, only Angie's shallow breathing barely audible.

"Angie, please, I need to know!"

"Respiratory disorder?" Angie responded hesitantly. "My Dad runs every day, does marathons and things like that. He's not got any breathing..."

He closed the phone and ran. He leapt up onto the next desk in his rush across the rows of seats. It happened to be the place where the delegate for Argentina had been sitting. He did not have time to consider the irony of that moment. Kiltman jumped from desk to desk towards the podium as he heard the countdown for New Year starting. Everyone was joining in noisily shouting out the numbers: 10, 9, 8, 7, 6...

Omar was still puffing hard on his inhaler. His other hand was inside his jacket pocket. He extracted a glass cylinder about the length of a water bottle, containing a murky green liquid. He lifted his hand in the air, in a motion that would allow maximum impact when it landed on the marble floor. Kiltman understood that in seconds the hall would be filled with a lethal chemical contained within the container, most probably Ricin or Botulinum - everyone in the hall would be dead within minutes. Only Omar would survive as a result of the antidote he had been inhaling greedily in advance of his deadly act.

5,4,3...

As Omar's hand moved in a swift downward movement, Kiltman dived across the podium, knocking the US President and UK Prime Minister to the ground.

2,1...

He managed to reach across and wrap his fingers around Omar's wrist, punching him hard on the chin with his free hand. Omar dropped the cylinder, its downward trajectory spiralling haphazardly to the marble floor. Kiltman felt a sense of doom when he realised he was not going to be able to catch it in time, both arms engaged with a struggling Omar.

The lethal liquid was barely six inches from impact; its glass casing about to burst into tiny fragments before projecting its poison up into the air to envelope the hall in a lethal gas. A petite, soft hand appeared from nowhere. Kiltman recognised the unusual mole in its palm, a mole he had kissed many times before. The hand was inches away from the cylinder; close enough to give them half a chance of stopping the horror.

Far enough away to be considered a last futile attempt to save the world leaders.

Saved by the Belle

Wilson's lunge towards the cylinder came at the end of a frantic chase to follow Kiltman across the auditorium. She had not taken the time to think, to even consider what she was doing. She had seen Kiltman's desperate rush towards the podium, barging through world leaders. Whatever flash of madness had inspired him to do this, she would have to follow. That is what partners do. She had trailed his awkward path of mayhem along the aisle and across the desks.

"Happy New Year!" bellowed across the speakers as the bells clanged for midnight. The majority of the people in the hall were cheering, kissing, and hugging, while a relatively small number had watched in incredulity at Kiltman and Wilson smashing into the Scottish representative. To see him collapse in a heap, unconscious, a plastic inhaler bouncing off the floor beside him.

As gravity took over, Kiltman could not avoid landing squarely on top of Wilson. He felt her small frame buckle underneath his weight. Out of the corner of his eye, he saw her strong, thin fingers wrap themselves even more tightly around the glass cylinder.

After a few seconds of lying there, catching his breath, he heard a quiet groan emanating from underneath. "Oww, Kiltman, can you please get off me? I swear, I'll never mock your New Year resolutions again."

He clumsily fell to the side off his partner, who pushed up with her free hand into a sitting position, gasping greedily for air. Kiltman was sitting on the ground, arms wrapped around his knees, wheezing with the excesses of their bizarre welcoming of the New Year.

She was aware of the silence surrounding her as she stared at the green liquid inside the cylinder. The cheers and shouts had stopped, and a hush had descended across the UN Assembly – reflecting a frightening realisation that something catastrophic had been avoided.

Security guards were rushing from every corner of the hall towards Wilson and Kiltman, and a motionless Scottish delegate.

"Happy New Year, Wilson!" Kiltman said before three guards grabbed his arms, and two pounced on Wilson pinning her to the ground. For the second time in a minute.

"Oww!" she groaned again.

Gemmill Debrief

"Okay, Wilson, let me be clear. I've just gone to bed after bringing in the New Year here in Glasgow. My head is nipping, I've slept one hour. I'm still in my pyjamas having had to answer a phone call at six o'clock in the morning. What on earth has happened?"

"Okay, sir, I can see why you might be peeved," she looked at Kiltman, a hint of a smile creasing the corners of her mouth. She was not trying to enjoy this - it was just too hard not to. They were sitting in a quiet room just off the main UN assembly hall, having spent the best part of an hour explaining to the security services why they had toppled Lafit. He was already in a downtown jail under maximum security having been carried by stretcher to the ambulance. He had still been unconscious after smashing his head on the marble floor on Kiltman's rugby tackle.

"The last update I gave you was when we prevented the girl blowing up the museum. But we knew that Mask was still out there somewhere. We just didn't know where. In the absence of a plan, we went to the UN assembly because Tommy MacGregor, the guy who helped us against Skink during…"

"Wilson, I'm not interested in how you blagged your way into the UN. Come on, it's six in the morning here!"

"Okay," she was no longer hiding the smile. "I'll pass to Kiltman at this stage."

"Oh, here we go!" said Gemmill. They could practically hear his eyebrows rising.

"Well, Chief," he leaned forward to the mobile phone's tiny speaker. "It was coming up to midnight and I noticed that Lafit was using an inhaler. I had thought at first he was ill and reacting badly to something. You know, we were in a hall full of world leaders. Goodness knows, what he may have caught." Wilson was holding her sides, trying to avoid eye contact with Kiltman.

"Forget the rubbish jokes, Kiltman!" Gemmill shouted. "Just cut to the chase!"

"Nice one, Chief. I would have been proud of that one myself. Chase, get it? We were chasing Mask," Kiltman was looking at the floor concentrating on keeping control. Gemmill's silence told them that his blood vessels were most probably at bursting point by now. Kiltman decided to continue rather than await a response.

"Anyway, you see, I had never known him to use one of these before, and it seemed odd. At first I was worried for his health. But then I saw how aggressively he was sucking on the inhaler." He chose not to mention the call with Angie, although he would need to deal with that after the Gemmill briefing. He was not looking forward to speaking to Roddy later.

"He then pulled a cylinder of what I was sure was poison from his pocket. He was ready to smash it on the floor. When the liquid was exposed to air, it would have morphed into a lethal gas that would have filled the room in seconds. I managed to get to him, but it was Wilson who made the critical intervention of catching the vial before it smashed."

They decided not to spend time explaining how they had been marched to a secure room in the basement and detained by the security guards. Fortunately, it did not take them long to realise that Lafit was the criminal, and their priority should be in finding a safe place for a cylinder of deadly poison. The guards had taken on board Wilson's warnings to make sure Omar Lafit was securely restrained, even in his unconscious state. There was silence on the other end of the phone, as they waited for Gemmill to assimilate the information.

"Okay, look. Why on earth would Lafit want to poison the UN assembly on a day when he was giving a speech on self-determination? It doesn't make sense."

She stepped in. "Lafit was not from the Middle East, like he had made us believe. At least not originally. He was from Argentina. He grew up in a home where the father was an escapee from Germany in the second world war. The father had indoctrinated him with his Nazi idealism and beliefs. We don't know why, but he ran away from home as a boy. He disappeared for a few years, then showed up in the UK as an immigrant from a war-torn region in the Middle East. Nobody would have doubted his credentials considering the number of people being allowed into the country at that time. It was the perfect opportunity for him to create a new identity, while staying close to his fellow zealots back in Argentina. Together they plotted to wreak destruction in Milan and in New York."

As Wilson explained Lafit's true background, Kiltman could not stop a rising concern as to how Angie would react to this news of her father. He expected she would be inconsolable. Then there was the question as to her welfare when her father would be in prison for the rest of his life. Kiltman pushed it to the back of his mind. His Kenny Morgan persona would need to deal with that one.

"Okay, it all sounds very far-fetched," Gemmill grunted. "But where does Skink fit into all this?"

"Lafit, whose real name was Alois Mann, although technically Alois Schmidt since his father had changed his name before he was born…"

"Are you trying to confuse me, Wilson?"

"Sorry, sir," she paused and took a long sip of cold, but strong, coffee. "Lafit did not have the capability to create bombs and poisonous liquids. It was not his forte. But it was Skink's. We believe last summer when Skink was arrested, Lafit got the idea to use his bomb-making skills, before, well, before topping him in Tolbooth Steeple."

Gemmill went quiet again, but they could hear him breathing heavily down the mouthpiece. Not a pleasant sound, Kiltman thought.

"Look. I think we got off on the wrong foot at the start of this case. Wilson, you've done a remarkable job over the last week. You should be proud of your achievements." She nearly fell off her chair. He sounded genuinely appreciative.

"Oh, thank you, sir, but…"

"I know, I know! I was getting to him. Kiltman, you too. You're not everyone's cup of tea, but we would not have wrestled these maniacs to the ground without your quirky superpowers. Thank you, too!"

"Well, Chief…" he began.

"Stop! There have been enough speeches for one evening. Where is Lafit, or Mann, or Schmidt now?"

"He's under surveillance with NYPD. He was still unconscious when he was carried off."

"Okay, I'll check in with the commissioner now and see what the state of play is. We'll need to make sure he's kept under maximum security surveillance." He waited a moment; they could hear him scribbling. "This is not something you should be concerned about. Why don't you wrap up and get yourselves some well-deserved kip. Cheers for now. I'll see you when you get back home."

The phone clicked off.

She turned to Kiltman and spoke wearily, "I'm ready to go home. What about you?"

"Home is where my heart is, Wilson," he answered with more meaning than she appreciated.

VIII

In with the New

Maximum Security

Mask's eyes were closed as he banged his head slowly against the wall. The blows were not hard, just impactful enough for him to recite silently and rhythmically the speeches he had practiced ad infinitum over the decades. The words of the great leader he had never met but had watched throughout his childhood on videos his father had kept in the attic.

The chains wrapped around his arms and legs and the orange jumpsuit were medals he wore proudly as a temporary reminder of the sacrifice he was willing to make. It is never easy to lead a double life, no matter what one is trying to achieve. That did not stop him from achieving what many people would have considered impossible. To change a UN Assembly resolution and convince the world leaders to accept his message. Maybe one day when Scotland benefitted from this intervention and chose its own fate, its people would see him as a man of visionary resolve and character. Despite his politician face being a cover, he had still been able to achieve incredible things, changing political outcomes for future generations.

How much more powerful would his true persona be in delivering the philosophy and masterplan of his father and their Führer? Imagine what he could achieve when he is not hindered by the distraction of his alter ego. At least now his quest for achieving the master plan would not be diluted by trying to fit in.

All he had to do was escape from what they considered a maximum-security prison. He would prove that he was capable of the impossible, by dropping his chains and fleeing like a ghost. He had an ally on the outside who would help in making this happen. Yes, she was young - some would say, too young - but he knew what she was capable of.

The thought gave increased momentum to his head banging, encouraging him to add just a little bit more pain to the incessant thumping. It felt good to start again.

Maggie's Epiphany

He watched the sun setting in the distance, beyond the beautiful island of Islay. During moments like these he remembered why he had agreed to build Uisge Beatha near the top of the Old Kilpatrick hills overlooking the Firth of Clyde and beyond. It was a brisk January 2nd, the air carrying a slight breeze making him feel refreshingly cold on his deck - comforted by a flask of hot tea.

The trip back on New Year's Day had been as uneventful as a transatlantic flight can be. He had tried to watch the inflight movie while Wilson snored gently beside him. Her peaceful sleep reflected her brief conversation with Tas before she had boarded the plane. He had apologised for being so cryptic in his New Year text message. He had consumed a couple of beers too many and had become overly melancholic. He emphasized there was nothing for her to worry about; and that he was immensely proud of his *wee sister* and how she had saved so many lives.

Gemmill had managed to contact them before the flight left to say that Alois Mann/Schmidt had awakened from his unconscious state to see that his worst fears had been realised. He had failed. He was immediately transferred to a maximum-security prison in Colorado - and would stay there until his trial. With the weight of evidence against him, he was facing a number of life sentences.

The press had taken time to react to the event in the UN assembly. There was something surreal about a politician being so evil and cruel, that the media held back waiting for several confirmations of the authenticity of the story. Once they had become satisfied, the news broke with the impact of an overflowing dam. Despite the fact he had fooled so many people for so long and had become a trusted member of the community, the Scottish National Party were not vilified for how he managed to climb their ranks. The public seemed to understand that he had played the system astoundingly well.

It was Angie that Kenny felt for. She had lost her mother at an early age and now she would never see her father again. When Fiona broke the news to her, she apparently accepted it surprisingly well. She admitted to sensing there was something not right about her father. When they were at home together, he barely spoke to her, delegating most of his parental tasks to the nanny or the school. She was part of the cover he had layered around himself to create the perfect image of the immigrant refugee who had risen above his challenges. Her lack of remorse in losing her father to a life in prison in a faraway continent spoke volumes to her relationship with him.

Fiona had mentioned to Kiltman that she would be willing to adopt Angie if the social services allowed. Angie adored Fiona and Roddy, they were already a mini family in many respects, spending any free time together. Kenny had reached out to Shuggy just after his flight landed on New Year's Day. Shuggy had built up a network of contacts and strong associations throughout Scotland's social services system. He immediately understood Angie's circumstances, and the complexity of her emotional reaction to her new situation. He was going to make sure the best case was put forward for Angie to join Fiona's family.

On New Year's Day Angus had contacted Fiona to tell her he would not be coming back. He admitted to not being ready for a relationship, hinting at Roddy being a nice lad but an imposition on their privacy. Considering her desire to adopt Angie, she knew she was far better off without him. She had already moved on from Angus and did not even consider mentioning her plans for Angie.

The doorbell's tinkle startled Kenny from his reverie.

"I'll get it, Dad!" Roddy shouted from the kitchen. He had spent the day with Angie until she had to go home to collect an overnight bag. They were going to have a sleepover at Fiona's later that night. Hopefully, he mused, an indication of better times to come.

A couple of minutes later, the door to the deck opened and Maggie walked through. He rose from his chair and enveloped her in a hug she desperately needed. She fell into his arms enjoying the security of feeling protected. Over the last week she

367

had spent her waken hours looking after others, it was comforting to know that Kenny was doing the same for her.

He directed her to a chair alongside his own facing out towards the river and the sunset. He poured some tea from his flask into a cup he had waiting for her to arrive. She picked it up, cradling the warm mug in both hands, the steamy vapour rising up into her face. She closed her eyes and sipped slowly. "Aaaahhh, you don't know how good that feels. You don't know how good this feels." She made a sweeping gesture with her arm, looking out to the peacefulness of the evening.

"Kenny, there's something I need to tell you." She placed the cup down on the table.

"Maggie, hold on. Before you do that, I have my own topic for discussion," he responded, hands in the air inviting her to wait. "It's important to make sure you've completely finished the Mask case you've been working on."

She had called him earlier that day and explained many of the details of what she had been doing over the past week. He felt he had done a fairly good job of pretend surprise as she talked about Vienna, Milan, Argentina and New York. She had made a point of saying that her telephone call to him was to get the discussion of the investigation out of the way, to make sure that their evening was not dominated by her talking about Mask and his accomplices. She would rather they focused on each other, which suited him perfectly.

She looked at him curiously, not knowing how to respond.

He continued. "While I've been out here thinking, I realised there is something quite biblical about what you've been through recently."

Her eyes narrowed a notch, barely noticeable but enough for him to see he had her attention.

"Goodness knows what you've had to endure since Cullen Skink escaped on December 21st. Would you believe that was exactly 12 days ago? And in that time, you've had to adapt and transform yourself to cope. I would even suggest you are probably much more like the person you should be now than you were before his escape."

He waited a moment - when she did not take the bait, he said, "12 days after Christ was born, the three wise men arrived. That day is called the Epiphany because it's the Greek word for 'reveal' - Jesus was revealed to the world when presented to these men bearing gifts." He waited a moment for this to sink in, then continued, "Well, today is going to be your Epiphany."

"Kenny, you do say some weird and wonderful things," Maggie whispered, an edge of tension in her voice. "But at the moment I can honestly say, I am completely bamboozled."

"I know. I'm sure you are. Look, would you be allowed to show me the clue you and Kiltman were working on, the one that Skink left you?"

She furrowed her eyebrows and placed a hand inside her coat pocket. Taking out the A4 copy of the clue she had carried with her over the last few days, now dog-eared and dirty, she placed it on the table. She was waiting for him to speak.

He pointed to the last line.

PS. Rules of Riemann hypothesis apply to identities too. My last gift to you.

She studied the words, realising that in their haste to close the case down, they had not focused on that line. "What about it?" she asked. "Kenny, I'm struggling to see where you're going with this."

He looked at her for a moment, feeling more nervous than he had expected. "Hold on, I'll be back in a sec," he said.

He walked quickly to his bedroom; and reached up above the wardrobe. Taking down his sporran, he placed it gently on the bed. He reached his hand inside and extracted the item he prized more than anything else. Seconds later she looked at him distractedly when he walked out onto the deck. She was feeling annoyed she had missed that *PS* line - and was beginning to wonder if there was another act of terror out there, something she and Kiltman had not focused on, and should have been chasing down.

He sat back in his seat. "Okay. I think I can help you with the last part of that clue."

"Really? You've only just seen it! But go on."

She was wondering if he was feeling jealous and having some sort of Kiltman envy. In the background she could hear Roddy walking around the house banging a drum with a brush drumstick. It added a soothing hum to the silence of the evening surrounding them.

"Okay, you do know that Donald MacKenzie, Skink and I, went to university together."

She nodded, not knowing where this was going but her interest had peaked.

"Well, during our third year we worked for months and months together on the Riemann hypothesis, considered to be the greatest unsolved puzzle in the world of mathematics. Most people don't know what the Riemann hypothesis is. So, let me explain."

He took a deep breath. "In the world of mathematics, there has always been a desire to understand the pattern that prime numbers follow. You know, numbers only divisible by themselves and 1. Well, nobody has been able to figure out why prime numbers appear in the order they do. It seems random. But then, nobody can believe mathematics would have a random element in the core of how numbers operate. It has been a mystery since time began." She nodded, pleased that she was following so far, although concerned that Kenny had been drinking again.

He continued. "Donald and I worked ferociously hard on the Riemann hypothesis. There were weeks we would not sleep, addicted to solving the holy grail of maths problems. Then one day we had the eureka moment when we were convinced that we had it solved. We tested our answer a hundred different ways and were sure that we were correct.

"You have to understand that the solution to this mystery is worth a fortune. Incredible minds, including Einstein, were not able to solve it. Yet, Donald and I believed we had the answer." He could feel his excitement rising with each word of his story. "Since we knew we were sitting on a goldmine, we were also fearful as to the exposure this would bring. So, we agreed never to divulge the answer to this mathematical problem unless we both shook hands and agreed to do it together. Unfortunately, in the end, we realised that we had not solved it. Our testing had not gone far enough, and while we had made progress, we had to admit defeat."

He stopped and looked at her. Roddy's drum playing had stopped and the quietness that filled the air started to become slightly oppressive.

"Interesting story," she said. "But why's it relevant to Skink's clue? And why would he reference something about you in there?"

He put his hand in his pocket and removed the object he had just taken from his sporran. He placed it carefully on the table. She studied the bright white feather as if hypnotized by its whiteness, slightly tinged by the grey streak. Memories of pistols and crazed Nazis flooded back making her heart skip a beat.

"Kenny, that feather," she mumbled. "It's the same shape and colouring as one that I saw in Argentina. In fact, in some ways a feather like that saved my life." She paused then looked at him. "Why on earth would you want to show me a feather?"

He was looking into her eyes waiting for a glimmer of understanding to register as to what he was trying to say. She was becoming increasingly perturbed why he was presenting objects and concepts to her that smacked of extreme coincidence. Roddy was still quiet in the background. In some ways she wished he would start banging the drum again with that gentle brush stick in a languid, steady rhythm to slow down the heartbeat picking up pace in her chest.

Roddy had become distracted. He had wandered into his father's room looking for a book he thought he had left there. On the bed he was surprised to see the sporran - his father had not worn a kilt in years. He picked it up and enjoyed the texture of soft leather on the back and the clunky tassels on the front. On the back of the sporran, he saw some dials and understood he would need to find the code to open it. This was becoming much more exciting than practicing his drums. What code would his father use, he wondered? If it had been Roddy's, he would have used his father's birthday. So, his father, he assumed, using the same logic, would have used Roddy's birthday.

He entered the numbers 1402 and the sporran popped open. Nestled inside, a gleaming, silver flask looked too inviting for him not to investigate. Reaching in carefully he took the shiny container in his hand. He tried to twist it open it but realised it was locked. On its surface he saw a design of a man and boy in what must have been the Highlands - he had no doubts that was meant to be him and his father. On the other side, his father's initials, *K M*, sat alongside a Celtic Cross, so striking, he instinctively pressed his thumb against it. The top of the flask sprung open unlocking an incredibly pleasant aroma that immediately wafted through the air up into his small nostrils.

Outside on the deck, she was beginning to perspire, ever so slightly, but enough to express a physical manifestation of her overpowering sense of confusion. "Kenny, what's going on here? What are you trying to say to me?"

She wanted to get up onto her feet and walk across the wooden deck. To stop that sedentary sensation settling into her limbs, rooting her to the chair. She could not move a muscle, barely able to speak. Her mind was being invaded by recent memories of foreign countries, evil people, new friends and the one constant through it all, Kiltman.

He reached across slowly and took her hand in his, feeling her fingers relax into his grip. He squeezed with exactly the same firm but gentle pressure Kiltman had applied in the back row of the UN assembly hall two days earlier when she had been concerned about her brother.

That was the moment she understood. The moment it all made sense. The moment Kenny reached across and kissed her gently.

The moment when Roddy raised the flask to his mouth and took his first sip of Hair o' the Dog.

Acknowledgements

Kiltman 2 was born out of lockdown. It would be a stretch to thank a virus for giving me the time and energy to write a sequel so soon after the original Kiltman.

Yet while COVID-19 was the unlikely catalyst, there are many special humans to thank for their love and support.

I would love to say home-schooling Max and Bruce was an absolute pleasure. But in truth, neither they nor I could get them back to school fast enough. As they laboured at their desks with homework, while trying to get phones, ipads, laptops and printers to work, they still managed to provide the inspiration I needed to tap the keyboard. It never ceases to amaze me how much love, fun, ingenuity, and imagination can be squashed into two wee boys.

My gorgeous Georgie was hugely supportive throughout (well, maybe except for when she realised Max's lockdown homework had not been submitted). She always found the time to encourage me as she battled with teaching history through a tiny computer screen - when her natural style requires a spacious classroom, white boards, and props - to bring the magic of the past to life. Georgie had the natural ability to see beyond the words, providing invaluable edits and suggestions I greedily captured and included in the final publication.

I believe the expression '2020 sucks' is an apt way to describe a year that still has two months to go at time of writing.

Our sister, Margaret, was the inspiration for many of the characteristics and antics of Maggie Wilson. Margaret was loved and respected by everyone who knew her and her trademark qualities: kindness, dignity, wisdom, and grace. She did the ordinary things extraordinarily well, and the extraordinary things with humility and humanity. Our hearts were broken when she left us this year. Leaving an unbearably hollow vacuum. If ever children were a credit to their mother, Billy and Michael have shone through it all, embodying their mum's strength, compassion, and generosity of spirit.

Margaret has gone to be with our mother (another strong, caring Maggie), and brother George - born with one extra chromosome that embodied an extra-large dose of love and charisma. I am sure they are enjoying a good old knees up to welcome our *wee* sister Maggie.

I always knew my sisters, Anne and Angie, had a huge capacity for love and kindness. When I saw them drop everything and focus on Margaret's comfort and needs, I was reminded of how truly amazing they are. The quantity of selfless love and tenderness compressed into this dynamic duo of altruism and compassion cannot be measured.

John, my big-hearted, uniquely affable brother, who has likely driven the equivalent in miles of a hundred times around the planet, is a constant inspiration for Kiltman's wacky one liners and edge of reason humour. He made me realise there is nothing more bonding than sharing mutual grief for an amazing person.

2020 saw Jack McVitie leave us during the summer. A man of wisdom and strength, a true titan in all senses of the word - he left a hole the size of a planet... filled with memories of fun and wonderfully unique times. We just needed many more of them.

Malcolm McConnachie, the *New Yorker*, was there with his beautiful family - Lucinda, Cole and Jake - when the idea for Kiltman was born on the streets of Brooklyn. He is in heaven with Jack and Margaret sharing his boundless energy and compassion, his huge capacity for love.

Once again, Martin Delve prevents me from embarrassing myself through his eye for detail and challenging of logical inconsistencies. A great guy, one of life's rock-solid people, integrity and quirkiness intelligently entwined.

Tommy MacGregor's personality and antics are inspired by the quirky and affable Paul Gunn - who visited me in Estonia for a two week holiday in 1994 and is still there today, somewhere in the countryside growing vegetables while cooling his *Sovetskoye Shampanskoye* in the local stream.

To my other pals, if you see a character in here that sounds like you, then it just might be you!

Last but never least, the remarkable Phelim Connolly has done another incredible job on the cover, bringing my mind's eye to life. I am privileged my lifelong friend and brother from a different mother, Beannie Muldoon, and the gifted, ingenious artist, Eddie Kennedy, connected me with this God-given talent.